GW00853414

Turning Point

Barbara Spencer

Matador
9 Priory Business Park
Kibworth Beauchamp
Leicestershire LE8 0RX, UK
Tel: (+44) 116 279 2299
Fax: (+44) 116 279 2277
Email: books@troubador.co.uk
Web: www.troubador.co.uk/matador

ISBN 978 1783060 511

British Library Cataloguing in Publication Data.
A catalogue record for this book is available from the British Library.

Cover image: Jessica Carreras

Typeset in 12pt Garamond by Troubador Publishing Ltd, Leicester, UK
Printed and bound in the UK by TJ International, Padstow, Cornwall

Matador is an imprint of Troubador Publishing Ltd

To all the fans of Running, who asked for another adventure

ALSO BY BARBARA SPENCER

Young Adult
Running
Time Breaking

Childrens
Legend of the Five Javean
The Jack Burnside Adventures:
A Dangerous Game of Football and
The Bird Children
A Fishy Tail
Scruffy

For Younger Readers
A Serious Case of Chicken-itis

The man paused and glanced back, his hand on the doorknob. *'Kill them.'*

His words registered in Scott's brain like a solid weight. Surprisingly, he no longer felt scared. Drained of energy, tiredness swept through his body blocking every sensation. Too tired even to keep battling. He eyed the open door. Once that closed it was over – all the anguish and pain. The door closed and silence fell.

Pete drew his weapon. 'You always were a gutsy kid,' he drawled. 'I'm almost reluctant to kill you.'

Scott raised his head wearily. Like a juggernaut running amok, these people had become unstoppable. 'Then don't.'

'Sorry, kid.' He aimed the barrel of his weapon at Scott's chest. 'As I told you before – this isn't personal. It's business.'

Scott watched the finger on the trigger tighten and shut his eyes.

ONE

Summer

The porter tapped politely before opening the door a crack, coughing loudly to alert the occupants of the room to his presence.

'Mr Randal, sir, a visitor,' he announced, his voice carefully schooled to sound portentous.

The young man sitting by the window, his feet on the desk, was tall and dark with fine features that had stopped short of Homeric good looks by a broken nose and a kink in the jaw line – left from a high-speed collision with a tree while out skiing.

At the sight of the thin figure peering over the porter's burly shoulders, he leapt to his feet, a half-eaten doughnut dangling from his fingers.

'Great Scott, it's Terry.'

'You know this gentleman, sir?' The porter stated the obvious, although doubt was still uppermost in his tone. The gentleman in question was most likely one of those Yanks of Irish descent, badly dressed, not even bothering to shave. Not something the hallowed portals of Jesus College, in the fair city of Oxford, encouraged.

'Absolutely, Bates, we're old climbing buddies.'

'I see.' Pushing the door wide open he stepped to one side, almost grudgingly allowing the visitor to enter. 'In that case, Mr Terry, sir, you are welcome.'

'And to what do I owe this pleasure?' Beau's irresponsibly infectious tones burst out as the door finally closed behind the porter.

The middle Randal child ought to have been born on a Sunday. Nothing else would account for the ease with which he floated through life. Monday's child might have been fair of face and Tuesday's full of grace... But it was only the child born on the Sabbath day to whom the rhyme awarded gifts of being fair and wise and good and gay (in the old-fashioned sense of being happy). And his acceptance into the University of Oxford at seventeen had been as easy as everything else. Surprisingly he had applied to live in Hall and had been lucky enough to be awarded a room in his second year.

By contrast, the man standing by the door might easily have been mistaken for a down-and-out, someone who hadn't bathed, shaved, or eaten in months. The porter had been correct about his being an American, although for the inhabitants of the eastern seaboard showering and bathing were as much a daily routine as the saluting of the flag in middle-America. And, as Beau knew only too well, the whippet-like figure disguised muscles of unbreakable steel, the result of climbing mountains most weekends when not working. Only the stubble on his chin provided a genuine clue to the man's character, his entire being devoted to the American Secret Service and their pursuit of the men who had destroyed America's reputation as a world leader.

'Sit down and take the weight off while you explain what you're doing in Oxford,' Beau babbled cheerfully. 'Coffee?'

Sean Terry's steely blue eyes broke into a reluctant smile

and he collapsed his angular frame into a conveniently placed armchair. Beau disappeared into a side room, accompanied by the clatter of pottery and the abrupt click of an electric switch.

It was a large room overlooking the outer court with its immaculately kept lawn, the turf as sacred to the college authorities as any religious artefact was to the Church. The old-fashioned casement windows still retained their original wooden shutters, painted white and set deep into a recess on either side of the window. Thick walls and double doors kept sound in; the original oak door left in place as a gesture towards preserving the soul of building. Dark beams spanned a tall ceiling, which was sprinkled with ugly white cables running down the wall, splitting off into fire alarm, telephone and electric lighting, an aesthetically-challenging attempt to provide modern conveniences in a room five centuries old.

Beau stuck his head back into the room. 'Nice isn't it. Can you believe I also have a kitchen and shower? I'll give you the tour later. May I tempt you with a doughnut? They are quite divine – I pick them up from a bakery on the way back from my run. I hope you're planning on staying. You can join me in the morning if you are – best way to see Oxford, a ten-mile run at six a.m.'

'I'll not say no to a coffee and doughnut. I was up at five. I saw your dad last night. He said you'd taken up athletics.'

Beau reappeared carrying a tray which he placed on the table, passing across a steaming cup of black coffee. 'Had to,' he said, sitting down again. 'The old jaw won't take contact sports any more. That's why I'm still here – training stops for no man. Well…' He shrugged, 'Holidays anyhow. Most of the others have already left for the summer. So, Dad?'

Sean Terry took a cautious sip of the steaming liquid. 'Good man to have on your side if there's a spot of bother. Nice place you've got here. Historical!'

Beau grinned. 'Terry, you didn't drive nearly three hundred miles to discuss the wallpaper. What's going on? Did you lose another Cornish resident?'

'Give it time.' The agent rubbed his chin ruefully. 'It's only a few months since the last one.'

'Bill's okay, though.'

'We were lucky there. Fraction of an inch either way and Scott'ud be an orphan right now. He's home – and mending nicely but that's about all. Got one of my men stationed there permanently.'

'And Scott?'

'Still hates my guts. Thinks I'll try and involve his dad again.'

'And will you?'

'I need him to convince the UN that America didn't blow up Iran and we aren't the bad guys…'

Beau grinned. 'They already know that.'

Terry responded with a scowl. 'But getting them to admit it, that's a whole different ball game. In any event, he and the Styrus project should stay together. No one else really understands it…'

'So you are getting him involved again. Scott won't like that one little bit.'

Terry dropped back into his chair and gave a curt nod. 'I know. Still, it's only till the UN scientists get up to speed. Hey, give me some credit, I'm into good deeds these days.'

'*Lord above!* Things are definitely serious.' Beau grinned wickedly and took a bite of his doughnut. 'But with you at the helm don't be surprised when it backfires.'

Terry acknowledged the hit with a rueful smile. 'Okay, so in my walk of life good deeds are a sign of weakness. But they're a decent family and I like young Scott. He doesn't trust me, never has, and makes sure I know it; not by anything he says or does, but it's there deep down – tightly controlled. I admire that in a kid. That's why he can climb, because he's able to control his emotions.' He leaned back in his seat and picked up his coffee cup, wrapping both hands round it. 'Once Bill is totally recovered and the UN are out of the way, I'll drag them back to the States – they'll be safe there.'

'You mean they might still be in danger? How come? The bad guys ran away.'

'Did they though?' The agent stared across at Beau, his blue eyes deeply serious. 'I went over Bill's debriefing. It keeps me awake nights. I was talking to your father…'

'Dad again! Aren't there any Americans worth talking to?'

Terry ignored the jibe. 'Think about it. Somewhere in Europe is a man with dreams of becoming king. Then Bill and his little team of scientists come along with a world-beating computer virus…'

'Is Styrus really that good?'

'Bill says the only way to stop it is to switch computers off – permanently. He admits it was badly named – Black Death would have been more appropriate.'

Silence fell broken only by the sound of distant laughter. 'It's impossible to imagine a world without computers,' Beau said after a moment, his brow furrowed thoughtfully.

'Hell yes! That's why the UN must take it on. No one country – not even my own – can be allowed to wield *that* sort of power. Half the team that created it are dead, Bill captured, and it's not even out of the wrapping paper yet. Okay, so we managed to get him back, but the men responsible vanished with the computer discs, blowing up half of Holland on the way. We were lucky not to have more casualties.'

'But…'

'Ferdinand Aquilla, the mysterious Mr Smith's right-hand man, told Bill – and I quote, "In the big scheme of things, this doesn't even register".'

'Ah!' Beau dusted the sugar off his fingers. 'Hence the sleepless nights.'

'Yep!' Sean Terry's expression took on a grey glaze, his eyes bleak. 'I think it's about to get scary – and I've seen scary.'

Beau gave a whistle of surprise. 'The ace detective admits a weakness – whatever next? So what is this good deed you happened to stumble over?' Beau strung his long legs over the arm of the chair.

'Oh that!' Terry reached forward and topped up his half-empty coffee cup from the filter jug on the tray. 'I suggested Hilary should think about quitting the service.'

'Ah! Young love, eh. Very powerful stuff. My advice is: never get involved.'

'How old are you? Nineteen? Twenty?'

Beau hooted with laughter. 'A very old nineteen. I'm right though. Scott might forgive you his dad but not his girlfriend. So why are you unloading this on me?'

'I trust you.'

Beau leaned back in his chair, closing his eyes. 'Trust and faith – the most seductive words in the English language,' he said dreamily. 'Tell people you have faith in them, trust them, and they queue up to do your bidding.'

Terry shifted in his seat as if suddenly uncomfortable. 'Back at the hospital in Lisse, you said you might like to join our team.'

'Absolutely, once I've finished my degree – I'm your man.'

'Trouble is – it can't wait.'

Beau's eyes flew open again and he bent forward, his normal amused expression wiped off. 'I should have been a betting man. When I saw you standing there, I got this chill deep in my bowels, that was nothing to do with my run earlier in the day. Knew all along you had something up your sleeve. Spit it out.'

'I hope you are still acting this cheerful when I reach the end. It's refreshing.' Sean Terry's voice took on the texture of gravel – harsh and rough. 'Have you been keeping up with the news?' Beau gazed across the room, one eyebrow lifted questioningly.

'Two major conglomerates – rock solid for a century – gone into receivership. Debts galore. What's the betting our Mr Smith is behind it?'

Beau sprinkled some flakes of sugar into his coffee, stirring it briskly. 'So soon?'

'Told you it was getting scary. Do you know what I did last night, and the night before? Watched student riots on *News 24*. Belfast suffers riots most weekends; so does Paris, Lyons, Stuttgart, Rome, Lisbon, Brussels – you name it. On any weekend, the police throughout Europe are up to their asses.'

'Isn't that to do with unemployment?' Beau asked

'I don't think so!' The agent cut through Beau's words like a guillotine slicing paper. 'On the face of it, maybe,' he conceded, 'but behind the scenes, I believe they're being orchestrated, and rather carefully too. Aquilla actually boasted to Bill that Europe was packed with angry, unemployed youth who could be manipulated into doing anything.'

'So how can I help? I'm definitely not angry although you could say I'm unemployed.' Beau reached for the coffee jug.

'I want you to get yourself arrested.'

'*Arrested?*' He burst into laughter. 'Dad would never go for that. It would damage the fair name of Randal... ' Beau glanced affectionately round the small room, its white walls austere and lacking any form of embellishment except the memories of centuries. 'Besides, the College would chuck me out.'

Terry rubbed his ear lobe. 'Doug actually thinks it a good idea. Says, it's something he'd have wanted to do at your age.'

'Go on!'

'There's a rally planned for London in the next couple of weeks – royalists determined on bringing back the monarchy. It's an all-across-Europe thing. You know – a bunch of deluded middle-aged people who want to re-write history. Don't be surprised when violence breaks out. Join it. If possible, get yourself arrested. For minor affray you'll most likely end up at one of the new internment camps. All very practical and sensible. Everyone agrees that short, sharp punishments are the way forward.'

'But why?'

'Ten years ago, a young immigrant applied to me for a job. Brash chap. Wanted to serve America. I had agents coming out of the woodwork – they weren't needed any more with the US foreign policy in tatters – and reluctantly I sent him away, telling him to keep in touch. He wandered back to Europe and got hired by a nest of villains. To my surprise, he contacted me a few years later offering information in return for… peanuts, I guess.' Terry shrugged and took a sip of his coffee.

Beau rested both feet on the table, his glance absentmindedly flicking through the window where a couple of sparrows were bickering over a crust of bread on his window sill.

'A job was what he was after in the US, with a green card,' Sean Terry continued his monologue. 'For a couple of years he was involved in some pretty nasty goings on – feeding me information when he could, protecting our interests in Europe. A year ago, he asked me to meet him in Belgium. For some reason, pure instinct, I told no one. Thank God, he wouldn't be alive today if I had.'

Beau raised his eyebrows. 'Nice people you mix with.'

'If you look hard enough,' the agent's tone grated harshly,

like stone through a crusher, 'you'll meet up with murderers even in the most exclusive society – and don't you ever forget it. You won't live long enough to regret it, if you do.'

'Like that, eh?'

Terry gave a curt nod. 'The chap had changed, coarsened, and he admitted he'd killed. Swore it was necessary to stay alive and become trusted. Had a strange story to tell. One that involved computer scientists and underground cities, in which armies of teenagers were being programmed to set Europe alight... Those were his exact words.'

A fleeting expression, keen and penetrating, swept across Beau's his face. 'But that's your story!' he exclaimed.

'Exactly. What I'd struggled with for eight years, he handed me in a second. Only thing was, he didn't know who was behind it. Said he would try to find out. So I took him on and kept it quiet.'

'And you can do that because...?'

'I trust my boss and he trusts the President – they can do anything they like.'

Beau whistled. 'And he's been reporting to you all this time?'

Terry grimaced. 'Pretty much. So it's not only me second-guessing from watching the news channel. He's warning that corruption is rife throughout the entire establishment. Ministers think nothing of taking bribes, turning a blind eye.' His restless gaze flew round the walls, mimicking the action of countless students who'd been faced with an apparently insolvable problem presented to them by their tutors. For the brightest, those who got the answer correct, their reward was the chance to run for government or become a captain of industry. For the agent, success meant a handshake from the President and a brief *thank you*.

'Go on.'

'Haven't heard from him since that business in Holland, when Bill got shot. I need you to find him and get him out.'

Beau rose to his feet and stood by the window casually glancing down into the courtyard, its leaded windows and crumbling arches a testament to history. Very faintly, in the distance, the hum of cars and buses edging through the narrow streets could be heard. 'Do I get given a safety rope or are you expecting me to scale the tower wall using only my teeth?'

Terry glowered. 'Aren't you ever serious?'

'Naturally, if the occasion warrants. But so far this morning, life has been great. A good friend has come calling, and offered me a brilliant job even if it is only temporary. The sun has shone for a few hours and the coffee is excellent.' He waved his hands at the tray 'This new blend is first class and will definitely keep me awake all day. So – climbing gear – list of.'

'You'll wear a trace – that's it.'

'Like the one that was planted on Scott?'

Terry took a sip of coffee before replying, idly staring round the room. Then, as if happy no one was listening… 'Better than that. This one's decidedly hush-hush. Hardly anyone knows about it…'

'You mean *you, your boss, and the President*?'

Terry's saturnine expression dissolved into a reluctant grimace of amusement. 'Now you're getting it. It's undetectable.'

Beau slowly dragged his eyes up from his toes to his head, examining his body closely as if seeing it for the first time. 'The mind boggles!'

The agent barked a laugh. 'Doug happened to mention you lost a couple of molars in that skiing accident. We were thinking of an implant.'

'Again, the royal we. I presume you're still referring to: you, your boss, and the President? Would it be impolite to enquire why?'

'Because I had a snake in our organisation once, and it left me plenty shaken.'

'You mean Pete.'

'Yeah.' The response was dull, still painful. 'A rogue agent. You don't forget that in a hurry. If it hadn't been for Scott and Hilary, he'd have got away with it too.'

'So I'm to get myself arrested, hopefully adopted, and somehow track down your man. It all sounds a bit tame to me. I'm sure real spies have a much more exciting life.'

'I promise you, you'll thank me when you hear the alternative.'

'Go on, I'm all ears.'

'Besides telling me what a great athlete you'd become, your father happened to mention you knew more about computers than anyone he'd ever met. Apparently, at school you were always being sent to the head for inadvertently hacking into places you shouldn't and, on one occasion, only his influence stopped a bank pressing charges.'

'You could say I was somewhat misguided in my youth,' Beau's grin was broad but lopsided, the damaged side of his face a little reluctant to join in. 'So?'

'We toyed with the idea of you hacking into the Pentagon and having a warrant issued for extradition to stand trial in the States. With that sort of reputation, the bad guys would come running.'

Beau collapsed into his seat, his laughter echoing riotously around the high-ceilinged room. 'How long did it take you to cook up that little lot?'

The agent grinned. 'I told you, you'd thank me. This way might be dull, but it's relatively safe – as long as you're not caught snooping.'

'Gadzooks! I only hope you know what you're doing? From where I'm sitting, it all sounds a bit hit and miss to me. To begin, how will I know I'm even in the right place? And, this man of yours… I might recognise him but how on earth will he know I'm on his side? Before or after he sticks a knife in my ribs.'

'*If…* he's still alive! If it's humanly possible I want him out before the shit hits the fan. I owe him.'

'So where do you think these guys are now?'

'Not a clue – except if they are behind the riots they need access to cities. Lisse was perfect. From there you could dart in and out of at least four or five countries in a matter of hours. That's why my money's on the new detention centres.' Beau glanced up sharply. 'To my knowledge, there's three up and running – France, Germany and Spain. The time scale is…' The agent drew his arms through the air expressing his amazement. 'Even in America building takes for ever. My guess is, someone had either built or planned them well in advance. At the moment, colleagues back home are delving into European parliamentary reports to find out where the idea originated – someone had to come up with it. If we find that, it might lead us down the chain to the main man.'

Beau picked up his coffee mug. 'You said colleagues?' he said, his voice suddenly serious. 'How big is this thing?'

'It's big in terms of value but not manpower.'

'Not sure I follow you.'

Sean Terry's expression was suddenly bleak, making him all at once older than his forty years. 'Politicians come and go – it's money that calls the tune and there's an awful lot of it going astray.'

'Do I assume your little hobby has turned into a full-time business?'

The American nervously cracked his knuckles. 'You could

say that. Your father says these characters are the original *Gnomes of Zurich*. A secret society with vast power and influence; yet with all their resources, even they have been unable to track down Mr Smith. With Styrus in his hands, world-wide instability is the most likely outcome – and they're not about to let that happen.'

'I see. So, once we find him, they go in guns blazing?'

'Pretty much. According to my boss, one phone call is all it'll take. You game?'

Beau laughed. 'I like a good challenge and life's awfully dull at the moment. 'When do I start?'

'Now, if you're okay with it? I've already asked Doug to fix you up with a dental appointment – in case.' Terry got to his feet and strolled across the room, peering out of the window. He remained still for a moment, listening to the echo of feet on the ancient stone steps, watching two women walk across the quadrangle, carefully keeping to the paths, their black gowns billowing out behind them like wings. Their voices wafted through the open window, merging with the scent of wallflowers carried on the breeze. 'This is a nice place – sure you want to do this?'

'My dear man, I'd swap ancient Greek and Latin for danger and death any day of the week. Have another doughnut – we might as well finish them. If I'm allowing myself a visit to the dentist, I may not be able to eat solid food for a couple of days, by which time they'll be stale.'

TWO

Cheese and cuckoo clocks would probably have been Scott's answer to the question, *what is Switzerland famous for,* although in the hours since their arrival in the little alpine country, he'd seen neither.

Their flight from Exeter, late the night before, and the efficiency of the Swiss airport had left Scott with the distinct impression that the term *cuckoo clock* was a wind-up, a joke, a veiled reference to something only the Swiss would understand, since all they had met up with so far had been efficiency – plain and simple. Not only had the plane landed precisely to time but queues for immigration had failed to materialise, and the loo he had popped into had positively sparkled with cleanliness. By the time they reached the luggage hall, suitcases were already breaking through the rubber flanges at the end of the conveyor belt, dropping them off at their customers' feet rather like an obedient dog bringing in the newspaper.

He glanced across the limousine at his father wondering how he was holding up, his expression tinged with worry. It was a familiar expression; Scott saw it often enough when staring at himself in the mirror. Plain features, nothing to write home about, although so far his skin had remained clear of spots, his long fair hair neatly trimmed above stormy grey eyes that carried a permanent frown. When the obsession for styling gel had swept into school Scott had steered clear, deciding it smacked of narcissism. Besides, he didn't have time to bother with stuff like that; the life-threatening incidents of the past six months had left a very clear picture of what was important. On his list, number one was staying alive by any means possible.

The anxious look had appeared the day a bullet blasted his dad's shoulder to pieces, and had rapidly become a permanency. Even though doctors had assured anyone who cared to listen, that Bill would make a full recovery, the word *full recovery* still sat uneasily with Scott.

The limousine, black and elegant with tinted windows, its chassis reinforced with armour-plating guaranteed to stop anything other than a missile, followed docilely behind a long line of vehicles crawling along the lakeshore towards Geneva; the skyline to the south dominated by the unmistakable shape of Mont Blanc. A majestic silhouette, its crest was topped with snow all year round. In summer, when climbing the Alps became a pastime for both the skilful and foolhardy, it was possible to reach the summit and retreat down again in a little over five hours.

Lake Geneva lay unmoving, dark and uninviting, although the intense frost of the early morning had cleared, leaving a sky darkening towards snow. The travel brochure, which Scott had browsed through on the plane, proclaimed the lake a fun spot in the summer, with people flocking to the water to escape the heat and humidity of the city. Gazing now upon its sullen surface, it seemed impossible to imagine even donning a swimsuit and sunbathing. The heat gained from long months of summer sunshine had long since dissipated, like a flock of birds heading south for the winter. Only health fanatics would trespass on its shores now. The thought of dipping a foot into the icy water made him shiver uncontrollably.

'What?'

Scott grinned, embarrassed at being so feeble-minded. 'Nothing really, it was the idea of people taking a swim in that.' He pointed at the unmoving stretch of water.

'It doesn't look like this in summer.'

The man occupying the passenger seat next to the driver slid back the intervening glass partition. Shifting sideways, his jacket snagged against the back of his seat, the outline of a bulky strap clearly visible through the lined material. Without being told, Scott knew it was a holster for a gun – a M1911 – a semi-automatic pistol, magazine fed, with a .45 cartridge. And despite a somewhat controversial history, still the weapon of choice for many American departments. Scott knew this because Tulsa, who had accompanied them to Switzerland, often chatted to him about guns. And he did so with a sense of pride that marked him out as being American.

Guns were something that Scott had quickly become used to, ever since… He glanced out of the corner of his eye at his father, noticing how stiffly he still held the one side of his body. Ever since he'd been shot.

Nostalgically, he gazed through the window, his sight fixed on the jagged teeth marking the summit of the distant mountain range. As a child, his overriding ambition had been to climb Mont Blanc; his most prized possession a scrapbook about mountaineers who'd done just that until, on paper, he knew every step of the way. His father had promised they would climb the mountain together and they had spent a part of every holiday hill-walking and climbing, training themselves to meet the demands of the highest mountain in France, and the second-highest in Europe. Now that ambition lay in tatters and would never be realised – at least not by his father. His shoulder still gave pain on movement, although Scott didn't know how much because Bill refused to say. With the muscle strength all but cut in half, no way could it stand anything more strenuous than country walking. Even his father's beloved motorbike, the Suzuki, was left for Scott to use most of the time. Absentmindedly, he patted the pocket of his jacket where his new licence rested proudly in his wallet. Although legally he was still restricted to machines that pottered about, no one bothered much in the wilds of Cornwall.

Strange, it was almost as if the incident of the assassin's bullet had been Day One of a new style of living in which guns and suspicion replaced the freedom that comes with living in the country, although great efforts had been made to keep things as normal as possible. But how could they be when Scott was driven to school by an armed guard? And, when he awoke in the morning, it was to the sound of the bolt on an automatic being shot back, the incoming guard testing his weapon to make sure, if called upon, it would operate without a hitch; or the soft sound of the clip on a handgun being checked for rounds of ammunition. Each piece of equipment designed with a single purpose – to kill.

'You been here before, Tulsa?' Bill said.

'Yeah!' The security-guard inched himself round further, glancing into the back of the car. Mid-forties, dark with short hair, his complexion, once swarthy, had lightened considerably with the gloom of the wet summer, England suffering weeks of rain throughout July and August. Before the tragic events of last spring, Bill and Scott had spent the summers sailing and surfing. Now it was Tulsa who accompanied Scott to the beach, easily keeping up with his youthful energy. They had become friends, although the agent had communicated very little about his personal life. Taciturn in the extreme, all Scott knew was that he worked out when he was off-duty and back in Exeter.

It felt strange to see him so formally dressed, making him

all at once middle-aged. At the cottage, Tulsa always wore jeans and a blouson jacket; the latter zipped up in all weathers as a courtesy to the inhabitants of their small village, who would have been shocked if they had known he was toting a pistol. The only time it left his side was when he took a shower. Even then, Scott felt convinced it accompanied him into the bathroom. Being forced to travel unarmed, to pass through airport security, had left Tulsa nervous and twitchy like a first-time flyer or a heroin addict forced to go cold-turkey. Thankfully, a car sent by the US Representative to the UN had met them on arrival, its driver handing over a neatly wrapped package.

'In those heady days before Europe kicked our butt, loads of kids like me left the service and went into personal security. Some joined Special Forces.' Tulsa shrugged. 'I decided to see a bit of the world before I settled down. I'd already been to Switzerland.' He shuffled about, easing the strap on his gun holster. 'I done a tour of duty at the embassy here when I was in the Marine Corps. Liked the place – orderly, not like the States. Most of our cities are a sprawling mass of broken-down car lots and hoarded-up buildings. I got a job with a Nigerian diplomat for a year – he was okay.' Tulsa paused to switch the piece of gum he was chewing from one cheek to the other. 'After the quake, he didn't want me no more.' There was the briefest of pauses. 'Couldn't blame him. No one wanted anything to do with America back then.'

'I remember,' Bill said.

'So I went back home. Stupidly, my Nigerian hired a Frenchman who got him killed. There was a coup – the man had shot his mouth over corruption in politics. Crazy, eh…' he left the sentence unfinished. He grinned suddenly. 'Never did settle down.'

'Do you have family?'

'No one directly belonging to me. A sister in Portland.'

'Oregon?' Bill continued the questioning. 'I thought you came from Oklahoma?'

The agent produced another grin. 'Nope – Portland born and bred. Guess I'll go back one day when I retire. Got called Tulsa in the marines. Our little corps was code-named Oklahoma. We drew lots for cities – I drew Tulsa.'

The driver slowed to a crawl alongside a line of elegant vehicles waiting for the lights to change. The morning rush had long since ended; the men driving into Geneva now were mostly high-ranking civil servants, embassy staff or government representatives who gave lip-service to their work, arriving and leaving when it suited them. Scott, for the umpteenth time, checked his watch. It said half-past ten. Their appointment was for eleven-thirty.

Bill, noting the movement, closed the lid of his brief case and touched his son on the arm. 'It'll be over soon.'

'I guess. But it's like sitting in a condemned cell watching the clock.' Scott rummaged up a grin.

Bill laughed. 'Can't you dredge up something more cheerful? After all the UN are supposed to be on our side.'

'They took long enough getting round to it.' The lights changed to green. Scott nodded at the cars on either side keeping pace with them. 'I was just thinking, if that little lot works at the UN it's no wonder nothing gets done.' He heaved a sigh saying wistfully, 'Whatever happens, at least I've seen Mont Blanc.'

Bill's gaze was acute. He laid a hand on his son's knee. 'And one day you'll climb it, Scott, and I'll be there to cheer you on.'

The lines of traffic intensified. Bumper to bumper they edged from one set of lights to the next, the majority of the vehicles flying pennants. Scott identified the flags of at least a dozen different nations. All at once he felt nervous, his hands sweaty. In a few moments they would be entering the hallowed portals of the United Nations, the most powerful place on earth, where countries voted to declare war or push through economic sanctions against a renegade regime. Still, he wiped his hands on a handkerchief, once his father had given his address that would be the end of it – they would be free.

With a burst of acceleration, the chauffeur steered the heavy vehicle across lines of converging traffic, edging the cumbersome vehicle around the main carrefour in the centre of Geneva – a wide-open space filled with displays of art, giant posters advertising forthcoming exhibitions, adding a snapshot of colour to the monotony of the grey November sky.

Indicating right, the limousine entered a spacious avenue lined with elegant white buildings set back behind flower-encrusted pavements, scarlet geraniums in tubs still blooming vigorously in a last-ditch attempt to evade the biting frosts. Part way along, the flags of the Red Cross and the Red Crescent soared from the roof tops of adjoining buildings, endorsing Switzerland's claim of being a bridge between warring nations. Outside their gates, neatly dressed pedestrians waited politely on the kerbside for the lights to change before attempting to cross the road.

At the mouth of the avenue where several roads met, a brooding monolith of brown stone rose up, its dour façade broken by layers of identically sized windows – too small to be effective as a giver of light and too ugly to be an architectural feature.

'That can't be the Assembly Building?' Scott exclaimed.

'Surprising, isn't it? So different from the rest of the city.' Bill peered through the window as the limousine joined a queue of vehicles waiting to descend the ramp into the underground car park. 'It used to be the High Commission for Refugees but, when the UN moved to Switzerland, it was the only building large enough to house the General Assembly. According to the newspapers, it was rather like the Mad Hatter's tea party, with everyone moving down a seat. I was always sorry my life style didn't exactly permit me to come and see. The Swiss must have hated the confusion; they are such an orderly race.'

Scott grimaced. His father had spent fifteen years in hiding before eventually being traced and taken prisoner. Every single piece of knowledge he'd acquired during that time had been second-hand, picked up from the television or computer.

'So why didn't they build new, Dad?'

'The Swiss wouldn't give them the land. Besides, it would have taken too long,' Tulsa broke in. 'After the nuclear explosion in Iran, the UN went into panic mode and wanted shot of the States as fast as possible. Besides, the Swiss never wanted the UN in the first place; they're hell-bent on keeping out of international politics. They only agreed providing it was temporary. For a small country, they sure carry a lot of weight.'

Scott was surprised to hear the agent speaking up, never for one moment imagining him to be interested in world affairs. At breakfast he read the newspaper, back page first – sports not politics.

'Is politics always like this, Dad?' Scott said, gripped by the idea of actually being in the city around which the entire world revolved. It was all so different at home, buried in the depths of the Cornish countryside. There, it never made a scrap of difference who was in office.

'Pretty much. Ever since the wars of the last century, there's been a jockeying for position between Russia and America. It got worse after the wall went up.'

'What do you mean, wall?'

'You don't know about the Berlin Wall?' Bill sounded surprised.

'No, Dad,' Scott retorted, hearing Tulsa chuckle. 'That's why I asked. If you remember, I don't do politics. You've got me mixed up with Jamieson,' he added, thinking about his best mate. Whenever Jay came to stay, he and his dad spent much of the time talking about the unrest sweeping through the continent, and the need to get rid of President Rabinovitch. A self-made man, his family had originated in East Germany, and his meteoric rise through the party-ranks had taken place while the world had its eyes closed, battling with radiation and the effects of a devastating earthquake and tsunami. Once in power, he had brought in measures to quell any opposition, and had now been President for twelve years. And, in Scott's opinion, dictator or not, he seemed a permanency.

'It's not politics, Scott, it's history. The wall was built straight across the centre of Berlin and lasted thirty years – an ever present symbol of Russian dominance. You should read about it. In hindsight it's exciting stuff. Russia and America sparred like crazy, at one point threatening all-out nuclear war, with spies disguised as diplomats and embassy staff. It spawned hundreds of books and films... with unbelievable scenarios. Umbrellas tipped with poison, cyanide pills in case of capture, double agents living the high life in Washington and Moscow; with captured spies exchanged in the dead of night on a bridge somewhere in Europe...'

'You serious?'

'Deadly. Since the wall came down, Russia has dwindled into a something and nothing country, its satellites breaking away to become part of the Eurozone.'

'Don't they mind?'

Tulsa twisted round, an impish smile on his face. 'They like to pretend they don't.'

The chauffeur, his grin reflected in the rear-view mirror, winked at Scott. He brought the heavy car to a stop, his route into the car park blocked by a barrier manned by Swiss police. An officer checked their pass against the television monitor in the small gatehouse.

The building in front of them was loathsome, reminding Scott of cartoons in which giant bugs, from an alien galaxy, plonked themselves down in the middle of civilisation, demolishing everything around them. It certainly didn't look like a harbinger for world peace. As they descended into the underground car park, he cast a despairing glance over his shoulder watching daylight slowly reduce to a mere slit. Even the feeble electric lighting made little impression on heavy-set pillars of a cement-lined cavern. An irrational thought flicked at Scott's mind of being swallowed alive, rather like Jonah and the whale.

Glass doors fronting a corridor splashed with brilliant illumination beckoned. But still nothing welcoming – nothing that deserved a place in a building dedicated to world peace. It was the weirdest of sensations but Scott, after the events of the spring, had become used to trusting his instinct. Nothing good would ever come out of this building.

THREE

Tulsa was out of the vehicle before it had even stopped, quickly opening the rear door.

'Stewart Horrington, Mr Anderson.' The man waiting for them grasped Bill's hand in a warm handshake. 'US Representative. You made it okay then. Glad to see you.'

The grey-haired, neatly suited figure greeting them was not alone. A secretary, carrying a stenographer's notebook in one hand and twirling a pencil with her other, nestled into his right shoulder. A few steps behind, a mass of eager attention, stood two somewhat younger versions of the statesman – their clothes and hairstyle as close a copy to their boss as it was possible to achieve without being thought a clone. Behind them again, a tall man leaned against the nearby wall. To the casual observer he might have passed for a broken-down reporter on the staff of a tabloid newspaper, someone whose ambitions had faded at forty and who would never be paid well enough to afford decent clothes. He looked unkempt, his button-down collar and narrow tie ill-fitting, his dark hair unruly and in need of cutting – and he hadn't shaved. He raised his head from his contemplation of the carpet and a pair of tight blue eyes under fiercely frowning brows raked the newcomers.

Scott felt an irrational sense of dislike sweep over him. He knew it was unwarranted but couldn't prevent it. Sean Terry had saved his father from certain death. And he was grateful, he really was.

When Hilary had pleaded to stay on in Cornwall and finish her education, surprisingly Sean Terry had agreed, carefully pointing out to the young secret service agent that since only their friends, Travers and Mary, were aware of her real identity, it might work – but…

'If you stay in the service, no getting matey. Staying close to Scott… it's an assignment… a job. That's all. Got it?'

He had dragged the two of them into a corner of the room to lecture them, the steel of his eyes blazing like a laser. Hilary had flushed bright scarlet, taking an instant step backwards. It wasn't a big step and Hilary probably wasn't aware she'd done it but it was significant, and had changed everything. From being on the friendliest of terms, spending every spare moment together, they were once again strangers. Every time Scott tried to break through the cordon of frost that surrounded her, she backed away snapping a putdown. Only when Travers and Mary were about did she relax, becoming once again an ordinary teenager, fun to be with.

No wonder, Scott thought bitterly, everyone loathed Sean Terry. It was far easier to deal with Tulsa. He didn't bother about stupid restrictions becoming a real part of the family, even taking his turn with the washing-up and vacuuming.

'Sean Terry, you know.' The US Representative beckoned the stick-like figure forward.

'Of course I do,' Bill said warmly. 'Good to see you again. I believe I have you to thank for this.'

'Perhaps at the outset.' Terry shrugged off the compliment. 'Media wouldn't listen. Too much pressure from the top. But then… you know how it is – things change and now they want you – like, yesterday.'

Beyond a cursory nod, the agent had scarcely noticed their bodyguard's existence, yet both men worked for the Secret Service – if that was what it was still called. Changes of regime, whenever a newcomer entered the White House, often resulted in agencies being amalgamated. In recent years, it had fallen under the umbrella of Homeland Security. Despite that, it remained a powerful organisation, well-financed and answerable to the President himself. For Scott, Sean Terry's obvious rudeness was yet another reason for disliking the man, although Tulsa seemed undisturbed, concentrating on keeping his position tucked behind Bill's right shoulder, his attention focussed on the moving figures in the corridor ahead.

A short staircase emerged at ground level into an extensive foyer, built in the same brown stone as the exterior and garlanded with flags of the various nations. Once a gathering place for desperate individuals seeking sanctuary from their war-torn countries, it had been blitzed to create a café and public exhibition area and had quickly become a favourite meeting place of such diverse nations as Tobago and Swaziland, UN staff constantly finding excuses to slip out of their office for a shot of excellent Swiss coffee. Although that was another thing Tulsa had warned Scott about – the coffee: 'Strong enough to grow hairs on your chest. If I were you, I'd keep it down to one cup a day, otherwise you'll never sleep.'

Ignoring the bright lights and the aroma of freshly-ground beans, Stewart Horrington, a career politician who had served a number of terms in the senate, shepherded the little group towards a bank of lifts. Here, polished steel plaques inscribed in three languages – French, German and English – offered precise instructions as to which part of the twenty-storey building they served. By tradition in the UN, the higher the floor the more important you were. The Secretary General and his staff occupied floors 19 and 20. By mutual consent, the five permanent members of the Security Council had taken up residence on 17 and 18, while the General Assembly, consumed by a vast logistical problem of having 192 member states, was sited on floors 1 through 3.

'It's a great day for our country,' the US Representative made polite conversation. 'I had a call from the Secretary of State earlier. She commented it was like emerging from forty days in the wilderness. For the past fifteen years, diplomacy has been conducted behind closed doors, yet the Iranians have known we weren't responsible for their nuclear debacle for at least a decade. It took regime change for them finally to admit it publicly.' The lift slowed to a halt and the door opened. 'You don't sit on the floor, Bill, that's for the representatives only; guest speakers are raised higher than that.' Stewart Horrington grimaced to show he was joking. 'It means everyone can see you. And my assistants will be there – they are fully briefed and can answer anything you struggle with.'

'I'm sure I'll be fine.'

'Not unless you're wearing shark repellent, you won't,' the grit-laden voice of Sean Terry broke in.

Bill grinned at the agent. 'Don't worry. I'm determined to have my fifteen minutes of fame. I've waited long enough, heaven knows. Can Scott wait in one of the side-rooms?'

'Jane.' Representative Horrington beckoned his secretary. 'Show Scott into one of the visitor booths.'

Flashing a perfunctory smile, the young woman headed down a corridor leaving Scott to follow, every pore of her narrow frame oozing with indignation at being forced to pander to the needs of a sixteen-year-old. In the past six months, Scott had met up with dozens of officials from the US Embassy, making several visits to its hallowed portals in Grosvenor Square. Jane Oliver, with her blond streaks and lithe figure, was no different; so obsessed with American resolve and ambition there was little margin for genuine interest in people. To her, teenagers were hardly worth a moment's notice unless they happened to be an outstanding athlete or mega-rich, when doubtless she would have encouraged them to become her best friend.

The corridor, lined on both sides from floor to ceiling in maple, was curved, its seamless outline interrupted by door knobs regularly spaced along its polished facade. Above them, inset into the surface of the wood, were flat steel plates on which the number and status of the room – occupied or vacant – were displayed. According to the hieroglyphics, they were on the third floor, heading west.

Opening the door, the secretary casually nodded towards the front of the booth, where a wide panel of reinforced glass offered a perfect view of the proceedings taking place in the hall below. Above it a black-panelled speaker. 'If you flick that switch, you can listen to your dad,' she said before hurrying out of the room, her footsteps muffled by the carpet in the corridor.

Scott, who had been expecting something grandiose in a world-renowned organisation, was disappointed to find the room plain and rather drab, a run-of-the-mill-type office no better than they had at school. Inside the door, a raised area had been allocated for meetings and furnished with a glossy conference table, six chairs tucked neatly around it. Glancing up, he noticed hinged wall panels, allowing the space to be doubled in size if required.

Closing the door behind him, Tulsa followed Scott down a couple of steep steps to a line of seats fronting the screen of toughened glass.

'Aren't you staying with Dad?'

'Terry's there. Besides I figured he's safe enough. Not so sure about you, though, don't want you getting into trouble.'

Like stalls in a theatre, the meeting place for the delegates occupied the lower of the three floors, a vast area scooped out to create a feeling of space, with lights set into the ceiling seeming as far distant as stars. Representatives of the world order sat in rows behind curved swathes of polished wood, which were liberally sprinkled with white-printed name boards, microphones, and plastic water bottles. No pecking order in the seating other than the obvious: Afghanistan at one end, Zimbabwe the other.

Mimicking the curve of the corridor, the long sweep of tables faced front where a grandiose stage presided over the proceedings. It reminded Scott of a courtroom. Presumably the chairman of proceedings, the Secretary General, sat there, the blue flag of the UN draped like a backcloth across a high-fronted desk. On either side, at a lower level, were microphones for use of guest speakers and, lower again, desks set aside for clerks responsible for recording the proceedings. To the rear of the delegates, and partially obscured by an overhang, secretaries and assistants milled about, while a battalion of linguists, the backbone of the UN, overlooked the proceedings from glass-fronted work-stations on the upper floor. Fascinated, Scott watched dozens of mouths moving without sound. What a feast for a lip-reader.

On the flight over, his dad had briefed him about the United Nations, a new leader elected every five years who could serve two terms. The new man was from Iceland, a country that steered clear of international affairs. 'Whatever people say about the United Nations, it does give little nations a chance to hold their own, and it does try to maintain a spirit of cooperation and good sense between its members. Of course people, like the Secretary General, have risen up through the ranks and have more loyalty to the body than their own country.'

There'd been tons more but Scott hadn't bothered to listen, gazing through the small porthole on the fuselage at the staggering view of snow-capped mountains, far more interesting than one of his dad's lectures.

Idly, he picked up a pair of ear-phones built into the seats, fiddling with the dials in the arm rest, annoyed that the secretary couldn't be bothered to demonstrate how they worked. The cryptic symbols meant nothing, and he had no clue as to which one controlled sound from the floor of the Assembly. Impatiently, he zoomed them backwards and forwards, hoping something would burst through. He jumped startled as voices emerged through the ear-phones.

'I tire of these prancing lunatics in Europe. Their devotion to democracy I find frustrating. The timetable for their descent into chaos must be moved up.'

And a soft, almost caressing reply: 'Remember, Europe is not the Middle East; you cannot expect civil unrest to take place in a day, with regime change following in a week. But it *will* happen – and probably within a year. That I promise.'

The words sounded theatrical, the voices accented as if English was not their first language. And while one came over the airwaves as a menacing growl, the terse style of someone in authority used to being obeyed, the other seemed more hesitant, almost gentle, patient sounding. And very scary.

The destruction of Europe – what did they mean? And why would anyone say such a thing unless they were joking – except, the voices didn't sound like they were joking. Puzzled, Scott peered through the window, wondering if he had caught a conversation between two of the delegates on the assembly floor, but could find nothing obvious in the groups of men and women listening diligently to the speaker – a woman, her arms waving vigorously with the force of her argument. But it had to be a joke, didn't it?

'Is she even aware that bankruptcy stares Norway in the face?' The voice pounded his eardrums, on certain words the accent very marked and Scott could sense the frustration hurtling over the line. 'How long before she is once again on her knees, begging help for her own nation's economy.'

'Lotil Oil continues to resist.'

'You have obviously warned them of the penalty of delay.'

'Naturally.' The softly-spoken syllables slithered their way into the airwaves, like a rattle snake through grass, setting Scott's teeth on edge.

'A small explosion might hurry them along.' The words, loudly spoken as if to offset the crackling on the line, came across as a statement not a suggestion.

'That would prove rather difficult. Security on oil rigs is very tight.'

'So! They will concede – they have to – there is no alternative.'

This wasn't a translation of the debate, this was someone plotting revolution. Whipping his ear-phones off, Scott gazed down at them as if they were about to explode. Yet, there seemed nothing odd about them. Neatly packaged, with soft foam ear pieces, they were identical to those handed out by a cheerful stewardess whenever you embarked on a long-haul flight. Anxious not to miss a word of the illicit conversation, he clamped them back on grateful that the language was English. Had it been any other it would have passed straight over his head, for languages were definitely his worst subject at school.

'I agree. We are like a hoard of mice that creep into the forest at night, silently nibbling away until they topple even the strongest tree.'

'Who do you expect to fall on its sword first, Greece?'

'Naturally. As always its heroic posturing is nothing but hot air. And then Denmark perhaps… the most settled of all to show our strength.'

Scott swivelled round in his seat. A map of the world, circled by flags, had been stencilled onto the back wall. The Scandinavian country, north of Germany, looked little larger than a small pimple, and was bordered on all sides by sea.

'A small country with an even smaller army; the perfect starting place. If we only incite a few protesters onto the streets, we will bus in a crowd from Germany. Enough to create a little delicate mayhem. A few rounds of live ammunition will do the rest. They're a stupid people and a mounting death toll will provoke even the most cowardly into action.'

A burst of cruel laughter sent a shiver through Scott.

Tulsa shot him a piercing look. 'Scott? You feeling okay?'

Impatiently, Scott flapped his hand at the agent to stop him talking. The conversation had to be taking place within the building, right? He squinted down at the row of knobs built into the armrest. If they were only for internal use, where had the hiccup occurred? His glance darted round the huge space seeking the speaker. It was easy to spot the translators at work, their eye fixed intently on the representative they were translating for that day. Around them, people stood up or sat down, coffee cups saluted empty air, doors opened and closed as meetings began and ended. Every word spoken would remain confidential behind the thick plate glass yet it was still in the public domain. No one could meet secretly; all were in full view yet private.

Out of the corner of his eye, Scott caught a movement as an overhead beam of light picked up an answering sparkle from a watch. The man, seated in the booth on the opposite corner, had a phone pressed to his ear. How come? He'd passed at least a dozen notices on the way up from the underground car park, advising that mobile phones didn't work in the building.

Swinging round, he spotted a telephone receiver tucked away on a narrow shelf next to the boardroom table. So that was it. Each of the viewing stations had access to an outside line. And somewhere it had become connected to the internal system. So how many more people were listening in?

'Naturally, in every ointment there is a fly. Bill Masterson – I understand he's speaking next. How sad that he survived. The Dutch are so unbelievably capable – it's disheartening. We need him out of the way before...'

Scott gasped and jerked backwards at the sound of his father's name.

The line was abruptly cut. The man in the booth opposite looked up, his razor-sharp gaze scouring the room and, for a brief moment, their glance met. Then, with equal suddenness he was gone, the glass shell with its polished conference table and chairs empty.

'Tulsa?' Scott pulled the ear-phones off and held them out, his hand trembling. 'They were talking about Dad.'

The agent smiled indulgently. 'What a surprise, he's on next.'

'No!' Scott beat the set against his knee in agitation. 'This was different. I heard them say he had to be killed.'

Tulsa clamped the ear phones his head. 'Nothing there now. Sure you didn't imagine it?'

'You think I imagine things after what's happened?'

'No, I don't. But your dad's fine. Look!'

Scott blinked rapidly to clear the mist from his eyes. At the far end of the room, a door had opened. He gasped out his relief at seeing the tall silhouette of his father, flanked by Stewart Horrington's two assistants.

The agent leaned across, twiddling a knob. The speaker

above them burst into life, a man's voice, the words marrying up with the person who had just stood up – the representative from Slovakia.

'You speak French?' Scott dropped into a seat beside him, his legs suddenly too weak to hold him upright. 'I'm sorry but...'

'Enough to make do.' Tulsa twisted a second knob and the voice changed, a woman now speaking in English.

'What's that?'

'That's the simultaneous translation.' Tulsa pointed to the floor of the assembly. 'See the light...'

Scott scanned the rows, picking out the faint glow of a light bulb set into the desk of the representative now speaking.

'This knob,' Tulsa pointed to the first in the little row, 'puts it up on speaker and these... produce a translation, into a couple of dozen languages: French, Spanish, Mandarin, Russian...'

'How do you know all this?' Scott said, hearing his voice still shaky, and anxious now to shrug off the lingering sense of unease that the unknown voices had left behind.

'Agents aren't just pretty faces, Scott. How could I possibly protect you and your dad, if I didn't know exactly where we were going and what to expect.'

'I never thought.'

'I don't suppose you did. But I can promise, when you do your homework, I do mine...' Tulsa's lip twisted in an amused grimace. 'Although, probably, I complain less. So what was all that about? Not like you to get in a panic over nothing.'

Scott twisted the ear-phones round and round in his hands, ashamed now of his outburst. In hindsight, it didn't sound like much – it could easily have been someone sounding off, someone fed up with the tortoise-like approach of the UN. After all, he was the same, spouting words he didn't mean and never remembered afterwards – like when his dad played the heavy father, and refused to let him go out on a Saturday night. *Even so, threatening to bring down Europe?* It was possible that was a joke. But the mention of his father? Killing him?

'Two men were talking. It had to have been a crossed line – it was horrid. They used Dad's real name too… Bill Masterson. No one knows…'

'I'm with you on that. Even your dad's passport says Anderson. Sure you got the name right?'

Scott frowned trying to remember the exact sequence of threats in the illicit conversation but they were gone, wiped out by his panic attack, like a careless finger on the back-spacer of a computer relentlessly deleting text. 'I think so.'

'OK! No point getting yourself in a state. We can't do anything right now anyhow, they're about to introduce Bill. First chance I get, I'll warn the boss. But I promise you, nothing can happen here, security's far too tight. So relax and enjoy the moment. You've waited long enough. Heaven knows.'

Scott watched the tall figure of his father climb slowly to his feet and walk to the podium. Tulsa was right. Ever since the events of the spring, his father had fretted about getting all the secrets into the open, to be free from a constant fear of assassination, only feeling safe at home in their cottage on the hill. Now the chance had come.

'Ladies and gentleman, I am grateful for this opportunity to address you, the representatives of this august body.'

His dad was using reading glasses to decipher the neatly typed script – yet another change that had taken place since the shooting, as if the bullet had aged every part of his dad's body.

'Some twenty years ago,' Bill Anderson read out, 'the Styrus project was established. Funded by the US Government, it was set up in a research centre in California, and started out as an investigation into computer viruses. For a while, it seemed that every schoolboy's dream was to devise a virus that would cause mayhem.'

Bill paused to allow an appreciative laugh to break out among the English-speaking audience, waiting politely for the second wave as translators did their work.

'Unfortunately, before we could complete the project two tragedies took place. The first, as you know, was the nuclear disaster in Iran; the second, the earthquake in California followed by the tsunami.'

Scott listened to his father unravelling the tale. He came over as unemotional but Scott knew how painful the subject was. Thousands and thousands of words had been written about the Californian earthquake and its resulting tsunami, in which countries had been devastated and maps re-drawn. A decade and a half later, only media moguls still ferreted about in the ruins, plucking stories from the air and making fortunes from disaster movies that sanitised the true horror of losing your family to fire or water.

It was a sombre scene, rows of dark-clad figures broken up by a flash of colour from someone in native costume. Most were listening intently, their headphones in place, rifling through their notes to find the text. Only the odd one or two still conversed in muted whispers with their neighbour.

Scott still felt nervous and edgy, finding it difficult to listen. Crackling broke into his earpiece and he flinched, somehow expecting the voice of the anonymous caller to blast through again. He knew by heart the scenario of the gunmen bursting into the auditorium and mowing down their prey with machine guns; unsuspecting scientists, men and women gathered for a conference. He knew too that his father was the only one brave enough to speak out, while others remaining in hiding. Alarmed, his glance raked the auditorium from wall to wall, every muscle now on full alert.

A movement on the floor almost brought him to his feet, laughing shakily as an usher hurried across the space, his arms full of bottled water

Bill began again, his tone deepening under the gravity of his words, Scott murmuring the words of the speech under his breath. He'd heard it rehearsed often enough. For his dad the speech represented the key that would at long last open the gates of his prison cell. With the information in the public domain, all harm would vanish leaving them to live as they wished.

'In trying to recapture a normal life, I have passed the information to the United Nations. Even as I stand here…' Bill paused, his gaze flicking round the vast auditorium, scrutinising the rows of faces, making sure that every single person in the building – from the car-park attendant to the secretary drinking a glass of water – knew that he no longer held the secret alone. He had passed it on and was free. 'A dozen scientists are pouring over the programme. Too many people have died because of the power that Styrus wields. It would be wrong to let it continue. Thank you, gentlemen, for your patience and interest.'

It was over! From the speakers came a muttering of sound as translators completed their work. Emotion, like a blast of hot air, swept over Scott. He waited for the furore but none came. For nights, he had dreamed of delegates jumping up in their seats to applaud his dad's speech. 'I thought they'd be pleased.' He got to his feet, swallowing down tears of relief and disappointment pressing against his eyelids.

Tulsa grimaced 'I bet you thought the President of the USA would be hotfooting it to Cornwall to shake your dad's hand.'

Scott shrugged. He had. At the very least his dad should get a signed photo, *in gratitude for his role in maintaining justice and democracy*.

A voice broke the silence. 'Mr Anderson, this current global instability? Is Styrus to blame?'

Startled, Scott swung round. They hadn't expected questions. 'A short statement,' the US Representative had said, 'will be quite sufficient. They've been well briefed.' In any case, economic ruin wasn't a subject for a scientist, it was the preserve of bankers and investors, people who controlled the stock market.

'Possibly,' Bill admitted reluctantly.

Scott sensed a change in the atmosphere. Even blocked by reinforced glass, it was there – accusing his father. 'Tulsa – can't we stop them?'

Tulsa gave him a wry grin 'They've got to blame someone for the mess we're in. Don't worry, your dad expected this to happen. He'll manage.'

'Is there an antidote, Mr Anderson?'

'The representative for Norway has the floor.'

Scott picked out the speaker, a woman seated between Nigeria and Oman. His father's voice echoed through the speakers. 'Unfortunately not. It will take a few years.'

'And you are involved in the project?'

'In a consultancy role only. You have good people here.'

The representative for Lichtenstein rose to his feet, his expression fierce. 'But according to this – *not good enough.*' He struck the sheaf of paper in his hand making it flutter wildly. 'Until we have an antidote, we are all at the mercy of this individual you call Mr Smith. Is that correct?'

Scott watched Bill's expression change. 'I fear so,' he admitted. Scott caught the slight hesitation.

Alarm spiralled across the floor, the chairman calling for silence.

'As I stated in my notes, the organisation had already experienced limited success before they even laid hands on the discs. Fortunately, a colleague had encrypted them with just this scenario in mind. Hopefully, they will prove impossible to decipher completely. Even then, the virus may not work.'

'*You hope*, Mr Anderson, *you hope*. If it does work, can we expect the world to descend once more into chaos?'

The representative for Italy caught the Chairman's eye, indicating he wanted to speak, a frisson of murmurs running round the auditorium with everyone expressing concern at the use of the word *chaos*. It was a strong word, little used in an organisation in which gentlemanly behaviour, diplomacy and understatement were more likely than action.

'You met the man – what is his aim?' The Italian representative spoke slowly allowing the translator to do her work.

'In my report I use the words – *global instability*.'

'Do we not have scientists capable of arresting this…' the Italian circled his hands in the air, 'catastrophe?'

'We did once. Vast numbers of highly skilled individuals died in the earthquake – all of them leaders in the field of computer technology. I would hazard a guess that the long-term effect of this has been even more devastating to human progress than the tsunami. Without their knowledge all progress was stalled, which has left Styrus leading the field by a decade or more.'

Scott heard the surprised gasps, watching representatives turn to their neighbour sharing the sense of shock permeating through the long lines of delegates. But why? That snippet of information had been in their dossier – and it had been quite specific, the words written in italics for emphasis. He had read it; it had been tough going – not like the real story of his dad's kidnap, which was more like a horror movie. Even so, everyone working in that field understood that computer technology still languished in the doldrums. Perhaps, hearing the words spoken aloud made it all seem real.

More questions flooded the floor, delegates eager now to promote their own views and pin the blame for the mess on someone – anyone. Scott slumped back in his chair, not bothering to listen, his sense of disappointment overwhelming.

'He did what was expected of him, Scott.' Tulsa pulled his ear-phones away, his expression sympathetic. 'I know you wanted a magic wand, a ticker-tape parade… it was never going to happen. Diplomacy works through private meetings, brandy and cigars. Stewart Horrington will be quite satisfied with today's events. Your father has made it possible for the United States to get back into the ring and fight their corner, without everyone hurling bricks at them. Cheer up, you may not believe anything happened down there,' Tulsa pointed to the delegates, 'but that little speech is like a fresh dealer in a poker game shuffling the cards. The world order is about to change and some won't like that one little bit.'

FOUR

A knock came on the door. A young man peered round, his expression so serious and full of portent Scott expected him to come out with something earth-shattering. 'Representative Horrington has asked for you to join him upstairs.'

Scott got to his feet, glancing back for a last look at the Assembly, its members continuing to talk in levelled tones as if discussing the weather. Miserably, he retraced his steps to the bank of lift shafts, Tulsa silent behind him.

The lift glided to a stop on the seventeenth floor, its doors opening onto a spacious lobby with three sets of double-doors, highly-polished and firmly shut. Two bore the flags of China and France, two of the five permanent members of the Security Council. The third boasted not only the Stars and Stripes, but also marines. Standing to attention on either side of the doorway, they looked smart in their navy and blue uniform with white belts and gloves, a workmanlike rifle perched at their side.

'I am told they come with the Secretary of State.' Bill Anderson greeted his son. 'Apparently, she never travels without them. Swears they're better than a handbag.' He put his good arm round his son, hugging him tightly. 'Well, Scott, we did it. And we're still here. Come on, let's celebrate.'

Scott grinned, the black cloud hovering above his forehead fading abruptly. It was over and his dad was safe. Nothing else really mattered.

A hubbub of noise, a dozen people or more making small talk, greeted their entrance into the suite of rooms – a lookalike of their hotel suite, its neutral colours instantly forgettable. Framed photographs of past presidents decorated the end wall, the present incumbent in solitary splendour facing the doorway, all at the correct height for comfortable viewing. A woman was waiting. Not tall, but upright as if determined to make the most of her inches, her grey hair tailored into a severe bob, every pore oozing power and charm.

'Glad to meet you, Bill. Quite some experience by all accounts.' The Secretary of State welcomed them.

'Not one I want to repeat. My son and I are celebrating by taking a few days holiday in Europe. Our first ever.'

'So I gather. And this is your son. Scott isn't it?' Her voice was sharp, its accent that of the north-west.

Scott nodded, suddenly tongue-tied. It was one thing to read about powerful people, quite another to find yourself talking to them. Besides, all he'd done was try and find his dad – nothing special.

'We're grateful for your tenacity, Scott.'

The Secretary of State fixed her penetrating gaze on his father and took his arm. 'Come along, Bill, there's someone here I want you to meet.'

Scott relaxed, happy to remain insignificant if it meant skipping complicated conversation, especially since he wasn't quite sure what *tenacity* actually meant. Hopefully, it meant being stubborn, because that's what he was. But if he'd given the wrong answer, he'd sound like a real dork.

Left on his own, he wandered over to the window and pulled back the blind. Seventeen stories below, the cars and people appeared no bigger than ants. A long black limousine, its pennant sharp and clear even from a distance, pulled away from the underground car park. Casually, his gaze followed it, watching it peel off round a traffic island and recognised the Russian flag, with its three horizontal bands of colour, white, blue and scarlet. Whoever it was had either finished work for the day… or had a lunch engagement. Lucky them.

Suddenly starving, Scott moved away from the window. A waitress carrying a tray of drinks approached, a teenager, little older than him. He smiled his thanks, accepting a glass of orange juice from the heavily laden tray, wondering if he dare ask if there was anything to eat.

He glanced round the room noticing Llana Brigson, the Secretary of State, locked in conversation with his father and another woman. Scott vaguely remembered her putting a question to his dad and wondered which country she represented, although it didn't take a genius to guess what they were talking about – research into an antidote for Styrus.

'Who's that?' he said to the waitress, pointing with his glass.

'Emma Arneson, the Norwegian representative.'

The waitress's dark hair was tidied away under a half-cap perched on the back of her head. It was thick, the strands heavy and long. Idly Scott wondered, how long. She wasn't wearing make-up but she didn't need it; her skin tanned and her brown eyes large and luminous even without mascara. And, despite that awful black uniform with its white apron, very pretty.

'You Swiss?'

The girl smiled flirtatiously, her smile twisting the corners of her mouth. 'Would it make a difference if I was?'

Scott blushed and hastily took a sip of his orange juice. 'Well… er… *no*,' he admitted, surprised by his boldness.

This wasn't like him at all; he usually hung back when it

came to girls. He had to be desperately bored to actually start up a conversation – except she was nice, and far more interesting than the people busily chatting up his dad. He eyed the Secretary of State who had moved across the room, her voice like a river in full flood, a little circle of people gathered round her listening respectfully.

Scott found himself smiling again. When in Rome do as the Romans do. 'Where do you come from then?'

'I'm Turkish, a student.'

'So have you been working here long?'

Scott caught the sentence. How boring was that? Why couldn't he ever dredge up something fascinating that would keep her glued to his side? The flashback of that fateful voyage on the river hit him; trying to talk to Hilary – and failing miserably. The girl leaned on one hip, gazing up at him. It was a great feeling. Girls should always be shorter; it made you feel strong and invincible.

'I do a couple of days a week; it pays my tuition and lodgings.' Her English was good, although she hesitated before speaking as if thinking of the words in Turkish first before translating them. But that only added to her charm. She shifted the heavy tray from one arm to the other, staring down at it. 'There's no spare cash for socialising or boyfriends,' she said, all at once sounding shy. Her eyes flew up to meet Scott's. He took a hasty step backwards, startled by their intensity.

'What about you?'

'I'm here with my dad,' he said, his confidence increasing by the second, hunger now only a vague memory. 'He was addressing the General Assembly earlier.'

'Isn't he that scientist – the one they're all talking about who invented that germ that gets into computers?'

'It's a virus. They're different. Germs are what we catch.'

Scott caught a glimpse of his father at the far side of the room. He hadn't moved, still wrapped in conversation with Emma Arneson. He watched the Secretary of State step out of the group she was addressing, and call across the floor.

'Bill?' she beckoned. 'A word?'

Scott bit his lip, feeling absurdly proud. It was his dad and his team who had created this unique virus that everyone was talking about, a virus powerful enough to override the commands on any computer. 'Yeah, that's my dad.'

'So how does it work?'

Sean Terry's acid tones sliced across the conversation. 'How about a sandwich, I'm starving.'

The girl swivelled awkwardly, nervously clutching her tray. 'Of course, sir.' She smiled mechanically. 'Right away.'

'What did you do that for?' Scott protested indignantly. 'She's really nice and I've not got anyone else to talk to.'

'Then stay silent,' the agent snapped. 'If I hadn't come along, you'd have been spilling your guts to that pretty face.'

Scott blushed for the second time. He hadn't thought. 'But we're on American soil, *and in the UN*. Don't they have security checks?' He tried to sound confident but it was tricky with that gimlet gaze piercing your brain.

'Sure, and it's still as leaky as a sieve.'

'No way! I mean… I never thought,' Scott ended lamely. 'I mean she's like me, a teenager.'

'That's your problem, Scott. You never think. I know you resent it like hell, but why else would I keep Hilary away from you. Because, if you're all lovey-dovey you'd never notice a thing – and, for someone in your position, that can get you killed. As for that wretched Brigson woman…' Sean Terry glared in the direction of the Secretary of State. 'She travels with a bodyguard of marines and has a mouth big enough to hear in Russia.'

Scott rummaged up a reluctant grin. 'Do I guess from that, you vote Republican?'

'To keep us safe? Like hell I do – I've had enough of this US bad guy stuff.'

'But, Mr Terry, now the UN own Styrus, we're off the hook. We don't need to hide any more.'

'Yeah, sure!'

Suddenly, Scott recalled the gasp of astonishment that had greeted his father's statement – that Styrus remained light-years ahead of present day technology. He felt the blood drain from his face, the hand clasping his glass of orange juice suddenly clammy. If that was true, that put his father and the remaining scientists in the 'beyond price' category. So valuable, they would need to be carefully guarded – like diamonds in a safe, hidden from the light of day in case they were stolen. His father might have bravely told everyone that he was free. *But he wasn't* – none of them were.

'You mean it'll never be over?' Even to his own ears, Scott's voice sounded shaky, rather like a dying man gasping out his final words.

'We'll get them – eventually. I'll make damn sure of that. Till then, you'll need a guard. Think of it this way.' Sean Terry's eyebrows were raised mockingly. 'If the US President can deal with it, so can you. I don't promise it'll be pleasant, but it will keep you safe.'

'Is that why you kept Dad's visit to Geneva a secret?'

'Sure it is. Far easier to control the country area where you live than a metropolis like Geneva. In your village, a stranger would be spotted straight off.'

Scott reached out a hand to steady himself. Why hadn't his dad told him? Warned him? He stared across the room, his father still deep in conversation.

'So what's all this about you eavesdropping on a weird conversation?'

'Sorry, *what was that?*' Scott shook his head to clear the buzzing, the agent's voice hitting him from a long way off.

'The telephone conversation?'

'They said about killing Dad.'

'What else?'

'I don't remember… I was so het up…'

'Try.' The word struck Scott like the bolt of a carbine snapping into action.

Scott glanced wildly round, as if the walls could tell him what to say. A tray of sandwiches and plates in her hands, the waitress smiled at him – a warm, sympathetic smile. Embarrassed, he quickly slid his eyes over the portraits staring down from the wall.

'Honestly, I don't remember much. When the man said Dad had to be got out of the way, I was so freaked I stopped listening. It was about oil, I think.'

Across the room, the Norwegian Representative, an experienced politician who had been Foreign Secretary in a previous administration, was still talking with his father. In contrast to the American Secretary of State, Emma Arneson was immensely tall, her dark eyes on a level with Bill Anderson. An Olympic athlete, she had taken the bronze in the cross-country skiing event before retiring and entering politics.

Scott observed the group enviously, hearing his father's laugh ring out, wishing he were part of that conversation. Laughter had been in very short supply in the past few months – and it was great knowing his dad felt comfortable enough to find something amusing, despite Sean Terry's tale of gloom and doom. Besides, anything was preferable to being stuck in a corner talking to his most hated enemy.

'Lotil Oil?'

Scott blinked taken aback by the tone. 'I th-think so,' he stuttered. 'The word sounds familiar. Yeah, I'm pretty sure that was it. Something about... stopping it working. They said an explosion... an explosion on one of the rigs.'

Sean Terry grabbed Scott's arm. 'Come with me – *now.*'

Scott felt like a naughty schoolboy being frog-marched out of class for bad behaviour. All around talking was paused. Convinced everyone in the room was watching, he dropped his head and stared at the carpet.

'I suggest we take this somewhere secure,' the agent interrupted the three-way conversation, his tone brooking no argument, 'preferably to a room that was swept for bugs this morning. And not another word.' Deliberately, he focussed his gaze on the waiting-staff, the doors to the kitchen swinging open as a waiter carrying a tray pushed through.

'Come off it, Mr Terry, we're all friends here,' the Secretary of State bridled, shocked by the agent's forceful manner. How dare he speak to a top government official in such a fashion? That was the problem with the Security Service: too big for their own boots. They considered reporting directly to the President gave them carte blanche to ride roughshod over everyone else. At the very least he could have waited till the end of the sentence before barging in. She glared round at the peaceful scene.

'Apologies, ma'am, but I insist.'

Stewart Horrington, noticing the rigid body language, hurried over. 'Can I help?' he said diplomatically.

'We need a room.'

'Oh... right... that would be my office.'

The agent flicked his head at Tulsa, who was conveniently leaning against a nearby wall. The agent opened the door marked, *US Representative*, and disappeared inside.

The assistant, who had been sent to collect Scott and Tulsa

from their viewing post on the third floor, took a step towards the main door. For a moment it seemed as if he was about to call in the marines to arrest this maverick cop, who appeared to be holding the Secretary of State to ransom. As if he had antennae in the back of his head, Sean Terry swung round and fixed him with a gaze so bleak it froze him to the spot. The other guests, most of them American including the assistants, watched, their expressions muddled and confused, anxiety uppermost. Conversation lapsed altogether and a rigid silence descended.

'Agent Terry has our full confidence.' Representative Horrington leapt into the breach. 'Something awkward has come up…' He tailed off, seeing Tulsa emerge from the room something gripped tightly in one fist.

Scott had only ever seen a bug once before, but he knew what they were – and they weren't woodlice that had somehow managed to hibernate through the winter on the seventeenth floor.

'Not a word, Mr Horrington, but I suggest you instruct the marines not to let anyone leave. Do you have a back– '

A door slammed. Sean Terry swivelled round sprinting for the kitchen. Scott caught a glimpse of startled faces and a tray, loaded with sandwiches, left unattended on the buffet table.

FIVE

The sound of feet jumping their way down concrete steps reverberated throughout the fire escape stairs. It faded abruptly as the discordant jangling of an alarm took over – warning staff throughout the building of an emergency. Scott caught the heavy thumps and guessed Sean Terry was taking the stairs three at a time, Tulsa hot on his heels.

Scott eyed the roomful of people, their expressions both shocked and dismayed. Most had collapsed into a conveniently placed chair, waiting anxiously for news – although what was the point? Every word that had been spoken, every telephone conversation, identities of the speakers verified and noted, not a single sound would have gone unnoticed by a bug that remained on duty twenty-four hours a day. And for how long? That morning only? Longer? Two days, three days…more? Were these men and women even now wondering if they would become the target of an assassin's bullet on their way home that night?

The Secretary of State, her expression unchanged, stared impassively at the photograph of the current president; the diamonds on her fingers creating shafts of brilliance as she moved her wrist to check the time. But it was the change in Emma Arneson that really shocked Scott. The woman had turned as white as a sheet. He caught sight of her hands trembling before his father covered them with his own, turning her away from the room so no one else would witness her distress.

But why? What had she been saying? It had to have been something pretty catastrophic to produce a reaction like that.

A feeling of guilt swept over Scott, rumbling around like the hunger pains of a moment before. Fancy chatting up a terrorist. And she was so pretty too. How could anyone that pretty possibly belong to a terrorist organisation? Holy crap! *How could he have been so stupid!* He'd never live it down.

The kitchen doors swung open. Heads jerked round. Sean Terry, his expression grim, stood in the doorway. He didn't speak, still panting harshly from his manic pursuit of the girl. Instead, he drew his finger across his throat and shook his head.

She'd got away? *How could that be?* Sean Terry was fast, Scott knew that. The girl had obviously been faster or had an escape route already planned. The horrendous thought that someone so innocent-looking needed an escape route knocked Scott's breath out of him. He drew in a lungful of air, ashamed at what he might have let slip if Sean Terry hadn't arrived in the nick of time to stop him.

Nodding, Stewart Horrington picked up the phone. 'Most embarrassing!' he muttered, pausing long enough to punch in a group of numbers.

Scott caught at a bubble of hysterical laughter in his throat. Coughing to disguise it, he swung back to the window, staring down at the streets of Geneva where normality reigned. It certainly didn't in this office. *Embarrassing!* The man had to be joking. He had a roomful of people on his hands, most of them scared silly, including him, and the only word he could come up with was embarrassing. *Devastating, disturbing, horrific, unbelievable* – any of them would have fitted the circumstances better.

'I'm afraid, ladies and gentlemen,' the US Representative continued, 'we're in for a long session. I suggest you make yourselves comfortable while we wait for the all-clear. Help yourselves to drinks and something to eat.' He spoke briefly into the phone, glancing back at the agent over the receiver. 'How on earth could this happen? Here, of all places; the seat of civilisation. And why?'

For Scott, the need to laugh vanished as quickly as it had come. The *why* was easy especially after what Sean Terry had just said, but only if you believed in the global mastery of one man, Mr Smith, and could accept he had a mole in the newly refurbished American Embassy in London. It was too much of a coincidence otherwise – a listening device turning up the same day as his father addressed the UN. No way. Besides, he no longer believed in coincidences.

Stewart Horrington had assured them that the date had been kept secret, known only to him, his staff, and a colleague in London who had arranged the flights. His staff were totally trustworthy, hand-picked from families he had known since childhood, for generations solidly Democrat. And it was his car, with his personal driver, that had collected them from the airport and hotel. The Embassy in Geneva knew nothing of his dad's visit, purposely kept out of the loop. Neither did any of the other delegates; the appearance of his father unscheduled until early that morning when a confidential memo had been delivered by hand. It had to be London. Knowing when they were travelling, it would have been so easy to bug the suite. There could be no other explanation unless bugs were commonplace in the UN?

Scott swung round glancing briefly across the room. Emma Arneson looked better, less green, although the fingers gripping her glass were still rigid. And the people scattered around the room? The majority of them worked in the building on a daily basis and all of them were influential. These were the men and women that had striven to bring Styrus to the notice of the UN and were now being thanked with champagne, caviar, and smoked salmon sandwiches. The eager expressions they had worn on first encountering the Secretary of State had been wiped off, leaving their faces haunted, sombre or blank.

No, this was not an everyday occurrence.

But the waitress? *No, not her,* it couldn't be. Perhaps she ran because she was working illegally and didn't want to be picked up by the Swiss authorities and deported. Scott clutched at the idea. *That,* he could believe. But not that she was a terrorist, someone evil. He scowled angrily. The thought that, once again, someone might have betrayed his father to that elusive person who called himself Smith made him feel sick.

Behind him the American staff, out of a sense of loyalty, tried to maintain a cheerful front pushing waves of conversation at anyone capable of listening. The sudden and haphazard outbursts of noise reminded Scott of toadstools erupting from a grassy bank. Innocent-looking on the outside but containing toxins lethal to the unsuspecting – exactly like a word spoken out of turn.

Unashamed, he eavesdropped on a conversation nearby, hearing the words *snow* and *Christmas* repeated with monotonous regularity, as if they were imbued with magical properties and, if you said them often enough, everything would be all right. The speaker, a woman, spotting his interest, bridled with indignation and, turning her back, lapsed into silence.

The door to the suite banged open; eyes like startled rabbits caught in a car's headlights riveted on the uniformed figures blocking the doorway. Half-a-dozen men stood there, their appearance so formidable it was practically hostile.

Wearing their caps perched at an angle and their hair shorn close to the scalp, a knife-like crease ran down the front of their grey uniform trousers, and the polish on their black boots was so bright the overhead light was reflected in it. Armed and with an identity tag pinned conspicuously to the breast of their uniform, they paused for another couple of seconds racking up the tension in the room before striding in. Four out of the six carried black rectangular boxes and a wand, rather like an electric toothbrush, and certainly no larger. The remaining two had a heavy leather belt strapped to their waist, with household tools, such as hammers and screwdrivers bulging out of it.

If Scott hadn't been one of the victims, he would have found the whole procedure curiously comical. Like at school, when guys joined the auxiliary training corps. The act of putting on a uniform seemed to change their behaviour and qualities emerged never before noticed: pride, leadership, discipline, and on the other side bullying and aggression. There was no doubt girls loved uniforms, fancying guys they wouldn't give a second glance to in ordinary gear. It was like that now. The officer had said nothing but he was obviously quite aware that his appearance could stop a room in its tracks. And, rudely, he'd not even bothered to acknowledge the importance of the guests, particularly the Italian Ambassador and the Secretary of State.

Gesturing with his hands, he directed the guests into a line in front of him, running his wand up and down the victim's clothing before waving them abruptly away. One of the waiters, ignoring the gesture to be silent, hurried forward.

'*Ce n'est pas nous, monsieur,*' Scott caught the words and guessed it was French. The man sounded nervous and defensive. Not receiving a response, he tried again. 'It not me,' he said painfully, his speech so severely accented it was almost unintelligible. 'We many, many years here. No problem. Not us.' He swept an arm round the other two figures, a man and a woman, both middle-aged. 'I promise.'

'*Attends!*' The office in charge silenced him with a finger.

The head waiter said nothing further. He collapsed into a chair, his head nestling against the wall as if it was a pillow. Almost absentmindedly, he picked up a sandwich and nibbled at it, the majority of guests ignoring food in favour of alcohol, its properties well-known for deadening both guilt-ridden and despairing thoughts.

The office beckoned Scott forward. He flinched nervously. Accidentally talking to a terrorist wasn't a crime, but maybe she'd planted something on him – she'd certainly stood close enough, with her fingers brushing the sleeve of his jacket. He froze, holding his breath tightly as the electric wand swept over his clothes and sneakers. The machine remained silent and Scott sighed, an equally silent breath.

He stepped out of the line and moved to the window, his place taken by the Secretary of State, her turn to be prodded and poked like some species of cattle, the expression on her face glacial. It matched the weather outside. Even with double-glazing Scott could sense a drop in temperature. Snowflakes tumbled from the sky, the roofs and pavement already carpeted with a blanket of white, only the heavy traffic keeping roads free.

The sight of a line of vehicles exiting the underground car park like a gigantic centipede did little to alleviate the dark cloud hovering above Scott's brow. The emergency obviously had its upside, with some offices suspending work and giving their staff an unexpected bonus or an afternoon off. The absurdity of the situation made it worse somehow. That something so delicate and fragile, no bigger than a caterpillar's cocoon (and almost identical in colour and shape), had the power to create fear in people – even in the modern day.

'Come on, Scott, lighten up, you look like you've just lost the winning lottery ticket.'

Scott spotted the grin on Tulsa's face before being hastily wiped off. At least someone was happy. He glowered at the agent. 'Stop gloating.'

Tulsa seemed surprised. 'I'm not. I'm trying to cheer you up. Even with this mess, you can find something to smile about. For starters,' he pointed out of the window towards the snow-swept scene. 'I bet every single one of those people rushing to exit the building is desperately trying to remember conversations they've had since the place was swept last Monday. Some of them won't sleep tonight – remembering. In a way, you can blame the Swiss,' Tulsa chatted on, his voice quite light-hearted as if discussing nothing more serious than a day at the fair. 'They pride themselves so much on their diligence and efficiency, I'd like to bet their sweep of the building is performed at the same time each week.'

Scott caught sight of his father making his way across the room. The security officers appeared to have already swept the inner offices and cloakrooms. Now the men were on their knees in the reception room, carefully lifting the carpet around the edges and rolling it back to expose its brown underlay. Circling around them, Bill manoeuvred a path to his son's side.

'How long till we can get out of here, Dad?'

'Soon, I hope. I have asked Jane Oliver to check on flights – we may have to divert to London. We can catch a train from there.'

'We're leaving? But we planned to spend the day in Montreux tomorrow.'

Scott had been looking forward to his visit to the fabled lakeside resort ever since he'd known of their meeting with the UN in Geneva. On the edge of the lake was a statue of Freddy Mercury – one of the all-time greats. He kept a photograph of the pop star pinned to the wall in his bedroom. A legend like Elvis Presley, both had died far too young. Now, only their music lived on. Even Hilary agreed he was a great songwriter.

'I'm afraid that won't be happening, Scott. Another time, perhaps.'

'But it's all arranged,' he protested. 'We've never had a holiday outside England before and you want to cut it short…' Scott heard the stutter of indignation in his voice, his tone readying itself for an argument. 'That's so unfair, Dad. Besides, if they already know you're in Geneva, a day's not going to make much difference. We could see Montreux and go back tomorrow night, that's if we really need to go. But…'

The young officer in charge of the sweep headed towards Stewart Horrington. The Representative got to his feet, his eyes fixed on the man's clenched fist, and passed an unsteady hand across his mouth and chin.

'Bad news?' he managed.

'Five, sir.'

The American groaned silently.

The officer, his young face amiable and unconcerned, opened his fingers; the five miniscule objects sitting on his palm like dried peas that had rolled under a refrigerator and been forgotten about. He gave a brief smile, nodding to where the two men with work belts were carefully inching the edges of the carpet back into place, fixing brass carpet plates into position with small screws.

'Fortunately, nothing deep cover, sir,' he said, his English impeccable. 'Randomly distributed – it would take five minutes.' He pointed to the lamp on the desk. 'Standard placement. You lean against something, attach a bug and walk away.'

'So most likely it was the girl?' The American rubbed his chin, his voice hopeful.

'Could be anyone, sir. That's the point.' The officer stared round the room. Scott, catching his eye, immediately felt guilty again. It was gross, this guilt by association. Without being aware he was doing it, he straightened up, his hands by his sides, almost standing to attention.

Overhearing, Bill Anderson joined the two men. 'I doubt that,' he broke in. 'Among the many unforgettable memories of my captivity is the knowledge that these people are waging war with the help of teenagers. They even boasted that they are happy to use drugs to bend their supporters' minds to their will.'

'I read your report, Mr Anderson, very interesting.'

'You did. But why?' Bill said with astonishment.

'Part of my job, sir,' the young officer explained.

'You're based here?'

'Yes, sir. It's essential. This might have been a bomb scare – it has happened.' He tapped his watch. 'It took thirty minutes today to sweep these offices. We have twenty floors.' He nodded to the US Representative. 'We're done here, sir. One of my men will stay behind and finish up.'

'Ladies and gentlemen, you are free to go…' Representative Horrington indicated the officer standing by the door, who had begun to check security badges, noting the details. 'Please don't be alarmed when a security check is run on you. It's standard procedure. Can you imagine,' he confided to Bill, 'how much paperwork this is going to create.' He sounded despairing. 'We'll be up to our ears for the rest of the day.'

Sean Terry appeared in the doorway. He squeezed past the little line of guests blocking the entrance who, like competitors at the start line of a half-marathon, were frantically trying to get away. He collapsed his long frame into an easy chair, conveniently placed opposite the line of presidential photographs.

The suite of rooms was now almost empty. Waiters milled about clearing dirty plates and glasses, Stewart Horrington and his assistants had vanished into one of the inner offices, leaving the Secretary of State to chat with Emma Arneson, and Jane Oliver notebook in hand was telephoning.

Abruptly, Sean Terry shrugged his shoulders, as if ridding himself of the snow falling outside. 'Damn good job it wasn't a bomb scare.' He nodded towards the departing horde. 'The elevators would have been out of action and that little lot would have found themselves walking down twenty floors. Most look so unfit they'd have struggled with five and you'd have been up to your asses in heart attacks by the time they reached ground level.'

His face relaxed into a suggestion of a grin, something Scott knew was a very rare occurrence and, after the events of that morning, unlikely to reoccur for some time. The idea that innocent people often felt guilty for no reason appealed to SeanTerry's skewed sense of the absurd. Well, it would, Scott thought. The agent was so obsessed with his pursuit of justice he had little patience with normal behaviour.

Bill, carrying a plate of sandwiches in his right hand, side-stepped one of the men still packing his gear away and joined the group by the window.

'Bad day all round.' he held out the plate. 'Sorry Scott… Change of plan. We're probably not going to be able to leave for a while. And you must be starving. Tuck in. You too, Tulsa.'

The agent took a sandwich regarding Bill thoughtfully. 'We just witnessed something far more serious than an overheard conversation,' he said. 'The woman you were talking to, the Norwegian. When I found that bug, she looked like she'd been dealt a death sentence.'

'You're right. Emma Arneson had confided that Lotil Oil were being blackmailed,' Bill kept his voice to a low murmur.

'She was warned not to say anything. If she did, the price would be doubled. At the moment, it's twenty billion dollars…'

Tulsa whistled.

Bill smiled apologetically. 'Lotil is partly government owned and supplies sixty per cent of the country's needs. It's what we feared, Scott, that Styrus would eventually work. They proved it by stopping one of the rigs for a week. The computer system simply melted away without the slightest warning, every firewall bypassed. She begged for help and unfortunately I admitted I could…'

Scott gasped. 'But you told the United Nations you couldn't…'

'That was for your dad's protection,' Sean Terry broke in. 'No one knew it but him and me.'

Scott looked miserably at the agent. He loathed him and didn't trust him; yet… he was the one man they dare trust. 'Now, *they* know about it,' he said bitterly. 'Dad, I'm so sorry I made a fuss about Montreux…'

'You weren't to know, Scott. And, if anyone should apologise, it should be me. I let the cat out of the bag, speaking about Styrus in public.' He shrugged. 'I never imagined the UN would be bugged.'

Sean Terry spun his arm round the now empty room. 'There's still an outside chance the bugs are Europe's way of keeping an eye on us. They don't want us taking over again. It's possible, Bill, but I think unlikely. So they know about this and probably a lot of other stuff too. I've already asked for more men.'

Tulsa looked up, his glance speculative.

'I suggest, Bill, we move this little party to the Embassy. Bugs are like lice. Once you know you've got them, you never feel clean again, wondering if somehow one has slipped through and been missed. Tulsa, you take Scott back to the hotel and get your stuff together. Use the limo. We'll finish up here.'

SIX

Scott slumped back against the plush leather upholstery of the limousine, annoyed that he'd been dispatched back to the hotel with Tulsa to pack their suitcases, while everyone else went to the Embassy, to continue their conversation about the plight of Norway and how to fix it. But it was no good arguing – not with Sean Terry at the helm.

Yet, more than anyone there, he had the right to know what his father was getting himself into. After all, for months now, he'd been patiently helping his dad get better, trying to put the events of the spring behind them, working towards an ordinary, possibly even humdrum existence. Like the villagers who were content with growing dahlias for the annual flower show or taking part in a sponsored walk or hike, they no longer craved excitement and neither did he. In a moment of weakness, Scott had confessed to Tulsa, *excitement they'd had in spades*.

It had been a pretty good summer too, once exams were over and his dad fit enough to get about. Several times they had been invited to spend a day on the river, with Doug and Catherine Randal, Travers and Mary, peaceful days in which nothing more strenuous than trailing your hand through water was expected of you. The visit to Switzerland had been eagerly discussed and as eagerly awaited; the days counted down, hopeful that the long-awaited day of liberation was fast approaching – like rain for farmers who have experienced the worst drought in living memory.

Now, once again, his dad was thinking about getting involved. Okay, so he hadn't actually admitted it but Scott recognised the look – steely-eyed and stern-lipped. It was his favourite heavy-father expression, the one he adopted every time Scott was due for yet another tongue lashing about his untidy bedroom or throwing his dirty socks and pants under his bed instead of in the washing basket. Hadn't his dad learned his lesson? Last time they'd been lucky to escape with their lives. Couldn't he understand how terrifying it was to be at the mercy of men that killed on a whim? He was always moaning to Scott that he must work hard at school. What was the point, when you needed both eyes to look over your shoulder for an assassin?

Scott glanced across at his bodyguard, relaxed, staring idly through the window of the limousine at the sights, what you could see of them through the snow. It didn't involve Tulsa. He wasn't paid to worry or express an opinion. His job was quite specific, to keep them alive, and for doing that he earned a hefty salary.

The chauffeur slid open the partition. 'We've picked up a tail.'

Wanting to see for himself, Scott shifted round. Immediately Tulsa's hand was across his chest keeping him in place.

'You don't look round,' he said. 'How long?'

'Two blocks.' The driver's eyes flicked into the rear-view mirror. 'Brown Peugeot, four cars back.'

Tulsa took a small mirror from his jacket pocket, slowly raising it. 'Okay, got'em, they didn't waste much time.' He pulled out his mobile phone. 'How attached are you to your clothes, Scott?'

'Why?'

'Because you won't be getting them back for a while.' He raised his voice. 'Can you lose them?'

Scott caught the driver's smile in the mirror. 'Definitely, but they'll know we've tagged them. And then where?'

Tulsa spoke rapidly into the little machine. 'The Embassy. They might pick us up again there, but that won't matter.'

'Not the way I go. You belted up?'

'Will be, Scott?'

Scott fumbled for his belt, impatiently tugging at the strap where it had become tangled. Leaving the UN building after being told to take himself off, like a kid sent to bed after gate-crashing his parents' party, why would he even bother with anything as trivial as a seat belt. Catching sight of the time, an unexpected shiver tore up and down his spine making his hands tremble, the buckle snagging against the rim of the metal holder. It was only half-past two now, less than five hours since the driver had picked them up at the hotel, free as birds, no one the slightest bit interested in their activities. All this had been arranged since. Who on earth wielded that sort of power? Or were there vehicles stashed all over Geneva, like a colony of bumper cars, waiting for just such an eventuality – his father exiting the United Nations building? And who were they? Through the blacked-out windows, he saw a group of pedestrians waiting for lights to change before crossing the road. It could be anyone. How on earth would he recognise them in a city full of people – they wouldn't be carrying placards with the words: *repent now or die.* Scott caught a robust click as he slotted in the clasp on the seat belt. 'Got it,' he said.

The chauffeur nodded. 'Hang on.'

Scott watched him put the heavy vehicle into manual drive. Like the Suzuki he'd ridden all round Scotland, gentle noises, like the contented rumbling of a great cat, were indications of power and speed. Expensive indications too, the limousine a top of the range Mercedes, most likely powered by petrol rather than diesel, and built for a lightning-quick getaway.

Wondering what the man intended, Scott leaned forward watching the limousine cruise slowly towards an intersection, a four-way crossing with lights suspended above the roadway. Ahead, vehicles were filtering into three lanes – two of the three angling right or straight on, only the outer lane turning left across oncoming traffic. Four cars ahead, the lights stood at red. Four cars behind – their tail. The heavy vehicle glided to a halt, waiting patiently among the little queue of cars selecting the *straight on* option, and carefully keeping its distance from the one in front, like it was playing the children's game of *"Dare"*.

An instant before the lights flicked to green, as if the driver had been counting off the seconds, the engine roared, its rear tyres screaming in protest. Then they were moving. The heavy vehicle squeezed through the gap between lines of waiting vehicles to the front of the queue, the massive acceleration hurling Scott deep into the luxurious upholstery. The chauffeur spun the wheel and, at the same time stamped hard on the brakes. The rear of the car slid away. Scott's shoulder collided heavily with Tulsa's as the limousine performed a U-turn, the approaching cars bursting into movement the moment the lights hit green – burned rubber flying into the air from their tyres.

Hastily Scott screwed his eyes shut, his brain somehow taking its own decision that it might also be sensible to stop breathing because, at any second, there would be a fierce crunching of metal, followed by a blow that would knock him sideways. Startled, he hit the window frame with his other shoulder. His eyes flew open, to see the bonnet of a car sliding helplessly towards them. All around, mayhem spread as quickly as an infectious disease. Car horns broke into furious alarm calls, matched only by a screaming of tyres as brakes came into action, like the screeching of monkeys sirening an alarm call at the approach of a predator. Close by, Scott caught the loud bang as a car, unable to stop in time, tailgated the one in front. The lurching faded away and the engine cut back to a satisfied purr. He glanced down at his legs and arms, surprised to find them still in one piece. On the far side of the street, separated now by a strip of raised paving, Scott spotted the brown Peugeot, the driver impotently thumping his horn, his head turned to watch them drive past. A loud report struck the air, like a series of strident backfires, and gravel smacked into the window next to Scott. Automatically, he ducked.

'What the hell...?'

'They're shooting at us, sir,' the chauffeur said into the rear mirror. 'A bit rash, don't you think, in the centre of Geneva. Lucky though, it gets us off the hook nicely.' He waved an arm at the traffic, fast backing up. 'Plenty of witnesses.'

'You okay, Scott?'

Scott felt Tulsa's arm on his shoulder and raised his head. 'I forgot it was bullet-proof,' he admitted, a little shamefaced.

Tulsa grinned affectionately. 'I promise you, ducking is something all sensible people do. Besides it's a knee-jerk reaction, like blinking, nothing to do with bravery at all.' In the distance, sirens wailed. 'That was fast.' Again, he pulled out his mobile, quickly dialling. 'Can you get someone to trace a Peugeot?' He reeled off the licence plate. Scott heard the words. 'I doubt you'll get anything, its occupants will be long gone by the time the police arrive.'

Scott peered at the pockmarked window, star-shaped ridges of chipped glass smeared right across it in a neat line level with his head. Okay, so ducking was self-preservation but did that also account for his heart? He felt it pounding away, beating like a drummer in a rock band as if it wanted to break through his chest wall. He caught the words, 'no idea' before Tulsa closed the connection.

'Terry asked if you stuck your tongue out at them.'

Scott pulled a face. 'He was joking, wasn't he?'

'The boss joke – never. *Did you?*'

'No!' Scott exclaimed indignantly. 'I looked out of the window – that's all. Why?'

'Because this is Geneva.'

'But I've had people firing at me before.'

'Where?'

'At the motel in Birmingham…' Scott stopped, glancing once again at the damaged window. 'I see what you mean. High-speed car chases with bullets flying are only supposed to happen in movies – not in civilised countries like Switzerland. I promise you, I only caught sight of the car for a split second.' He noticed their driver staring at him through the mirror and shrugged apologetically. 'Besides, it's my dad they want, not me. But thanks,' he produced a sickly grin leaning forward, 'you were amazing. Where did you learn to drive like that?'

'Goes with the job – manoeuvring a limo like this one is child's play,' the man replied. 'It's the traffic and lights you need to learn about. That's what takes the time.'

'I ride my dad's bike, a Suzuki, a thousand cc. I'm pretty good with that.' Scott couldn't resist the boast.

Still concerned, he swivelled round in his seat, wondering if somehow the Peugeot had duplicated their manoeuvre and was once again on their tail, only to find his view blocked by a bus.

'You won't find many of those in Switzerland. Americans and English love their bikes. Swiss and Italians: their cars.'

Expertly, their chauffeur steered the heavy vehicle into a

narrow side road, more used to an average family-size saloon than a limousine. Scott guessed they were heading for the Embassy and taking the scenic route, the long way round; except it wasn't scenic. The elegant mansions of the centre had been left behind, hopefully like their pursuers, and a bank of tall concrete structures now criss-crossed the skyline.

Street after street fell behind the powerful vehicle, its speed reduced to a modest crawl unlikely to attract attention, although, Scott noticed, the driver kept a wary eye on his mirror. The streets narrowed further. Mostly empty of traffic and pedestrians, terraced houses lined both sides of the road. Cut from an identical pattern, with four windows and a door opening straight onto a narrow pavement, not even a clothes line with washing on it or a wall smeared with graffiti to break the monotony. At every junction identical blocks of apartments rose up, the shrubs in their communal gardens obliterated by a covering of snow. Even cars conformed to a rigid pattern, neatly parked in marked bays next to the kerb. Scott recognised the word *stationnement,* which meant parking in French, embossed on metal signs. Nervously, he checked the time. It was forty minutes since they had left the UN and for almost thirty of those they'd been locked among streets that seemed identical. Scott watched the driver indicating left and right with monotonous regularity and wondered if they had blundered into a maze and were trapped on a circular path that took them back to the beginning time and time again. No city could be this big – they had to be doubling back.

Abruptly, the residential quarter vanished, replaced by a single-track roadway with gated factory units. The signs pinned to the walls meant little to Scott, a series of names mostly ending in the words: *et Cie.* Parked cars were dotted about, like dice on a board. All at once he remembered it was Wednesday – an ordinary, uneventful working day for everyone in this city, bar him and his dad. The idea that no one knew or cared what had happened to them seemed both illogical and unreal. It was difficult to accept that the momentous events at the UN had passed over the heads of the residents like a cloud of radiation, unseen and unfelt.

At the far end, a forklift truck trundled back and forth unloading a lorry, drawn up alongside a raised loading bay, its cab facing outwards and blocking the roadway. Noticing the limousine approach, its driver swung up into the cab and started the engine, pulling the vehicle to one side. Abruptly, the limousine turned in through the factory gates and passed through a pair of double-doors, a mere thickness of paint between them.

'Apologies, this is the back entrance.'

The building appeared to be a storage depot, though for what Scott hadn't a clue, their chauffeur carefully manoeuvring the heavy vehicle along a narrow pathway between tall metal racks stacked with crates and boxes. As if by magic, sliding doors at the far end drew back. At first sight, it looked a dead end. Then Scott spotted a walkway, obviously intended for pedestrians and bicycles – not armour-plated vehicles. Edging slowly between high brick walls, they veered off into a second building and stopped. Behind them, doors slammed shut sealing them in. In the background, Scott caught the faint hum of machinery. Then, to his astonishment, railings grew up out of the concrete floor, encircling the limousine like an alien army of monsters. He felt the ground shudder and realised they were on a moveable ramp. He clutched the arm rest, watching the walls around them slowly descend.

'I thought they'd got rid of this entrance?' Tulsa said in an amused tone.

'They had sort of. But the present man thinks Europe is heading for trouble so he reinstated it. Today, it proved its worth. I bet they've got the front entrance well and truly tied up. Still, they won't hang around long in weather like this. When night hits, the temperature'll drop like a stone. They'll give up after a couple of hours, convinced you've already left the country.'

The ramp jerked to a standstill opposite what looked like a solid wall. Scott was just beginning to form the words *where do we go from here* when the wall slid to one side, exactly as if someone had called out 'abracadabra'. They were in a working garage, an air-gauge hanging off its walls, with a rack of spare tyres beneath it and a petrol pump next to the open doorway.

The chauffeur casually, as if passing through walls was as normal as buying a sandwich from a street-vendor, headed out into a yard full of cars, its surface criss-crossed with frozen tyre tracks, parking next to a wall. Intrigued, Scott released the catch on his belt and climbed out, watching the wall draw silently back into place. You'd never guess. Even knowing it was there it was pretty much invisible, the wall no different and equally as solid looking as the rest of the garage.

Swivelling on his heel, he examined the building at the far side of the yard. Even its rear view was imposing. With squared-off windows, it extended several stories high, its walls a gleaming white to match the snow that now covered every available surface to a depth of ten centimetres. He didn't need to be told they'd arrived, even though he'd never visited the American Embassy in Geneva before. In the middle of a wide driveway, leaning against a gated entrance that led out to the street, stood a figure that he recognised. No overcoat, despite the whirling snow and a bitter wind, his collar tight and buttoned down and his tie askew: Sean Terry.

SEVEN

Scott gazed out through the window of the four-by-four, a low mist curtailing his view. It didn't matter, every inch of the road was seared into his brain after cycling it almost daily for the past three years, ever since he had turned thirteen and decided he was quite old enough to ride the five miles into school on his own. It was a pleasant road especially on a fresh summer's morning, a tidy dual-carriageway bordered by fields in which the occasional horse or cow peered over the top of a gate; but he was still grateful that school was located on the edge of Falmouth and he didn't have to struggle through packed lanes of vehicles inching their way into the centre. Only when he was staying with Jay did he head straight through the town to his friend's house.

He still felt tired. It had been a long journey back to Cornwall and he'd slept badly too, concern for his father keeping him awake. It was all very well for Tulsa and Sean Terry but his dad had a family, who incidentally had seen very little of him in the past fifteen years. If he went back to his computer fixing other countries' problems, they were likely to see even less of him in future.

Their luck in getting the last two seats on an early-evening flight to Bristol had quickly changed to a desperate desire to be anywhere except circling a fog-bound airport. They had circled for a couple of hours before the pilot had been diverted to Gatwick, explaining to his exhausted passengers that the fog was persisting without an end in sight and the fuel situation now made landing a priority – a remark not particularly welcomed by nervous flyers. That morsel of information hadn't bothered Scott. Planes didn't run out of fuel in a country as small as England with more airports than days of the week. What did rankle was not being offered free food to compensate for the delay. The flight attendants had offered a dismal selection of sandwiches; chicken with slabs of bacon that looked and tasted like cardboard, tuna and sweet corn, or plastic cheese and pickle, all of them carrying a price tag which Scott considered an insult and, by the time he set foot on terra firma, he was absolutely starving. As promised, they had been met at Gatwick by one of Sean Terry's agents, but hadn't bothered to stop and eat wanting to get home. The fog had added a further hour to their journey and it had been almost two in the morning before they turned into the lane that led to their little cottage.

The west of England had been badly damaged by the tsunami sixteen years before, which had swept across the Atlantic leaving a dramatically changed coastline. Somerset had been worst affected and, for several years afterwards, tales of the Abbot of Glastonbury fishing for sea bass seemed self-evident as tourists gazed into lakes of salt water fifteen miles inland. Conversely, to the delight of historians and palaeontologists, in other spots the water table had dropped leaving areas of marshland never seen before. Fortunately, despite operating problems in heavy fog, Bristol airport had continued to operate during this period of world-wide turmoil without any closures at all.

During the flight, his father and Tulsa had chatted about

everything under the sun except what had taken place in Geneva, another clue as to how serious those conversations were likely to have been. Although to be fair, a conversation about gangsters trying to rub you out and taking pot shots from a moving car was hardly the right topic for a plane loaded with a hundred nervous passengers.

'What's going to happen now, Tulsa?'

'With your dad, you mean?' The agent didn't look round, concentrating on the road ahead, their fog-lights making little impression on the lingering mist. Tulsa had always found driving on the left difficult. More at home in Switzerland, he had confided to Scott that people there understood *which side of the road was which,* referring to the quaintly narrow Cornish tracks with their solid hedgerows as *flaming death traps* every time an oncoming vehicle forced him to back up. 'You'd better ask him – he won't thank me for telling you. Didn't he say anything before you left?'

'You know my dad, cheerful subjects only at breakfast. Besides, I got up late.'

Scott muttered the words, not wanting to admit he'd got up late on purpose, needing to talk to Jameson before putting forward his reasons why his dad shouldn't get involved. Jameson was brilliant at giving advice even if he hated taking it. And Travers and Mary would understand his point of view and sympathise. They'd travelled with him and Hilary to Holland, and knew first-hand about being scared for someone you love. Anyway, it was stupid to get involved in an argument with a morning ahead of geography and maths. 'A' level maths was difficult enough, without starting the day with a row. But what his dad was planning was bang out of order and all the explanations in the world didn't make it right. No way could he forget the last fifteen years, scarcely ever mixing in village life, the warnings relentlessly drilled home – *never say anything about your family, Scott, even to best friends.* If he had grown up in some ordinary family, without this huge weight of secrets on his back, he might have been like Jameson, easy-going, able to attract girls like they were bees and he the honey pot.

Scott twisted his head round, pretending to be absorbed in watching the countryside, impatiently waiting for the familiar outline of the school building to appear. Being a proper family… that's what had been promised. Now it was going to be snatched away.

Tulsa swerved the heavy vehicle around the carcass of a badger, its innards splattered across the carriageway. 'I miss possums, noisy chattering critters but friendly somehow.'

Scott's face broke into a reluctant grin. Tulsa was so laid back it was difficult to take stuff seriously when he was about. Whatever happened in the future, he would never regret having the agent as part of their little household – even if the house was really too small for three guys. Even that hadn't fazed the American for long. Within a few days of his arrival, he had installed a thin plywood partition across the living room to make a third bedroom, explaining to Scott that his family had been carpenters for three generations. 'My dad wanted me to go into the family business. I wanted to be a soldier.'

The last few months, Tulsa had taught him a lot. Responsible for his welfare while his dad remained in hospital, he had driven Scott to and from school, the silhouette of the four-by-four unfailingly parked by the entrance to the school yard, well in advance of the bell, although it became quickly apparent that no one was interested in him, the little country area as peaceful as it had always been. One week, for lack of anything other than births and deaths, the front page of the local newspaper had shown a picture of a heifer that had trampled down its fence and galloped wildly along the village high street, stopping only to munch flowers and grass as it passed, leaving gouges on lawns like the devil's pitchfork.

'When you finish with us, why don't you go back to the States and become a possum warden. It'd make a change from guarding people,' he said, half-joking. He didn't particularly want Tulsa to go but his absence would mark a turning-point; freedom from danger – something he prayed for every night.

'Do you want me to pick you up at the usual time?' Watching out for stray pedestrians, Tulsa indicated and slowed.

'Wow! There's Hilary.'

Before the agent had a chance to stop, Scott opened the door and leapt out, waving at two girls strolling towards the school gates. The taller of the two, Jenny, had been swimming captain all the way up the school. Not content with that she had recently added *school sports captain* to her growing list of titles, competing in both swimming and athletics at national level. To a stranger, Jenny would have been marked down as the tough one. Tall and athletic, she made Hilary walking beside her look quite petite and yet, as Scott knew, Hilary didn't scare easily and was a crack shot. Exempt from school uniform, sixth-formers were permitted to wear casual clothes, provided they were clean and tidy, and nearly all the girls now wore their hair long and loose. Even Hilary had given up on her pony tail, her ash blond hair sweeping across her shoulders in the light wind.

'Yes, that's fine. Thanks, Tulsa,' Scott spoke over his shoulder, not paying any attention. 'Hi, Hilary. Good half term? Did you miss me?' A delighted smile swept across his face.

'Not long enough – but it was good to see Mum.'

A dark-haired, serious-looking boy, his heavy spectacles refusing to stay put like his hair, which flew up and down as he moved, jumped his way through the queue of cars waiting in line to deposit their load of students. Placing his hand on the bonnet of a Range Rover to stop it moving, he peered through the passenger window on his way past, smiling perkily at the driver.

'What's your sister doing here, Travers?' he called to a tall, well-built youth busily dragging his sports kit and school bag from the back seat.

'Hi, Jay, she's got a shoot.' Travers slammed the back door and raised his hand in a salute. 'Thanks, Tash. See you at dinner.'

Flashing a friendly smile at Scott, Jameson wrapped his arm around Hilary's shoulders, planting a brotherly kiss on her cheek.

Okay, so it was only Jay, and he saluted all girls this way. It was part and parcel of his character, over-the-top excitability that gathered people around him in droves. It was only when Hilary became involved that Scott felt a twinge of jealousy, rather like indigestion circling his guts, wishing he could be as casual.

'The problem with you, Hilary…' Jameson began.

'Oh! So now I have a problem,' Hilary retorted, a spot of pink erupting on both cheeks. Even after nine months in an English school, she still found it difficult to relax and let the ragging wash over her.

'My dear girl, we all have problems. Scott, as you well know, has about two zillion…'

'Hey – I protest!'

Travers grinned. 'Jay's spot on. Everything with you is so serious.'

'Hang on a minute.' Jameson regarded Scott, a bewildered expression on his face. '*Is this a doppelganger I see before me?* You're not supposed to be here. You said you were back Saturday. What happened?'

'I…' began Scott.

'So, what's my problem?' Hilary interrupted, smiling gamely.

'*Darling girl.*' Jameson beamed down at her, instantly diverted. 'When a guy asks if you've missed him, not only is it impolite *not* to respond – after all, common sense will tell you that he wouldn't have asked the question in the first place if he hadn't missed *you* – but when someone like Scott who openly adores you…'

'*Watch it!*'

'Deny it, and go to hell,' Jameson retorted, a wicked glint in his eye.

'I'm not going to hell.' Scott suddenly grinned, his grey eyes leaping into life.

'You must let him down gently,' Jameson continued his lecture. 'Pointing out that it was good to see your mother, is not the way to go about it.'

Hilary glared around the circle of friends. 'Honestly, you lot, why I ever became friends with you in the first place…'

'Because we're the nicest guys in the class.' Mary, her dark hair now shoulder-length tiptoed up behind Travers, placing her hands across his eyes.

He knocked them away and, wrapping his arms round her, dropped a kiss on her hair.

Mary smiled at Hilary. 'Don't take any notice of Jay, he obviously ate sugar for breakfast.'

'I did not,' Jameson said, switching his manner to lordly, 'I will have you know…'

'New girlfriend!' Scott exclaimed, remembering that Jay mostly got out of hand when he'd met someone new. 'A new girlfriend – I bet you. Someone he met at half-term. So who is it? Come on, Jay…'

Mary kicked him on the ankle, surreptitiously jerking her thumb.

Scott caught the direction and his eyes widened. He swallowed down the words 'tell us all about her'.

'So let me tell you my news,' said Hilary quickly, picking up on Mary's gesture. 'You'll never guess…'

'Hang on a minute, you lot. Get in line.' Jameson darted to where Jenny was standing next to Hilary, head bent, pointedly scrabbling about in her bag trying to give the impression she hadn't been listening. Jameson grabbed her hand, raising it in a victory salute. 'This, in case you have never met her before, is Jenny – my new girlfriend. Jenny, meet my friends.' He gave a mock bow, ignoring Jenny's discomfort, her face scarlet.

'For the last time, Jay, I am *not* your girl-friend,' she retorted in a flustered tone. 'We happened to spend last weekend together, that's all.'

'Whoa!' Travers backed away, his hands up in the air as if fending her off. 'Come off it, Jenny. You can't go round spending weekends with guys and then say you're not their girlfriend. I mean – think about your reputation.' Travers grinned mockingly.

'Shut up, Travers. You know perfectly well it wasn't like that, because you were there. It was indoor athletics, you know, the nationals,' she quickly explained. 'Travers' brother Beau was scheduled to compete in the hurdles so Jay and Travers went along to watch. I was in the four hundred, and we sort of got talking. But don't you dare tell people I'm your girlfriend – I'll sue.'

Jameson placed his hands over his heart. 'It's not for want of trying. Give me the word, tip me the wink, and I'll be there. I have been your devoted slave, ever since… um… help me out here, someone!' He gazed dewy-eyed round the little circle of friends. Removing his specs, he batted his eyelashes at them, and even Jenny spluttered with mirth at his antics.

Scott could tell his friend had, once again, fallen under the spell of a girl and was covering his real feelings with play-acting. That's what girls never cottoned on to with Jameson, believing him shallow and flippant when they first met him, not realising that his charm and gaiety disguised a very serious and quite brilliant thinker. Eventually, though, even the most resistant succumbed to his charms.

Travers, on the other hand, was the opposite. Good-looking and athletic, girls swooned before him, even though he was not a great talker unless you got him onto the subject of his particular sport – rugby. He and Mary had been together now more than a year and seemed a permanent fixture.

He eyed Jenny, guessing her show of annoyance was play-acting too.

'Besides, Jay,' the sports captain struggled to keep her expression serious, 'I never go out with guys shorter than me.'

'Ouch, ouch, ouch!' Jameson hopped up and down on one foot. 'Below the belt. Besides, I'm only shorter because I had my hair cut yesterday.'

In the distance they heard the loud clanging of a fire bell. Automatically, the groups chattering in the school yard looked down at their watches, knowing it was the five-minute warning.

Still laughing, the six friends made their way through the school-gate, the year-sevens, who had only been at school for a couple of months, drawing politely back to let the sixth-formers into the yard first.

The comprehensive school had had its origins in the grammar school system, which had been popular in the previous century, although none of the present generation had even heard of grammar schools and, some years previously, in pursuit of modernisation the red brick turrets of the old school had been torn down to make way for a two-storey glass building. The severity of the radiation leak from the Iran nuclear disaster had forced school authorities to coat the windows with a special polymer, which meant lights were needed twenty-four-seven. It was only in the last few years that levels had dropped low enough for sports to take place outside again. Now, in summer, the grassy playing fields had once again become a gathering place rather than the school library.

Travers gave the youngsters a friendly grin as he passed. 'Were *we* ever this timid?'

'You weren't but we were,' Mary said. 'So, Hilary, your news?'

'Later, later, later,' Jameson chanted. 'And we will be, if we don't hurry. I've got important stuff to tell you, too.'

'And me.' Travers wrote a word on his hand to remind him what it was.

'Let's meet up at break and you can tell us then.'

The bell rumbled into life again. Automatically students broke into a run, aware they had less than two minutes to get to class, and anxious not to earn a late penalty. With a wave the six friends parted. Jameson clutched Scott's sleeve to stop him moving, his gaiety vanished.

'You weren't expected back till the weekend? What happened and why didn't you call me.'

'A lot happened.' Scott smiled gratefully. 'And two in the morning was too late. Come on, it can wait till break.'

Hilary's voice rose to a squeak. *'They were shooting at you?'*

'No, that's just the point,' Scott frowned. 'They were shooting at Dad – I was simply in the wrong place at the wrong time.'

'But you might have been killed,' she spluttered.

Scott shrugged, outwardly trying to appear calm and unconcerned, his pulse racing, thrilled that the possibility of his being killed had really upset Hilary. So she did care after all. *Damn Sean Terry and his veto.* 'They obviously still want him dead – and if he gets involved again…'

Heads nodded sympathetically, knowing how seriously injured Bill Anderson had been, escaping death by millimetres.

'But a secret entrance into the Embassy,' Jenny added. 'How cool is that?'

'Oh,' Scott gulped, his expression uncomfortable as if someone had trodden on his toe. 'I shouldn't have come out with that bit – it's not supposed even to exist.'

'Who are we going to tell?' Jameson said. 'A donkey looks over my fence most mornings until I feed it a carrot, and the neighbours live in France.'

'Honestly, Jay.' Jenny poked him in the ribs. 'This is serious. So what are you going to do, Scott?'

'Stop Dad going ahead with it,' Scott said, glad he had spoken out. It didn't come naturally though, not after years and years of keeping his thoughts hidden. It was nice to share and it made everything… Scott paused, trying to find the right words… *less intense, more ordinary.*

'Good luck with that.' Jameson peered round the little group their feet bunched up against the wall, the three girls facing the boys. It was a tight squeeze for six but no one complained. At least it was quiet without class mates barging in and disturbing their private conversation.

The previous year, Jameson had discovered a half-empty cupboard in the basement corridor. Realising its potential, he had immediately put a '*Hazardous Materials*' sticker on the door then, swiping the key from the secretary's office, had made a copy before replacing it on its hook.

'If anyone asks,' he said when Scott questioned the wisdom of his action, 'I shall freely admit to conducting an experiment into the unquestioning obedience of the great British public.'

Scott groaned. 'You'll never get away with it.'

'Course I will,' Jameson grinned. 'I have a reputation for conducting strange experiments and no teacher is going to admit to being taken in, especially not Fallowes, our beloved leader. Besides, no one ever comes down here. Even Wesley hasn't weaselled it out yet.'

He'd been right, and they'd now had sole occupation for almost a year, something Scott considered quite unbelievable in a school strapped for space.

'Jenny, did you bring the cake?' Jameson said now.

Jenny nodded, carefully easing a chocolate cake from a plastic carrier bag.

'What's it in aid of?' Mary eyed the cake covetously. 'That looks... oh! I could eat the lot, I'm starving; I didn't have any breakfast.'

'Don't you dare,' Travers muttered. 'Remember your poor starving boyfriend. Besides, I don't want you developing strange bumps.'

Mary blushed and kicked him with her foot. 'So why the cake, Jenny?'

'Because,' Travers broke in, 'Jenny won the four-hundred and is now British Schools Champion.'

A chorus of congratulations hit the air, Jenny's face as red as a beetroot.

When it had died down, Scott said, 'How did you get involved, Jay?' He nodded his thanks as Jenny handed him a piece of cake, unravelling a roll of kitchen paper to use as a plate.

'Travers wanted to meet up with Beau...'

'Haven't seen him for months,' Travers added. 'Not since summer. He rang to tell us he was competing in London, so I thought I'd go up and surprise him. I figured he'd probably fly us back and check in on the parents at the same time. You know what he's like. Anything for a lark.'

Beau, Travers' older brother had always been Scott's absolute hero at school. The most eccentric of the three, his maxim in life was never to sit if you could sprawl and never to drive if you could fly; and he had become the proud owner of a twin-engine Cessna on his eighteenth birthday, which he now kept at a local airfield near Oxford.

'Anyway, we went to the games but he was a no show. I rang Natasha. Luckily, she was coming this way for a shoot in Plymouth and she offered us her floor for a couple of nights.'

'And I tagged along.' Jameson ignored the interruption. 'You were busy swanning around Switzerland, and I thought a jolly in London just the thing for half-term. Good dinner and a show.'

'What did you see?'

'Jenny,' he announced with a grin.

Jenny ducked her head, staring down at the floor.

'I refused to go,' Mary said, 'when Travers told me they'd be flying back. You know how I hate those little machines.'

'But Beau's good.'

'I know that, Travers, it's the size of the aircraft I object to. If I fly, I want something that's bigger than me, with four engines.'

'You'll have to go a heck of a long way to find that,' Travers said indignantly. 'Besides Beau's Cessna is top-range – Dad made sure of that. You'd never find better even in a commercial aircraft.'

'Stop arguing, you two,' Hilary broke her silence. 'How you're ever going to survive fifty years of marriage when you can't get on for five minutes without arguing...'

'*Married?* Travers and Mary? That's not news; that's a bombshell.'

'No way, Jay, Hilary's yanking your chain. Besides, Mary understands perfectly well that I'm off to play rugby for at least the next five years. If there's a chance I can make the England squad, I'm going for it.'

'*Oh my God!* Travers, you're such a liar. Last time we spoke about it, it was, "possibly three to five years". Now, it's "*at least five*"!'

'You've got to be sensible, Mary,' her boyfriend retorted indignantly, his face flushed. 'In five years, we'll only be twenty-one. That's no age to get married.'

'So we're breaking up?'

A chorus of protests hit the air. '*No way!*'

'Hell will freeze over first,' Jameson added.

'But why athletics?' Scott said when the laughter had died away.

'Ah,' Travers beamed. 'Beau decided, since he couldn't play rugby because of his jaw, he'd take up athletics for a lark. Knowing Beau, he's only good at it. But that's not what I wanted to tell you. You remember that company that makes our specs?'

Scott nodded.

'Well, after the shenanigans in Holland, the European Court of Human Rights got involved.' Jameson took over the story. 'Don't you know about it, Scott?'

'Well, no.' Scott frowned. 'I was too busy getting Dad right. I wonder why he's never mentioned it?'

'Why the fuss?' Jenny said. She pulled her specs out of her pocket. 'We all wear specs outside – it's sort of normal.'

'I know, but we don't need to now – that's the point. Radiation's way down. Besides, that wasn't the real reason,' Jameson broke in eagerly, his normally studious face vividly alive.

Scott sighed. Even though they were best friends, it was difficult sometimes not to envy Jay who picked up snippets of information without any effort. He'd always found learning difficult, preferring to be out in the fresh air on his motorbike exploring new places to sitting studying.

'It's all because they planted secret identity chips inside the frames. The European Court decided this was *totally* unlawful and against human rights.' Jameson's eyebrows rose up above his glasses. 'Well, you'd never believe it, but the idea for this was traced all the way back to the offices of the President. There's a private member's bill in front of the European Parliament right now, censuring Rabinovitch. And he's furious. First time there's even been open criticism of him.' Jameson shook his head. ''Course, he denies it. Said he knew nothing about it. He's fired a lot of his aides – saying they must have acted independently. *We've simply got to get rid of him this time.* What's he ever done for Europe– '

'So, Scott, you're dad's a blinkin' hero.' Travers interrupted Jameson's excited tirade. 'We still have to carry identity – but it's no longer secret. They're rushing the new cards through and, Beau told me this, if you're found without it you don't automatically go to jail. You are given twenty-four hours to produce it. Dad's already applied for ours.'

'There you are, Scott, what did I tell you?' Hilary said, her tone gloating. 'I told Scott it was all a scam. That's absolutely brilliant. So me next, please.'

'Make it quick. Bell's about to go.' Jameson reminded his friends.

'I'm leaving the service.' Hilary smiled – a smile so wide and joyful it made Scott go weak at the knees. She didn't often smile, but when she did. Oh boy, was it ever great!

'When, why, how?' A chorus of voices hit the air.

'That's the best news ever,' Scott said.

'Effective immediately. I've already handed in my badge and side-arms.' Hilary rubbed her haunches. 'It feels sort of cold back there, as if I've forgotten to put my knickers on.'

'But...?'

'But Sean Terry had nothing to do with my decision.'

'That's impossible,' Scott exclaimed. 'You can't stick the guy. Now, you're standing up for him.'

'Okay. Maybe I do loathe him but that doesn't stop him being right.' She smiled apologetically. 'It took me a long time, Scott. I was like you. I hated him for interfering in my personal life. But he's right – you can't guard people you care about. You're a danger to them and you, because you're thinking more about them than what's going on around you.'

'So why?'

Hilary grimaced. 'It sounds silly coming from me. But I couldn't cope with the violence. I thought it okay at first but when I saw your dad, I knew I couldn't do it anymore.' She smiled gaily. 'I'm so relieved it's over – you'll never believe. So everyone meet Hilary Stone, sixth-form student, staying in Cornwall and studying English, art, and drama at "A" level.' To Scott's total astonishment she leaned forward, saying seriously, 'And if you ask me out, Scott Anderson, I'll say *yes.*'

Before Scott had time to respond, a loud clanging noise rent the air.

'Why does that wretched bell have to be a party-pooper, just when things are getting interesting,' Jameson said crossly. 'And I've not told you my news yet. Get a move on, Scott, or the Newt will be after you. You can leave the proposal till later. *Wow! What an incredible day.* Hilary has finally joined the human race.'

EIGHT

Scott gazed out of the window lost in a rose-coloured bubble of happy thoughts, oblivious to the diagram on the white board highlighting the rock strata of the Pennines, the backbone of England. He had chosen for his course work to contrast Snowdon in Wales with his all-time favourite, Mont Blanc in the Alps. Today's investigation, into the drawing of a cross-section of rock, seemed of little importance when compared to meeting up with Hilary to make a date for the weekend. Tragically, none of their lessons coincided so after school it would have to be. Surreptitiously, Scott huffed his breath into his hands, grateful now they hadn't stopped for supper when they landed and eaten food with garlic in it, because of all things Hilary hated garlic the most. Where could they go? A first date needed to be special if there was to be a second. Thoughts of taking the Suzuki and exploring the north of Cornwall faded as he watched rain streak long rivulets down the window pane. At least the fog was clearing. Perhaps they could go ten-pin bowling – the six of them. Scott smiled at the word *six*. It had been a long time coming.

His mobile in his jacket pocket began to vibrate and he slowly eased it out checking the sender. Hilary?

"got 2 go, leave early, urgent meet Terry. Speak later."

'Scott, if your head would connect with your body sometime today, I would appreciate it,' Mr Newman's sarcastic tone broke in. 'And I'd appreciate it even more if you would turn that wretched phone off. You know the rule – it applies even to sixth-formers.'

'Sorry, sir.' Scott quickly replaced his phone in his pocket, feeling his ears begin to burn. Still, who cared, he was going on a date with the most fabulous girl in the world. The thought left his knees weak.

By the time the afternoon bell rang, a downpour of rain had cleared away the last of the fog. Not seeing any of his friends, Scott made his way to the gate, his school bag bulging with books, praying Tulsa had parked nearby and he wouldn't have to struggle up the road. Spotting the dark blue four-by-four he broke into a jog, his heavy bag slowing him down. Opening the rear door, he dumped his bag on the seat, responding to Tulsa's cheery 'hi' with a nod, still wondering if his choice of maths, geography, and biology for 'A' level had been the right one. With Hilary about to become a permanent fixture in his life, he might well have made a serious mistake. Before then it hadn't mattered; he'd actually been grateful for something that kept him busy, too busy to daydream about a wide smile, perfect teeth, and legs to die for. But even forgetting Hilary – which was impossible – it was pretty stupid choosing subjects none of his friends were taking. Except for maths, which he shared with Jameson, none of their options were the same and he never saw them except at break and lunch. Mary had the same problem, with her choice of languages and English. She was always moaning on about not seeing Travers except on a Sunday because he was off somewhere playing some rubbish game.

Scott scowled and punched his fist into the canvas side of his bag in frustration. He might as well join a monastery. He'd got a ton of work to get through before Monday and Dad would never let him out till he'd done it. If only he'd been sensible and opted for sports psychology, like Travers and Jenny, or perhaps drama even though he couldn't act for toffee, then he and Hilary could be together. Still frowning, he climbed into the passenger seat.

'What?' Tulsa pulled out, crawling behind a line of cars heading for the main road.

'Work – that's all. School thinks you have nothing better to do.'

'And do you?'

'Definitely.' Scott grinned, once again feeling as light as air. The thought of seeing Hilary tomorrow… A dozen questions rampaged through his head. At long last he wouldn't need to sit tongue-tied as he'd done that first meeting, searching for something interesting to say. 'Hilary's leaving the service,' he said cheerfully. Restlessly, he fingered his mobile knowing exactly what he was going to do the moment he reached the privacy of his bedroom, ring her. He pulled himself upright in his seat. If this was what having a girlfriend felt like… it should become law.

'I heard.' Tulsa changed down, the engine note deepening as he accelerated up the hill towards the dual carriage-way.

'I'm over the moon about it. The Secret Service is definitely no job for a girl.'

Tulsa chuckled. 'For God's sake, don't say that to Hilary, she'll join up again just to prove you wrong.'

Scott lapsed into silence, not feeling the need to make conversation. That was one of the great things about Tulsa – he was quite happy with silence. Scott glanced affectionately at him wondering what his friend would do when the day eventually arrived and he had to quit the service. It was his life. Somehow he couldn't image the American sitting on a balcony in a rocking chair.

He peered out of the window watching sea mist creep along the river bed, coating the fields in a dark shadow. November was a horrid month – something you had to get through; the jollity of Guy Fawkes' instantly forgotten after a day back at school, with half-term over and five-long-weeks to go before the Christmas break. Most of the time it never got light at all, the sun struggling behind a thick pall of cloud, with days of frost followed by mild, soggy weather. The ferocious gales, which brought down leaves that clogged up the drains, left stagnant pools of water for midges to breed in. In biology, they had begun the autumn term examining the life-cycle of Culicoides furens and Culicoides impunctatus, the Highland midge, and why, despite all evidence to the contrary, they could survive temperatures well below zero.

Tulsa slowed, indicating left into the narrow lane that ran uphill towards the cottage where Scott and Bill lived. The land on either side belonged to a local sheep farmer, George Beale, whose family had farmed there for generations. Some years before, his father or grandfather had sold off the cottage, building something more grandiose further down the hill. The old farmer still lived in the same house, although it was no longer grand. Since his wife died George had not bothered with the upstairs, using two rooms on the ground floor. In contrast, the small cottage had been renovated by a series of wealthy owners before Bill had bought it. He had added the small studio and a wind turbine, which had been erected on the hilltop on a pocket-sized patch of land belonging to the cottage.

In summer the entrance to the lane was obscured by a dense thicket of oak and poplar, and tourists, eager to explore every inch of the Cornish countryside, swept past without noticing. Only in winter was the lane visible, its trees reduced to hollow silhouettes against a darkening sky. Along its western boundary a bank of spruce dwindled into a sparse hedgerow of blackthorn and elder. Atlantic gales had deformed the tall conifers and they leant forward as if trying to pat their stunted neighbours on the head. In the field below, the white fleece of sheep appeared like daubs of white paint in the rapidly fading light. When he was little, Scott imagined the trees to be giants running a race and turned to stone by an ogre. He smiled at them fondly, grateful the recent gales had left them unharmed.

The gate at the top of the hill stood open, which was odd. It was always kept closed… always had been. That was part of staying safe. Then he saw why. Neatly parked next to the studio was an old black Citroen.

'Oh no!' he groaned. 'Not again! What's he doing here?' He glared at the black car as if it was responsible for everything bad in his life.

'Nice way to greet my boss. You can do the garage doors.'

It was no good pretending. No matter how much people tried to tell him otherwise, the devil never changed its spots. Scott glared at the car, uncaring that he'd mixed his metaphors and had actually meant leopards. As far as he was concerned, it was the same. The presence of Sean Terry was an alarm call echoing through the jungle. He was at the UN – next minute, what happened? Someone threatened to kill his dad. And they'd tried too. Today, poor Hilary had been called in to meet with her boss one last time. What earth-shattering event was going to happen now?

Scott opened the rear door to get his bag and stopped dead. 'He wouldn't?'

'Who?' Tulsa swung round in the driving seat.

'Mr Terry. Hilary had to see him. He wouldn't…' the words caught in his throat, 'stop her leaving…'

'Scott…' The revs died away to a whisper. 'Enough of this phobia. It's stupid and childish. Not like you at all.'

'Sorry. But I don't trust the guy.'

'*You don't say!*'

Scott caught the sarcasm and laughed a little shamefaced. But what he'd said before was true. Bad things *did* seem to happen when Sean Terry was around.

Leaving his bag on the ground, he headed over to the garage doors and yanked them open. The noise startled some sparrows perched on the guttering and, with an outraged chirping, they flew off into the garden. It was a large space, amply big enough for two vehicles, although here the second vehicle was a motorbike, a Suzuki, in a brilliant fire-box red. The walls of the garage were festooned with camping and climbing equipment – none of it, except when he and Tulsa had gone to Dartmoor, used since the accident. Scott paused. And unlikely to be ever again, if his dad got involved. Surely he wouldn't let himself be suckered in by this stupid talk of Sean Terry, about a citizen's duty to his country. Dad was no longer an American. And he certainly wasn't responsible for Norway's problems. He drew in a long breath. *Sod the homework.* After dinner he'd go out. Nothing like riding fast for clearing your head and getting things back in their proper perspective.

Tulsa slid the heavy vehicle efficiently into its parking space, his gaze fixed anxiously on Scott.

'Scott…'

He hesitated, his hand on the garage door. 'What?'

Tulsa cut the engine, the silence almost deafening among the angry vibes swirling round the yard. 'Tell your father how you feel.'

'Tell him what, Tulsa? That I want to live as a family, with a mother and grandparents, and not have to look over my shoulder, every second of the day. That I want him back whole and able to climb cliffs, keeping me safe when I slip. He knows all that. Did you see that woman – Emma Arneson's face? He's not going to listen to me.' Scott shrugged. 'Mr Terry will make damn sure of that.'

'My boss isn't the bad guy here.' Tulsa climbed out of the vehicle and, closing the driver's door, flicked the button on the key fob. 'He's okay with Hilary leaving the service. Told her, she'd done a good job.'

'He did?'

'Yeah! Come on – let's get in out of this weather. I won't be sorry to get back home and leave this behind.'

'You're going! *Not you too!*' Scott's anger ignited again.

Tulsa turned his back and, leaving the garage door unlocked, headed towards the kitchen door, scooping up Scott's bag as he passed. 'Talk to your father – and calm down.'

As Tulsa opened the door Sean Terry, perched on one of the stools by the breakfast bar, acknowledged his presence with a brief nod. It was the same picture Scott had carried with him from their first ever meeting; the long frame constantly restless, alighting briefly, always leaving one foot on the ground ready to move at the slightest excuse, like a crow illegally foraging among the farmer's new seedlings.

As usual Bill Anderson was settled in a chair facing the television. There were two of them, old favourites, worn in the middle and on the arms. Before the accident, he mostly perched on a kitchen stool, except on the rare occasions when they watched television or returned to the house tired after a day's sailing or climbing. These days, it was the only place where he was comfortable, his shoulder frequently too painful to lie on in bed. Scott had become used to finding his father asleep in the chair when he woke in the morning.

It wasn't a large kitchen but a sunny one, facing south over the yard and the gate to the lane. To gain a few extra centimetres, the door to the hall had been taken off its hinges leaving an open corridor, narrow bookshelves lining one side, leading to the sitting room and bedrooms at the rear. To keep housework to a minimum everything had its place, with kitchen surfaces remaining empty and uncluttered. Except right now; Scott noticed a row of empty coffee cups standing by the side of the sink.

For years, Scott had made tea on first arriving back from school. It had been a tradition, carrying their cups out to the small studio where his dad worked. Doing what? That had been the question for which Scott had never had an answer – not until this year. At school he had said '*my dad stays at home*', leaving his class with the impression that his dad was unemployed and living off the state. He could have been for all Scott knew, except his dad never looked like someone that didn't work. And he'd always said he'd been busy, when Scott asked. Jameson had been his only friend in primary school and he never cared if Scott stayed silent because he said enough for both of them. In secondary school, it was Jameson he had to thank for Travers and Mary becoming his friends. Looking back, it had been a harsh upbringing, watching every word he did say, anxious not to slip up.

But as unnatural as it had been, it was still preferable to the ominous silence that greeted his entry. Even knowing from biology that one's heart was held firmly in place by muscle, it still made no difference, and a great sinking feeling flooded Scott's frame.

'Dad, what's happened?'

Bill Anderson looked exhausted, his face tinged grey with deep black rings circling his blue eyes.

It was a look that Scott had seen every day for weeks, damped down by heavy painkillers, but always present until the shattered bone had started to mend. 'Dad? Are you hurt – your shoulder? I knew the journey would be too exhausting.'

'I'm fine, Scott, stop worrying. It isn't me. Someone placed a bomb under Emma Arneson's car.'

Tulsa was filling the kettle with water for coffee and didn't look up, his expression unchanged. So he'd known about it already.

'She's dead?'

'No, her chauffer and bodyguard are – she's hanging on. We have to move you.' Sean Terry's bleak tones cut across the air like a bullet, sharp and decisive brooking no argument.

'But you said we were safe here in the village.' Scott shouted the words, remembering Hilary's magical smile when she had told him she was staying in England. 'You can't do this, it's my home. My friends, my school.'

'Scott, you said you wouldn't mind living in America. Remember?' Bill said his voice scarcely above a whisper.

His dad sounded as exhausted as he looked. They'd obviously been talking about moving back to America for hours and hours, depleting his father's fragile strength.

'That was before,' Scott reined his tone in. His dad never listened when he lost his temper and shouted. As a small boy he'd been sent to his room, to come back out when he'd cooled down. 'Losing your temper doesn't win friends or influence people,' his dad had lectured him. 'It only makes things worse. It's cold logic that wins an argument, not temper.'

'What about the British police?' he said more quietly.

The American shrugged. 'They're not interested. The Ambassador contacted Scotland Yard but they dismissed the connection as... unlikely.' He ended the sentence, using forceful sarcasm on the final word.

Bill got to his feet and wrapped his arm round Scott's shoulders. 'I know you think it unfair. Why should the politics of a country like Norway load themselves onto your back? They're not your responsibility. But because of me, you are involved, and so are Sarah and Nancy. We're all in this together. They're safe because they're hidden, and we're going to be safe too. Sadly, it won't be here. I know you love this place,' he hesitated. 'But the bugging of the offices in Geneva, and now this… It's changed everything.'

Scott shrugged off the arm, the thoughts in his head like a whirlwind of spikes as long as cactus thorns. He felt a sharp, piercing pain as they stung him.

'This is all *your* doing.' Uncaring, he hurled his words at the person responsible. 'We were happy till you burst on the scene persuading Dad to go to the UN. If we'd never gone we'd still be okay and Emma Arneson wouldn't be fighting for her life. If she dies, it's your fault, Mr Terry.' The words bounced accusingly off the kitchen walls. 'Dad, you can't do this again,' he pleaded. 'You're not strong enough and I won't stand by and see you hounded and killed by those men.' The angry flow of words faded away. 'I know what I said but even I can see they've grown too powerful. One day, Dad. One day! That's all it took and that… and that… woman is blown up.' Scott floundered unable to recall her name.

'That's why you have to leave.' Sean Terry's expression was bleak, his words unemotional. Histrionics played no part in his life. 'Your ticket is booked for Saturday. That gives you a day to say goodbye. Your dad argued for it. Reluctantly, I agreed. Left to me, you'd have gone out of the door now. Tulsa will go with you, while your dad heads for Norway. We'll send your stuff along afterwards.'

Scott spun on his heel. 'So you're in it too, Tulsa. That's what you meant by the weather in America being different. Why didn't you tell me? I trusted you.'

Tulsa backed away, holding up his hands in surrender. 'Scott, it wasn't my job to tell you. Anyway,' he shrugged. 'I thought it'd be better coming from your dad. It won't be so bad – new horizons, new places to explore. Somewhere you won't be looking over your shoulder. It'll be great. You'll see.'

'Well, you enjoy it because I'm not going. I'm quitting this cat and mouse game. I'm giving you formal notice, Mr Terry. Leave me alone.'

Grabbing his jacket and school bag, Scott backed out of the house slamming the door. Breaking into a run, he tore into the garage. How could he possibly leave now when he and Hilary... and his dad? He was far too ill to help. He should have been left alone to get better. Fumbling about, he grabbed a handful of books, stuffing them anyhow into the compartment under the raised pillion seat on the Suzuki, wedging his empty bag in on top. Pulling his keys from his pocket he turned the ignition, the machine bursting into life.

Bill appeared in the garage doorway. 'Scott, come back in. Going off in a state like this – it's so childish, it's not like you.'

'I agree... *it's not like me*. Perhaps seeing you blasted off the face of a building changed me. I'd be surprised if it didn't,' Scott spat out. He glanced miserably at his father his tone changing. 'Don't do this, Dad. I'm begging you.'

'I have to, Scott. There's no one else.'

'Let them use the experts at the UN. You said yourself they were good. Make *them* do some work, that's what they are being paid for.'

'It won't be so bad, Scott. And it'll be over soon.'

Scott shook his head helplessly, tears pricking at the corner of his eyes. 'So everyone keeps telling me. But it never is, Dad.'

Compressing his lips into a tight grimace, he opened the throttle. As responsive as always, the heavy machine soared effortlessly into motion. Helmetless, a brisk wind streaking through his hair, he tore through the gate and down the slope towards the main road.

NINE

Travers opened the door. 'Sorry I took so long,' he said, nodding in a friendly way to Scott, his finger poised to ring the bell for a second time. 'I thought it was one of Natasha's hangers-on. Can't stick the current one... chinless wonder. Even cash can't make up for his lack of brains. All he can do is drive a car. I mean, I'm not too bright in the upper storey,' he prattled, his smile friendly and welcoming. 'Compared to him, I'm Einstein. So, to what do I owe the pleasure?' Travers peered over Scott's shoulder noticing the Suzuki parked in the driveway next to the garage.

'Can I stay the night?' Scott followed his friend into the hall.

The house on the river had been designer-built especially for the television star. A world-famous rugby player, responsible for England winning the World Cup on two separate occasions, retirement had taken Doug Randal into television where, in addition to regular slots as a guest on talk shows, he now produced many of its sporting highlights. A house in London and a place on the river gave him a base to entertain celebrities, and an elegant motor launch, in constant use in the summer for exploring the river and coast, had been given a purpose-built home in which to spend the winter.

"Course. So what's up?' Travers replied good-humouredly 'Does there have to be something?'

'No, but there usually is. Mum's about somewhere, I'll ask her. Dad's missing, as usual. Messing around on the boat, I expect. As I said, Tash is about to go out, so it'll only be us. Ah, here's the guy now.'

A long, silver Maserati swung into the long drive, its soft-top raised against a chilly north wind, its engine almost soundless. It drew up behind Scott's bike.

'This guy gets a new car every year on his birthday,' Travers whispered under his breath, his tone pitying. 'He told us – several times.'

A willowy, fair young man climbed leisurely out of the sports car. Carefully latching the driver's door behind him, he removed his specs, pausing to check his appearance in the wing mirror, casually flicking a lock of hair into place.

'Hi, Scott, not often I see you twice in one day. You stalking me?'

Natasha, the oldest of the three Randal children, appeared at the top of the wide staircase. At twenty-two, almost six years older than Travers, she had always seemed so grown-up and far too grand to notice a scrawny schoolboy. Scott gazed admiringly, watching her trip lightly down the steps, her legs, which seemed to go on for ever, encased in a pair of tight jeans. She might almost be within reach age-wise now but she was planets away in terms of sophistication.

Travers grinned wickedly. 'Your ride's almost here, only he had to stop first to check his make-up.'

Natasha broke into giggles, all at once looking absurdly young and pretty. Guiltily Scott remembered Hilary.

'Shush, he'll hear,' she hissed. 'And it was so kind of him to pick me up.'

'Where's he come from?'

'The other side of Bath.'

'But that's a hundred and twenty miles away.'

'I know,' Natasha cooed. 'Isn't that sweet.'

'More fool him,' Travers retorted indignantly. 'You in tonight?'

'Not likely.' Natasha pointed to her overnight bag. 'I've been invited to stay overnight at the parental pad in…' She waved her arm vaguely through the air. 'Wherever the shoot is tomorrow. That's how we met.'

'Well, I suggest you get rid of him before Beau hears about it. And don't let them meet. You'll never hear the last of it. You know what he's like. I can accept that you're a weak and feeble woman easily attracted by bright and shiny things – and I don't mean him. *I mean the car,*' Travers growled out.

Natasha caught Scott's grin. 'You like cars, Scott?'

He nodded, all at once tongue-tied as she zoomed in on him, her dark eyes intense under her long lashes.

'My two pathetic brothers seem incapable of understanding that I worship cars. When I was a kid, I wanted to be a racing driver.' Natasha spun round, twirling on her scarlet stilettos, and casually raised one arm into the air. 'Hi, Jonathan, be with you in a minute,' she called waving merrily. Lowering her voice to a murmur. 'I promise you, it's worth an evening of deadly boredom if I get to drive that car. Dad's loaded but even he can't afford a Maserati.'

Scott smiled. They were a great family, Travers was so lucky. His own sister, Nancy, was only a kid and there'd been no chance to get to know her yet. *Nor will there ever be,* he thought wearily, not if Dad becomes involved in Norway's problems. They'd be under starter's orders to get running again, as fast as they could, to keep one step in front of their killers. For a moment he felt almost thankful for Sean Terry and Tulsa keeping them safe, quickly banishing his gratitude at the thought of leaving Hilary.

'So what are you doing here?' Travers repeated, closing the front door on his sister.

'Went to find Jameson but...'

'Naturally,' Travers interrupted good-humouredly.

'You forget, he's lives closer,' Scott protested.

The Brody house in Falmouth, although large, was not in the same league as the mansion the Randal family occupied. But when it came to the question of a sleep-over, or storming out after a quarrel with his dad, Jameson's was the obvious choice, within easy distance of the small cottage. It was only after passing his test, and with access to his dad's bike, that Scott could reach Travers' house. Besides, Scott had known Jameson since day-one of primary, the Randal family moving from London to Cornwall a few years later.

Whenever Scott thought about it, he still found it astonishing to have Travers and Jameson as best mates. Both were destined for stardom, whereas he... Scott paused, thinking... he wasn't especially good at anything. The best he could hope for was a half-way decent job when he left school.

'Yeah, and you've known him for ever. May I remind you, that I now know more about you and your dad's problems than even Jay does.'

Scott started back. He'd never given it a moment's thought. But it was true. Being present in Holland at every step, from his own capture to his father's injury, had given Travers the edge. Scott screwed up his face. To be honest, Travers was probably easier to deal with too. Jay was so swept away with everything he did, on occasions he couldn't bring himself down to earth long enough to listen to someone else's problems... even his best friend.

'Mary's upstairs.'

'She live here?' Scott said with a grin.

'I wish. But tonight we're actually doing some work. I'll tell Mum you're staying.'

Scott pulled out his mobile. 'I'll give Jay a call. He wasn't picking up a while back.'

Travers nodded, padding off towards the rear of the house, leaving Scott to make his way upstairs to the family sitting room, where he knew Mary would be. He liked both houses, the Randals' and the Brodys', feeling equally at home in both, even though they were at opposite ends of the spectrum – like the two families. The Brody house was cuddly, exactly like Mrs Brody. She had never gone out to work, devoting her life to her children, and three children apiece was pretty much the only thing the two families had in common. Two boys and a girl – except in the Brody family Jameson was the eldest and his sister the youngest.

The Brody house in Falmouth, although recently built with solar panelling as standard, had few pretensions toward grandeur, only the lounge sacrosanct and kept for visiting guests. The rest of the time, including Christmas, the family were to be found either in the kitchen or the conservatory; a huge room furnished with soft chairs and sofas covered in cotton chintz, its pattern of silver-pink roses hidden under piles of magazines and bags of knitting wool. It was here everyone congregated in the evening to talk or watch television.

By contrast the Randal home resembled a show home, with original paintings, including a full-length portrait of Catherine Randal at the top of the stairs. She had worked in the fashion industry until five years previously, starting her career as a model in London. Both she and Doug were often in the capital on business and a housekeeper had been employed to look after the three children, plus several women whose job it was to keep the house spotless.

Scott paused on the top step gazing back down into the hallway, admiring the elegant pattern of floor tiles in a soft yellow – absolutely perfect. The river house radiated a Mediterranean feel of warm summer sunshine, its floors covered with Persian rugs in the winter. On the first floor were five bedrooms, including one for school friends, plus a second sitting room for the exclusive use of the family; guests being housed in an annexe that also contained a small kitchen, a swimming pool and a billiards room.

Scott had realised ages before that there was nothing majestic or Mediterranean or chintzy about the cottage he shared with his dad. It had four walls and a roof – plain and simple. With no one but them to do the cleaning and cooking, possessions had been kept to a minimum; no pictures, knick-knacks, or even souvenirs of a holiday – not that they ever took real holidays. Not even photographs decorated the surfaces, except for one of his mother by the side of his bed. At the time Scott had thought it was to save on housework because most of his fights with his dad were about the mess in his bedroom, never tidying it to his dad's satisfaction. And how many million times had his dad sarcastically commented, 'Your bedroom would be greatly improved if it had less dust in it. The spiders might enjoy their environment, I certainly don't.'

It was only now Scott understood how possessions might have provided clues to his dad's past and identity, something that had to be avoided at all costs; a past which, for fifteen years, he had successfully kept hidden. Okay, so it might be a box with walls but it was still home, bursting with memories of growing up, and no one, least of all Sean Terry, had the right to make him leave.

Mary glanced up smiling as he opened the door.

'Surprise,' he said sounding rather lame.

'I saw you coming up the drive.'

'Jameson's not home and he's not answering his mobile.'

'Jenny said he was off to London.' Mary patted the seat next to her on the couch.

'London? He never said anything to me.'

'He confided in Jenny that he didn't want to steal Hilary's thunder by talking about it because the news had made you so happy.'

'You sure you've got the right guy? That doesn't sound like Jameson.'

Mary broke into giggles. 'Travers thinks he's desperately smitten and wants to come over as all caring.'

'Even so,' Scott replied indignantly. 'Jay always answers his phone. He's paranoid about missing stuff.' He collapsed onto the sofa, feeling strangely restless. Not only about himself but Jay too – he had the strangest feeling. 'It's not like Jay not to answer his phone,' he repeated.

'Jenny said he was going for an interview.'

Travers' head appeared round the door. 'You staying for dinner, sweetheart?'

'I'll stay for ever if your mother's cooking.'

Scott heard his friend shout down the stairs. 'Yes, Mum, please.' He came back into the sitting room and closed the door behind him. 'Who's going for an interview?'

Good humouredly Scott shifted to one side, allowing Travers to take his place. 'I was only keeping it warm.'

'Jay is,' Mary said. 'Jenny said he was over the moon about it. Apparently, some global conglomerate is head-hunting him. He was coming back on the late train. He left school early and went up after lunch.'

'He never said anything,' Travers protested.

'You're right, he didn't,' Scott agreed. 'Weird, even for Jay.'

'To be fair,' Mary jumped in, 'you didn't give him much chance. You were telling us about Switzerland, remember? And then Hilary took over the conversation. Ring Mrs Brody. She'll know. *Stop blowing on my neck and distracting me, Travers.* You promised you'd work if I came over,' she said, her tone reproving. 'Honestly, you'd think I'd have learned by now.' She flipped her hand sharply, making Travers jump. 'I said *quit... I'm not fooling.* I've got English to do.'

'Shush!' Scott hissed. 'Mrs Brody, it's Scott. Any news? Oh, good! I was worried. Yeah, it's not like him. I guess he was in the interview. Well, that's good news anyway. Speak to you tomorrow. Bye.' Scott beamed, closing the connection. 'It's okay. Thanks, Mary, glad I called. He's staying over for a second interview in the morning. Apparently, they're waving big money to start straight away – an internship.'

'But what about his "A" levels,' Mary said, sounding concerned.

'And university,' Travers added.

'I know!' Scott picked up Mary's book on English poets, flicking through it. 'Isn't that just typical! For years, it's been Oxford-Oxford-Oxford. Someone waves a bunch of notes in front of his face, and Jay jumps at it.'

'We don't know that. Hi, Mr Randal.'

The door opened and Doug Randal peered in. 'He's right here, if you want to speak to him...' He held the phone out. 'Bill wants a word.'

Scott leapt to his feet, shaking his head violently from side to side. Travers and Mary gazed at him in astonishment.

'Apparently, the feeling isn't mutual.' Doug Randal raised a hand before disappearing again, the door closing on the words 'I guess we can hang on to him.'

'Scott?' Travers and Mary spoke together.

Scott sighed. 'We had a blistering row and I walked out.'

Travers got to his feet, pushing his friend down onto the sofa next to Mary and perching on the arm.

Mary slipped her arm through Scott's. 'That's not a bit like you.'

'So everyone keeps telling me.'

'You're always so worried about your dad.'

Scott reined his anger in. 'I know, Mary. I am worried – desperately – and he can't see it.' He leapt to his feet, pacing up and down. 'That Norwegian woman from the UN, someone tried to kill her. Blew her car up.'

Travers and Mary exchanged horrified glances.

Scott continued his restless prowling. 'She might already be dead, for all I know. Someone tried to kill Dad too. That's why we cut our holiday short. Remember, I told you they took pot-shots at me.' He shrugged. 'I just want him safe. Not going to school every day, wondering if he'll be okay.' Scott swallowed loudly. 'Is that too much to ask? And now Sean Terry says we have to leave the cottage…'

'What! When?' Mary broke in.

'When what?' Scott stopped dead, staring at his friend as if he'd never seen her before.

'When are you leaving?'

'Saturday… didn't I say?'

'But that's…'

'The day after tomorrow! I know, Travers. Have you ever heard anything like it? Two days! Not even two days… to close up my life of sixteen years,' Scott fumed. 'Placing everything into a neat package for that…. Oh, I hate that man,' Scott swore. 'Why couldn't he leave us alone? We were fine till he came along with his grand ideas about the United Nations.'

'Your dad's really in that much danger?'

'And some!' Like a balloon bursting and letting out the air, Scott dropped down into a chair, all fight gone. 'I know we have to go. And I know I didn't help any by walking out. But I couldn't stand it another minute. It's like… the walls are closing in.' He gave a wavering smile. 'Sorry, you two. Didn't mean to bore you with my problems.' He shrugged. 'It all seems so hopeless.'

'But… but Hilary?'

'Yeah, don't you just love it?' Scott glowered at the floor, his arms wrapped over his head. 'Talk about timing. She arranges to stay here at the exact same moment Terry is planning to take us to the States. He sorted that out well.'

'Your dad? Does he know?'

'Not about Hilary. There's no point.' Scott's voice was muffled. 'Terry's made up his mind for him. He's so fired up about Norway's troubles he's forgotten how his own life was destroyed. Now he's planning to do it all over again. And, however much I shout and holler, there's nothing I can do to stop him.'

TEN

Scott slept badly. Overnight the stark reality of the situation hit home. Doug Randal had said he could stay – and another night might be on the cards. Even then, he'd still need clean clothes. His jacket and jeans would do for a couple of days but not his underwear. Travers had offered and, worst come to worst, he'd accept.

Except, he had rocks in his head if he believed that could happen. He hadn't got a couple of days and it was stupid to pretend otherwise. This wasn't the sort of row where he could storm out and not return until it had blown over. This was something over which neither he nor his father had any control. He couldn't stay because the danger didn't stop with his dad. Their enemies had attempted to get hold of him once before. He was the weak link – if they found him, they could force his dad's hand.

Mrs Brody had always said that he and Jay were as close as brothers and he could live with them anytime he wanted. In any other circumstances… But where was Jay? Scott flipped open the cover on his mobile, hoping to find a text. Jameson had called at break and left a message but nothing since. And, once again, his phone was switched off.

He glared at Mr Newman who was chatting to one of the

students about their geography project, holding him personally responsible for the missed call. *No phones in school. No exceptions even for sixth-form.* That's what the Newt had ordained at the beginning of term and he'd broken the commandment once already this term. But today of all days, why hadn't he left his phone on? He knew why: because he didn't want to speak to his dad. He had to go and he had to leave Hilary but he'd be damned if he was going to talk about it.

In his head, he saw a removal van crawling up the slope, its interior full of boxes. Their lives. Uneasily, he shuffled his feet finding it difficult to sit still, wanting to reach the cottage before that happened. He simply had to get his stuff, especially his mother's photograph before the removal van appeared and shredded his life into strips of bubble wrap. Scott tried to banish the images crowding in, seeing the cottage empty, the garage a vast cavernous space without its climbing and sailing gear, the rooms inside echoing after the removal men had cleared everything out. Nothing left but an empty shell full of memories, stripped and deserted like a building scheduled for demolition, surrounded by barbed-wire to keep out the homeless.

And Hilary! What could he say to her? How could he tell her he wouldn't be seeing her again, watch the excitement of yesterday fade away at his news? Just when they'd reached this unspoken agreement, it was over before it had even begun. But, whatever he told her, he had to make it sound good. Try to act cheerful, even if he felt like dying inside.

Scott watched his class-mates flock out of the room the moment the bell sounded, unable to throw off the feeling that he was riding a runaway train, overwhelmed by a series of unstoppable events crowding in on him. Despairing, he slammed his fist on the desk top. He couldn't deal with all that now. First things first… Jay. Clamping the phone to his ear, he replayed Jay's message. He'd already listened to it a dozen times trying to work out – what? If his friend was scared or worried? And why the Weasel? Scott listened again, silently repeating Jameson's words as he spoke them.

'It's me. Got to be quick. Told them I needed a pee. Did you hear about the interview? I don't think I'm going to accept. I guess that makes you happy. Why? Too much money for a kid like me. Something's wrong. It's got to be a scam. Weasel set it up. Thought it too good to be true at the time. Check with him and ring me back.'

That's when Jay's mobile cut out.

Scott dialled again, the answer-phone breaking in... *leave a message.* Where was the Weasel? And why listen to him in the first place? He was a snivelling rat. He'd always been a snivelling rat, ever since he'd joined their community the year previously, no change there. So what had he got to do with this? And why hadn't Jay called back?

Leaping to his feet, he hurried out into the crowded corridor heading for the canteen. 'Gangway, coming through. Anyone seen the Weasel?' he called, elbowing the chattering groups impatiently aside. He flung the question left and right, scarcely noting heads shaking and ignoring a muttered, 'You have to be joking. I keep well away.'

'Scott? *What's going on?* I missed you at break.'

Hilary pushed her way through the queue towards him. Scott smiled at her, all his problems wafted out of sight on a rose-coloured cloud that was Hilary. It felt like he was seeing her for the first time; newly born, every inch of her skin soft and waiting to be touched. Without thinking, he hugged her to him, kissing her hair, soaking up the fresh aroma of her shampoo.

A chorus of whistles broke out and Hilary stepped back her face scarlet, her fair hair glistening, the overhead light reflected in her blue eyes – now furiously scowling at him.

'What's that in aid of?'

'I've wanted to do that for ages,' he admitted.

'But not in school, you... imbecile,' Hilary said forcefully.

'I'm just making sure I get it in before we're torn apart.'

'*Torn apart?* What's got into you, Scott? Tell me? *Tell me?*'

'Later! I have to find the Weasel first. You see him anywhere?'

'He's in the canteen. Why?'

Scott grabbed her hand, pushing hard against a row of backs. 'Jay's gone missing. Come on, you lot, let us through. We're not eating.'

Reluctantly the herd of students split in two, leaning casually apart, not for one minute ceasing their noisy chattering. Scott forced his way through the gap dragging Hilary after him.

The cafeteria was busy. Fifteen hundred students attended the comprehensive and lunchtimes needed to be staggered to cope with its daily influx of hungry bodies. The senior school drew the short straw making do with both a later lunch-hour and a truncated one, which gave them a longer day, afternoon school finishing ten minutes after the juniors.

Wesley was sitting on his own reading a book, wading through a lunch of jacket potato, beans and salad.

Scott rattled the chair opposite him to get his attention, quickly sitting down, while Hilary remained standing. 'I want to know about Jameson?'

The boy didn't resemble his nick-name in the slightest. Slightly overweight, he was neither long nor thin, and his face was round rather than pointed. The nickname had arrived almost immediately after Wesley had joined the school because of his interest in Jameson. 'Weaselling out my life-history,' Jameson had complained indignantly to his friends – and it had stuck. It was the boy's persistence, following Jameson round like a puppy dog, that had led to their taking up residence in the broom cupboard every lunchtime and break.

'What about him? He went for an interview. I arranged it.'

The accompanying smirk infuriated Scott. 'I know that, he phoned. What I want to know is – who with? Who are these guys?'

Wesley shot upright. '*What do you mean?* They're business people. They want Jameson to work for them – that's all.'

'So why is Jay phoning me to say he's nervous about accepting?'

'He can't *not* accept. That's so crazy.'

'Why can't he?' Hilary broke in, her tone fierce. 'What are you playing at?'

The teenager leapt to his feet, leaving his lunch unfinished on the table. 'Nothing! I… I… applied… they didn't want me. Jameson's so lucky.'

Hilary grabbed his arm, staring intently. 'Why, you weasel. You're on a commission.'

'So what!' Wesley pulled his arm free. 'So what, there's no law against it. He's made for life with this job. I did him a favour. You ought to thank me.'

Almost breaking into a run, he vanished through the swing doors, the queue of students separating into two lines as he barged through using his elbows as a battering ram.

Hilary screwed up her eyes, staring after the fleeing figure. 'So Wesley's on a commission. How come? It's not like he works for an agency. And why the vanishing act? Did you notice how riled up he was? Here…' She subsided into the empty chair, her hand outstretched for the phone. 'Let me listen to that message.'

Scott passed his mobile across the table. Hilary listened in silence. 'And he's not answering?'

He shook his head. 'I rang his mum. She's starting to worry. I mean Jameson acts cuckoo sometimes but he'd never go off anywhere without letting his mum know. I don't know how much they're paying Wesley, but we'd better get an address of the hotel out of him before she calls the police.'

The five-minute warning bell sounded for the junior school, a clattering of chairs making conversation impossible as students hurriedly stood up. Hilary got to her feet too, her hand on the back of her chair. 'I've got to go. I've got a tutorial now.' She fixed Scott with a look, which he understood to mean she still had something to say. He waited patiently for the noise level to drop.

'Look, meet me after school. Meanwhile, I'll find out his home address from the school office…'

'You can do that?' Scott smiled gratefully. This was the Hilary he loved. He blinked at the word 'loved' quickly substituting 'liked'. So different from him, clear cut and precise. He specialised in woolly round the edges. Except now. For the first time ever he knew what he wanted. Dad to stay put and Hilary in his life.

'Sure. We'll go there after school. On the way you can explain your remark about being torn apart.' Hilary giggled suddenly. 'I should be flattered that you are feeling miserable about spending an afternoon in isolation studying… er… what do you study in geography…'

'Biology.'

'Whatever!' Hilary waved her arm nonchalantly. 'While I am the other side of the campus acting out Shakespeare.'

'I wish it was only that.' Scott bit his lip, quickly swallowing the rest of the sentence. There wasn't time to explain properly. Not even a superhero could come out with the words: *after today, two thousand miles of water will separate us,* and still make it to class.

Scott stared unseeing at the line drawings on the table in front of him, showing the various stages in the development of an amphibian. His thoughts whirled silently like a hover fly, flittering past Jay's vanishing act to land on the words he wanted to say to Hilary. He began rehearsing them over and over – *that fate was about to drive a wedge through their friendship* – alighting briefly on what he was going say when he did get home. The nerves in his belly griped with anxiety and hunger. Like Hilary, he'd not bothered with lunch, roaming restlessly round the school yard desperate to leave and get home… and sort that out. And he would have, except he'd promised Hilary they'd meet up. And nothing, not even war, would stop him doing that. Besides, he wasn't wrong, not this time, and he wasn't apologising to his dad just to keep the peace – no way. His mind flipped, seesawing violently up and down. What Sean Terry had done was totally vile. He was the professional. He should have known what would happen if his dad got involved. You couldn't put people's lives at risk like that – it was grotesque.

Under cover of the lab table, Scott pulled his mobile from his pocket, anxious not to miss a message coming through, willing it to burst into life, and quite happy to accept the consequences if it did. Jameson… Jameson… he silently repeated. *Get in touch.*

'Scott?'

He jumped, quickly glancing up at the sound of his tutor's voice. 'Sir?'

'You have a problem? I can't see you doing much work.'

'Sorry, sir. Daydreaming.'

Scott picked up his scalpel, glancing sideways at the skewered dead frog on the bench in front of him. Why the hell did he opt for biology? If he'd been sensible and chosen drama like Hilary, at least they could have spent a couple of hours together, not the few minutes they'd had in the canteen.

By the time the school bell rang for the end of the day, Scott's nerves were in shreds like his finger-nails, bitten down to the quick. Shoving the mangled remains of his frog into the lab refrigerator, he was out of the door first.

The decision to allow juniors to finish school before the seniors had been taken some years back, after one of the year-sevens had been injured, stepping out into the road in front of a car accelerating away from the kerb. Staggering the end of the day was supposed to reduce the chaos and lessen the chances of a similar accident happening. In practice, it made little difference. Teachers often used the extra minutes as punishment time, holding an inattentive class back for ten minutes or so; and coaches, hired to carry pupils to and from outlying villages, still had to wait for the seniors. As Scott pushed open the outer doors, he was struck by a wall of sound. He gazed round indignantly wondering why the juniors needed to shriek across the yard to their mates, like they'd not met up for a year or two.

Beyond the gates, it was worse – total chaos. The side road was narrow and already littered with the parked cars of residents. Parents, dropping off and collecting in the morning and afternoon, shape-shifted into wild beasts using horns and teeth to win a parking space over a rival, and frequently forcing their vehicle into spaces far too small, leaving the bonnet or rear sticking out into the road. Those arriving late only added to the confusion, stopping on yellow lines or in prohibited parking bays, their engines impatiently running, pounding their horns to alert offspring of their arrival. Departing cars were forced to hang back, waiting for the road to clear.

Scott spied the familiar shape of the four-by-four and Tulsa, his arms casually folded across his chest. He was parked quite close to the school, which meant he had arrived early obviously expecting Scott to return with him. But, whatever was happening at home, however mad his dad got at him, there'd be no clue in the agent's expression. Always the same, cheerfully polite, giving nothing away. That's what made him such a great companion, even if he was old enough to be Scott's dad; never patronising or judgemental, frowning or critical, giving everything Scott threw at him the same relaxed attention.

Spotting Hilary exiting from the side entrance of the school theatre behind a group of her class-mates, Scott waved madly to attract her attention. Flashing a smile, she broke into a jog, pushing her books into her bag as she ran, carefully side-stepping a couple of boys jostling about throwing mock punches.

A little way down the road, the same scenario was being repeated at the primary school where kids were still wildly chasing round and round the playground uttering loud screams of pleasure, until dragged away by an already-fraught parent; others noisily thumping a football against a wall and notching up the decibel level to blast-off proportions.

From behind the queue of cars came the sound of a base drum, the echoing sound momentarily drowning the noisy chattering and roar of car engines, and a knot of garishly garmented figures inched into view. Outlandish amongst a sea of navy blue blazers, their costumes appeared creased and dirty, slung together haphazardly as if, at the last moment, the wearers had decided to enter a competition for the worst-dressed pantomime character. On one side of the road, a barrel-shaped clown was handing out leaflets, passing them through windows to bemused-looking motorists. The colossal shape belonged exclusively to his trousers, the man underneath tall and skinny. Scuttling about like a crab, the skirt-like trousers were attached by a wide hoop held up by scarlet braces. It swayed alarmingly, banging noisily against the side panels of cars and making their occupants jump.

Idly, Scott wondered what they were advertising. Mostly, events like this were for a new fast-food outlet. The figure on the right, in a badly fitting red wig and garish white face-paint, was thrashing a drum in a monotonous repetition of two beats – dumm – dumm – more likely to repel customers than attract them. A third member, also a clown, was parading about on stilts. He lurched along the road, trailing one hand along the roof of parked cars for balance, using them as leaning posts while he passed over a leaflet to its driver. Dangling from his waist was a trumpet. Whenever he went to play it he teetered helplessly, rocking dangerously backwards and forwards, until the drummer reached up a hand to steady him. But it was the fourth member of the quartet that everyone was staring. Dressed as a storm trooper from an ancient *Star Wars* movie, all the rage when Scott was a kid, they had vanished off the scene years ago replaced by demons, vampires, and mutants. The suit was obviously old, the white pre-formed plastic cracked and ill-fitting. Designed for someone shorter, a pair of blue jeans peeked through its plastic knee joints. The man was prancing along the street, scrutinising every person as he passed, aiming his black E11 blaster at an audience of watching children. They jumped back in mock-surprise, squealing and with excitement.

Hilary arrived at his side and slid her arm through his. 'Are they for real?'

Scott smiled down at her. 'I expect it's advertising a new restaurant. And they've timed it brilliantly.' He pointed to the line of cars stuck behind the procession. 'No one's going to forget them.'

Hilary screwed up her nose. 'But they look gross. No one with any sense would eat there, including me. So…? *You missed me?*'

Scott's heart skipped a beat. Hilary was joking he knew that, turning his own words back on him. Somehow, she seemed so different like another person, light-hearted and fun, the same as that morning at the loch when, for a split second, she forgot her ambition to become the best agent in the world. It was great. And he was to going to ruin it.

'Of course!' He exaggerated his tone to show he'd got the joke. 'But that's not it.' He pointed to the gate. 'We have an escort. I left my bike at Travers' house and he's in the sports hall – trampolining.' Scott's mouth twisted in a grin. 'It'll be ballet next.'

'I got Wesley's address.' Hilary smiled triumphantly. 'Don't ask how. I'd have to kill you if I told you. Do you think Tulsa will take us there first?'

Scott hesitated. The dreaded confrontation with his dad would happen whatever time he got back. 'Let's ask Tulsa to drop us at the Randal house. We can pick up the bike, check out Wesley, and then go somewhere quiet to talk. I'll tell Tulsa I'll be back later.'

'Not going to happen,' Hilary bellowed the words as the drumming and shouting of the children grew nearer. She pointed towards the agent. 'He wants you to go with him now.'

'How do you know that?'

'His arms are folded,' Hilary yelled into his ear.

'That's it? His arms are folded?'

Hilary screwed up her face, grinning triumphantly. 'You forget I've worked with him. Right arm on top of left means he'll use his gun if you don't go quietly.' She grabbed his hand. 'Let's go see what he wants.'

ELEVEN

Tulsa grinned at the two laughing teenagers. 'That makes a change. So, you coming home?' He nodded at Hilary.

'If I have to, but – '

'You have to.' He moved away from the heavy vehicle, its side-panel covered in mud from the deep puddles in the lane.

'I need to pick up the bike first.'

'And we have to go via a school mate,' Hilary shouted. 'It won't take a moment but it's…'

'What?' Tulsa cupped his hand behind his ear. 'Can't hear,' he bellowed. 'Get in, it'll be quieter. You can't hear yourself think with that racket.' He pointed to the procession now only twenty metres away.

Holding the rear door open, Tulsa glanced casually towards the quartet of gaily caparisoned figures that had brought the entire street to a standstill. His amused expression froze into disbelief. Scott, about to open the front passenger door, felt a blow like a sledgehammer. It toppled him head first onto the pavement, the air around suddenly peppered with strident blasts of sound, splinters of concrete viciously striking his arms and head. For a split second, the air became densely silent. Scott raised his head feeling Tulsa's body, heavy and unyielding, pinning him to the ground. Then, a flood of high-pitched screams severed the air saturating Scott's eardrums and blocking out every other sound. He twisted round struggling to see, the scene frozen in time – stalled. Hilary was looking down at him, her mouth moving silently – her words drowned out by the strident shrieking. Behind her, like statues, their arms suspended in the air, were a crowd of people.

Bewildered, Scott stared at the figures, now pooled into a blurred mass of vague shapes, unable to comprehend what had happened. Then he saw what the figures were staring at. He grabbed his bodyguard's arm. 'My God, Tulsa! What have you done?' He gasped the words into life. 'It was some kid dressed up. Not real and *you've shot him!*'

He pushed himself free of the heavy weight and dragged himself onto his knees, staring bewildered at the scene. In the centre of the narrow street, bodies lay strewn across the ground like ninepins. Spread-eagled amongst them, the figure on stilts, one leg spiralling skywards like a beacon. Gradually, the blurred figures began to move, to become focussed, pulling themselves upright, every eye fixed on the spaceman his white suit pooled with scarlet.

Scott swung round, angry words ready to blast into life. Struck dumb, he watched blood trickle slowly from a corner of Tulsa's mouth, his body slumped against Scott's.

'Ah…' the word flickered and died. Scott swallowed noisily. 'But how could you possibly know?' he whispered.

'Finger on trigger… taut.' The words were scratchy, whispered on an outgoing breath. Scott felt a searing pain flash across his own chest as if he too had been shot, instinct sensing the monumental effort it had taken to get out those four words.

Biting his lip, he gazed hopelessly round – his eyes begging for help, for it not to be happening.

'*Oh my God, oh my God!*' Wringing her hands, Hilary slid

down onto the pavement beside him. She stared down at the agent's jacket, the impact of the bullets tearing it to shreds. 'This is all my fault. I let down my guard. I'm so sorry.'

Tulsa's mouth twitched and his eyes flicked open. 'Not your problem. You quit...' Scott caught the sound of air being dragged in. 'Get Scott to safety, take my gun. Hurry!'

'I can't,' Hilary gasped wildly. 'You just said it. I don't work for the service any more... '

'Take... it... and... get out of here.' Tulsa's voice faded and his eyes began to glaze. Scott watched him drag in another breath, the silence deafening. In the distance a police siren sounded. 'Shooters hunt in twos,' Tulsa gasped out, the words faint under the strident sound.

Hilary stared briefly into Scott's eyes, her gaze haunted. Then she was on her feet, dragging him up with her. 'Let's go!'

'We can't just leave him... ' Scott hesitated, wanting to lift his friend up – take him, save him.

'We have to.' Ducking back down, she fished in Tulsa's pocket searching for the car keys. 'Hang on, I beg you, help's on the way,' she whispered. She yanked at the passenger door. '*Scott?* Can you drive this thing?'

He nodded. 'But...'

'Quit arguing!' Scott saw her hand on the passenger door shaking wildly. 'If you want to live, you drive. Now!'

Scarcely aware of what he was doing, Scott crawled across into the driving seat. Leaping into the seat next to him, Hilary threw him the keys, slamming the heavy door. Immediately, sound from outside faded cocooning them in an eerie silence, the heavy glass muffing the screams and shouts of the terrified schoolchildren.

'Tulsa's right,' Hilary muttered checking the weapon in her hand and sliding the safety on. She pulled out her mobile, hurriedly scrolling down the numbers on the speed dial, constantly twisting round to check over her shoulder.

The ignition fired. Scott pulled out, his foot heavy on the accelerator making the engine roar. He'd rarely driven the four-by-four – not much interested when there was a powerful bike on display in the garage. He looked down, fumbling with the heavy gears and momentarily taking his eye off the road.

A spray of bullets like angry hornets ruptured the windscreen, flashing through the space his head had occupied a second before. Out of the corner of his eye, Scott saw Hilary's mobile disintegrate into a meteor shower of dark matter exploding through the air. She screamed out and automatically he ducked. Shards of sharp plastic struck his head, cutting a pattern into his cheek. He put up his hand and felt a trickle of blood.

'I can't see,' he gasped. He peered through the star-shaped cracks in the windscreen rubbing his hand against the blurred glass, momentarily forgetting it wasn't like the vapour you encountered on a frosty morning, that you could simply wipe away. Another round of bullets twanged against the rear bumper and he snatched his hand back as if burned.

Hilary stretched across striking the butt of the heavy pistol against the shattered windscreen, a trail of blood smearing the dashboard. Wind roared through the hole she'd made, sweeping tiny pieces of glass into the air.

'You're hurt.' Scott said, seeing blood trickle down her arm.

'I'm okay,' she shouted back. 'It's only my hand. A flesh wound. Just go. *Oh my God, what are we going to do?* That was my mobile… and I never memorised the number. Terry said I should and I did, but there's a new one and I didn't ever think I'd need it again.'

Scott caught the sound of rising hysteria, painfully reined back. He wanted to comfort her, but didn't dare ease his foot off the accelerator, the heavy vehicle pounding along the narrow stretch of road. Flashing amber lights ahead warned him of a school crossing. He flew past, momentarily shutting his eyes, uttering a prayer for there to be no kids waiting to cross because he wasn't stopping. 'There's a duster in the dashboard.' Easing back slightly, he flew a cautionary glance left and right, checking the main road ahead. 'Which way?'

'Doesn't matter – just lose them.'

Scott floored the accelerator and cut across the dual-carriageway, the tyres on the heavy vehicle screaming in protest. Behind them, a horn blasted out angrily and brakes screamed, the oncoming motorist swerving to avoid a collision. 'They still there?' he shouted above the hissing of the wind through the windscreen. He steadied the vehicle, changing up into fourth gear.

Hilary twisted round in her seat. Scott saw the duster wrapped around her left hand already spattered with blood. 'You need a hospital.'

'We need a lot of things, Scott,' Hilary's voice was cold almost angry sounding, as if her earlier lapse into near hysteria had been something alien and unacceptable. 'Most of all, to stay alive. Can you shake them?'

Through the rear-view mirror, Scott spotted the car that he'd cut up, a red Peugeot Estate. Behind that was a black saloon – low-slung and reminiscent of Sean Terry's souped-up Citroen. 'Honda,' he said, 'old model but fast – faster than us.'

'You know these roads, Scott.'

'Yeah, but that doesn't help much on a dual-carriageway.'

'Then get off it.'

'Can't! I need five minutes.' Scott noticed the speedometer, the needle nudging ninety. Sixty miles an hour was a mile a minute; he needed to stay ahead for another seven miles – two miles past the turning to the cottage.

'Then you'd better pray the driver behind is so angry, he'll not let them through.'

Scott peered anxiously through the side mirror watching the black saloon swerve out, trying to pass and not succeeding. 'I'm praying!' His hands on the wheel were shaking out of control, flashbacks from the scene outside the school breaking into his concentration. He couldn't think about that. Not yet. He had to get them to safety.

A stretch of trees flew towards them round a steep bend. Scott spotted a break in the concrete strip that formed the intersection of the dual-carriageway, allowing vehicles to turn right into the lane on the far side. Praying in earnest that his pursuers were strangers to the area, he swerved the vehicle through the gap on two wheels, feeling Hilary's body lurch against his own. Then he was across the intersection, ramming the vehicle into a lower gear as he hit the muddy track.

'Thank God,' Hilary said in a relieved tone. 'What is this place?'

'It's a dirt track. I learned to ride a bike down here. No way off for miles now. They'll backtrack and follow but it won't get them very far. You need a four-wheel drive to cope with this little lot.' Scott slowed before engaging the mechanism, the tyres both front and back biting into the muddy surface. 'Dozens of paths. With luck if they do follow, they'll head downhill and get stuck.' He spun the wheel into a sharp right-hand bend, slowing even more as they pitched and stumbled over the bumps, ridges of dry mud keeping their speed down to twenty miles an hour.

Ahead of them, the wooded path split into two. The left-hand track slanting downwards was wider and drier, and beckoned enticingly. Ignoring it, Scott set the heavy vehicle to climb the hill, keeping the revs low so as not to spin the wheels. Ahead of them the path narrowed even further, winding between outcrops of spruce and yew which swallowed up the light and left it dark and gloomy.

Hilary leant forward reaching for the light switch on the steering column. Scott pushed her hand away. 'No, they'll see them,' he murmured craning forward to see through the hole in the windscreen. The light deteriorated as the trees grouped together, their spindly branches scraping across the bonnet and hampering his vision still further, the heavy vehicle inching its way upwards. Abruptly, they crested the hill, the pathway dropping away steeply into the gloom. Hilary squealed and clutched Scott's arm. Banging the gears into first, Scott edged cautiously down, his foot clamped firmly on the brake, the four- by-four listing and slipping almost out of control. Then, with equal suddenness they were down. The heart-wrenching drop levelled into a steady gradient.

Scott heard Hilary's sigh of relief but didn't speak, concentrating on keeping a steady course in the worsening light. An accident now – that would be unimaginable. They had to reach the cottage.

He felt the path smooth out and changed up, steering round the worst of the muddy patches, knowing them to be deep enough to spin even the wheels of a four-by-four. Abruptly, the trees jumped back and it was possible to see the stretch of meadow in front of them, a five-barred gate blocking their entrance into the gravelled lane beyond. Hilary was out in a flash and, leaving Tulsa's gun on the seat, ran over to the gate and pulled it open. Scott eased the vehicle back into first, jolting over the deep ruts left by the huge wheels of a tractor.

'We safe?' Hilary swung the gate shut and climbed back into the passenger seat.

Scott nodded. He switched off the engine and let his head drop onto the steering wheel, the silence of the open countryside seeping through the shattered windscreen.

'What time is it?' he said.

'Just after four.'

'No way! God, I'm so exhausted, it could easily have been midnight.'

He sat up and, like the engine of the four-by-four, forced his shattered senses back into gear. 'Thank you.'

For a moment she didn't reply, her face guarded. She sighed. 'If only.'

He stretched out his hand, taking her hand gently in his. She flinched back but didn't pull away. She didn't need to, her gesture was sufficient. Scott bit the inside of his cheek, wishing he didn't feel so helpless.

'Hilary, this is nothing to do with you, no one's to blame.'

'You're wrong. This is all my fault.' She kept her gaze lowered refusing to make eye contact. 'If I hadn't been so happy to see you, to tell you about my plans...' She picked up the gun and gazed at it for a moment, as if memorising its shape, then dropped it back down. 'I would have spotted the danger!' She raised her head, glaring at Scott as if she hated him.

Shocked, Scott flinched back. 'But you'd already left the service,' he protested. 'You said you couldn't stand the violence.'

'I know what I said... it's still no excuse. Sean will tell you, once an agent always an agent. I forgot that.'

Scott closed his eyes on the guilt, hurt and anger circling round the interior of the vehicle. Hilary was no more to blame than he was for storming out. Neither of them were. But it was too soon for her to come to terms with what had happened, not with every one of the body's emotions skewed, like the spokes in a wheel that needed the firm hand of a mechanic to straighten them out. Only time would put things back in their proper perspective. And time they didn't have.

'How's your hand?' he said, changing the subject.

Pulling off her specs, Hilary rubbed at her eyes with her undamaged right hand. She held up her left, wrapped in its blood-soaked duster. 'I'll live.' The portent of her words echoed round and round. 'Great driving, Scott,' she hastily slotted in.

Too late. Scott's thoughts flew to the figure left lying on the pavement. He kicked open the door and hurled himself out, staring blindly into the hedgerow, a few skeleton leaves still clinging to the matted layers of beech and blackthorn. He felt Hilary behind him and swung round to see the blue of her eyes faded and full of pain. Without thinking, he stretched out his arms. She took a step forward and he wrapped them round her slight frame, hugging her tightly to him.

TWELVE

For a long moment neither of them spoke or moved, no thoughts, no anguish, a sense of peace from the gentle countryside enveloping them like a warm blanket, the pain of events absorbed into the blue haze of darkening sky.

Eventually, it was Scott that broke the silence, whispering into the soft strands of Hilary's hair the words that were uppermost in both their thoughts. 'He's not going to make it, is he?' He felt Hilary respond with a tiny movement, an infinitesimal shaking of her head. *'He was going with us back to the States.* It was all arranged. I didn't want to go. I didn't want to leave you.' The words came out on an agonising shaft of pain, Scott imagining, yet again, the savage pain of bullets tearing through his body.

Hilary pulled away. She stared up at him as if trying to penetrate his mind, her face intensively white. *'Why you, Scott?* Why do they want you dead?'

'Me? That's r-ridiculous,' Scott stuttered. 'It's Dad they're after. They want him dead... I heard them say it.'

Hilary grabbed his arm, her nails digging in. *'No. They were waiting for you, Scott.* Tulsa saw it and got between you. That's why he's dead. I should have seen it too. He jumped in front of you. *Get it!* They wanted *you* dead. But w*hy? Why?'* She screamed the words into the air and a scavenging magpie alarmed by the sudden noise took off with a loud rustle of its wings.

Puzzled, Scott replayed the scene in Geneva over and over again, remembering the busy streets of the capital city so different from here, where the evening sky was quiet and tranquil. Did the gunman fire at their limousine before or only after catching sight of him? He sighed. 'I don't know.' Pulling open the back door, he grabbed his bag ferreting inside for his phone. He pulled it out, dialling quickly. 'God, no! The answerphone's on. *Dad, get hold of Sean Terry and call me back,*' he said into the receiver. 'Did you hear? There's been a shooting at school; Tulsa's...' He stumbled over the word and came to a breathless halt. 'Call me, *please.*' Quickly closing the connection, he dialled another number. An empty ringing tone floated out from the black plastic rectangle. 'His mobile but he won't answer, he never does.'

He leapt back into the driving seat. 'We must warn him. When they can't pick-up our trail, they'll head for the cottage.' He beckoned, every instinct screaming at him to hurry, to get home. 'Try and remember that number. I may loathe Sean Terry, but we desperately need him now.'

'Scott, I'm so sorry. I'm hopeless with numbers.' Hilary fumbled her way into her seat, using her undamaged right hand to shut the door. 'It'll be on my computer... Sean said to memorise everything and use disposable cell phones, so there's no record. But that didn't work for me. I entered my numbers in code on my computer – just in case.'

'Where you live?' Hilary nodded. 'Hell! That means going all the way back into Falmouth!' Scott turned the ignition key. 'We'll check Dad first. Sean Terry could well be there. If he isn't, Dad's bound to have the number. As a last resort, we'll find a way to get to your place.'

'I'm sorry.'

'*Stop saying that!* I told you. You can talk about honour and devotion all you want, but none of this is your fault.' He took a deep breath attempting a lighter tone. 'Besides, having your mobile blasted to bits is not an everyday occurrence. I'm not sure if there is even a clause in the insurance contract to cover bullets.'

He pushed the car into gear and moved off along the narrow lane, his head twisting awkwardly to see out through the hole in the wind screen. 'This lane runs parallel to the dual-carriageway from here on.' Scott said, keeping his tone in neutral. 'I know I shouldn't say it – and I know you'll hate me for saying it – but I'm ever so glad you're here. Last time, I was alone without anyone to trust. I didn't even trust you.'

There was no reply.

Shifting sideways, he saw Hilary staring through the shattered glass, her expression rigid and unmoving, her hands gripped tightly together. He knew what she was seeing, the blood-soaked body of Tulsa on the ground.

He switched his gaze back to the lane, the rapidly vanishing light making it almost impossible to distinguish between solid bits of road and treacherous rain-soaked verges. Anxiously, he reduced his speed still further. Slipping the gears, he let the heavy vehicle free-wheel to a stop, the entrance to the dual-carriageway only a few metres ahead. The road seemed deserted. He checked again, searching for the tell-tale trace of sidelights or evidence that a vehicle might be waiting for them, ready to pounce. He flinched back as a solitary lorry came into view heading south along the main artery that criss-crossed Cornwall, its dipped head-lights cutting a neat pathway across the tarmac road. Then, taking a deep breath for courage, he gunned the engine and flew across the wide carriageway, slowing as he hit the muddy surface of the lane on the far side, the mirror image of the one they had just left, its tall hedgerows hiding its occupants from the view of anyone travelling along the main road.

'Where does this come out?' Hilary's voice sounded wooden, her words emerging through clenched teeth.

He gave her a painful half-smile. 'Another field. Runs up to the back of the cottage. George Beale, the local farmer, owns it but he doesn't use it much. Says the grass is only suitable for silage. Dad and I use it as a short-cut to the village. He doesn't mind.'

The surface of the lane was badly pitted, their vehicle jolting savagely from one pothole to the next. Branches and twigs armed with long thorns scratched noisily against the side panels as they lurched past, making Hilary jump. She reached over. 'You can't see a thing, Scott. Get your lights on.' She pointed to the hedgerows, their tops taller than the car by almost a metre

'No.' Scott slowed to a bare crawl. 'We daren't risk it. Anyone up high looking down would spot them and come running. We haven't exactly got much of a population round here. Except for George Beale and us, most people live in the village.'

Abruptly the lane came to an end, a padlocked gate barring their way. Hilary made to get out but Scott stopped her.

'I'll turn first.' He swung the steering wheel hard round. 'I don't know what the insurance company's going to say about this little lot when they see it.' The tyres grated over the rough surface as he pulled forward facing the way they had come. 'It has to be a write-off.' Hilary leaned back to pick up her bag, briefly glancing at the mess of glass littering the floor. A pattern of holes had ripped across the back seat where bullets had strafed it exposing the wire springs, cotton stuffing gaping out of the wound like the innards of some sea monster. 'Don't bother with that, you can get it later. Come on, we need to hurry.'

In only a few minutes full darkness had taken over. Under their feet, individual blades of grass had dissolved into a general sense of nothingness, making it difficult to identify anything except by touch. Knowing the path blindfold Scott strode on ahead, leaving Hilary to catch him up, a terrible sense of foreboding crawling its way into his chest. If the men had lost him, they would have headed for the cottage, aware he'd have to return sooner or later. He found himself fixating on Sean Terry's words, that he had sent for extra men. Surely Tulsa would never have left his dad alone.

A noise cut across the gentle silence of twilight, a settling of leaves in a ditch, a crumb of earth breaking. Recognising the staccato clattering of a sub-machine gun, Scott broke into a run. The sound had always reminded him of a tribe of belligerent woodpeckers, their busy tapping amplified a million times. That had been one of the lessons Tulsa had taught him. A single round took so many seconds, with a number of seconds between rounds – long enough to take cover or draw a weapon and fire back. A fourteen-bullet magazine in a pistol – equally as quick, and much more accurate, much more deadly.

The high rattling vibrated through his head, making him want to scream out.

'Scott… No!' Hilary hauled on his arm.

'Give me the gun.' He lunged for the weapon in her right hand.

'It's too late,' Hilary backed away.

'I can shoot – Tulsa taught me. I've got to do something… please.'

'No, Scott. There's two – listen.'

Scott caught the sound he'd missed before, a second

rhythm, a slightly different pitch, much lower, a different make and model of gun.

Catching Hilary off guard, he grabbed the pistol from her hand. 'I don't care.' Fumbling for the safety, he ran towards the menacing sounds that had vanquished the silence of early night. He ducked behind the low wall edging the garden, cautiously peering over. The firing had stopped. No one in sight, nothing moving. A light flared briefly and he heard a door slam. An explosion rocked the air, hurling him to the ground.

He crash-landed against a cattle trough, striking his head on its metal side. Dazed and bruised he sat up, the pistol dangling forgotten in his hand. A ball of fire was sweeping through the cottage, flames spiralling into the sky like an ancient warning beacon alerting villages to the approach of invaders. Except, the warning had come too late. A second explosion brought Scott back up onto his feet, watching the studio vanish in a pall of smoke and flame; a tearing of wood and metal battering his senses as its roof caved in.

'Dad,' he screamed heedlessly into the noise. His mobile burst into life, the strident bars of music piercing the roaring of the flames like an arrow.

A shout from the yard. 'It's the boy – get him.' A figure cut through the gloom ahead.

Then Hilary was tugging on his arm. *'For God's sake, run, Scott. Come on.'*

'Dad!' he shouted, ignoring her. 'I have to find Dad!'

Bullets struck the ground behind them; clods of earth flew into the air striking him in the face. Dazed, Scott stared round as if he'd been sleepwalking and had abruptly woken up.

Clasping Hilary by the hand, he tore back along the field, leaping the tussocks of grass oblivious to the ground beneath his feet, Hilary stumbling along beside him.

'Slow down,' she screamed, 'I'll fall.'

Thunderous footsteps sounded in the darkness behind. Ignoring Hilary's protest, Scott accelerated, dragging her forcibly along. Seeing the gate ahead, he dropped her hand and leapt over, diving headfirst into the four-by-four. Cramming the keys into the ignition he started the engine, impatiently leaning across to open the passenger door, waiting only long enough for Hilary to get her foot in.

Using his headlights now, he flew along the narrow lane, ploughing straight through the ruts and ignoring the ominous swaying of the vehicle. At the end of the lane he accelerated automatically turning towards Falmouth, fishing in his jacket pocket for the betrayer, the Judas, the mobile phone with its noisy ringing tone that had exposed them to the enemy. He tossed it over. 'Who was it?' he muttered, keeping his eyes on the road.

'I'm sure your father's okay, Scott.' Hilary patted him on the arm, her tone soft and compassionate.

'Stop treating me like a child.' He flung the words into the air. 'I'm not. I'm old enough to work things out for myself.'

Hilary rubbed the tears from her eyes and flicked up the caller ID. 'It's Travers.'

'Get him back.'

Travers picked up straight away. 'Scott there?'

'Yes, he's driving. We're in trouble.'

'I'll say you are.' Travers' voice on speaker phone echoed loudly across the silent interior. 'I caught the news on local radio. They said Scott killed a man at school.'

'I didn't,' Scott shouted.

'I know that. Where are you? For God's sake, don't come here, it's the first place the police'll look.'

Scott screeched to a halt. Ramming the gears into reverse, he jammed his foot on the accelerator, hurtling back along the dual-carriageway. Cars speeding towards Falmouth swerved past blasting them with their horns, the occupants turning to glare. Scott ignored them, concentrating on keeping a straight course. He swerved the vehicle into a side road impatiently pulling on the handbrake, rocking to a halt.

'So where can we go? I need the bike; the car's a wreck. If they're looking for me, they'll be searching for it too. And someone's just blown up the cottage.'

'My God, no!'

'Dad's missing. Is yours there? Let me speak to him. He may know something.'

'That's just the problem. It's only me and Natasha. Mum's going mad; she can't get hold of Dad either. He told us he was running across to France but he seems to have disappeared. She's on the phone to the coastguard right now. She's no use. Can't get a sensible word out of her.'

'Travers, can you meet us somewhere with the bike?' Hilary took over, her voice icily calm.

'I guess but... hold on.'

Silence.

Scott bit his thumb, drumming his fingers nervously on the dashboard.

Travers' voice sounded again, the line crackling as if the battery was about to die. 'The police are at the door,' he said softly. 'Looking for you. Mum told them you've not been here – but they're not buying it. She's phoning Dad now. What the hell's happened to him, why doesn't he pick up? Listen up, Tash says she'll load your bike on the boat trailer and slip out the back. But where? You'll never get through Falmouth. Hell!'

'What?' Hilary yelled.

'They're flashing Scott's picture on the telly. How did they get hold of that?' Travers said indignantly, forgetting to whisper. 'They don't waste any time. It says you're armed and dangerous. Scott, what have you done?'

'Nothing! I promise. They were trying to kill us…'

'Who?'

'Men… we don't know who… it doesn't matter anyway… but it was Tulsa doing the shooting. He shot the man trying to kill me and he…' Scott twisted round in his seat, his face blotched and patchy. 'Why do they want *me* dead?' he repeated helplessly. 'What have I ever done to them?'

Hilary flung her arms round him. 'I don't know but let's get away from here and then we can work it out.'

'Hilary, let me speak to Scott.'

Hilary passed the phone across.

'Scott, remember when Jay was water-skiing and got tangled in a rope and nearly drowned.'

Scott dragged his brain into gear. 'You mean at—'

'You got it!' Travers cut him off. 'We'll meet you there. But it'll be at least an hour – maybe longer.'

'Travers?'

'What?'

'We need money.'

'And bandages,' Hilary called out.

'Who's hurt?'

'Me,' Hilary shouted. 'We also need warm clothes and food.'

'Just like old times.'

'It's not a joke, Travers,' she snapped.

'I know that.' Travers lazy-tones floated into the air. 'But there's enough people in hysterics without me joining in.'

'Sorry.'

'No sweat.'

'Travers!' Scott yelled the words, panicking at the thought of his only friend in the world closing the connection and leaving them stranded. 'Can you get hold of Beau?'

'We've already tried. He's not in. Left a message with the

porter. I dunno. Fine life he leads; always out on a jolly somewhere. Why him?'

'He may know where Sean Terry is. We've got to find him. Hilary's phone was smashed to smithereens when they were shooting at us.'

For a moment Travers' voice changed, becoming grim. 'This makes no sense. I can understand them wanting your dad out of the way. But why you, Scott? Why is someone trying to kill you?'

THIRTEEN

Scott had no idea of time, nor any awareness of his surroundings, cold and damp seeping through the shattered windscreen, the air outside bitter. At some point, and on some level in his subconscious, he had made the decision not to run the engine to keep them warm in case the noise carried across the lake and someone out walking a dog reported it. He neither remembered making the decision nor why such a decision was needed in the first place. Instead, flashbacks tore relentlessly through his mind, his inner eye fixated on a scream of bullets raking the yard followed by the double explosion, with flames so high they would have been seen in Falmouth. People would have come running – fire-fighters, police. The thought was recognised but thrown away next minute, the scene continually rewinding to the moments before the explosion. Were the men firing at people in the cottage? Scott fought to make sense of the scene; a dark silhouette pumping round after round of ammunition through the kitchen door. Why? To kill living and breathing people?

Did that mean his father was dead?

No, he couldn't be!

Scott swerved away from the thought, unconsciously fixing his gaze on the phone in his lap, completely unaware of Hilary curled up against him trying to keep warm. *No messages.* If his dad had been okay, he would have phoned. For the tenth time he scrolled through his messages. Nothing!

'Scott? Scott?' Hilary's voice penetrated the layers of confusion. 'Travers and Natasha are here.'

Scott glanced up, his eyes dull and flooded with pain.

'Scott,' Hilary laid her hand on his arm. 'I'm sure…'

'Don't!' He snapped, unable to stomach kindness. Taking a deep breath, he forced a flicker of a smile. 'If you can do this, I can too. But, please, don't expect me to talk about it.'

With relief, he watched the lights of the family Range Rover swing off the country road and circle the woods. He rubbed his arms vigorously, all at once noticing he was frozen to the core. 'What time is it?'

'Gone eight.'

'Holy crap! We've been here for hours. I'm so sorry, Hilary. This isn't your problem. As you said, you're no longer a member of the service. You left, remember. For my sake, go home with Travers, at least you'll be warm. It's not you the police are bothered about.'

'Sometimes, Scott Anderson, you say the most stupid things.' Hilary's eyes flashed angrily. 'I'm not involved! So, I'm not involved when a friend gets gunned down. So I'm not involved when someone I care about…'

'You care about me?' Scott felt hot tears override his rigid self-control and push their way to the surface.

'Now is not the time, Scott! Remember what I told you? It's never been more true than it is now. If we're going to stay alive, we have to remain focussed. You need someone to protect you and I'm a better shot than you – that's all. So I'm staying, thank you very much. I only hope Travers has brought something to eat, I'm starving.'

Hilary wrenched open the passenger door and stumbled

out. Scott followed her, watching the headlights slowly change direction, inching down the steep incline that led to the lake shore, its asphalt surface in constant need of repair as winter storms and ice broke through the layers.

Quarrying at Budock Water had been abandoned some thirty years previously, after it became cheaper to import gravel from the Baltic, and the shallow diggings had quickly filled with water. Warning signs, ignored by intrepid youngsters anxious to pit their skills against the elements, eventually led to a local water-sports company renting the site. Scott, Travers and Jameson had been among their first customers wanting to learn how to water ski, although Jay had only gone the once, put off by a freak accident with the tow rope. The enterprise survived a few summers then sailing took over. Discovering this to be a social sport, in which drinking and partying were essential elements, wealthy city dwellers found it a pleasant way to pass the weekend. Now, well landscaped and with an elegant clubhouse, the lake was clearly marked on local maps, with owners of small sailing dinghies honing their skills on the inland water before making an assault on the tidal estuary at the mouth of the River Fal.

Scott had often sailed there, both with his father and Tulsa. Tucked away from civilisation it was the perfect place to hide out, totally deserted over the winter months. Littering the shoreline like beached whales, a scattering of hulls covered with tarpaulins lay in wait, in the hope of an early spring.

Travers looked the more worried of the two, an expression rarely seen on his face unless his team were being thrashed on the rugby field.

'I've got a flask in the car – you must be frozen, poor things. Get in and get warm,' Natasha called out, skilfully manoeuvring the trailer into position so Scott could run the Suzuki down the ramp.

Scott patted the bike affectionately, its solid presence, with its red paintwork gleaming even in the dark, somehow reassuring. As long as he had the bike, everything was bound to turn out okay. Like it had before.

Reluctantly he turned away and climbed into the back seat of the Range Rover, hoping that Hilary had already relayed the happenings at the cottage.

Natasha was tying a bandage round Hilary's hand. Fastening the last knot, she bent down and pulled a thermos flask and two mugs from a bag on the floor.

'Here, drink this,' she said, pouring the steaming liquid into a mug and handing it to Hilary.

'Natasha did a good job on my hand.' Hilary wrapped her fingers round the pottery to warm them. 'It definitely looked worse than it was. Now she's cleaned it up, I don't think I'll need stitches.'

'That's a relief.' Scott caught the tremor in his voice. Taking the cup Natasha held out to him, he took a sip and cleared his throat. 'Did your father return?'

'No!' Travers shook his head, his dark eyes expressing his obvious concern. 'Even I am beginning to worry – especially after this business involving you.'

'Could they be connected?'

'No way!' Travers exclaimed frowning fiercely at his sister.

'Come off it, Trav. Dad's into some pretty weird stuff with the monarchist party.'

'But it can't have anything to do with this.'

'It might.' Natasha nodded at Scott and held up the thermos, silently asking if he was ready for a top-up. He shook his head.

'Jameson's gone too,' Hilary said.

'*What!*' Travers exclaimed. 'You never said anything.'

'Only because it's not as important as some of the other

stuff we've got to deal with. Besides, he's probably on his way back now – at least I hope so. Me and Scott, we were planning to chase Wesley up after school and ask him.' Hilary took a sip of the hot soup. 'That's before we were shot at. Thanks for this, it's a lifesaver.'

Travers scratched his head, a look of bewilderment on his broad face. '*Wesley?* I know he's a pain but how come he's involved?'

'He was the one that set up the interview for Jameson,' Scott broke in.

'And he bolted like a scared rabbit as soon as we tried to question him,' Hilary said. 'He's obviously on a commission. But he has to know who they are. He told us…' She caught sight of Scott's puzzled expression. 'What?'

Scott screwed up his nose. 'I'm not sure. It's something…'

'To do with Wesley?'

'I don't know, that's the problem. I can't put my finger on it. Maybe it's something I read or heard or…'

'Don't bother with that now,' Travers said, his tone of voice brooking no argument. 'Like Hilary said, you've got enough to worry about. Leave that one to me. I'll go over to his place tomorrow early. If he's not willing to play ball, believe me I'll use him as one.'

'My God!' Natasha slowly shook her head from side to side. 'This is worse than your worst nightmare – there's no end to it. First Jameson, then Dad,' Natasha ticked off the names on her fingers. 'Tulsa, your dad…'

'He's vanished, that's all,' Scott blurted out, the word echoing round and round in the empty night air.

Travers and Natasha picking up on Scott's panicky expression eyed Hilary in alarm.

With the slightest of movements, she shook her head in warning. 'And we can't get hold of Sean Terry,' she broke into the painful silence. 'By the way, did you manage to contact Beau?'

'Not yet! He'll probably ring in,' Natasha said. 'You know Beau – he's decided he wants sun and has flown out to spend the weekend at a friend's villa in Spain.' She shivered. 'I don't blame him, this weather's the pits.'

'He was our last hope too.' Hilary dropped her head, burying her face in her mug.

Scott shifted round to face her. 'We'll find him. People like Sean Terry are indestructible.' Realising the double-meaning, he leaned back against the upholstery furious with himself for not picking his words more carefully.

'What did happen to your mobile?' Travers said.

'A bullet caught it.' Hilary held up her hand. 'I was lucky.'

'But if the SIM card's okay…'

'Burned to a crisp.' Scott said. 'We already thought of that.'

'So what is it you know that makes you such a threat?'

Scott shrugged, the mug gripped tightly in his hands. 'I've been wracking my brains, Travers, the only thing…'

'Yes?'

'Well… you know in Geneva… when we arrived at the UN…' Scott blinked and bit his lip. 'Tulsa and I were dumped in a booth overlooking the auditorium. They're glass-fronted so you can see what's happening, and there's ear-phones fitted into the armrest of every seat, so you can listen to the speeches. The secretary, sent to show us the way, was so snooty…' Scott screwed up his face remembering. It was a relief to talk, to think about something other than what had happened to his father. 'She couldn't even be bothered to show us how they worked. And all the dials were marked in a foreign language – well, French anyway.' He shrugged. 'I started fiddling with them – you know, like you do – and accidentally tuned into this weird conversation.'

'Go on,' Natasha broke in.

'They were talking about Norway,' Scott rushed on, 'the voice on the phone was saying about destroying it. That's why I was convinced it was him… Dad… they want.' Scott forced the word out, his face like an automaton's, expressionless. 'I heard them say he had to be killed. This stuff happening today, it doesn't change my mind any. You see, they admitted to using Styrus to blackmail Norway's oil industry. Sean Terry said they'd asked for billions, enough to bankrupt them, so Dad was determined to help, to stop them. He was…' Scott faltered to a stop. 'He *is*…' he glared fiercely, 'the only one that knows how to override Styrus…'

'Oh my God!' Natasha exclaimed. Reaching over, she placed a comforting hand on Scott's arm.

He shook it off. 'I'm okay. The only thing is…' Scott stopped again, his hand crawling up to cover his mouth. 'I never thought about it at the time… they knew I was listening.'

'Who?' Hilary stormed impatiently.

'I dunno – that's the point. I was so shocked when I heard them use Dad's real name… Masterson…'

'Your name's not Anderson?' Natasha broke in.

'No, Dad had to change it. Mr Randal knew but…' Scott paused, his words coming out stilted, 'hardly anyone else.'

'Go on.'

'Well, I was so taken aback; I remember… I sort of… gasped out loud. They must have heard, and realised someone was listening to their secret conversation. *Of course!*' Scott's voice changed, all at once sounding terrified. '*He was looking right at me.*'

'Who was?' Hilary repeated.

'The guy in the booth. It had to be him. Everyone else was busy; you know… translators… people having meetings… ordinary stuff. I remember now.' Scott's hands shook up and down in agitation. 'But so much happened after, with them shooting at us…'

'*Shooting?* Scott!'

'Shut up, Tash, I'll tell you later,' Travers growled.

'He was foreign.' Scott reined in his panic, trying to speak slowly, to dredge up bits of information that had been forgotten till now and create some sort of picture for his friends. 'He spoke English but with a really thick accent. You know that old joke about Americans?'

'Which one?' Hilary glared suspiciously.

'How the hell did you ever pass for English?' Travers grinned at her.

'I tried hard. Go on.'

'That Americans never learn languages, they just speak louder.'

Travers snorted. 'Sorry!'

'Only you would find that funny,' Hilary snapped.

'I bet it's true,' Travers protested.

'You don't know any Americans except in old movies.'

'Okay, point taken.'

'I wish it was a joke, Travers,' Scott said miserably.

'I know. Go on.'

'Well, the man sounded like that, bullying, convinced if he spoke loud enough, he'd get through.'

'Did you get a good enough look to recognise him again?'

'I-I think so.'

'What about the second voice?' Natasha passed over a pack of neatly wrapped sandwiches.

Scott nodded his thanks. 'Quiet, you know that menacing quiet that sends shivers down your spine. He was talking about the destruction of Europe. Funny, I can still hear it.'

'So that's why they want you dead – because you can identify them. But why is that so important? Important enough to kill you.' Natasha spoke the words slowly, thinking aloud.

'Because they can't be seen together?'

'Sometimes, Travers, you're a genius.' Natasha smiled triumphantly. 'That's it! Nothing else makes sense. That's why the phone call from a public building. Because it would make world-wide headlines, if they were ever caught talking to one another. *But why?* Enemies talk all the time – it's called diplomacy, and you were in a building dedicated to diplomacy.' She paused. 'What is it they're so desperate to keep secret? What can possibly be so important that you – a sixteen-year-old schoolboy – instantly becomes public enemy number one?'

'You *have* to go to the police.'

'How can I, Travers? They're trying to arrest me.'

'But they're not trying to kill you.'

'Like hell they're not. Didn't you just say, *armed and dangerous?* You think I should chance it and wind up dead.'

'So, if they want you dead, what Natasha said is right. They can't afford to be identified because that would be too damaging for what... their cause? Hilary stopped, her eyes frightened. 'What you said, Travers, about the monarchists. *They* want to break up Europe.'

'That's crazy talk.'

'But is it? All those riots – the head teacher was talking about it in school. She said the riots were about one thing only, restoring the monarchy – Belgium, Holland, Sweden, Spain... all of them. Even the United Kingdom. There were protest marches in all the major cities last weekend. People going on strike. They're trying to destroy the European Union, put it back the way it was. Okay, as an American, I'm all for that – I hate Europe.'

'Not now,' Scott shushed her.

'So they might, Hilary,' Travers picked up the conversation, sounding angry. 'But Dad doesn't believe in violence – he'd never go along with it.'

'But...'

'Stop it, you two,' Natasha called out. She patted the air. 'This isn't helping any. What will you to do now, Scott? You can't come to our place if there's a chance they're still watching it.'

'How come they weren't at the cottage when we needed them?' Scott burst out suddenly. Hilary flinched and dropped her sandwich. 'Sorry, but it's been bugging me all this time. Tulsa was at the school – who stayed with Dad? Why weren't your blokes there if it was as dangerous as Sean Terry made out? He said he was taking us back to the States this weekend. But what if that was a smoke-screen and he intended to get rid of Dad all along.'

'Scott, stop it!' Hilary screamed the words. She bent down, fumbling around, trying to pick up the broken pieces of bread from the floor. 'You can't start all that up again. I know you hate him but he was the one that saved you.'

'No, he wasn't. That's exactly my point,' Scott gasped wildly. 'It was you and Travers. You followed me, remember. He had no choice with all those people about. Mr Randal... Beau – too many witnesses.'

'Hold on, Scott, this is crazy talk.' Travers broke in. 'A moment ago, Hilary was all set to accuse my dad. You're grasping at straws – and it's not getting us anywhere.'

Hilary leaned across and, taking Scott's face in her hands, peered at him intently. 'You don't believe this any more than I do. You don't believe Sean Terry would kill one of his own men...'

'Pete did,' Scott insisted stubbornly.

'He's not Sean. I know you don't want to talk about it – because talking about it will make it seem real. But this is real,

Scott. It's happened. *Deal with it.* Tulsa's most likely dead and your dad… *he's gone too.* And exactly like before, we're working in the dark. But – exactly like before – we've still got friends.' Hilary leaned back indicating Travers and Natasha. 'I promise you, we'll work this one out. But you've got to help me. I can't do it alone. And no more conspiracy theories.'

'As a rule, I don't believe in conspiracy theories,' Scott said more quietly, 'but, you have to admit, this is one hell of a conspiracy theory. The police… government. Who else?'

'It's okay, Scott.'

'No, Hilary, it bloody isn't,' Scott burst out again, his face strained and white. 'And it's never going to be.' He took in a large gulp of air. 'I'm sorry but I'm staying angry, if that's what it takes to keep focussed. Travers, will you ring the Brodys. See if they have police watching the house. I don't want to use my phone… in case.'

'Good job I brought my old one along then. It's a pay-as you-go. Haven't used it for years but it still got some credit on it.' He fished in his pocket, handing the phone to his friend.

'Thanks.' Scott keyed in the eight digits. It rang once and was picked up. 'Mrs Brody, it's Scott.' There was a burst of high-pitched noise. 'No, I'm okay. Thank you, I wish you could convince the police I'm innocent. No, I can't, not yet. They've blown up the cottage…' Scott listened; his friends stared anxiously, watching his expression change running through a gamut of emotions – anger, alarm, disbelief, incredulity. 'How can it be all tied in?' he burst out. 'Yes, I know Jay was into computers like my dad. But… *That's it! I knew there was something.* No, Mrs Brody, I can't explain. But, you might be right, it could all be linked.' He paused. 'Yes, I know exactly where we're heading… course I can't say. Mrs Brody… please, *please,* don't cry. We'll get him back, I promise.'

'No prizes for saying what that little lot was about,' Travers said as Scott closed the connection. 'No word from Jay, the police have called there too, and Mrs Brody thinks Jay's disappearance and your problems are connected.'

'That's what was bothering me. It was ages ago now. We were talking about kids disappearing. Don't you remember, Travers?'

'Sorry,' Travers rubbed his forehead. 'Brain's gone dead.'

'It was the day I…' Scott stopped dead. He fixed his gaze on the pack of sandwiches in his lap, his ears tinged red. 'It was the day I first spoke to Hilary,' he mumbled.

'Aah! No wonder you remember it so clearly.'

'Honestly, Scott?'

'Yes,' he glanced up, his expression shamefaced. 'But it didn't get me anywhere. You hated me, remember.'

Hilary smiled. 'Admit it, you were rather a pain.'

'Come on, Scott. Put us out of our misery?'

'I was mucking about, Travers, boasting that Wesley was trying to steal Jameson's brain. You see Jay was…'

'I remember that,' Hilary interrupted. 'Jay was telling us how he was obliged to hide in a cupboard to avoid the Weasel, who was always tagging along wanting to know what subjects he was going to study at university. *Oh my God!*' Her tone changed as did her expression. 'I'm so sorry – I never swear. And I've done it twice now.'

'I know,' Scott tried hard to rummage up a grin, still angry with himself for losing control. It only made things a hundred times more difficult and things were grim enough without his help. 'But you have to admit, there are some occasions where swearing is the only thing that helps. So?'

'Maybe they were planning to abduct Jay even back then,' Hilary said.

Travers whistled his astonishment. 'If they were, I'll find out. You can most definitely leave that bit to me. Look here,' he glanced down at his watch. 'We need to get back, pronto. Mum'll be having a nervous breakdown. 'So where are you heading?'

'Exeter – that's where the guys hang out.'

'Where in Exeter? It's a big city.'

'An industrial centre – don't worry, I'll find it. And they'd better be there. Scott and me, we did this once before – only somehow, this is worse.'

'I don't think you should go anywhere,' Natasha said, her voice sombre, sounding deadly serious, totally at odds with the light-hearted girl whose ambition it was to drive a Maserati. 'Stay here till Dad gets back. He'll sort it. Or Beau! He could fly you out of the country if need be.'

'That's all very well, sis,' Travers argued. 'Ideal scenario and all that guff. But where? We can't take them to our house – theirs is in ruins, and a hotel's out of the question. They'd be picked up in no time. Besides, what happens if Dad doesn't appear, we do this all again tomorrow?'

'No point arguing about it,' Hilary responded fiercely. 'We can always head for London, if we have to. I can claim asylum at the American Embassy – and take Scott in with me.'

Scott bit his lip, to stop himself coming out with the words, *but they can't be trusted.*

'I don't like any of this – it's like fishing in the dark.' Natasha pulled out her phone, scrolling down a list of contacts and quickly dialling. 'I've got a friend – she'll let you borrow her floor for the night. 'Gladys, it's Natasha. I know, darling, it's ages since we've met up. I'm based in London now – come up and visit, why don't you?'

Scott tuned out, his attention focussing on the dense blackness of the wooded shoreline, a hint of moonlight reflecting off the lake, wishing they could hide out in the woods until everything was sorted. Natasha was right – they should stay. It made a hell of lot more sense than wandering about. But where? They'd already checked the building for an open window or flimsy door and found both covered with impenetrable steel mesh, designed to stop hooligans and ram-raiders. A distant star glinted on a patch of frost already decorating the grass and leaves. Abruptly, he shivered. There really was no choice; a night in a bullet-ridden car wasn't an option unless they wanted to wake up dead. Scott flinched, wishing his mind would stop honing in on that particular word – like the words of a song, remorselessly repeating over and over.

'I promise they'll be no bother. Bath, blankets, and breakfast – that's it. Key under the mat. Eternally grateful, darling. Love you, do the same for you any day. Kisses!' Natasha snapped her mobile shut. 'All arranged. You'll be quite safe there. Gladys – God, what awful names some parents cripple their kids with – is the stay-at-home type; bookish, never ever watches television. Absolutely perfect.'

Hilary flung her arms around Natasha, hugging her tightly. 'I was dreading spending the night in the open. Now Scott can wait in the flat while I go searching for Sean Terry.'

'No way,' Scott retorted. 'I'm not letting you go anywhere without me.'

'Why are you always so stubborn, Scott Anderson?' Hilary flared angrily. 'You know perfectly well, you can't go chasing about Exeter as if nothing had happened. You're wanted, remember?'

'No one will recognise me on the bike. Not with a helmet and goggles.'

'They will if there's a police post checking identities.'

'We'll avoid them then – that's what we did before.'

'Shut up, you two. I've thought of that.' Travers fished in his pocket pulling out two plastic cards. He passed them to

Scott. 'They're our new IDs – me and Natasha's. Came by courier this morning.'

The pictures on the squares of plastic were small and slightly blurred but still identifiable as Travers and Natasha. 'You'll need to change the colour of your hair,' Travers muttered. 'You, too, Hilary.'

'That's all under control.' Natasha unzipped her holdall, pulling out a couple of cans of non-drip hair-dye. 'Dark chestnut. But, first, I need to trim your hair, Scott.' She showed him a large pair of scissors. 'Don't worry, I'm pretty good at it; I moonlighted in a hair salon on a Saturday when I was in the sixth form.' She opened the car door. 'I know it's bitter out, but be an absolute darling and perch on the step for a few minutes while I wave my magic wand.' She brandished the scissors in the air. 'Hair is an absolute beast to get off upholstery and, even for you, I refuse to spend tomorrow vacuuming the interior of the car; I've got better things to do.' She swivelled round inspecting Hilary closely. 'I think you're okay, Hilary. Your hair's a bit longer than mine – but it will pass.'

'That's a relief.' Hilary watched intently as Natasha quickly and expertly began to reduce the length of Scott's hair. 'I hate myself with short hair.'

'Me, too.'

'Me, too.' Scott added. He stuck his hands firmly over the crown of his head. 'No way are you shearing it as short as Travers wears it. His face can stand it; mine can't. I'll look like a dork.'

'Honestly, guys!' Natasha heaved a sigh. 'They're worse than us girls.' She peered in her bag and pulled out a hand mirror, passing it to Scott. 'Here! Though what good it will be in this light… And I don't much care what you want, Scott,' she snipped briskly at the layers, 'if it will keep you safe.'

Scott gazed into the mirror, the interior light bright enough for him to watch the face he knew so well disappear under a shower of falling hair. The one emerging looked at least five years older, the planes of his cheeks more angular, his expression grim and determined.

'Whoa!' he exclaimed.

'That's amazing,' Hilary echoed. 'You look so different.'

Travers grinned. 'He might look different but if anyone asks, you play fly-half. You're too light to play prop.'

'Shut up, Travers.' Natasha rounded on her brother. 'You know perfectly well, hobbies and pastimes don't appear on your identity card.' She dusted off her hands, replacing the scissors in her bag. 'First thing in the morning, change the colour of your hair. And you'll have to buy some coloured contacts too. If police stop you to check, Hilary, you won't stand a chance with fair hair and blue eyes. They won't bother about height – they never do…'

'You mean this has happened to you?' Travers butted in suspiciously.

'Happens to everyone in London, if you visit the clubs. Beau's always being picked up. As I was saying, they won't check any further as long as you match the general description and look approximately the same age. Being dark'll make you look older too.'

Travers nudged his sister, showing her the time on his wristwatch. 'Mother'll be spitting poison if we're not back p.d.q.'

'I'm sorry.' Natasha kissed Hilary on the cheek. She scrambled down to the ground, shivering violently as the cold struck.

Leaving Hilary to stow the canisters of hair dye into the box on the back of the bike, Scott climbed reluctantly onto his feet, shrugging on the helmet and gloves Travers had brought with him. If only something could happen to stop them leaving. It felt like he and Hilary were in a boat, being cast off from a jetty heading out… to where? Last time, it was the thought of tracing his dad that had kept him focussed, spurring him on. This time, there was nothing except an empty space where his dad had once stood.

The engine of the Range Rover broke into life, Travers and Natasha waving as they edged the vehicle with its trailer back along the path. Scott raised his hand, overcome by the weirdest of sensations that it would be a very long time before he saw his friends again. Shaking the thought away he turned the ignition, the familiar roar of the engine cutting loudly across the silence. Opening the throttle, and with a burst of speed as if wanting to fly the bike across a hundred miles of countryside between them and Exeter, he headed for the main road.

FOURTEEN

The wind cut across the open terrain like a knife forcing Scott to ease back on the throttle, conscious that Hilary was only wearing borrowed gear, her jacket neither heavy enough nor windproof at high speeds. Natasha's own career as a model dictated the wearing of clothes that were a fashion statement rather than practical and, although Scott felt grateful for her forethought, it would be an unpleasant ride for any pillion passenger in those clothes. His headlights picked up the sparkle from a thick covering of frost on the grass verges. Momentarily, he considered handing over his own jacket, instantly recognizing how stupid that would be. No one except an idiot would ride a motorbike in sub-zero temperatures, wearing only a light sweater. Even on a hot day the wind chill was considerable and while people strolling were okay, on a bike you still needed windproof gear. Tonight, with temperatures plummeting, he would never make Exeter except on a stretcher suffering from frostbite and exposure; the cloth of his jacket built for town wear, not a seventy-mile-an-hour bike chase across a hundred miles of open country. The sensation of warmth against his back, as Hilary nestled tightly against him, was very welcoming and reminded Scott of Scotland – a good memory.

He dropped his speed back to fifty, frustrated at not being able to go faster, to get the journey over and done with and track down the furniture warehouse where the American Secret Service had their headquarters. Still, it was ludicrous to imagine anyone would be on duty this late. With a long night ahead waiting for dawn, when honest people would be up and about their business, there was no point breaking the speed limits. Even so... he remembered Travers' warning; he would be forced to stay put until the shops opened and Hilary could buy some tinted lenses.

Scott patted his jacket feeling a thick wad of notes that Travers had stuffed in his pocket before driving off. Travers was never concerned about money, he didn't need to be, but it was still good of him, especially now when it seemed unlikely Scott would ever be able to pay him back. He was like that, always had been, do anything for a mate. A good friend. Scott smiled ruefully, wishing he was still with them. Somehow Travers' larger than life appearance, so laid back and casual, created an aura of dependability which reduced panic to calm common sense. Perhaps Tulsa *had* survived and they were getting in a state for nothing. Perhaps his father *wa*s safe. Perhaps tomorrow everything *would be* all right. Somehow, with Travers on your side it all seemed possible. He'd inherited that calm air of assurance from his dad. Whenever Doug Randal was about, nothing ever went wrong.

Scott frowned, remembering Hilary's accusation. She couldn't possibly have been serious. Not Doug Randal. That was bang out of order. Like him going on about Sean Terry. Scott bit his lip, angry with himself for sounding off. He had behaved like a man drowning, casting around for something, anything, to hang on to. And yet, it *was* possible for Sean Terry to be a sleeper. It would explain why the bad guys caught them off-guard, turning up where they were least expected. Only someone in the know could organise that. Angrily, he blinked away the vision of Tulsa lying on the pavement, covered in blood. No! Hilary was right, it was crazy thinking. There was too much evidence to the contrary. Okay, maybe his manner and appearance put the agent in the category of archetypal villain, caustic, impatient, dangerous, but it's was still prejudice on his part, pure and simple. He resented the man's influence on Hilary. Because of him, they'd wasted an entire summer and it had taken Hilary resigning to change things.

Briefly, he removed one hand from the controls and flexed his fingers, reaching back to touch her leg.

'What?'

'You okay?' Hilary jerked her chin against his back in confirmation. 'Won't be long now,' he added, sensing a change in temperature, the wind lessening as the warmth of the city seeped out past the welcoming street lights. 'We'll stop and get a takeaway and then head for the university.' He caught the muffled word 'bath' and grinned. Girls and their baths. Still, she had to be frozen solid.

Gradually, the lights of the town closed in around them. He glanced down at the time, a twenty-four-hour digital clock set amongst a myriad of dials, controlling fuel, speed, amps and revs, and saw it had gone eleven.

'We'll be lucky to find anything to eat at this hour.'

'Head for the centre, then,' he heard her say.

He'd visited the city once before but that was in the daytime when the streets were thronged with traffic and shoppers. Now, it felt strangely alien, silent in a way that only sleeping cities possess, the streets washed clean with rain from an earlier shower and deserted except for stray cats, and a solitary car returning home. Following the signs through the suburbs, with its rows of houses woven tightly together, Scott spotted lights ahead. Next moment, it was as if the bike had passed through a parallel universe, the streets as bright as day and thronged with party-goers. Young and skimpily clad, they surged in and out of an open doorway like waves on the seashore, the steady punching out of a base rhythm identifying the building as a nightclub, well and truly open for business.

The air was still cold and the sight of girls, in nothing but micro-mini skirts and strap tops, waiting in a line outside a kebab shop, sent shockwaves down Scott's spine. Noticing a burger bar open for business, he slowed to a stop then quickly sped up again, identifying the neon yellow of a police van, a row of black-clad police leaning against it their gaze fixed on the nightclub doorway. Nervously, he wove his bike through the partying jay-walkers, seemingly unaware they were standing in the road. Noticing a side-turning, he swept into it and pulled to a stop. 'I daren't go any closer, the place is crawling with police,' he called over his shoulder. 'And I'm starving.'

'I'll go,' Hilary said, 'but you'll have to help me off. My legs have gone dead.'

'Why didn't you say, I'd have pulled over sooner?' Scott jumped off the bike and lifted Hilary to the ground, momentarily hugging her to him to generate warmth. 'Sorry,' he murmured, wishing they could stay like that for ever, not moving, and simply ignore all the bad stuff happening around them.

'Not your fault.' Groaning, she rubbed her legs. 'But I'll be glad to get in.' Hilary peered down the road, the monotonous rhythm of the music reverberating into the side road. 'I bet they just love weekends.' She nodded towards the darkened windows of the house nearest the corner, grimacing sarcastically. 'What do you fancy eating?'

'Doesn't much matter. Something quick,' Scott muttered, fishing in his pocket for a twenty-euro note. 'And something to drink. Wait – that won't be enough. Here, take this.' He passed over a second note.

Hilary nodded and, still rubbing her haunches, disappeared round the corner. Scott waited, anxiously picking at the fabric on his glove.

All at once, the noisy mayhem of the main street accelerated into strident hoots of derision, followed by more authoritarian shouting. Scott was forced to picture what was happening, not daring to leave the bike and look. No doubt it was guys, too drunk to know any better, taunting the police. Silence descended for a moment and he guessed some sort of arrest had been made and the perpetrator was now cooling his heels inside the police van.

A bitter smile broke the edges of his mouth as he watched Hilary's neat figure appear round the corner. She waved and broke into a jog.

'What?' She quickly unlocked the box at the back of the bike – a shallow compartment doubling as her seat.

Scott shrugged and smiled ruefully. 'I was just remembering my marvellous idea, to take you out for an afternoon somewhere nice. Some great idea that was.'

At the corner of the street, two guys were slumped on the pavement a girl bent over them. 'It's the thought that counts.' Hilary gave him a brisk smile and climbed back on the bike. 'It'll happen one day, Scott. And when it does, let's go somewhere warm. Romantic walks in England should be outlawed in winter. Brrrr!' She shivered violently like a dog shaking off drops of water. 'It's freezing. Come on. We passed the sign for the university back up the road.'

True to her word, Gladys had left a key under the mat – and a note. 'If you're burglars I've nothing to steal, so don't bother. If you're Scott and Hilary – welcome.'

A series of other notes led them upstairs, a line of paper

arrows pointing to one of two doors on the first-floor landing – a second key waiting for them under the mat.

'She's very trusting.' Scott stared round the little room. Except Gladys was right; there was nothing worth stealing, the poky little sitting room cluttered up with a shabby sofa and chairs, and a work table. A threadbare carpet covered the centre of the room, its colour long gone leaving behind faded strings of grey yarn. The only thing burglars might have pinched were the curtains; long dark green velvet that reminded Scott of James Nicely's room in Scotland, with its cosy warmth countering blasts of bitter air from the open moor. Why did trouble always arrive when it was freezing outside? He frowned, remembering the road-side near Loch Lomond and his early-morning walk through the empty streets of Lisse. Everything was so much simpler if it was warm. Okay, so perhaps the temperature hadn't exactly been below freezing. Maybe it was the memory of being scared that made it colder than it really was. It had been April, after-all. Still!

From the kitchen came the hum of a central-heating boiler, a sense of warmth closing in on him. He peered round the door seeing Hilary had already unpacked their supper onto two plates.

'How come girls always know where the kitchen is?'

'What do you see when you go into a strange place?'

'Never given it much thought. I guess... um... a refrigerator with food in it?'

Hilary flashed a smile, passing him a plate and a tray. 'Girls check out the bathroom followed mostly by the kitchen because, somehow, you guys have it in your head that girls automatically know their way around a kitchen.'

'I wouldn't dare think that,' Scott returned the grin. 'Besides, Dad always made me do my own...' He stopped abruptly.

'It's okay.'

Placing his tray on the worktable, Scott shrugged his jacket off. 'I know. Take no notice. Whether he's dead or alive, the word still exists and I have to deal with it.'

'For what it's worth, Sean Terry may be a scumbag but...'

Scott forced a smile. 'Nothing we can say will make a scrap of difference. Let's leave it for tonight. And, for my sake, if I get stuck on a word, ignore it. This is one situation where talking doesn't help.'

Hilary nodded, her face full of sympathy. 'Do you want to talk at all?'

'Is it too late to ring Travers?'

'It's nearly midnight, Scott. Can't it wait till morning?' Hilary perched on the shabby couch, tucking one leg under her. 'He would have called if he had any news.'

As if Hilary had pressed a secret button, the mobile in Scott's pocket burst into sound. Scott grabbed it. 'Travers?'

'Just checking you made it.'

'Anything?' Scott pressed the button for speaker phone and Travers's deep tone rang through the small room.

'No, nothing. The police called again while we were out. They want to interview both Jay and me. Trying to find out where you are, I expect. Jay's still not back...'

'You serious?'

'Not a word. Mrs Brody's that worried. Mum told them I'd gone back to London with Natasha. She's the best at lying – she's that charming, no one ever suspects. She's going spare about Dad though, threatening divorce when he does get home.'

'No!'

Travers chuckled. 'The coast-guard said there'd been no reports of an accident.'

'Will you...'

'Scott, I'll talk to him as soon as, and call you. Oh yes, and Mary says…'

'Is she there?'

'No! She had to wash her hair, but my guess is there was something on telly she wanted to watch and didn't want me butting in and spoiling her fun. I'm picking her up first thing. What was I saying?'

'Something about Mary,' Scott reminded.

'Right. We need Weasel's address – you forgot to give it to us.'

'So I did.' Hilary leapt up, fishing for the piece of paper which she had put in her jeans pocket. 'Twenty-two Upton Court.'

'Got it! Get some sleep.'

'Travers?'

'Leave the thanks till we're in the clear, okay? Bye.'

Scott flipped the cover on his mobile shut, once again overcome by that sensation of being cast away in a vast ocean without a trace of land anywhere, nothing but a wall of dark grey water rolling relentlessly towards a bare horizon.

'Scott? Scott?'

Scott blinked and the pictures vanished.

Hilary slipped her arm through his, squeezing it tightly. 'What is it? Tell me!'

Scott gazed round the shabby little room as if seeing it for the first time and a deep well of unease soared through his body. 'I don't know but it wasn't very nice. Come on, let's get some sleep.' All at once, he felt unbearably sleepy. He got to his feet and delved into a pile of blankets and cushions left on the sofa, yet another note pinned to them.

'You haven't eaten.'

Scott took a hurried bite of his burger. It had gone cold, the fat in the meat congealed. He took a hasty swig from his

Coke bottle to clear away the taste. 'I'm not that hungry. You having a bath?'

'You know me, prickly as hell if I'm not clean. And it'll warm me up. Get some sleep. I'll try not to wake you.'

It was deep, dreamless sleep of total exhaustion; so deep that Scott neither heard their hostess get up and leave the flat nor Hilary moving about. He eventually awoke to the telltale click of an electric kettle switching off.

'What?'

'It's gone ten.'

Scott struggled out of the nest of blankets he'd made on the floor, leaving Hilary the couch. He must have been tired, not even noticing the rigid hardness of the floorboards under the thin carpet.

'You look awful. Here.' Hilary passed over a mug of coffee. 'I got some lenses.'

'You've been out?'

'I was their first customer. The shop assistant was curious so I told her I wanted them for clubbing tonight. I took the money from your pocket. Hope that's okay.' Scott nodded only half-listening, a dull throbbing headache pounding against his temples. 'By the way, your photo's in the paper.' Hilary handed across the newspaper that she'd picked up at the supermarket.

Instantly wide awake, Scott stared down at the front page. It wasn't a particularly good likeness, but the grainy black and white image had already gift-wrapped him into someone definitely guilty of something. 'They didn't waste much time,' he said, his tone as bitter as the coffee he was drinking. Cheap supermarket stuff made from the dregs of floor sweepings. He rested his mug on the carpet. 'I can't drink this. Isn't there any tea?'

Hilary shook her head. 'Couldn't find any. It tastes horrid, I know, but try and drink it.'

Scott got to his feet and wandered into the kitchen. A square box with a frosted-glass window for light, ramshackle cupboards hung from one wall posing as fitted units, with an old stove, its burners dulled with fat and grime, a sink, and a fridge lined up underneath. He hadn't seen the bedroom but guessed, like the rest of Glady's flat, it was equally poverty stricken and soulless – without any sense of personality – exactly like he felt. He'd slept fully clothed. It wasn't a big deal but a shower would help. Opening a cupboard, he peered in. 'There's always a tea bag.' Hilary caught the sound of tins being moved around. 'Yep, thought so,' Scott called. 'One, lost in a corner. At last the day is beginning to pick up.'

Scott came back into the sitting room, his face buried in his mug. Hilary hadn't moved. She held the newspaper rigidly in front of her, the fingers clutching the edge white with strain. 'I'm sorry.' Her voice broke. Dropping the newspaper on the couch, she fumbled through her pockets, pulling out a tissue.

'Tulsa?' She nodded, burying her face in her hands. 'And Dad?' Scott said in a dead voice. His tea forgotten, he stretched out his hand for the newspaper.

'It's on page three. Scott… please don't!'

Ignoring the anguish uppermost in her voice, he flicked over the pages his eyes skimming the paragraph. Then, his expression steely and unflinching, he read it again as if trying to make sense of the words.

The cottage on the outskirts of the village of Oddisham is the property of Mr William Anderson, the eminent scientist. Recently returned to his home in Cornwall after addressing the United Nations in Geneva, Mr Anderson is still missing. His sixteen-year-old son, Scott, is being actively sought by police in connection with a shooting incident outside Falmouth Comprehensive in which two people were killed. A body recovered from the fire has been sent for forensic examination. It's thought likely to be that of the owner.

George Beale, who farms the land around the cottage, when interviewed described the father-son family as quiet, always keeping to themselves. 'Nice kid, used to ride a bike,' he commented to our reporter.

A great bleeding void cut across Scott's chest. He rattled the pages savagely, wanting to tear them into shreds to match his life, now reduced to a few paragraphs in a newspaper. Okay, so he still had a mother and a sister – except he didn't, not really. He'd only met them a couple of time; the last fifteen years had been all about his dad. And now he was gone.

FIFTEEN

It was a stop-go road to nowhere, endlessly trawling streets and criss-crossing the city, frequently stopping just long enough for Hilary to ask directions; only to be met with, "Sorry, can't help you, I am a stranger meself."

The directory in the library had offered a bewildering list of industrial sites, an army of black blobs dotted around the map of the city like nettles in a field of corn. Hilary had visited only the one time, and not having an address they decided to check them alphabetically. The weather didn't help, the frost of the previous night replaced by a cold drizzle, the air thick and unmoving under its pall of steel-grey cloud. None of the sites were particularly easy to locate. Twice, they'd been directed back to a site already checked and it was one o'clock before they finally found where the furniture depository was located, Hilary recognising it by the position and number of the CCTV cameras. Besides that, its tin-clad units were no different from any of the other sites they'd visited, a line of concrete posts strung with barbed wire around the boundary, and double gates at the entrance tightly shut and accessible only by key code. Except here the gates stood open, blocked by a row of scarlet fire-engines. A pall of acrid smoke hovered over the site and heaps of smouldering rubble lay everywhere, yellow hosepipes straddling the concrete surface.

Scott skidded to a halt. He felt a tug on his jacket and caught the muttered, 'Oh my God! We're too late.'

He swivelled round, alarmed by Hilary's wide-eyed stare, the fake lenses masking the obvious anguish in her expression. 'What's happening, Scott?' she whispered. She grabbed at her mouth. Snatching off her helmet, she flung herself off the bike and ducked behind a wall.

Scott kicked the bike stand into place and quickly followed. He caught the sound of retching and saw Hilary crouched in a corner, her body shaking.

'I can't do this any more, Scott,' she whispered wiping her mouth. Keeping his face averted from the pool of vomit on the ground, he pulled her upright. 'I thought I could but I'm terrified. The men behind this – we can't fight them, they're too clever. They know what we're doing even before we do.' Her voice rose hysterically. Wrapping his arms tightly round her, he hugged her to him.

'You all right, miss?'

A policeman stood next to the motorbike, watching them curiously. Hilary pulled abruptly away. 'I think it was the burger I ate last night. I was feeling rotten all night.'

'Yeah, tell me about it. We're not using that place again.' Scott gabbled the words, his face burning up.

'Okay, then, if you sure you're all right.'

Hilary's lip quivered. 'Yes, thank you,' she said her voice faint.

'What happened over there?' Scott nodded in the direction of the fire-engines, desperate to direct attention away from Hilary, the officer examining her white face with concern.

'Witness says the place blew apart when they opened up. It was a furniture store – went up like a rocket. The fire brigade had their work cut out to contain it, I can tell you. Fortunately, they managed to stop it spreading to the other units.'

'An accident?' *Hell!* Scott gulped at his stupidity. His girlfriend was sick and he was showing more interest in the fire than her wellbeing. Rigid with fear, he eyed the officer relieved to find his grave expression of concern unchanged.

'Most likely someone with a grudge.' The officer seemed happy to chat and Scott relaxed a little.

'Was anyone hurt?' Hilary said. She clutched at her stomach, leaning against the wall. Worried she was about to throw-up again, Scott tucked his arm through hers. She needed to be strong now – one false word and they'd be for it.

'One fatality; another seriously injured. Why are you interested?' The policeman's tone was suddenly keen, penetrating.

'We're not… except… you know… curiosity.' Scott felt himself tense up. With enormous effort, he tried to relax his shoulders aiming them into a shrug.

'Live round here, do you?'

Scott forced a smile. 'Visiting – a friend from uni.'

'Okay, then. Off you go – if you're sure you're all right, miss.'

Hilary smiled briefly. 'I'm fine except I've gone off burgers.' With her face angled towards the pavement, she busied herself tucking a strand of loose hair into place. Replacing her helmet, she climbed back on the bike.

Scott flicked the ignition, the bike responding instantly.

'Good bike, that. New, is it?'

'Not really; it just gets polished a lot.' Scott muttered, feeling sweat break out on his forehead. *Holy crap!* What if the policeman asked to see his driving licence? His hands began to shake and he tightened his grip on the handlebars to keep them from betraying him. Anxious not to give an impression of being in a hurry, he raised his hand in a brief salute, easing the bike slowly away from the kerb. Swinging round the corner, away from the sharp eyes of the watching policeman, he took in a much-needed breath. 'Do you think he recognised us?' he called over his shoulder.

Hilary didn't reply. There was no need, Scott already knew the answer. A crime had been committed and the police would check everything including a couple of nosey parkers asking questions. It would be standard practice to check the number plate.

He pulled to a stop and, fishing in his jacket pocket, pulled out his wallet. 'Half-way through, I realised I was carrying my licence. It's got my real name on it too. I can't believe he let us go without asking to see it.' Pulling out the credit-card sized piece of plastic, he dropped it down the drain.

'But, Scott...' Hilary protested.

Scott jerked his head at the empty street behind them. 'Want to bet he's checking up on us right now. I'll ditch the bike in the university car park, it should be safe enough there. We were so lucky. I hate to say it but thank God you felt sick. Come on, let's grab you something to drink and phone Travers. His dad must be home by now.'

Keeping his speed low, he set off again picking up a stream of traffic as they joined the main road. 'Scott?' He felt a tug on his jacket and, indicating, pulled to a halt.

'What?'

'Pete would have known about that place so why didn't they move?'

Scott didn't reply, he couldn't. His head was bursting, a swirling mass of confusion, flipping from event to event. Nothing made sense. 'I don't know,' he groaned. 'I'm making it up as I go along. But I tell you this...' A little way down the road, he spotted blue signs directing them to the university.

He swivelled round, seeing the black and white signs to the industrial site behind him. How ridiculous; they'd spent several hours combing the city looking for the place, and it was ten minutes away. How senseless was that? The way forward had been there in front of them all this time... and he'd ignored it.

'Scott?'

He jumped. 'Sorry! Let's get back into town. We'll ditch the bike on the way and walk in.' Swallowing painfully, he revved the engine. Indicating, he pulled out, his mind made up. Strange how everything suddenly had become clear, like the road to the university. They could have saved hours if only they'd made the right choice at the start and begun their search in the local vicinity. However much he wanted and needed her company, he should never have allowed Hilary to come. It was so selfish belly-aching about how bad he felt, he'd never given a moment's thought to the effect Tulsa's death would have on her. All she could see was her own body lying blood-soaked on the ground. Besides, his problems were his and his alone. They always had been. Dad had taught him that. It had been the focus of his childhood learning, to become self-reliant in case the day ever came when it was needed. Dad had taught him to cook and keep house, row, climb, swim and play ball. Behind every lesson was that single-minded aim.

Uninvited, images of a body burned beyond recognition swept through his mind. He blinked them away. Hilary was right. Two kids alone couldn't fight an enemy that was always one step ahead – they *were* too powerful.

Powerful enough to control government departments?

Scott's hands on the brake lever tightened and the bike slowed. The thought was horrendous – too horrific to put into words. Before, it had only been a suspicion. Now, it was a certainty. Somewhere, hidden away among the corridors of power was a man that played chess with people's lives, casually destroying any piece that stood in his way. And so colossal was this man's power, no one ever questioned his right to give orders, however wrong or evil they might be. Unnoticing, the roadway slipped past, Scott automatically steering around potholes, slowing for lights and pedestrian crossings. If this were a game of chess he would be a pawn, a solitary little piece of no importance. Except – he grabbed at the thought like a lifeline – even a pawn, if it chose the right move, was capable of changing the course of the game and bringing down the king.

Another thought jabbed at the corners of his mind, one he dreaded bringing to life. Pieces on a chess board could be swept away and the game begun afresh with no lasting damage. In real life, the dead stayed dead. *And they wanted him dead.*

The bike swerved and he felt Hilary tense up. He flexed his fingers tucked inside their handlebar muffs, bought with the money his dad had given him on his sixteenth birthday. He couldn't think like that. There had to be some good, honest people around. Like that policeman. He'd been genuinely concerned about Hilary. If he told him what had happened in Geneva, that people were hell bent on killing him, maybe… just maybe… he'd be believed, especially after the fire today. Okay, so he'd be arrested but at least Hilary would be safe.

The bike swerved and a horn blasted out behind them.

'Scott, what's up – you're scaring me.'

Scott opened the throttle, his mind made up. 'We're going back. I'm giving myself up.'

SIXTEEN

They were running along a dual-carriageway, a busy ring-road that circled the city. In theory, it allowed through traffic to bypass the congestion of the shopping streets. In practice, it made little difference, traffic expanding as fast as throughways were built. Along the centre of the dual-carriageway ran an unbroken concrete strip, tall lampposts like tree trunks sprouting up every fifty metres or so. On the near side, a narrow pavement overlooked council allotments and, beyond them, a forest of roofs, and the reason for the continuous stream of heavy traffic.

Scott scanned the road ahead searching for a possible way off, running the bike through a series of traffic lights with no right-turn. Frustrated, he cautiously edged his way through the long line of cars, slowing to a crawl as traffic ground to a halt. Behind him, horns broke out over the steady rumble of a dozen idling engines.

Noticing a left-hand turn some twenty metres away, Scott stepped the bike around the stationary cars ignoring a battery of angry looks. Lined with terraced houses, a hopscotch pattern in yellow and grey stone accompanied the bike downhill, mirroring the direction of the dual-carriageway; the narrow road made narrower by a line of parked cars. At the bottom of the hill, Scott spotted a T-junction, a couple of vehicles waiting to turn into it, their progress stalled by a procession its participants waving placards and chanting. Impatiently, he crawled to a stop. Anyone stuck behind that was going nowhere fast.

'At least we know why the traffic,' Hilary said.

She got off the bike rubbing her haunches.

'Feeling better?'

She gave a nod and taking off her helmet handed it to Scott, fiddling with her hair. Scott smiled. It was odd how a change of clothes and hair colour could affect someone's personality. In Natasha's borrowed jacket and with dark hair, Hilary appeared quite the stranger; even the shape of her face seemed different, more vulnerable somehow, ringed by its halo of dark chestnut hair, the bossy fair-headed agent vanished. Scott glanced down noticing that Tulsa's pistol was no longer tucked into the waistband of her jeans.

'What did you mean back there about giving-up? You're not serious, are you?'

Scott flipped up the guard on his visor, his smile edgy. 'It's the only way...'

'*No!*' she flashed back. 'You can't – not on my account. Park the bike somewhere and we'll get a train to London. The American Embassy – they'll shelter us.'

Scott took her hand in his. It was warm. 'I want to, Hilary, believe me, I want to. But I'm almost sure it was the embassy that betrayed Dad and me in Geneva.'

Hilary looked shocked, her face under its dark mop drained of colour.

'*Watch where you're going, you effing twerp* – you nearly ran into us,' a voice bellowed.

Scott glanced back over his shoulder. A group of youths had spilled into the side-road, their placards made from squares of brown cardboard stapled to a wooden pole, thick black marker pen used to write the slogan 'up with the monarchy.'

A little way away was a minibus, its rear doors open.

'But I wasn't moving,' he protested.

'Yes, you was,' a voice shouted back. Scott eyed the gang, searching for its owner. 'Ran over me toe, ye did.' Even their clothes were designed to intimidate; black jeans with garish T-shirts streaked with artificial blood, skulls and daggers. He caught the glare from a bearded youth at the back of the group. Head and shoulders taller than the rest, he was covered in tattoos like a piece of graffiti on a motorway underpass. ''Ere, lads, how about this for a poncy bike? All right for some, innit. Does yer dad know yer out?'

Hilary gripped his arm tightly and snatching her helmet back, climbed up behind him hastily putting it on. 'Scott, let's go,' she muttered, poking him in the back.

A burst of chanting filled the air.

What do we want – Monarchy. When do we want it – now!'

A youth clutching a loud-hailer darted onto the street, pushing his way to the front of a line of students, their arms tightly linked to show solidarity. Much to the amusement of the crowd, he pretended the procession was an orchestra and began conducting them. Wearing an outrageous mohican, dyed every colour of the rainbow, his skin-tight jeans were liberally sprinkled with silver chains above long black boots. He pranced backwards waving both arms in the air, one still clutching the loud-hailer, occasionally interrupting his arm-waving to shout into it. Laughing, the students rose to the challenge, more and more joining in the chant.

'We students,' he bellowed, 'are marchin' for the friggin' monarchy. Join us. Make yer voice count. Demand a referendum. *We want it back. When do we want it?'*

'NOW!' the herd obediently roared and waved their forest of placards.

People on the pavements began to applaud.

Grateful for the diversion, Scott nervously edged the bike round, aiming to step it through the gap between some stationary cars.

'I said, *ged-off.*' The bearded youth erupted into view elbowing his way to the forefront of the gang surrounding the bike. Up-close, Scott noticed dried flecks of white foam ringing the sides of his mouth. The guy pressed his leg up against the front wheel to stop it moving and raised his banner aggressively, grasping it like a battle-axe. Alarmed, Scott glanced down and saw steel-tipped boots. No way was this a university student, even the wildest didn't go round with steel-rimmed toe-caps on their shoes.

Panicking, he gunned the accelerator hoping the noise would scare him off. A hand grabbed his arm. Scott looked into empty eyes devoid of humanity, nothing he could appeal to. Expressionless, his pupils dilated, the youth stared back. Instinct warned Scott; it wasn't him the guy was seeing, it was something else – something he needed to destroy. Panicking, he pounded at the boy's hand, trying to break his grasp.

'I said *ged-off.*'

Out of the corner of his eye, he spotted the placard aiming for his head. He ducked and it crashed down on his visor, momentarily blinding him. Hands dragged at the handlebars, and the bike tilted alarmingly. Scared, Scott got his feet down bracing them against the ground, the strain on his calves unbearable. Hilary screamed and he sensed her being dragged backwards, a feeling of space and air replacing the warmth of her body. There came a series of thumps and he guessed her place on the pillion seat was being fought over.

Leaping off the bike, he ran over to Hilary. A dark figure

was bent over her. Instinctively, his fist flew out striking the guy on the shoulder. Scott felt pain power up his arm and gasped.

'No need for that, I was only tryin' te help.' Scott recognised the guy with the loud-hailer.

Ignoring him, Scott pulled Hilary onto her feet. 'You all right?' he said, brushing her down.

''Course. But the bike!'

A deluge of scrabbling figures obscured the streamlined silhouette. Helpless, Scott could only watch. The writhing figures reminded him of maggots in a tin of fishing bait, squirming endlessly round and round. No sooner did one gain a perch on the saddle than he was pulled off and left on the ground, another figure using their fists to take his place. The bearded guy sat at the controls laughing like a maniac, the engine thundering out of control and making those in the bike's path skip nervously to one side, for fear of being run over. Behind him a figure crawled his way up onto the saddle. He stood up, his arms outstretched for balance, the guy sat behind grasping his ankles to keep him upright. Two others tagged on behind, using their boots as skateboards. Screaming like a banshee, the guy at the helm manoeuvred the machine round the parked cars, their occupants staring out with glassy, frightened eyes, their fingers firmly pressed on the door-lock.

Hilary tugged on his arm. 'Scott – let's get out of here.'

He pulled himself free. 'No, it's Dad's bike. I have to get it back. He'll kill me if anything happens to it.'

'Scott! No!'

By now, the march had come to a halt and a wide gap had opened round the rioters, still scuffling among themselves for possession of the bike. Scott dived into the crowd, fights breaking out left and right. 'Let it go,' he yelled trying to keep pace with its rolling wheels. Next moment, something heavy hit him across the back of the head and he toppled headlong into a solid wall of milling shapes. He felt boots trampling him down into the concrete. Dazed, he fought his way back onto his knees, unable to see the bike anywhere. In the distance, police sirens sounded, growing louder.

Hilary grabbed his arm, pulling him up onto his feet. 'Scott, we have to get out of here,' she screamed, trying to make herself heard above the racket, 'the police are coming.' She swung her helmet at a youth armed with a knife and it clattered to the ground. Scarcely aware of what he was doing, Scott shrugged her away and plunged back into the sea of squabbling figures, ducking the blows headed in his direction.

The sirens stopped abruptly, the noise from the fighting once again taking over. Whistles sounded. Suddenly, as if a starter's gun had sounded, an avalanche of fleeing figures fought their way through the crowd leaving the red bike alone on the ground, its wheels still spinning. Then Scott saw what the crowd had already seen – smoke spiralling into the air.

'*Run!*'

A huge explosion knocked him to the ground. For a moment he felt nothing – then he did, his hip and knee screaming in pain at the force with which he'd been hurled onto the roadway. Dazed, he looked up to see the air saturated with acrid black smoke, flying debris still tumbling to the ground.

'*Right, you're nicked.*'

He was yanked roughly to his feet. Scott recognised the black stab vest. 'But I haven't done anything,' he protested. 'Hilary?'

'If that's your girl-friend, I reckon she's nicked too.' The officer dragged him into the little side-road, the crowd of onlookers pushing back to let them pass. Over their heads Scott saw a police-van and an ambulance. In the distance another siren sounded purposefully. A second van swung off the dual-carriageway at the top of the hill, driving at speed along the narrow road, its siren blasting out.

'Bloody yobs and your petrol bombs.'

'But I…'

'Shut-it! You'll get your chance at the station. If it was up to me… Bloody good hiding is what you lot need.'

In the middle of the street lay a pile of smoking metal where the bike had been, nothing remaining of the elegant scarlet machine. 'But I wasn't even riding it,' he protested.

'Pull the other one. Next, you're going to tell me you wear your helmet and biker's gear to yer ballet class.' Scott didn't bother to reply; the insult had been intentional, a sneer uppermost in the officer's voice.

'I say, mate…'

The driver of the ambulance looked up as Scott was dragged past the open doors of the police van. Briefly he glanced inside, waves of dizziness sweeping over him with the movement. It was full – two officers busily taking names. Relieved he spotted Hilary hunched up in the far corner, her hands over her ears as if trying to block out sound. He guessed, like him, her ears were still ringing from the blast. But at least she was all right – and safe. It didn't matter what happened to him as long as she was okay.

'This chap's had a bad crack on the head. Check him out; then stick him in with the others. But keep his helmet – I need it for evidence.'

The paramedic was a middle-aged man, mostly bald, a narrow fringe of hair circling the back of his head where the rim of his cap perched, his demeanour open and cheerful. 'Here, let me give you a hand with that,' he said as Scott fumbled with the strap on his visor and tried to pull it off.

'What's going to happen to me?' He nodded gratefully

feeling the pressure on his head lessen as the medic slowly eased his helmet off. He gasped in horror. One side was almost completely crushed.

He flinched away, feeling fingers prodding his scalp.

'It wasn't half your lucky day. If you hadn't been wearing that helmet – and I don't care what the reason was – most probably you'd be lying here with a fractured skull instead of nursing a bad headache. I think you're okay but, to be on the safe side, I'll get a doctor to check you out.'

'Thanks but I'm okay, honest.'

'In a hurry to get arrested, are you?'

'My girlfriend's in there.' Scott said, watching the doors to the police-van slam shut. He heard its engine start up. 'Where are they taking them?'

'Central station to be booked in, followed by a few hours in the cells to cool off, then an appearance in front of a magistrate. Most likely that will be arranged for later in the day. Disorderly conduct carries a mandatory sentence – a minimum seven days in a youth centre.' Scott swayed, still unsteady on his feet. 'Here, lad, sit down, you look all in.'

Scott collapsed down on to the side of a stretcher, his legs giving way. 'What about a solicitor?'

'Never been arrested before?' The middle-aged man smiled kind-heartedly.

'No!'

'It's just like speeding. There, you attend a course on safe-driving for a few hours, pay your fine and *Bob's your uncle,* you don't even get points on your licence. Same thing with misdemeanours – like drunk and disorderly. Magistrate decides if you're guilty; you do your seven days. It's like community service, except you get board and lodging. You're given the chance to pay back by cleaning streets and drains. Then you're home free, not a stain on your character.'

'But why – what if you're innocent?'

'It saves on money and time, lad. The Union doesn't want courts cluttered up with solicitors, only there to make money. *Great!* He raised his arm in a salute. 'You're in luck.'

A small white car squealed to a halt, the words *Doctor on call* printed on the side. A young man flew out carrying a brief case.

'I heard petrol bombs – told people were hurt.'

The ambulance driver shook his head. 'Nothing serious bar this lad. Nasty crack on the head. My mate's checking the crowd. We were lucky this time.'

'A petrol bomb? Is that what blew up my bike?' Once again, Scott felt fingers rifling through his hair. Automatically, he pulled away.

'Hurts, does it?'

'A bit of a headache, that's all.'

Ignoring him, the doctor pulled a small torch from his briefcase. 'Cover your left eye.' A narrow beam searched his right eye. 'Now the other.' He snapped the torch off. 'I think he's fine – but you'll ache like the very devil tomorrow.' He smiled down at Scott. 'And it's not wimpish to admit you've got a massive headache. Your headgear says it all.' He nodded in the direction of the flattened helmet. 'Take two of these now, and I'll leave you some for later. Officer?' A police officer standing nearby looked up. 'He's all yours but I want him checked every couple of hours.'

The officer nodded. 'In you go, lad.' He pointed to a second police van – half empty. 'Don't look so worried – we do this all the time and we never lost a client yet.'

He grinned cheerfully at the paramedic inside the police van. A girl in her twenties, she was dishing out painkillers and plasters to a row of youths, sporting cuts and bruises.

Nervously clutching a handful of foil-wrapped painkillers

and a cup of water, Scott climbed awkwardly into the van, his back protesting loudly with every movement. A hand flew out, helping him up the steps.

'You hurt?'

Scott recognised the guy that had led the chanting. He had pulled off his mohican and it sat forlornly on his lap, like a cat that has fallen into a river, its spikes reduced to question marks. His own hair had been layered with clippers creating a pattern across the crown of his head and leaving a long back and sides, lank greasy strands falling down over his face.

'Got a bad crack on the head,' the police officer answered cheerfully. 'What's ye name, lad?' He pulled out a clipboard.

'Ss… er… er…' Scott fumbled for the card in his pocket, and pulled it out. 'Travers Randall,' he muttered, averting his eyes from the officer's gaze.

The young guy whisked the card from Scott's outstretched hand, examining it intently before handing it back. 'Never seen one of them before. New, are they?'

Scott hesitated, uncertain how to answer.

''Ere, take the weight off.' The guy smiled in a friendly fashion and flapped his wig at the officer in charge, who had moved on still recording names. 'He's local. They're generally okay. It's the bastards from county you want to watch out for.' He held up the remains of the loud-hailer, its edges flat and bent out of shape. He gazed at it ruefully. 'Made the mistake of beltin' one of them rioters on the head with it.'

Scott leaned back against the side of the vehicle and closed his eyes, his head throbbing. Nervously, he fingered the plastic card in his pocket, wishing Travers had kept it. If he was caught with a phoney ID it would only make matters worse. Besides, it was Travers' finger prints that were recorded on it – not his. Waves of misery blasted in behind his headache. A week ago they'd been happy – looking forward to Switzerland.

Now, there was nothing. He leant forward and, wrapping his head in his arms, gulped back his tears.

'No need to worry, mate, they'll let ye go. You ain't done nothin'.'

Scott peered through his eyelids at the guy next to him, the loud-hailer still gripped in his hands, his dark eyes friendly. *Let him go.* He had to be joking. He was Scott Anderson, masquerading with forged documents and wanted for murder. And he'd just taken part in a riot. Who would believe him after that? He huddled deeper into his seat, ignoring the conversation around him. At the edge of the darkness, he spotted a kernel of light and reached out for it. At least, in a police station surrounded by rioters, he should be safe.

SEVENTEEN

True to his word, Travers had rolled out of bed on the Saturday morning at eight, early for him and, by dint of threatening Natasha with *dire consequences* if she didn't get up immediately, managed to get them both out of the house by nine, collecting Mary on the way into Falmouth.

Mary, an only child of elderly parents, lived in a small Victorian villa and a bigger contrast between the two family homes it was impossible to find. Built around the turn of the twentieth century, when house building was in its prime, it had offered an inside bathroom and toilet – an unbelievable luxury in those times and greatly envied, especially by the less well-off who were forced to make do with a WC at the end of the garden. Over the following century, its solid construction had survived both the bombing in the Second World War and modernisation, although new drainpipes and double-glazing had been fitted, and it remained solid and enduring despite being unpretentious. The Randal house, by contrast, was a product of the twenty-first century. Built on a large parcel of land overlooking the river Fal where it flowed into the bay, it had been chosen for its mooring and the sea-going cruiser was usually to be found tied up at the end of an equally large garden. By force of habit, Travers' gaze focussed on the river when he got out of bed but the mooring remained empty, his father not yet returned from his trip to France.

'Mum's going spare,' he replied in answer to Mary's question as to his father's whereabouts. 'Dad'll be for the high-jump when he does appear.'

'But he's always off somewhere, Trav,' Natasha butted in. Like all the Randal family, things came easy when she applied herself. Like Catherine Randal she was tall and willowy, and modelling school had been glad to accept her – earmarking her as a supermodel of the future. She was also a good driver, when she wasn't chatting on the phone and, more than once, Travers had to refrain from grabbing the wheel as the Range Rover headed, at what seemed unstoppable speed, for the car in front.

'I wish you'd get off the phone,' he grumbled. 'It's dangerous and stupid, especially in a town.'

'I was talking to Gladys.' Natasha snapped the phone shut, dropping it back into the open mouth of her handbag. 'She says that Scott is probably still asleep on her sitting-room floor but she met Hilary on the way out.'

Travers heaved a sigh. 'Thanks, sis, I was that worried, it nearly kept me awake.'

In the back seat, Mary gurgled. 'I assume, Tash, that since you've known Travers since birth, "almost staying awake" counts as ten out of ten on the worry scale.'

Natasha eyes flashed to the rear mirror, smiling.

'No use you two ganging up on me,' Travers retorted indignantly. 'You know perfectly well what I mean. And it makes good sense to leave the worrying to someone else. Besides, I did try and check in with Scott this morning to see how he was but his phone was switched off, so I guessed he was still sleeping.'

'It's unbelievable,' Mary said. She leaned forward and

placed a hand on her boyfriend's shoulder. 'I wish Mr Randal was back – he must know someone who could unravel this mess.'

'I agree – Scott was a real state last night. You could see the suffering plain as plain. I don't suppose you caught the local news, Trav?'

Travers shook his head. 'You know me. I never listen to bad stuff before breakfast. Why?'

'They found a body... '

'At the cottage? Oh my God!' Mary gasped. 'You don't think... his dad...'

'I don't know what to think. From what Scott said – could anyone have survived that firestorm? Hilary said Scott is blanking her – refusing to talk about it. I mean, what if it is his dad? Mum's practically a basket case already and dad's only been missing twelve hours. It's not like her to panic. But a whole gang of media guys have been invited for brunch tomorrow and she doesn't know whether to cancel or keep hoping he shows in time. But she's definitely...' Natasha broke off. 'Did you say Upton Street, Mary?'

'Twenty-two Upton Court.'

'Okay, this is Upton Street, so I guess it's along here somewhere. Yes!' Natasha indicated left, pulling to a stop in a red-brick courtyard, fronting a collection of two and three-storey townhouses; a *For Rent* sign pinned to the ground-floor window of two of them.

'Let me go, Travers.' Mary opened the rear door. 'I'm not as intimidating.'

Travers wound down the window in time to see the door open and a woman in her early sixties, her iron-grey hair neatly curled, come out onto the doorstep.

'I thought you were the postman,' she said to Mary. 'Can I help?'

'Are you Mrs Davis?'

'Yes, and you are?'

'A friend of Wesley's from school.'

'Oh!' The woman took a step backwards as if surprised. 'I'm sorry, you've just missed him. He's gone back to London.'

Travers opened the door and jumped out. 'For the weekend?'

'No, permanently.'

'So you're not his mother?' Travers demanded belligerently.

'*I beg your pardon?*' the woman retaliated, her tone fierce. Her hand curled round the edge of the door, ready to shut it.

Mary kicked him. 'Sorry, Mrs Davis,' she smiled her words. 'My boyfriend got out of bed the wrong side this morning. We said we'd give Wesley a lift to the station to save him struggling with his suitcase on the bus. What a shame. What train did you say he was catching?'

Automatically, as if wearing a timetable on her wrist, Mrs Davis glanced down at her watch. 'I didn't.' Her tone cut the air like a knife. 'How extraordinary, after months without friends suddenly three turn up on the doorstep. What did you say your names were?'

'We didn't,' Travers said abruptly, drowning out Mary's response. He pushed her towards the open door of the Range Rover. 'Get in.' He slammed the door, turning with a ready smile on his face. 'Don't worry; we'll catch him at the station.'

'I wouldn't bother. You'll be too late.' She spoke confidently, once again checking her watch.

Natasha swung the heavy vehicle swiftly round in a three-point turn. She waved her arm at the woman still carefully watching from the doorway, and called, 'Thanks!' through the open window, before speeding back the way they had come.

'Anyone find that conversation a bit odd – or was that just me?' Travers buckled his seat belt. 'If you want to break the speed limit, sis, I'll ride shot gun and look out for coppers.'

'No problem.' Natasha shifted into fifth gear, the engine responding smoothly. Spray flew into the air from the wet roads as they pounded along between rows of garish hoardings advertising mobile phones, retracing their route back through the centre of town. Not many people were about, the sudden squalls keeping pedestrians to a minimum.

'Odd, in that you thought he lived with his parents?'

'Mr and Mrs Davis, yes,' Mary said. 'It's on his school record so why...'

'Absolutely, Mary, bull's-eye!'

'Will someone explain?' Intent on the traffic ahead, Natasha's face took on a bewildered expression. 'Mary might understand your code but I don't.'

'It's quite simple. Wesley arranges an interview for Jameson. Jameson disappears. Scott questions Wesley. Wesley disappears.'

'And the woman at the door had the same name but she wasn't anybody's mother,' Mary added. 'She might have been once – but she was old, like someone's grandmother. And did you notice how her manner changed. She was all friendly at first.'

'That could have been meeting up with Travers. He does tend to be full-on.'

'Come off it, sis. I wouldn't hurt a fly, you know that. Another thing, she took our number. I saw her watching as we turned into the main road. Put your foot down, Tash. If we miss him at the station, we'll pick him up in Truro. He has to change there for the London express.'

'Right!' Natasha accelerated, the heavy vehicle leaping the orange traffic light. 'I agree, if we're to help Scott we need answers and, after what you've just said, I can't help feeling Wesley knows more than he's letting on.' She swung the vehicle round an island, its neatly dug beds of earth waiting for the spring. 'I wish Dad were here.'

The single-track line from Truro to Falmouth earned its keep in the summer when thousands of visitors flocked to the area to explore its fine beaches and walks. For twelve years, the threat of radiation had reduced outings to the seaside to a single-day affair; even then few people had ventured into the water for fear of contamination. Now, with beaches and rivers at a safe level, tourism was once again the main industry in the town, with cruise liners visiting its deep-water harbour. As yet, though, nothing had been done to update the century-old station, giving passengers the choice of waiting on the platform or in an apology of a waiting room. Dingy, its windows smeared with salt spray, it boasted an out-of-order vending machine and half-dozen plastic chairs, which had been bolted to the floor, its only source of heat placed high-up on the wall out of reach of vandals. From time to time, an attempt had been made to smarten it up with brightly coloured posters of the region but these were instantly reduced to pornographic message boards.

Before even the Range Rover had come to a stop, Travers was out charging into the building in the exactly the same way he charged down a rugby pitch – at full pelt – with Mary racing after him. Natasha switched off the engine, flicking the button on the key fob to lock the vehicle before following. They came to an abrupt halt, the diesel locomotive with its two carriages already in the station.

'Start that end,' Travers bellowed peering into the end carriage. 'Got him!' Flinging a quick glance at the station master, who was standing by the train whistle and flag in hand, Travers yanked the door open and dived in. He reappeared, carrying a suitcase in one hand and dragging the struggling figure of their schoolmate in the other.

'Left without paying his bill,' he called out to the station master who had taken an anxious step towards them.

'Want me to call the police, sir?'

'Don't bother.' Travers smiled reassuringly. 'Mum only wants to be paid. He can wait and catch the next train. Can't trust anyone these days.' He glared down at the squirming figure. 'Not a word, if you know what's good for you,' he growled.

'You don't understand,' Wesley gasped out over the strangle-hold on his collar. 'They'll kill me if I say anything.'

'I doubt that and you're staying – so get used to it,' Travers muttered, watching the train glide into movement. The station master, after casting yet another suspicious glance in their direction, vanished into the booking office and shut the door behind him.

'We'd better go – he's bound to call the police,' Mary said timidly.

'Might be a good thing if he did,' Travers agreed. 'All this cloak and dagger stuff is doing my head in. Why are you running away?'

Wesley glared defiantly and his small eyes narrowed even further.

'You might as well tell us because you're not leaving till you do.' Travers dragged the still struggling figure over to the Range Rover and manhandled him into the back seat. 'You go in the front, Mary,' he said passing over the suitcase. 'And dump that in the back.'

'Wesley,' Mary patted his hand in a friendly fashion. 'I'm sorry you missed your train, but we need you to tell us where Jameson is. Everyone's worried to death.' She unlatched the rear compartment hoisting in the suitcase before climbing in beside Natasha.

Natasha turned the ignition, switching on the windscreen wipers as a rainstorm blew in from the sea. 'Which way?'

'Somewhere quiet. The beach, it'll be deserted.'

'Jameson's fine.' Wesley glared defiantly. 'I told Scott. Ask him, he knows where he is.'

He flinched back into the upholstery Travers' fist an inch from his nose. 'You're lying.'

'No! Ask him. Ask Scott.'

'It was Scott that sent us,' Travers said calmly.

Mary flashed a worried glance at Natasha. 'I think we should go and have a chat with Sergeant Halliwell,' she said, naming the local police officer. 'He'd be very interested in talking to you, Wesley, particularly since you arranged Jameson's interview and he hasn't been seen since.'

'Okay!' Wesley's eyes flashed. 'But you've just made one hell of a big mistake. When my boss hears about it, you'll be the one with a fist in your face and I'll be laughing.'

The coast road was empty except for dog-walkers braving the sudden squall. Natasha pulled to a halt. 'I think we'll risk it.' She turned round. 'My brother is a kindly soul and he'd think twice about kneeing a guy where it hurts most. I wouldn't… and I can spot a lie at ten paces.'

Mary glanced admiringly and bit her lip to stop from laughing as the older girl winked at her.

'Okay, then. I'm not sixteen,' Wesley spat out. 'I'm almost eighteen and for the last two years I've been a recruiting officer for a top European force – very hush-hush. Only a few people know about them.'

'Is that why you move about?' Mary guessed.

'Yes, I stay six months checking out the local area…'

'So why did you pick Jameson?'

'Because! He's totally brilliant with computers, which is what they want. He'll be trained up and earn shovel loads of money. He's lucky. I was only ever employed to recruit.' The boy's tone sounded genuinely envious.

He had to be telling the truth, Mary thought. 'But why the

secrecy and why did Jameson go without telling his family. It doesn't make sense.'

'That's the price you have to pay. It's a secret task-force, I told you. Stands to reason – it wouldn't be secret if everyone knew about it,' he said, his tone shrill.

'You're lying,' Natasha smiled.

'No – I promise!'

'Don't!' Travers leaned in close and Wesley licked his lips nervously. 'No way would Jameson have gone along with it. No one would. This is real life, Wesley, not a film script.' He grabbed the boy's jacket, twisting the collar in his large fist. 'Something happened to Jameson at that interview and you're not leaving till I know what, and where he is.'

'He's somewhere in France,' the boy whimpered. 'I don't know where. I promise that's the truth. *Please, let me go.* They can't hear about this. I wasn't kidding; I'm done for if they do.' Noticing the sceptical expression on the faces of his three captors, he babbled, 'Look, I didn't want to do it but they made me. One more and one more… I made up my mind. I told Mrs Davis I was heading back to London but I'm not. I'm going back up north. *Oh God* – why did I ever believe that advertisement.' Wesley dropped his head in his hands. His face crumpled, his skin tinged yellow like an old newspaper. 'I promise you, he's fine only he can't come home yet. Not till they can trust him.'

Mary held her breath, feeling the atmosphere tense, spine-chilling. She stared through the rear-view mirror. 'Wesley, if you need help, Travers' dad, Mr Randal, he's knows all sorts of people.'

'What advertisement?' Travers' tone was ice-cold, implacable.

Mary stared at her boyfriend, unable to believe it was the same person. He was always so easy-going, never put out by anything – not even her nagging. And then she remembered Scott and Hilary.

'Mega-bucks and a job for life.'

'Go on,' Travers said.

'I was brought up in a kids' home.'

'What a shame.' Natasha's tone was tinged with sarcasm.

'You try it,' Wesley flashed back. 'You'd have done like me if you had. There was this advertisement. It sounded too good to be true – and it was,' the boy said bitterly. 'There were loads of kids – not many English; mostly Turkish and from the Middle East. I went to Holland – it was exciting, I'd never been abroad. Except it wasn't abroad – because you didn't get to see much, as I said, not till you'd proved your loyalty.'

'To?'

'A new world order. For years the west has been dominated by big business led by the American dictators. Any country that dared stand against them has been invaded and turned into yet another capitalist state.'

'You believe that?' Natasha said.

'It's totally true. Ask anyone. South America, the Middle East – every country with reserves of oil and precious metals, the US have dredged up an excuse to invade them. They ignored poverty-ridden countries – like Africa. Not interested in people starving to death. Finally, they got their just reward.' Wesley lifted his head, smiling almost boastfully. 'Only, it wasn't finished because Europe became corrupt then – just like America. Fat cats everywhere – while people like me live in gutters and starve.'

'You're not starving and you weren't living in a gutter,' Natasha retorted dryly. 'Sounds like you learned your lessons a bit too well. Is that why you were sent to England?'

'England's my home and I was glad to help.'

'So what changed your mind?' Travers interrupted.

'Nothing!'

He peered closely at the trembling figure. 'Something did. It was Jameson, wasn't it?'

'Okay! Yes! I wanted him to be my friend but he wouldn't – he hated me.' Head down, Wesley mumbled the words.

Travers and Mary exchanged astonished glances. 'No!' Travers mouthed, raising his eyebrows in disbelief.

'I wanted to call a halt but by then it was too late – the interview was all arranged.'

'So what about Scott?'

'Scott! What's he got to do with it?' The guy sounded genuinely surprised.

'Didn't you hear? He's wanted for murder. It was on the news last night. Two men got shot outside school, one of them Scott's bodyguard.'

Mary watched Wesley's face turn an unbecoming shade of green as if he was about to be sick.

'You have to let me go – *please, I'm begging you.* I've got to catch that train.' His head flicked from side to side searching the empty road and beach. 'They can't know I've been talking to you.' Wesley drummed his fists on his knees, his tone pleading. 'I beg you; if you've any pity – let me go.'

'Okay, okay.' Travers held up his hand to stop him babbling on. 'Tash...'

Natasha nodded and started the engine, the steady rumbling seeming to calm the hysterical boy.

'Look – come home with us,' Travers urged.

'No!'

'If you really are scared, Dad'll...'

'NO!' The word came out on a shriek. 'They'll find me. You don't know them. They're everywhere.'

The station came into view, the little commuter train already in view on its return leg from the city.

Wesley leaned over into the back, dragging out his suitcase. 'When you find Jameson, tell him I'm sorry.'

Travers watched the rotund figure hurry into the station and disappear. From a distance, a whistle sounded. 'Did you believe him?'

Mary nodded. 'He was terrified when you told him about Scott. No one's that good an actor. Whatever's going on?'

Travers glanced towards the departing train, his face grim. 'Whatever it is, it's not nice.'

EIGHTEEN

Scott followed the broad back of the desk sergeant through a series of long corridors, a notice board, its brown cork surface scarcely visible under a deluge of bulletins, the only thing breaking the monotony of bare walls. For the past two hours he'd been locked in the sick bay waiting for a doctor, worrying about what was going to happen, yet determined to speak out, to tell someone. So far he'd been lucky and no one had taken his fingerprints. At the station, he'd been left in a side room while the rest of the group were processed, lining up to pass through a scanner to check their ID. As far as he knew, only the one guy had had his prints checked.

The young constable, assisting the officer in charge to book them in, had definitely been local, his accent pleasant and friendly, peppered with long slow vowels, but no way senior enough to offer help. The desk sergeant fitted the bill except Scott disliked him on sight. With his flushed face, he appeared to be suffering a bad case of heartburn, greeting the long line of detainees with a heavy scowl. Finally, it had been Scott's turn to confirm his name and address, the inner door swinging shut behind the last of the group.

'Turn your pockets out,' the man ordered, his manner abrupt. Scott piled a handful of broken pieces of plastic onto the desk in front of him. 'And what are these supposed to be?'

'My mobile. It was smashed when I was hurled across the road by the blast from the petrol tank. Can I phone my parents. They'll be worried.'

The response was a blistering negative. Scott swallowed, trying to keep the anger from his voice. Determined not to seem intimidated, he placed his eye drops and lens container on the desk. 'I *really* need these. I suffer from dry eyes.'

The sergeant nodded taking no further notice and, gratefully, he returned them to his pocket, still smarting from the put-down.

He'd been on his own in the sick bay, an apology for a room, its two beds covered in paper roll to protect them from muddy boots. He'd been glad to lie quietly though but couldn't stop his thoughts festering like an unlanced boil, relieved when the door did eventually open to see a doctor standing there.

'Anything of concern that you need to tell me, lad? Double vision, sickness…'

Scott took a deep breath. It was now or never. Even if the doctor didn't believe him, he'd have to take it further. The door opened again. The sergeant from the front desk stood there, a grim scowl covering his face, swinging the set of keys dangling from a chain on his belt round and round.

Scott felt a muscle clench in his jaw at the sight of the impatient figure. 'No, I'm fine.'

'Right, off you go then. And do try to keep out of trouble.'

The building was modern, the holding cells a huge barracks of a place, vaguely reminiscent of a changing room at a swimming pool, a line of doors either side of a narrow walkway, except there the doors were mostly of coloured preformed plastic. Here, they were reinforced steel with grilles at shoulder height to allow guards to see in; locked and bolted from the outside.

Impatiently, the sergeant flipped open one of the grilles, its flap tumbling down with a loud clunk. He peered in, counting names listed on the chalkboard outside before moving on.

'Bloody yobs. It beats me why you can't get a job and stay out of trouble like decent folk.' Pointing to a door on the far side of the corridor, he selected a key, its chunky length fitting neatly into the gaping aperture of the lock-plate. The door swung open. A row of heads jerked up and eight pairs of eyes stared towards it.

Scott hesitated in the doorway. 'I think my sister, Natasha, is somewhere about. Can you…'

'You should have thought of that before ruining my Saturday afternoon,' the officer snapped. Gesturing Scott to enter, he locked the door behind him. Scott heard his footsteps fading away all at once grateful for living in a country where there were laws to protect prisoners. The sergeant was the type who would happily have cast him into a watery dungeon and thrown away the key, blatantly more interested in watching a football match on television than caring for his prisoners.

'Thought you'd been let go.'

Scott glanced across the cell, seeing the guy that had led the chanting. He stared round seeing other faces he recognised from the police van, and gave a relieved smile. At least he was in with the walking wounded and not the same cell as the rioters. He winced, remembering the glazed expression on the face of the guy who had started it all by pinching his bike. How stupid had he been to try and retrieve it. If only he'd walked away when Hilary had begged him.

'I guess you been with the medic?' The guy patted the bench. ''Ere, budge up, you lot. It ain't much, but you're welcome to it.'

Narrow, double-stacked benches made of heavy-duty

plastic lined the walls, a couple of guys stretched out on the upper deck apparently asleep. The bunks didn't look particularly comfortable but Scott guessed comfort was furthest from the designers' remit; more important was an ability to withstand a drunken onslaught. No mattresses or blankets. Hopefully, if they were forced to spend the night, mattresses and covers would be provided. Scott wasn't confident, especially after sampling the hospitality of the sick bay. Nothing to look at or read, the plastic beaker so flimsy it had buckled under the weight of the water. And the officer escorting him even took that away, once he'd had a drink, in case he was tempted to use it as a tool for suicide or escape.

High up in the wall was a small barred window, its only role an indicator of day and night, too small to provide anything other than the merest suggestion of natural light. Hidden behind a metal grille in the ceiling, electric light burned steadily. In the uppermost corner, out of reach of marauding hands, a CCTV camera had been bolted to the wall and, at ground level, again built in to prevent their being smashed and used as a weapon, was a flushing toilet with a wash basin and cold tap.

'I'm Lightnin', by the way.' As the guy leant across to shake his hand, Scott caught sight of a strawberry birthmark on his cheek and neck, his hair dragged forward in an attempt to hide it.

S – Travers Randal,' Scott stuttered tripping over his friend's name.

'I know. I saw your ID.' Lightning grinned mockingly. 'Nice to meet yah, Travers.'

'Lightning's your real name?'

'Nah, it's Peter Sparks – god-awful name. Lightnin' suits me better.' He grinned cheerfully pointing to the chains and zips festooning his jacket and jeans. Scott recalled his hands loaded down with rings, at least two on each finger, including a cameo with a grinning skull. They were bare now, and he guessed they'd been removed by the custody sergeant.

'Is your head, okay?' The guy seemed friendly enough and, despite his ripped shirt, relatively clean, although at first glance the coloured spikes of his mohican, like a dirty comb, had been a real turn-off.

'I'm sorry I hit you. I thought... you know... you were one of them.'

'Think nothin' of it. She your girlfriend?'

'No... my sister,' Scott remembered just in time.

'Okay.' Lightning sprawled out on the bench squashing the guy next him, who hastily moved along. 'Still the march was goin' fine till you came along on that bloody-red bike.'

Scott flinched. 'Were you injured?'

'Nah! Limp's put on.' Lightning grinned and straightened up. 'You get a damn-sight better treatment if you act injured,' he added amiably. 'The rest will be herded in like pigs. At least here you get to sit down. You still at school?'

'Yes. Doing A-levels next year. Maths, biology and geography.' It felt good to talk about something normal. Being alone in the sick bay had almost driven him mad, worrying about what was going to happen. 'Why?'

'No reason.' Lightning shrugged. 'Bit young to get arrested though.'

'Doesn't all this bother you?' Scott asked, his smile tentative.

'Not much. You never joined protests before?'

Scott thought about shaking his head then decided against it – his headache bearable only if he remained perfectly still. 'No,' he said. 'The paramedic who treated me said we'd get seven days.'

'*You're joking!*' The guy opposite jerked upright. The

198

movement dislodged his glasses. Old-fashioned with thick lenses, they hung drunkenly from one ear, a strip of white tape around the earpiece holding them together. 'You've only to look at the CCTV,' he exclaimed in a shrill voice. Tall and weedy his chest wall dipped inwards, and his blue jeans were loose and ill-fitting with ragged hems that dragged along the ground, his trainers scuffed and worn down on one side. 'We didn't have anything to do with it. Any idea where those characters came from?' He glanced hopefully round the cell.

'They were bussed in, I saw them getting off.' One of the guys occupying the upper bunk, who Scott had thought sleeping, propped himself up on one elbow. Older than Scott and brown-skinned, his checked shirt was liberally stained with blood, his face covered by a large wad of cotton wool which he clutched across his mouth,

Lightning sat forward, regarding the guy intently. '*You're jokin'*.'

'*Not!* Ouch!' Scott noticed his bottom lip was swollen and split. He obviously found speaking painful. 'James...'

He pointed to a guy nursing a black eye who raised a hand, his fingers stained yellow with nicotine. 'That's me.' He gave a cheerful grin.

'He was organising the student protest,' the guy mumbled, 'and I was late. Took a short cut across the car park. They were on a minibus.'

'I saw them too,' Scott volunteered. 'They must have been parked up waiting. I was trying to avoid the traffic and I swear the road was empty when I came down. No one about. Next minute, these guys showed up.'

'So where did you spring from?' James pointed across the cell at Lightning. 'You're not one of us. I'm the union rep and know most of the faces on campus.' He stared accusingly.

Lightning held his hands up in mock surrender. 'Hey, don't

pin this on me. Remember, I'm the dude with the loud-hailer…' He grinned mockingly. 'You should be thankin' me, I got the crowd laughin' – always a good sign.'

'So where do you come from?'

Lightning wriggled his shoulders against the wall as if he had an itch. 'Nowhere special. I heard about the march and I'd nothin' better to do.' He pulled his jeans pocket inside out. 'No money for footie and Exeter were playing Cheltenham. I wanted to see that match. Besides, I like marches, you meet a nice class of people there.' He frowned, twisting his mohican round and round. 'I'm as puzzled as you lot how it set off.'

'*Puzzled*? I'm bloody furious. This yob came straight up to me… socked me straight in the eye,' a voice called out from the bunk above. Scott caught sight of a head leaning down over the edge. Noticing Scott staring up at him, the guy lifted away a pad of cotton wool concealing the lower half of his face. The area under one eye was cut and swollen, a purple bruise covering his cheek bone. 'Bloody oaf had a knuckleduster.' He pointed to the cuts. 'Came prepared. I thought at the time he was all coked up.'

'That big guy, the one they called Tyson…' Blank stares greeted the name. 'You know, the one on the bike,' James said, eager to talk. Scott nodded, remembering the blank stare and uncalled-for aggression. 'He was as high as a kite; it took three cops to load him into the van.'

'Did they all get pinched?' Lightning asked, his question greeted by shrugs.

'We were all too busy checking we were in one piece,' the tall nerdy guy replied.

'That's right. I heard someone call out the rozzers were on the way. That's when they blew up the bike.' James leaned back against the wall. 'Never saw nothing after that, I was too busy trying to pick myself up off the ground.'

'Was it your bike that caused all the trouble?' the student on the top bunk called down.

'Yeah,' Scott aimed for a smile and failed miserably. 'But I promise you, I wasn't planning on being a part of the march. I wasn't even riding it at the end. You said the guy's name was Tyson? I'll remember that. He owes me a bike.'

'The cops said someone blew up your petrol tank.' James said.

Scott nodded, still angry. 'So why were you marching? Do you really believe protesting will bring the monarchy back?'

The guy with the broken glasses shrugged. 'We're not actually about the monarchy, it's more about democracy. Our country fought two wars to keep democracy alive and now we're letting bureaucrats make decisions that affect everyone in this country. And no one says anything. I mean, it was the European parliament that got rid of the monarchy, we never had a say…'

'And I doubt you'll get it,' Lightning butted in, 'however much you march. Not while Rabinovitch is President. Bloody dictator. You might as well save yer breath. I'm like you – but we're on a hidin' to nothin'.' He swivelled round in his seat. 'What that paramedic said – he's right. And so are you, er…'

'Chris!' the boy twiddled the arm on his broken spectacles.

'Okay, Chris, it's another law the government never voted for. If you're found guilty of affray or even bein' in the wrong place at the wrong time, justice is swift and unmerciful. Has bin ever since the riots in London and Paris a few years back.'

'You a lawyer?' a voice piped up from the bunk above to the accompaniment of relieved laughter.

'But that's only if you're found guilty, right?' James said. He got to his feet, prowling restlessly round the cell. With his stocky build, he gave the impression of someone in a hurry; short and bustling, his whole demeanour was quite different from Chris sitting next to him. His posh accent alone would have given Scott cause to avoid him, since egg-heads tended to use words he didn't understand about subjects he'd never heard of. But they were obviously friends. Scott remembered they'd sat next to one another in the police van.

'I checked with the college authorities. They don't like you marching but will grant you permission provided it's peaceful. It wasn't our fault. Chris is right and the CCTV will prove it. I mean... the worst that can happen is we spend a night in the cells while they check the tapes.' He stared round the bare cell, his glance hovering over its single toilet.

Without warning the bolt on the door slid back noisily, two officers standing in the doorway.

'Right, you lot.' One of the officers beckoned. 'We've found a magistrate and you're off to court. You won't be coming back here so make sure you don't leave anything.'

'I'm all for that,' Chris said, getting to his feet.

'What about food? I'm starving,' a voice shouted.

'Don't worry.' The officer barked a laugh, the flashes on his jacket sleeve awarding him the rank of sergeant. 'You'll get fed. But it'll be a while yet. Now fall in, single file.'

'Here we go.' Lightning got to his feet. He clutched the wall mimicking someone having difficulty standing up.

Scott didn't need to pretend, his heart pounding out of control against his chest wall. His head swirled uncomfortably as he got to his feet, the pain intense; the pain killers the paramedic had given him making little difference. Scared, he shut one eye testing it for focus and then the other, relieved to find he could see okay. Hopefully, the doctor was right and it *was* only a bad bump.

The little line of prisoners made its way up a flight of stone steps and out into a courtyard, the two officers bringing up the rear. All around were tall red-brick buildings stacked high with windows, a small patch of sky visible above their tiled roofs. The light was beginning to fade, its sullen cloud base darkening swiftly towards evening: a typical November day in which sunlight became a distant memory. Across the mouth of the courtyard, thwarting any attempt at escape, were a pair of heavy steel gates; on the far side the blacked-out silhouette of a coach, a second one parked behind it.

'Court's right there,' the officer said, pointing to a flight of steps leading downwards. 'As you leave, you'll be handed a pack of sandwiches, crisps, and a drink to eat on the coach. That'll have to do you till tonight. But you won't starve.'

Scott couldn't believe what he was hearing.

'But I didn't do anything,' he burst out, unable to stop himself. He looked up at the windows flanking the courtyard, silent and dark. The people that worked in these offices were at home – no one worked weekends. James was right. It was logical to assume they would be held overnight or even till Monday morning. By then Mr Randal would have made enquiries and got him out. This was all wrong; they were being sentenced and they hadn't even been tried. 'Isn't anyone interested?'

The sergeant stared over the line of heads, his gaze ferreting out Scott standing at the rear. 'I've worked in this job nigh on twenty year, lad. In all that time, I've never come across anyone that's guilty. White as driven snow you lot are! Stop belly-aching and accept your punishment like a man. Do your time and hopefully you'll learn a valuable lesson. Don't get mixed up in protest marches.'

Scott felt his face burning with anger. He opened his mouth to retort.

'Leave it.' Lightning grasped his arm. 'It's not worth it. And it'll make no difference except you miss out on the food.'

It was like being on a conveyor belt, everything speeding

by so quickly it became a blur, leaving Scott with a vague impression of a dark tunnel, a line of shuffling figures passing them on the far side, their heads lowered as if with shame. There'd been no sign of Hilary and that bothered him. The officer directed them up a flight of dark steps, a patch of light burning ahead. Scott saw they were in a courtroom, stout railings around the dock stalling any further progress.

It felt hot and stuffy although the windows on one side of the room had been opened to let in some air. Scott caught a murmur of voices and guessed that members of the public had also been allowed in. He didn't bother to turn round and check, unsure of how good his disguise was and nervous of being recognised.

Opposite the line of prisoners, and almost on a level with them, was a high-fronted bench, the golden-brown of the wood creating a splash of colour, the city coat of arms prominently displayed behind it. At ground level clerks, seated at a table made from the same colour wood, were busily writing. Opposite them a lone suited figure. As the line of detainees entered the dock, he glanced up briefly, his demeanour tired and dispirited. He looked away again, adding notes to the pad on the table in front of him.

The bench had been designed to hold a trio of magistrates but only one was present, a grey-suited figure. Seemingly oblivious to the prisoners shuffling into the dock, he was talking to one of the court officials, glancing casually as names were called, his gaze steely but disinterested.

'The charge is causing an affray and criminal damage,' the officer of the court read out. 'How do you plead?'

Scott heard the not-guilty pleas run along the line like tumbling dominoes, and quickly added his voice to the rest.

A police officer got laboriously to his feet and began to read from a typed script. He'd obviously done it several times before, speaking whole sentences without looking down, and Scott wondered how many people had preceded them, recollecting the line already exiting the courtroom as they entered.

'All six CCTV cameras in the centre of Exeter have been vandalised so no record of the march exists. The ambulance service report that twenty further people sustained injuries in the explosion, excluding the eight accused...' He paused long enough for his glare to hit its target. 'Four shop windows were smashed, and flying metal damaged three vehicles that we know of. Could have been extremely serious, sir.' He lifted his head not bothering to read the actual words.

Scott could sense the tension sweeping through the line of students as the officer painstakingly trawled through the details, and he guessed, like him, they had despaired of a happy outcome. He'd caught the thumbs- down sign as the previous group passed, which meant they'd been found guilty too.

The officer took his seat, silence echoing loudly around the courtroom.

Placing both hands on the bench in front, the magistrate leaned forward, running his eyes along the line. 'Do you know what I have spent the entire week doing?' he said in a tired voice. 'Judging scum like you intent on causing chaos. Seven days community service.'

Lightning, standing next to Scott, took in a sharp breath.

The man at the table climbed to his feet. Clutching a coloured file in his hand, he waved it to attract the magistrate's attention. 'Sir, I must protest...'

'Protest all you want, Mr Armitage, that's your job as a lawyer. It's not going to change anything.'

'But, sir, I must defend them... a number of these young people sustained injuries.'

'And if you'd been listening, Mr Armitage,' the magistrate

leaned even further forward, 'so did members of the public. The report said twenty innocent people and property desecrated by louts who find it amusing to go on the rampage.'

'But, sir, without CCTV…'

'Mr Armitage. Do you have anything to add to the statement you made ten minutes ago?'

Dispirited, the lawyer shook his head.

'Then I have heard all the arguments. It is simply a waste of time to go through them again.'

'But, sir, the defendant… er…' He peered down at a document on the desk in front of him, 'Travers Randal,' he read out. 'I've not yet had a chance to speak to him.'

'Put your objection in writing, Mr Armitage,' the magistrate's tone was dry and pithy reminding Scott of their headmaster, who delighted in sarcasm. 'Meanwhile, Mr Randal may serve his seven days. Were you present at the march, Mr Randal?'

'Well, yes, but…' Scott stuttered, taken aback at being singled out.

'There you have it.' He banged the gavel. 'Next case.'

A clerk sitting at the desk below stood up and passed the magistrate a slip of paper. Scanning it quickly, he leaned down to ask a question.

Scott saw the clerk shake his head.

The magistrate beckoned to a court official. 'The prisoners – bring them back in,' he instructed. The man nodded and scurried out through a side door, heads turning to watch him go.

Still irritated by his stupid response, Scott glanced down at the lawyer who had tried to stand up for him, wishing he could claw back time to a few minutes ago. But it had always been like that; he could never come up with a smart answer without thinking about it for ages first. That was him – that was his character. And he was stuck with it. If he'd known he was going to be asked a question, he could have prepared a proper answer, one that might have got him off. Hearing a ripple of conversation break out in the gallery, Scott risked a glance over his shoulder. Whatever was happening was unusual, that was obvious. Still, they were the lucky ones; they got to go home afterwards. He turned back eyeing the magistrate who, taking no further notice, was glancing through some papers on his desk. Calling the prisoners back didn't mean a change of heart; the man had no intention of sending them home.

The side door opened and a line of prisoners filed in, uniformed officers directing them across the courtroom. Anxiously, Scott scoured their faces, immediately spotting Hilary's dark hair, her small figure obscured by the bulky youth walking ahead of her. As if she knew he was there, she raised her eyes to the dock. For a brief second, their glance met and a silent message crossed the space. Hilary's face twisted in a half-smile that said she was fine and not to worry. Scott felt his heart pump loudly with relief. Hesitantly, he raised his hand to show he understood. Nothing mattered now. They could do what they liked to him as long as she was all right.

There was a restless shuffling as the forty or so prisoners moved to make room for the final few. The door closed behind the last one, the smirking faces of Tyson and his three mates at the back of the line.

A surge of indignation at the rotten unfairness made Scott want to call out, to tell the magistrate that those four were responsible for starting the riot. If he did, what could happen to him? Nothing worse than was happening now. He took a step forward and felt a warning hand on his wrist. 'Don't be so stupid!' Lightning hissed out of the side of his mouth. 'You'll get us fourteen days if you don't shut it.'

The clerk called loudly for silence, his voice echoing round the chamber and adding to Scott's misery, his head throbbing painfully.

The magistrate leaned forward, his glance frisking the line of prisoners, dwelling intently on each face for a moment before passing on. Ignoring the wooden gavel, he thumped both his fists on the desktop. It reminded Scott of the judge in their school play the previous Christmas who had vamped his role for laughs. This was the same except no one in the gallery was laughing, quelled into a nervous silence.

'I have brought you back in because I am appalled at the sheer number found guilty of affray. How can honest people go about their daily lives in safety with you at liberty?' Scott shifted from foot to foot wishing he could sit down, the close confines of the overcrowded courtroom making him feel sick. 'Community service seems to be ineffective, an alarming number of you reoffending almost immediately. I have therefore decided to make an example of you all and send you to a labour camp. I understand conditions there are more likely to have a lasting effect. Perhaps, this time, you will learn your lesson. Take them down.'

Gasps of horror ran along the little line of figures like an electric shock, intermingled with a muttered, 'yes!' Out of the corner of his eye Scott saw Tyson bang the air with his fists, his smile triumphant. Then the door opened and he was gone.

NINETEEN

Travers, Mary and Natasha reached home to find it deserted, the back door unlocked. Guessing their mother wasn't far away, Travers wandered out into the garden followed by the two girls, its wide stone paths fringed with giant green lollipops, its avenue of tropical palms carefully wrapped in green polystyrene to protect them from winter frost. The squall earlier had left the flagged paths wet and slippery, and they picked their way carefully down the slight slope leading to the river. As Travers had expected, their mother was camped out in the small boathouse, a flask of coffee at her side, scouring the grey waters of the bay through binoculars, a few desultory seagulls riding the waves close in shore.

Hearing feet on the path she swung round, lines of worry creased across her forehead.

'Every time I hear footsteps, I think it's Doug. Why hasn't he phoned? He'd better have a damned good excuse.' Shivering, Catherine tucked her thick jacket more tightly around her. 'A wretched day for a disappearing act, too. Did you see your friend?'

'We did,' Travers replied grimly. 'But he was half-way out of the door and reluctant to say anything about Jameson. Mum... what's that?' He pointed out over the grey water his keen sight picking up a smudge on the horizon. The River Fal emptied into a deep-water harbour which, in winter, was mostly deserted except for a few working boats. Only the shore line, littered with hulls wrapped in tarpaulins, like presents waiting in a cupboard for Christmas, displayed signs of activity; its jetties busy with owners of motor yachts taking advantage of a quiet Saturday to undertake pressing maintenance.

Catherine hurriedly put the binoculars to her eyes. 'Thank God; it's the cruiser. 'I'll murder him, you see if I don't. He'd better have a damn good excuse,' she repeated, her face pinking up with anger and relief.

'I expect it'll turn out to be something technical, Mum.' Natasha laid a comforting hand on her arm. 'Dad never goes AWOL.'

'Because he knows I'd kill him if he did. I had it written into our marriage vows.' Catherine smiled at Mary, her finely groomed eyebrows raised mockingly.

Mary smiled back. 'It's okay, Mrs Randal, I know you didn't mean it. And, anyway, I'd kill Travers if he disappeared without phoning for twenty-four hours.'

'Mum, we're going in to get a drink,' Travers said. He pointed towards the dot on the horizon, still a long way off and scarcely visible to the naked eye unless you had long sight like him. 'But we'll be back in plenty of time to watch your performance.' He winked at Mary who stifled a giggle. 'Hope you're not carrying anything lethal?'

Catherine glared fiercely. 'You can get out of my sight too. I was awake all night worrying and my temper is definitely uncertain – so watch it. And take this with you.' She waved her thermos in the air. 'It's gone cold and tastes gross.'

Travers nodded and walked off up the path, one arm clutching the thermos, the other round the shoulders of his girlfriend. 'You wanting coffee or Coke?' he said, opening the door into the kitchen.

'Coffee please. You're mother's right. It's a horrid day and a coffee will cheer me up.'

'Me too, please, if you're making,' Natasha followed them in. 'I feel like Mary – we shouldn't have let Wesley go.'

Travers opened a drawer, pulling out an assortment of coffee sachets in different colours, examining their labels. 'What do you want, cappuccino, latte? I don't think we could have stopped him.'

'I'll have a cappuccino please, if you've got chocolate sprinkles.'

'No problem.' Travers poured water into the elegant stainless steel machine, switching on the power. 'Tash?'

'Black, please.'

'God, you models, you miss out on all the good things in life.'

'You forget I've always hated milk,' she retorted sharply. 'But about Wesley…'

Travers shrugged. 'I sort of hope he does make it back up north. He was scared though.'

'The events of the past two days have left me plenty scared,' Mary added, perching on a stool. 'I don't like this sort of excitement. People vanishing or dead – it feels like the world's turning upside down.'

'At least Dad's no longer among the missing. Look, we need to tell him about Jameson…'

'And Scott,' Natasha interrupted.

'Course! That goes without saying. But Jameson… If there is an organisation behind it, maybe Dad'll know something. I tell you what though…' The coffee machine burst noisily into life, a cloud of steam erupting as the freshly made brew trickled into a cup. Silence fell as Travers concentrated on removing the full cup from the machine without spilling it. He placed it carefully on the kitchen table, an old-fashioned wooden affair that had come from a neighbouring farm. In the designer built mansion, the kitchen was the only room in the house that bore traces of a bygone age, with red quarry tiles on its floor and copper pots and pans hanging from hooks on a wooden frame suspended from the ceiling.

'Sprinkles in the drawer and, if you use that thing,' Travers pointed to a circular plate with a star shape cut into it, 'your drink will look professionally made as well.' He swung back to the slim-line machine, its stainless steel gleaming as brightly as the copper pans, fitting another sachet into the slot at the front. 'What Wesley was saying,' he continued, 'sounds like brainwashing to me. The capitalist governments of the west! Does anyone still believe that crap?'

Natasha nodded her thanks as Travers passed over her coffee, wrapping her hands round the cup to warm them. 'Don't you ever read the papers?'

'Travers only reads the sports section.' Mary smiled lovingly. 'He says the rest isn't worth the effort.'

'You can hear the gist of it every hour on the hour, if you want,' Travers argued, 'so why read about it too? Anyway, newspapers are the pits, always quoting some famous person's opinion, and the world-editor for every TV station giving his view too. You're better off sticking to sports and entertainment. Anything else fries your brain.' He glanced down at his watch. 'Changing the subject, I wonder how Scott's getting on. I hope they've found what they're looking for.' Thoughtfully, he took a sip of his coffee. 'I mean if you think about it, we've accepted without question that the American Secret Service have a base in the UK. Isn't that a sort of brainwashing? I mean who gave them permission? Come on, drink up. Let's go and welcome Dad home, then we'll try Scott again.'

By the time they reached the river mooring, the dot had

grown into a sizable white cruiser capable of voyaging long distances, and fitted out with cabins, a shower, and a fully-equipped kitchen.

The tall figure at the wheel waved, manoeuvring the elegant craft skilfully into its mooring, rubber fenders absorbing any impact as it came alongside. Even from a distance Doug Randal looked tired, his face drawn, and the cruiser showed signs of a voyage through bad weather, its polished wooden decking dulled with brine. He eased his tall frame onto the deck tossing the bow ropes to Travers to tie off. Impatiently, Catherine leapt down from the jetty and he caught her in his arms.

'Darling, you look exhausted. Tell me, tell me; I've been so worried.'

He hugged her to him. 'I know. I'm sorry. You must have been out of your mind. We hit bad weather in the channel and my mobile went overboard. I was in the middle of calling you when we got hit by a freak wave.'

Catherine peered at him anxiously. 'The coastguard said there was a big swell... but you could have used the ship-to-shore. That was working, wasn't it?' She scrutinised her husband's face.

'We had a problem there.' Dragging his wife with him, he leapt onto the dock wrapping his spare arm around Natasha and smiling warmly at Mary. 'Keeping Travers in check, I see,' he said in an amused voice.

'Not today, Dad. It's Scott. He's in real bad trouble...'

'And Jameson's vanished...' Mary butted in anxiously.

'And we've had the police here. Twice.'

Doug halted in mid-stride. He stared down at his wife. 'What did they want?'

'They were searching for Scott. They wanted to interview Travers. I said no. Not till you were home.'

'Did they have warrants?'

'To search the house? Whatever for? I told them we hadn't seen Scott. They obviously believed me because they left.' Catherine's tone rose impatiently. 'I tried to phone you... what happened? I was worried to death. *Doug?*'

'I need to get the ship-to-shore working.' He swung round. 'Come along for the ride, we can talk about it on the way.'

Travers stared at his father, instinct telling him that something had gone badly wrong. And it happened the moment his mother mentioned police. He examined his father curiously, surprised to find a look of strain overlaying his usual amiable expression.

'I think that's a great idea,' he said, taking Mary's hand. 'Can Mary come? We're spending the day together.' He took a step back towards the launch, the wind strong enough to swing the vessel round against its mooring.

Mary gazed up at him doubtfully. 'But...'

He wriggled his nose in warning.

'I was planning a working lunch, Doug. We need to go shopping; we've fifty people coming for brunch tomorrow, remember.' Catherine's voice dripped acid.

'I hadn't forgotten. I already picked up the wine.' Doug pointed to the cruiser. 'This won't take long. While we're fixing things up, I'll buy you all a late lunch in St Mawes – my treat. They do great lobster thermidor at the restaurant there. We can do the shopping afterwards. Natasha?'

'Can't it wait, Dad? We need to talk to you; it's desperately urgent. We promised Scott.'

'Tell me on the way. You got your phone on you?' Travers nodded. 'Didn't you just get a new one?'

'Don't you remember, Dad, someone nicked it, and I had to claim on the insurance. A real pain, I lost all my contacts.'

'Thought so, keep forgetting to take your new number.

Lend it to me, there's a good chap? I want to check this bloke's at home. Catherine, while we are out, remind me to buy a new phone.'

'If we *are* going out on the bay, I'll get a warmer coat.'

'Don't bother. I've got plenty of stuff aboard you can borrow. We really need to get moving.' Doug glanced up at sky. 'I'd like to get this fixed p.d.q and it'll be dark early today.'

'Really, Doug, this is so inconsiderate. I wouldn't be seen dead in your smelly old cast-offs. Especially lunching in St Mawes. Think of my reputation.' Turning on her heel, she stormed back up the path.

'Catherine?' Doug shouted after her. 'Wait!'

Natasha pulled a face. 'I agree with Mum,' she snapped. 'What's got into you, Dad? We've been waiting all night. I've never known Mum so scared, and all you're bothered about is your stupid boat. We won't be using it again till spring, anyway. Bags of time to get its problems sorted out. I'll come with you, Mum,' she called after the hurrying figure. 'I need something warmer too.'

Travers stared after the disappearing figures, a worried frown covering his face.

'You two coming? You can borrow a jacket, Mary, if you're cold. Whatever my wife thinks, they're clean and tidy. And very warm.'

'Dad?'

'Yes, Travers. Untie the stern, there's a good chap.'

'Dad?' Travers called out, his tone insistent.

Doug glanced up. 'Don't worry about your mother, I'll make it right.'

Travers shook his head, his expression grimly determined. 'I know you will and I'm not. It's not that. When we were little, you promised always to tell us the truth and you expected the same from us. I know Beau's the bright one –

but even I can tell you're lying. There's nothing wrong with the radio and I don't believe there's anything wrong with your mobile either. You wouldn't use it anywhere unsafe – that's not who you are.'

His father raised his hands in surrender. 'I have three amazing kids. Okay, then. The phone in the house is bugged, and probably the boathouse too. That's why I tried to stop your mother going back in.'

Travers stared, unbelieving. 'How…?'

'Did your mother invite the police in?'

He nodded. 'She took them into the kitchen and offered them a cup of tea while she tried to ring you.'

'Quite long enough. And I bet there was car waiting outside with officers in it?'

'Yes, is that important?'

'While she was phoning the people outside would hack into the landline and my mobile. Easy enough to do. Takes minutes. Planting a bug – not even that.'

Mary tugged at Travers' sleeve, her face pale. 'Oh my God, Wesley! What have we done?'

'But, Dad, you couldn't possibly know that,' Travers protested, still not convinced. 'You were at sea.'

'And I'm not into taking chances, especially with my family. The cruiser's okay – what about the boathouse? Did they search there?'

Travers hesitated. 'They insisted on checking the garage.'

'Then you can assume it's bugged too. Let's get back on board – it's cold out here.' Doug helped Mary down the narrow companionway. 'We need to go over everything you've said since their visit.'

Heading into the lounge, he flicked a switch for the central heating.

'Dad?'

'It's a long story, Travers. And, to be perfectly honest, Mary. I'd prefer to keep you out of it.'

Mary gave a timid smile and sat down, tucking her legs under her for warmth. 'The thing is, Mr Randal, I'm not very brave and if it was only me, I'd stay out of it and get Travers to take me home. But the thing is,' she repeated, 'our friend Scott's in terrible trouble. His father's been killed, so's his bodyguard, and now Scott is wanted for murder.'

'Scott, wanted for murder? When did this all happen?'

'Last night, Dad. That's what we wanted to tell you. Someone blew up the cottage. Tash heard it on the radio. They found a body.'

Doug Randal put up a hand. 'Hang on a minute, Travers! One thing at a time. Go on, Mary… '

Mary nodded painfully. 'If what you say is true and the house is bugged… ' She looked appealingly at Doug who nodded back slowly. 'Then we've put someone else in danger too.'

Doug heaved a sigh. 'What a mess! But if you want out, just say so.'

Travers smiled possessively down at her and folded his hand over hers. 'I'm so lucky to have you.'

'I know, so don't push it,' she retorted.

'This little problem is all to do with the monarchists,' Doug said. 'I've been a member for years but quietly so, very low profile. In the past year or so, prominent party members have found their phones bugged.' He picked up a plastic torch, the same size as a Cuban cigar tapering at one end into a steel probe, and waved it in the air. 'They bought this piece of kit from the States. I got one, too, in case. If a phone is bugged, it's so sensitive it picks up the electronic signal and buzzes. I rang to speak to your mother, to tell her where I was… When I heard the buzz, I put it down sharpish and didn't try again.'

'Dad!'

'It's okay, Travers – you weren't to know. So tell me about Scott. What happened?' He looked up. 'Give me a moment; I need to talk to your mother... alone.'

Travers glanced up, seeing Natasha and their mother coming down the path, his mother's expression cold and distant. He watched Doug leap onto the little jetty and, taking her arm, walk her back down the path.

Natasha came into the cabin. 'Oh Lordy, Lordy! There's going to be one-hell of a row. If Mum wasn't furious before, she is now. Dad'll get both barrels. By the time she's finished, he'll wish he'd never been born.'

'Never going to happen.' Travers glanced out of the window. 'Not when Mum knows what's really going on.'

'What?'

'Our house is bugged.' He held up the small gadget. 'And this is an electronic bug finder. Dad was in the middle of telling us about it. That's why he didn't phone.'

'You mean the police? Oh my God! That didn't take long.'

'You heard about the house then,' Catherine called out as she climbed aboard, Doug following her. 'It's like discovering we're infested with fleas.' She shuddered. 'I don't think I'll ever want go back in.'

'Travers, get the ropes.' Doug took the wheel, switching on the ignition.

Travers raced back onto the little wooden jetty, quickly casting off the bow rope before jumping aboard again. He coiled the rope neatly wondering how much of their story his dad knew already. And what he'd been up to for the past twenty-four hours. His mother hadn't said a word but he'd like to bet, during the past few minutes his dad had confided in her.

The powerful vessel gathered speed, surging across the bay and tossing water aside as if it was a combine harvester reaping gossamer strands of hay. The day remained overcast, the white of the hull luminous against the sullen grey of the waves moving steadily under a light wind.

'Scott should have stayed put,' Doug said as Travers came to the end of their story.

'Told you,' Natasha chanted.

'I never said he shouldn't,' Travers protested. 'But where? I mean… even our boathouse wasn't safe, according to you, Dad. And no one could have survived the night in a bullet-ridden car. They'd have perished. If we'd tried for a hotel, he'd have been picked up straight-off, and it was way too risky to bring him back here.'

'Is Bill's four-by-four still at the lake,' his father asked.

Travers nodded.

'Remind me on Monday to get it picked up.' Doug stared thoughtfully through the glass windscreen, the tailored shape of the hull giving a smooth ride through the vigorous swell. 'I can understand them wanting to kidnap Scott to get at Bill. But why try to kill him?'

'He thought it might be the conversation he overheard at the UN,' Natasha said.

'I forgot that bit, sis.'

'*What conversation?*'

'Scott wanted to listen to his dad's speech. According to him, he picked up the headphones and all he got was this two-way conversation about the destruction of Europe.'

'That's it, Travers. A bit feeble, isn't it?'

'I thought like you, Dad, at first. How could a couple of guys gossiping on the phone be that important?' Natasha agreed. 'I changed my mind after Scott told us that someone had tried to kill him in Geneva. They tried again two days later outside the school, only Tulsa saved him. And… well, you know what happened then.'

'So he saw or heard something he shouldn't,' Doug said in a thoughtful voice.

'The same thing happened with Wesley,' Mary added. 'We told him about Scott and he freaked.'

Travers got to his feet. 'Dad, do you have any food on board?'

'Honestly, Travers.'

'Thinking makes me hungry,' he protested to his mother.

'Tell me about it, I brought you up, remember.'

'Do you, Dad?'

The stories had taken some time to tell and they were nearing the far shore, dark grey smudges dissolving into individual polka dots before taking on the colour, shape, and form of waterside buildings. Doug eased back on the throttle, slowing their approach. 'Cheese and biscuits, and there's crisps in the cupboard. Otherwise, if you can't wait for lunch, use the microwave. There's lasagne in the deep freeze.'

Nodding, Travers got to his feet ferreting about the cupboards. He pulled out packs of crisps, passing them round. 'If we really are going to have lunch, I'll hang on.' He leaned against the cupboard, its door fitted with locks that stayed shut even in a force eight gale. His father was listening intently to the story of Jameson's disappearance, asking questions – good questions. Yet Scott's problems hadn't seemed to faze him. Travers started, his gaze raking his father's face. *It didn't bother him because he already knew about it.* He stared at his father, wondering how involved he was and in what.

'Dad, any chance you have Sean Terry's number? We tried Beau but he isn't answering.'

'I can find it. But I daren't use it, it's compromised. By now they'll have pulled off a list of all my contacts.'

'What about the bugs in our house, Doug?'

Doug spun the wheel, angling the heavy craft towards the

jetty. 'All of us, you too, Mary, we buy new sim cards with new numbers. First off, Travers, you get hold of Scott. Get him back here. The man I spoke to says they'll do a sweep of the house this afternoon. By the time we've had lunch...' He glanced down at his watch. 'Is it that time already... and done the shopping – they should be finished.'

'Who do you know, Dad, that's into bugs?'

Doug shook his head. 'I can't tell you that, Natasha.' He heaved a sigh. 'You are all far too involved as it is.'

By the time they boarded the cruiser for the return trip across the harbour it was already dark, the mooring lights of vessels riding at anchor never still under a rolling swell. As they pulled into the mooring, a man stepped from the shadows hailing the cruiser.

Telling them to stay put, Doug went ashore. There was some muttered conversation then, with a wave of his hand, the man vanished back towards the house, leaving the family to carry in the shopping.

'We're clear,' he announced stepping back on board.

'You're sure?' Catherine said nervously.

'One hundred per cent. These guys are like bomb-disposal experts; they can't afford mistakes. They've disconnected the main phone. So its mobiles only till I get the number changed. Come on, let's get this stuff into the house.'

'Are you staying, Mary?'

'I'd like to, Mrs Randal.' Mary picked up a large bag of groceries, following Travers up on deck. 'I'm worried sick about Scott and Hilary – Travers has been texting and phoning, but nothing.'

Travers dumped the bags he and Mary were carrying in the kitchen and, grabbing Cokes from the fridge, walked upstairs with Mary to the family sitting room leaving Natasha and her mother to organise the food into cupboards. Handing her a can of Coke, he collapsed down on the couch, instantly getting to his feet again and roaming restlessly round the room. Knowing people had been in the house, even though they were checking for listening devices, had left the place feeling different somehow. But then everything *was* different.

Catching sight of the wool jacket he'd left on the back of a chair, he was reminded of the time he'd caught a loose thread in the sleeve of his favourite sweater. He'd tried to break it off only to see it unravelling. The more he pulled the worse it got, with no end in sight. Until... Travers heaved an angry sigh, it had to be thrown out. All he'd wanted, ever since he could remember, was to play rugby. That and being with Mary were the only things that interested him – pretty much. The news report, twenty-four hours earlier labelling his friend a murderer, had changed everything. Now, all he could think about was Scott and Jameson, and what was happening to them. Dad wasn't helping either. Making it worse, if anything. Whichever way you looked at it, if he knew people that casually went around debugging buildings, he was into something seriously serious.

Desperate to drive the whirring thoughts from his head, he switched on the television, scrolling down the channels for something to watch.

Mary placed her drink on a side table and, pulling out her new phone, switched it on. 'When I get back home, I'll have to start replacing all my contacts. What a pain. Travers?'

He glanced up. 'Mm?'

'Do you think we're safe?'

'Not sure.' He slammed his fist against the top of the bookcase making her jump. 'Dad knows what's going on... I only wish he'd tell us. Put us out of our misery.'

'Tell you what?' Doug wandered into the sitting room carrying a bottle of beer.

'How you know experts in debugging and why the police are interested enough to bug the house in the first place. And how come you knew about Scott and his dad before we told you?'

Doug went over to his son, wrapping an arm round him. 'I know it's frustrating and I'm desperately sorry; because of Scott problems you've all become involved. Especially you, Mary. I would have done anything to keep you out of it. I can't answer your questions. I told you before, it's too dangerous. Lives are at stake here. So let's forget it, at least for tonight, and enjoy our family evening. Nothing more we can do, anyway. I've already spoken to people about Jameson and Scott.'

'You see, that's just it, Dad,' Travers broke in. 'You've spoken to people. It's doing my head in. I could help – I know I could help.'

'No, Travers. Forget it – you're sixteen.' Doug's voice was stern brooking no argument. 'You've done your bit. Come on, I want to listen to the Premier League results.'

'They're on in a minute.' Angrily, Travers increased the volume, the newscaster trawling through the items on the teleprompter. It was rare for his dad to lay down the law. When he was a kid, he'd never questioned it. But now – couldn't he understand that not knowing somehow made things worse?

The newscaster, a glamorous young twenty-something who had the job of relaying the early evening news, had already moved on to regional items, charity fund raising and a child who had beaten a serious illness against all odds. She paused. Closing the pages placed on the desk, left there to convey an impression that she was reading from a script, she stared into the camera, her tone changing. 'Earlier today, at Truro railway station a tragedy occurred…'

Travers caught the frightened look in Mary's eyes. He grabbed her hand knowing she, like him, had guessed what was coming.

'A young man fell to his death in front of an oncoming train. He has been provisionally identified as Wesley Davis, a student at Falmouth Comprehensive. Police are appealing for witnesses.'

Mary burst into tears. 'We did that – we sent him to his death. If we hadn't... '

The harsh sound of the phone broke the horrified silence. Doug picked it up. 'Yes!' Silence. 'Exeter? How can I help you, Mr Armitage?'

He looked meaningfully at Travers, his gaze swinging to Natasha who had appeared in the open doorway, her jacket over her arm. 'You say my son and daughter were arrested. What are they accused of?' Travers jumped to his feet, his face full of questions. He beckoned to his father who raised a hand silencing him. 'May I see them?' Murmuring came from the mouthpiece. Doug replied, his tone steely. 'I see. How thoughtful. You knew I would be concerned. Let me understand this correctly... They have already been taken in front of a magistrate, found guilty, and are in the process of being shipped to a camp. Can you find out where?' He listened intently, his face grim. 'Not England. And a protest takes how long?' More murmurings. 'And there's nothing I can do?'

Silence.

'Very well.' Doug let out a loud impatient breath. 'I will speak to you on Monday to see if you have further news.' His tone changed becoming terse and pithy, his words snapped off short, glaring at the figures staring rigidly at him.

Travers eyed his sister, passing across a silent warning. Oh Lord, they were in for an ear-bashing for giving away their precious identity cards.

'Would you do me one kindness and try to get a message to them. I see; they've already left.'

Doug replaced the receiver and took a sip of his beer. 'It gets worse by the minute. And I thought we could have a pleasant family evening and forget all this. It seems that you two have been arrested for disorderly conduct...' he said pleasantly. Travers groaned, aware he wasn't going to enjoy the next few minutes. 'Which is quite a surprise, since you are both still sitting here. I guess you forgot to tell me that bit.'

TWENTY

Scott felt his head drop forward onto his chest. He stirred and blinked, staring blearily round the dimly lit interior of the coach. 'Where am I?' he muttered, trying to see out of the window, before remembering there were steel shutters bolted across to stop light from seeping in and prisoners from seeing out.

Lightning, in the seat next to him, gave a shrug. 'Beats me, but we're here wherever it is.'

Scott groaned. 'What time is it?'

'Five-ish.'

'Morning or evening?'

'Evenin'.'

At first, Scott thought it weird how the guy had sought him out and befriended him, staying by his side as if glued. He'd wondered if he was gay except he didn't give out any of the usual signals. Then, as if Lightning had eavesdropped on his thoughts, 'In case you're wonderin', I owe you,' he explained. 'It's my fault you got arrested. I could see that guy was a nut-case. If I'd kept him away from your bike none of this would have happened.'

Scott didn't argue, glad of the company. He'd have been sitting alone otherwise, the students they'd met in the holding cell determined to stay together, only he and Lightning outsiders. He didn't agree with the guy though. Throughout the long journey from the court to the dockside, the whole scenario of the day, since the moment he had stupidly directed the bike into the side road, had replayed itself over and over in his mind. Every bit of that riot had been planned and if Tyson hadn't blown up the bike, it would have been something else – possibly much worse.

Much of the journey remained a blur, Scott's head pounding and demanding his full attention. Desperate to feel better he'd eventually swallowed four pills, twice the recommended dose, and that had driven it away. By then they were on a ferry to somewhere and the flat-bottomed craft, used to transport cars and lorries, had been tossed around like a matchstick. He'd closed his eyes on that scene too, relieved he'd felt too ill to eat on the coach and anxious to escape the sight of the detainees, their faces the colour of putty, throwing up.

He'd caught sight of Hilary only the once when she stepped onto the ferry ahead of him. One of three girls, they'd been allowed to board first, and he spotted her neat figure as she stood by the officer who was checking their numbers. That had been the final piece of indignity in a whole parade of indignities, designed to make you feel like a worm trodden on by hobnailed boots; your identity reduced to a plastic card worn on a cord round your neck, bearing your photograph and prisoner number. Hilary had paused and swung round, searching through the shivering line of guys desperate to escape the piercing cold of a wind blowing in off the sea. He'd waved to attract her attention but too late. Spotting the hold-up, the officer had yelled a rebuke and pushed her on, before turning to check another identity.

By the time the ferry landed dawn had broken, a pale grey

sky streaked with traces of pink and yellow hinting at a brighter day. Shivering with cold and lack of sleep Scot had trailed behind Lightning into yet another coach, one of two waiting outside the terminal, nervously eyeing the guards lined up by the side of the gangway. Different from the English police, who had been mostly cheerful, these men were stony-faced and armed. He wasn't the only one to feel scared then, at the mercy of strangers who used their batons to make up for a lack of English, slapping them noisily against the palm of their hands. The coaches were different too, fitted with metal shutters that obscured all sight of the countryside, a steel-mesh partition isolating the driver in his cab.

'So where are we?' he repeated. Groggily, he stared through the mesh screen. The driver's cab was empty. He could see him in the headlights talking to some men. A buzzer sounded, cutting angrily across the night sky. Scott jumped nervously, watching a heavy metal gate slide to one side.

The driver returned to his cab, muttering to the guard up front. The engine rumbled, the coach pulling forward into a lighted yard railed by spikes and barbed wire. Yawning loudly, the guard climbed to his feet. Stretching, he undid the padlock on the heavy metal screen. '*Allez*,' he grumbled beckoning his prisoners.

The sun had set, dusk creeping silently through the sky like a burglar entering a house, the dark shape of a building nestling against a backdrop of hills like a shadowy halo. Stumbling a little, he followed the line of detainees through open swing doors, noticing the second coach already parked up. After the darkness of the coach, the light was momentarily blinding and he flung up an arm to shield his eyes, the blurry confusion gradually clearing into a square lobby, broken up by a series of doors.

The guard pointed with his baton. '*Toilette.*'

Swinging on his heel, he kicked open a pair of doors to what looked like a classroom. A line of chairs faced a wall screen, each with a narrow writing table built into its frame. Desperately tired and in need of sleep, Scott trailed into the room and crashed down in the first empty seat. At the front of the room a man was waiting. In his forties and only of medium height, his dark hair had receded at the temples while a heavy stubble decorated his chin. His whole demeanour screamed soldier, his shoulders strained back as if locked there with constant exercise. He waited for the shuffling figures to settle, impatiently slapping the cane he was carrying across his palm, mimicking the action of the men at the docks.

'The first thing you need to learn,' the man said in English, his voice commonplace without any discernible accent, 'is that this is not a holiday camp. It is one of three specially equipped punishment centres set up to accommodate louts like you.'

Within five minutes, Scott knew they were in for a week of absolute hell, their instructor's gaze patronising, greedily relishing his role of power. It had been bad enough enduring the short walk from the coach to the ferry, noticing the contemptuous looks thrown at them by members of the public who had travelled in the relative comfort of the ship's lounge. Compared to a week in this man's company, that had been a walk in the park. So far, all they'd been offered was water and no sleep.

'Sleep deprivation is part of the course, so is lack of food. Grumbles and complaints will result in time being added to your sentence.'

James, across the aisle from Scott, opened his mouth to object and Chris hastily nudged him. Scott stared bleakly along the rows of guys, seeing anger, despair and fear in their expressions, and was surprised to find only eighteen – not the twenty he had counted onto the coach. Puzzled he checked again, wondering where they'd got to. Perhaps they'd wandered into the second group by mistake? There had to be a second group, although so far there'd been no sign of anyone apart from them. Still, Hilary had to be here. It was the same coach in the yard that had picked them up at the docks.

'Talking is not permitted other than the minimum. You are not here to make friends.' The man slapped the cane viciously against the side of his leg. Scott jumped at the hollow sound, suddenly registering it was a prosthetic limb. At some point in his career he must have been wounded and invalided out of the services, his left leg amputated above the knee. He stared at the figure pacing across the floor and picked up on a faint limp brilliantly disguised. 'Your goal is to be reinstated in society. Each of you,' the instructor swung the cane along the rows, 'has landed here because of a crime against the state and in my book that makes you a pariah. From this point you're on your own. How you survive is up to you. You'll find no friends here. Everyone is to be considered an enemy. For reporting misdemeanours, extra food will be awarded.'

James leapt to his feet, boiling over with indignation. 'You can't do that. Under human rights legislation, even prisoners have rights.'

'Rights?' The cane slapped against the wooden surface of the front desk so hard Scott thought it would crack. 'I agree. Human beings do indeed have rights. Turn round.'

James glanced back over his shoulder.

'You see a number on the back of your chair?'

'Yes, sir.'

'Yes, *Mr Reynolds-sir*.'

'Yes, Mr Reynolds-sir.'

'As long as you remain in this establishment, you are Number Thirty. And numbers do not have rights. Remember that.'

Scott swivelled in his seat to read the number printed on the back. The room had been built to accommodate twenty-four students, and a quarter of the seats remained empty. He and Lightning were seated nine and ten.

'If you show a willingness to learn what we have to teach you,' their instructor continued, 'an ability to obey orders without question, you will be side-lined into a special division where you will be offered a job with good money.'

The man clicked a remote and the screen flicked into life. Scott watched the images take shape into a re-run of the march in Exeter. Out of the corner of his eye, he saw a puzzled frown sweep across Lightning's face and knew he was asking the self-same question. How did they get hold of the tape when the CCTV cameras had been vandalised?

Familiar figures flooded onto the road where Scott waited with the Suzuki. He heard the hyena-like laugh ring out and caught sight of Tyson. He flinched back, almost expecting the guy to fight his way out of the screen. It looked worse in playback mode, angry figures throwing punches into the face of innocent bystanders for no reason that he could see, as if a bell had rung in their heads, a starting pistol for violence.

Even as the thought took hold, the scene switched to soldiers marching in perfect rhythm, heads turned, their bodies angled backwards not a foot out of step, saluting men standing on a balcony overlooking the parade ground – the antithesis of disorder. Tanks rolled past. The camera flicked again and Scott recognised Paris even though he'd never been there, the unmistakable silhouette of the Eiffel Tower in the background. A huge crowd surged along the street, their arms linked. They were chanting. Then chaos struck. Instantly, the volume on the soundtrack increased till the air vibrated with screaming and cries of terror, the noisy outburst jerking the drooping heads of the exhausted inmates abruptly upright. The marchers all seemed to be students, most of them carrying banners. Scott recognised the word, '*non*' but that was all. Police in riot gear were waiting. Batons at the ready they charged into the marchers, beating at them as if threshing corn in a field. Water cannon tore into the ones still resisting, the force of the jets tumbling them head over heels. Panic reached out from the screen, alarm and terror streaked across the faces of the marchers. The occupants of the classroom stared blankly and in silence. All Scott wanted to do was close his eyes and block up his ears so as not to listen, but the noise was everywhere, bouncing off the walls and ceiling. Silence. He opened his eyes on a scene of total order, a parade of stern-faced soldiers, the volume reduced so that only the dull thud of a thousand boots hitting the ground was audible.

It was like being on a switchback ride. You reached the unendurable, the summit of the ride, the pinnacle of pressure on your lungs, desperately shrieking out for it to stop; then the image changed and you were on a gentle slope, like a country walk, your senses soothed by order and calm. The repetition was endless. Chaos versus order. Unbearable images of youngsters being mown down by guns or beaten to the ground by men in authority. Scott didn't recognise to which country they belonged, there were so many and all different – constantly replaced by an orderly procession designed to caress the senses, a crowd applauding enthusiastically. Scott dragged his exhausted mind into gear. There had to be a purpose behind the showing of the film, but what? The embryo thought vanished, blasted by a tirade of new atrocities. Shattered, he shut his eyes, jerking them open as the cane slammed down on the table in front of him.

'Number Nine. You sleep when I say.'

Scott gulped, feeling his head slouch to one side, finding it difficult to hold it upright, his headache pounding away again.

The relentless switchback ride continued. Hunger came and went, fatigue followed and left by the back door replaced by visions of yet more violence. Several of the guys were openly crying, wiping their tears away as calm once again took over the screen. Scott found himself praying for those moments, to take a breath and close his eyes, no longer bothering to work out why, content to bask in the lull like sunbathers on a beach who, seeing a storm in the distance, are desperate to soak up the last rays of sun before it struck.

The screen flickered and blacked out and a collective sigh ran round the room.

'On your feet – you have twelve miles to do before your next class. Pick up a bottle of water on your way out.'

Scott crawled to his feet, grateful that the relentless battering was finally over. To his surprise, he felt a fist in his back pushing him to the head of the little queue of weary figures, most leaning against the wall, their eyes shut.

'You fit?'

'Why?'

'I said: you fit?' Lighting repeated slightly louder. Scott saw his hand resting horizontally across his middle, one finger angled upwards.

'Yeah.' Scott pounded his feet in a semblance of energy and glanced nonchalantly at the video camera in the corner of the room. 'Those marchers, I wonder how long it takes to get them perfect like that.' Lightning was playing some sort of game; he hoped he'd understood the warning right. He caught a faint movement of the guy's eyelid and then they were outside.

He was surprised to find it dark. Behind the little group, the building was a blur of silence as if everyone in the world was asleep apart from them, its windowless shape leaving no clue. Scott frowned, trying to recall whether it had been night or day when they first arrived. He glanced down at his watch, the luminous digits standing at three-fifteen. *Holy crap!* He stifled a groan. It was the middle of the night. His stomach griped confirming his worst suspicions. Twenty-four hours, and no food except for the sandwiches and crisps he'd shared with Lightning, once they'd recovered from the seasickness of their stormy crossing.

Silently, with Lightning matching him step for step, the line followed the instructor out of the gates, picking up a couple of guards on the way. False leg or not, the man set a fast pace and Scott felt grateful for all the walking he'd done that summer. The air felt good, reviving his shattered senses and, at long last, he could think.

Noises came from behind and with a barked 'keep following the path,' their instructor headed back down the line.

Their path was made of beaten-down earth and obviously well used. Lights, like those edging an airport runway, kept them company allowing a brief glimpse of grass and low-growing shrubs, their thorny spines reminding Scott of the gorse that grew on the moors, before darkness took over again.

Lightning grasped his arm briefly. 'Listen up. Inside that buildin' every move you make is watched. Don't trust anyone – that vindictive son of a bitch meant what he said. Hungry enough, even friends will dob you in for extra food. And for God's sake don't ask questions.'

'But... Hil... ' Scott floundered, stumbling over the word. '*Hell!* Sorry!' he sketched an apologetic smile. 'I'm that tired, I can't even get my words out. It's my sister, Natasha, I've got to find her.'

'Forget it. Until you're accepted as a model student, you won't see or speak to anyone.'

'Okay, so how do I do that?'

'Can you act?'

Scott blinked, finding it difficult to understand the question, his thoughts sluggish. 'Never tried.'

'This is how it works.' Lightning's tone was fierce, his voice showing no sign of the fatigue that flooded Scott's body. 'For two days we'll be starved and kept awake, by which time you'll want to stop livin'. Don't go the whole hundred yards. Find some way of convincin' that sadistic apology for a man that you believe his claptrap.' Scott glanced up at the guy's face, unable to make out more than his profile staring restlessly into the dark ahead. Had Lightning done this before – but why risk it a second time? No one in their right mind would go near a march after this. 'How…?'

'*Step up in the front, what do you think this is?* A walk in the park? It's punishment good and simple. So move it.'

The figure of their instructor moved alongside, glancing briefly at the silent figures, their heads bent to avoid tripping over loose stones on the sandy path. 'Eight more miles, and you get to rest,' he sneered.

Scott ignored the taunt, concentrating on keeping up the pace, his muscles protesting at their lack of fuel. Nothing except water for twenty-four hours wasn't a good way to start a twelve-mile walk. He caught the sound of a helicopter. It drew closer, buzzing the group like an angry mosquito, and lights flared illuminating the darkness around them. Unable to stop himself, Scott swung round watching the figure of their instructor head back down the line, guys in the rows behind toppling to the ground like ninepins, grabbing the chance to stop moving.

Remembering the warning, Scott stayed on his feet. 'You've done this before?'

Lightning shrugged. 'You jokin'? Only a lunatic would risk this twice. Got sent to rehab once. Learned about this place from an inmate there.'

Scott stared at the wall of hair framing the guy's face. He knew nothing about him. On the journey he'd felt too sick to talk. 'What they're doing, it's inhuman.'

'Yeah, in't it just! First off I guess they want to scare us, make sure we'll be good little boys from now on.' Lightning's voice changed. 'However tough it gets, never believe what you see on the screen.'

'I don't get it – why…'

'*And who said you could stop?* You at the front; one extra mile for stopping. And, you lot on the ground – you can join 'em.'

It was almost dawn by the time the barbed wire surround of the detention centre came into sight. Even then they weren't done. Back to the classroom, the hours crawling past in a daze of hunger and tiredness, Scott clutching at the tranquil scenes of peaceful countryside whenever they cropped up on the screen. Driven outside again to find it full daylight, the beginning of yet another endless day.

Determined not to give in, Scott battled against sleep. Even knowing he was being brainwashed made no difference. *You can have all that if you want it,* his mind nagged at him. Somehow, and he couldn't remember when, order became synonymous with eating. He jerked himself awake, trying to recall when the images of plenty had taken over the screen; mouth-watering steaks laden with tomatoes and mushrooms, curries and double-cheeseburgers, castles of ice cream. Each time these images flashed up, food was on offer, with people playing happy families to great gatherings of friends cheerfully toasting one other in lager or beer.

Shocked, Scott saw one of the figures in the row in front stretch out a hand to the screen. Next second, the image was snatched away replaced by a soundtrack of gunfire; women screaming, youths running, falling, covered in blood. Like a bomb exploding, the noise blasted from the speakers so suddenly the watchers flinched back, darting glances of fear behind them. Immediately, the silence of orderly marching replaced the chaos, interspersed with countryside scenes of flowing rivers and food… tables heaped with food. Scott felt his mouth salivate at the thought.

Order and obedience were now all he craved because if you had that, automatically you had a loving family around you and food… tons of the stuff. Anything you wanted, you could have. A voice shouted out "yeah" and began to applaud. Scott leapt to his feet applauding like a maniac as troops saluted their leader, pride in their every step.

The screen went blank and silence fell. The instructor stared balefully at the group of boys seated in the last row their hands on the desk, the only ones not applauding. Scott inched round in his seat, recognising James and Chris. Their tutor's bleak gaze swung on to include the guy with the split lip and one other.

'What have you got to say for yourself?'

James got to his feet clutching the desk for support. He looked like Scott felt, his eyes half-shut and drained of life. Sometime in the day, they'd been dragged out on a second walk or was it three they'd done now? Scott recalled the daylight but little else, needing every scrap of energy just to stay on his feet. If he remembered right, it had been cut short by heavy rain… or had he imagined that too?

James nodded his head respectfully, as he would have done to a college lecturer. 'I promise you, sir, none of us has any intention of ever getting into trouble again.'

The ex-army figure nodded and, picking up a clipboard, began calling numbers. Scott caught the Number Nine and staggered to his feet.

'The rest will stay here.'

Scott stifled a groan. Not another run; he'd never manage

it. He didn't care any more. They could shoot him if they wanted *but not another run.* No more, please.

Numbly, he stumbled into the lobby to find a guard waiting, the dull thud of his baton landing on his open palm like a call to arms. Behind him, the shiny aluminium doors leading to the courtyard remained closed, allowing no clue as to whether it was sun or moon that ruled the sky. Scott picked up his wrist to check the time then let it drop. It didn't matter. Nothing did. Beckoning the line to follow, the guard opened swing doors into a corridor. Heads down, the line followed. A few of the inmates picked up on the sound of the baton landing on the guard's open palm, beating out the rhythm of their footsteps, and tried to copy it. At the far end, swing doors opened inwards, light and warmth, and the smell of food, spilling out. Figures hurtled past Scott making a bee-line for the food, the swing doors crashing backwards and forwards with the force of bodies colliding with them.

'Eat – and when you've finished you will find dormitories on the far side of the room. You will be called at six in the morning. Take a shower. You will find clean clothes waiting.'

Scott gazed down at the clothes he'd worn since Friday, dirty and crumpled, dried bloodstains on the zipped front of his jacket, trying to work out what day it was.

Grabbing a bottle of Coke, he stuffed a slice of tomato and mushroom pizza into his mouth, swallowing it half-chewed. Elbowing someone aside, he picked up a plate and, loading it up, collapsed into the nearest empty chair. No one was talking; a couple of the guys had fallen asleep at the table leaving their food untouched. Taking a mouthful of the fizzy drink, he stuffed in another slice of pizza, almost stumbling in his haste to reach his bed. His thoughts lurched incoherently, like sheep lost and wandering in a thick fog, before oblivion finally took over.

TWENTY-ONE

Tuesday! It was Tuesday! Scott repeated the words over and over, determined to stay focussed and not be swept away by the subliminal imagery on the screen. He could feel it crawling around his head like a living parasite, whispering its sinister philosophy that black really was white. What he'd thought to be democracy was camouflage for something so evil it had to be wiped out before real peace could be achieved.

He'd slept twelve hours. Only on waking did he realise it must have been early Monday evening when, fully dressed, his head had hit the pillow. Except there'd been no pillow, the bunk beds supplied with mattresses covered in plastic. Sometime in the night the electric light had been switched off and it was this flashing on, the strip-light dazzling after near-darkness, that woke him. Even without covers he hadn't felt cold, but he felt gross – every bone aching, his stomach churning round and round, undecided if it was growling with hunger or about to throw up.

A hot shower helped. He stood under the spray feeling the knots ease and break up, his head still pounding. In a side room, stacks of clothing in multiple sizes lay neatly piled on slatted wooden shelves. He had already collected a jacket and trousers from a pile of track suits, all in an identical shade of brown, underwear, trainers and clean socks, remembering to change over the container and eye drops for his lenses, which he had stowed in his pocket.

The unit was small and compact, a medical room and toilet at the front of the building opposite the classroom. Behind them were the dormitories with an adjoining shower block, and what passed for a dining room, simply a collection of plastic tables and chairs, with a self-service counter dispensing hot and cold food. Scot had spotted only one other doorway. Bolted shut, it lay behind the counter and obviously led to other parts of the facility. There had to be more. Someone had to cook their dinner and someone had to wash their clothes, unless the outfits they'd arrived in were to be incinerated. Even so! His thoughts flew to Hilary. Was she on the far side of that locked door? He'd never have guessed by the silence in which the building was wrapped, so deep they could have been buried alive. Not a single sound invaded the space apart from their own breathing; not the slam of a door or the echo of distant laughter. They were entombed in a silence so vast that every member of the little group was affected. Scott stared around at his room-mates seeing their furtive glances, scurrying about like frightened mice trying not to make a noise. If this was what they had turned into after thirty-six hours, God help them.

He headed back into the dormitory wondering what to do with his dirty clothes. Lightning, already dressed in the brown uniform, was lying on top of his bunk staring at the ceiling. Evenly spaced down the centre of the room were rectangular grilles, providing the warmed air that was life-blood to a building in which there were no windows. Breathing was something you took for granted but it was a horrid thought that without that mesh screen in the ceiling pumping in a steady stream of oxygen, no one would survive. Scott stared at the nearest vent. More than likely, it also concealed a camera or listening device.

Lightning glanced up, as Scott walked past, giving him a half-smile. Scott replied with a brief nod, hoping if there was a camera, no one would bother with casual everyday greetings.

He turned away stuffing his clothes into an already bulging hamper. Through the open doorway, he caught sight of Chris still asleep on a top bunk in the second dormitory, James impatiently trying to shake him awake. What had happened to them after the rest had been dismissed? He wished he was brave enough to pass on Lightning's warning – at least it would keep them from being punished further.

He finally got an opportunity when partnered with Chris on the afternoon run. The four friends had been split up and Scott had got Chris. His feet pounded the path, trying to keep in step with the line ahead, the third time they'd been dragged out to do this particular run… or was it the fourth? He shook his head unable to remember, the blistering attack on his senses too exhausting to keep track.

The day had followed the same pattern; turmoil followed by enticing scenes of peace and plenty, in case anyone still needed a nudge in the right direction. Scott had joined in enthusiastically, never doubting for a moment the truth of what he was being shown. Any thought of dissent was swallowed up under an avalanche of graphic pictures detailing the consequences of disobedience – hard labour, solitary confinement with no food. Death by firing squad.

It was the fresh air that had clawed him back from the precipice, bringing with it a reminder of mornings spent jogging along the beach in Cornwall with his father, who often used the time for a speedy lecture. One of his favourites: *Take nothing at face value, especially when it sounds too good to be true, because it usually is.* That had come about after a particular sociology class, when he had arrived home, *spouting pure rubbish*, according to his dad. Surprisingly, Scott found himself thinking more and more about Tulsa and his father. Somehow, with hell on the doorstop, it seemed easier to accept that they were dead. The word no longer frightened him.

How simple it had been for them to be suckered in. Even now, he could still feel the insidious barbs lurking in the pores of his skin waiting to dig their sharp hooks in. Exhaustion didn't help, his legs still aching from a build-up of lactic acid the day before. They'd not been offered breakfast and all he'd managed was a half-bottle of Coke that had gone flat and the crusts of pizza that he'd left on his plate before falling asleep. Every cell in his body screamed out for food. He heard Chris's belly rumbling noisily and sympathised.

The rain of the previous afternoon had left puddles denting the sandy surface of the path, making it impossible to do more than a fast walk. The bog-like surface sucked at their feet and, although now dry, the temperature had dropped steeply with a biting wind. Shivering with cold, his trainers heavy with mud, Scott doggedly set one foot in front of the other. At this rate it would take more than three hours to complete twelve miles. The thought of battling against the cold for that length of time was not pleasant but it was way better than the alternative. Taking advantage of the gap that had opened up between them and the guys behind, he murmured, 'Did you get food?'

Chris glanced sideways at him. He didn't reply, concentrating on sidestepping a puddle, his feet moving sluggishly like someone unused to walking long distances.

'I promise you, I'm no threat. I've no intention of snitching on anyone. I only wanted to tell you… to warn you to go along with anything they want. Lightning said it was the only way.'

Chris gasped in astonishment. 'He couldn't survive this… not twice,' he kept his voice to a low murmur.

'No way! He says a guy at rehab warned him about this place. Told him, whatever they said or did, not to believe.'

'*Believe!*' Chris slowed, staring at Scott in amazement. Without his glasses to hide behind, his face seemed exposed and vulnerable, and a nervous tick flicked at the corner of his left eye.

Scott grabbed his arm, hurrying him on.

'Haven't you ever read George Orwell's *Nineteen Eighty-Four?* This lot have – it's classic. Three days into our sentence and the group are standing in line to do their bidding,' Chris's tone was bitter. 'I thought you were one of them.'

Scott flushed, feeling ashamed. 'No, I promise. But what do they want from us? It can't only be about keeping out of trouble in future. If it was, why keep you back and not let you eat with the rest of us?'

'If you get a chance, talk to James – his hypothesis is really freaky. He thinks their plan is an army of zombies to take over the world.'

Scott screwed up his face, not sure if Chris was joking or James really did believe such rubbish. 'Tell him, no way am I turning into a zombie.'

Chris stared at him pityingly. 'You didn't think like that this morning. I saw your face. If they'd told you to jump in a river – you wouldn't have hesitated.'

Scott flushed. Had it been that obvious? 'It's so hard, everything screaming at you till you can't think. Who else is holding on? If I know I'm not the only one it'll be easier.'

'James, me, Stephen and Max – he's the one that got his mouth busted. One of his teeth is still loose so he's not too keen about eating anyway. There's a few guys still swinging in and out but not many. '

'Stephen? Which one's he?'

'Nerdy sort of bloke – red hair – studying politics and economics. You didn't see him before; he was in one of the other cells. It would take more than a week's brainwashing to sort out his obsession with right-wing politics.' Chris took in a long breath, panting a little from the steep incline to the top of the sandy ridge, the ground rising steadily towards the hills. 'Hates Europe, loves the Thatcher era.'

'Lightning says they listen in.'

'We guessed that. Max and James know sign language – they do most of the talking. I can understand bits – enough.'

'*You two, you know the rule.*' The instructor came alongside. The detainees had learned his name on that first day; *Mr Reynolds-sir.* It suited him. 'You don't get friendly. Add two miles to the twelve – and that means all of you.' Groans ripped up and down the line. Scott winced, furious with himself for bringing retribution down on the entire group. It wasn't fair but then none of this was. 'Number Nine – at the front on your own,' Mr Reynolds glanced back down the line, his eyes bright relishing the group's discomfiture, his tone triumphant at being handed a God-given opportunity to inflict punishment. 'Remember, one of you fouls up, you all foul up.'

Breaking into a sprint, Scott overtook the figures walking ahead before reducing his speed again to a jog. The ground on either side of the sandy track was featureless and it would have been easy to get lost without the identifying stones and lights marking their path. He caught a quickly silenced groan from one of the guys but didn't bother looking back. He had no intention of setting a fast pace, only too aware of the over-riding sensation of fatigue dominating the group. You could feel it washing into the air like a spiralling dust storm. But at this dragging speed they would freeze to death, the wind ice-tipped against his cheek. He headed out across a flat expanse of dry scrub, nothing to focus on except a string of scrubby spruce, their leaves curled and brittle and their trunks spindly and bent over, as desperate to escape the wind as the runners.

After a few miles at a faster pace, Scott felt warmth begin to creep back into his body and, by the time the low silhouette of the facility appeared once more on the horizon, the ache in his legs had all but disappeared. He paused in his stride thinking how ugly the building looked, with its horizontal stripes of green and brown. Like a fat toad squatting on a piece of twig, perfectly suited to its evil purpose. Although, it didn't much matter what it looked like, there were no towns nearby to object to having a prison in the vicinity – not even a tumbledown cottage on the horizon. Out here, you'd never stumble across tourists drooling over the scenery – there wasn't any. The first run of the day took them across the plain, crossing the roadway along which the coaches had driven. The word *plain* was relevant in more ways than one, no trees to break the horizon and scarcely a dip or incline anywhere. It was only when they tackled the longer run, did they head out across the lower slopes of the hills. Wild-life seemed almost non-existent too. They had come across a weasel on their early-morning run... A six-mile jog at six, Mr Reynolds-sir had quipped as they had set out, still blurry-eyed. The weasel had caught a rabbit, its small carcass torn and bloody, but the heavy footfall made it leave its prey. And Scott had caught sight of a flock of birds, too high to identify. Other than that, the land seemed home to little else but gorse and grass. Yet even without beautiful scenery the feeling of freedom was a lifeline, something to grab onto when the ideas gushing out from the screen became intolerable.

In the distance, Scott spotted movement. Squinting, he made out a line of running figures turning in through the gates of the facility. Hilary's group? The ache in his chest returned, forcibly reminding him how much he missed her. The previous day and night had been all about survival – his – leaving no energy for anything else. Scott increased his pace again, glad he'd risked punishment to talk with Chris. It was good to know he wasn't alone. He pushed back his shoulders, feeling in control for the first time that morning.

TWENTY-TWO

Scott opened his eyes, wondering what had woken him. He glanced at his watch; it had gone midnight. After eating at six, most of the guys, including him, had gone straight to bed. The prison authorities hadn't bothered to supply books or television. Besides, there was nowhere to sit except for a scattering of hard plastic chairs in the little dining room. And, since conversation wasn't encouraged, Scott had found himself counting the cracks on the walls, or breaking his bread into squares moving them around like pieces on a chessboard, anything to avoid thinking – and sleep was the best option.

Since talking to Chris two days ago, he'd paid special attention to the detainees, noting the difference in attitude between those still holding out – and they didn't include Lightning, unless he was the most brilliant actor in the world. The atmosphere had become like a minefield; one wrong step and... boom. Although, to be fair, so far no one had done more than exchange morose glances full of suspicion as if jealous even of the air they were sharing. Thank God, it was Thursday. Only two more days to go. Hopefully, they'd be out before the explosion took place. There would be one; someone was bound to lose control unable to take any more.

Scott stared into the darkness, grateful his body was finally playing catch-up after sleeping like the dead three nights running. Even with only the one meal at night, he now found himself with energy to spare at the end of the day and it was boredom that carried him to bed so early, lacking even the will to brush his teeth. It was bizarre punishment routine, taking your prisoners to the edge of insanity before hauling them back.

Catching the sound of movement, he leaned up on his elbow wondering who was out of bed. From the toilet block, red emergency lighting swept shadows across the dormitory, a second light at the far end of the corridor marking their exit in case of fire. It was an unlikely scenario though, with cigarettes and lighters banned and the dormitory empty except for a double-row of metal bunk beds. They hadn't even been provided with a hanger for their clothes or a shelf or cupboard for their belongings; they had none. Their original clothes had been cleaned and stacked back on the shelves. Packed into a plastic carrier, they awaited the release date. He caught sight of a figure heading out of the dormitory and recognised the shorn head of Lightning.

On the Tuesday morning, after being fed and allowed to sleep, they'd been herded outside, one guard forcibly removing studs and earrings from lips, ears, tongues and eyebrows, while another wielded clippers. Lightning's shoulder-length hair had been quickly consigned to a pile of hair-clippings on the ground, exposing his wine-coloured blemish to view. Only Chris and Scott had escaped the clippers; Natasha's haircut sufficiently draconian for Scott to pass muster while Chris, uncaring about his appearance, already sported an economical short-back-and-sides that made his ears stick out. Scott had felt huge sympathy for Lightning then. A bulky ribbon of twisted scar tissue ran down the back of his neck, perhaps the result of a bad burn, and long hair had shielded him from curious stares.

Scott listened, catching the faintest of clicks as the door to one of the stalls was shut. A couple of the guys had suffered diarrhoea and sickness, gorging on rich pizza and curry after their enforced starvation, but Lightning hadn't been among them. Sleepily he lay back down, his thoughts drifting in and out of their own accord, still trying to work out the rationale behind their treatment. It made a sick kind of sense, especially if you treated the first couple of days as a painful yet permanent deterrent. It was rather like playing a game of good cop/bad cop only it wasn't a game. The ordeal of the classroom, bewildering and terrifying as it was, was the menacing negative and the constant exercise was the positive, leaving them fitter and stronger. The group as a whole had improved their times that morning and been rewarded with milky coffee and bread on their return – but no praise. Scott had come to the conclusion that you could have tortured their instructor to death – a task for which he would eagerly have volunteered if the occasion ever arose – before a kind word ever passed his lips. The man seemed incapable of anything other than a merciless stare more likely to render its victim incoherent and blubbing.

But the images on the screen… Someone had to possess a really twisted mind to dream those up. Now they were being fed, the food feasts had all but vanished. The nightmare images still played, often the same ones seen through a different camera angle, but it was educational films that occupied the screen now, men in white jackets droning on and on about becoming model citizens. Obeying without question had become the key to happiness, and the bright, cheerful images on the screen proved it.

None of it made any sense… unless James was right and they really did want to create an army of mindless zombies. Gradually, Scott drifted off into a dreamlike sleep, his mind haphazardly winding down, occasionally blinking back into consciousness, unable to recall what he'd been thinking about a moment before. He caught the sound of a footfall and an almost indiscernible creak from the bunk above. Sleepily, he scratched an itch on the back of his neck, catching sight of the luminous digits on his watch before subsiding once again into sleep.

He was out of bed the moment the electric light snapped onto his eyelids. That first night, he'd made the mistake of leaving his lenses in, and his eyes had been inflamed and sore when he woke next morning. Since then, he'd removed them under cover of darkness, dashing to the toilet the moment he woke to put them in again.

A deluge of coughing, clearing of throats, the odd expletive, and not a few groans, greeted Scott as he headed for the showers. But no friendly word hit the air. The threats of that first night remained, each inmate locked inside his own personal space. He picked up a clean towel from the pile. He felt the same. They'd been together since Sunday, it was now Thursday, and he knew no more about any of the guys than when he got on the coach five days ago. Okay, so their faces had become as familiar as his own, but forced to use numbers instead of names kept everyone at a distance. Besides, the warnings on that first night had labelled any overtures of friendship as suspicious.

Scott opened the hot tap, a burst of steam preceding a deluge of hot water. That had proved an even more important reason for getting to the showers early. If you left it late, the water was tepid rather than hot and the tiled floor became a death trap of slippery soap suds and scum. Scott angled the shower head at his bare legs, noticeably more muscular than when he'd arrived and gingerly, taking care not to slip, grabbed his towel, wrapping it round his waist.

He passed Lightning coming out of the toilets. The guy looked awful – his skin tinged grey from lack of sleep.

'Okay?' he said, the expression on his face enquiring.

Lightning gave him a startled look. Glancing rapidly over his shoulder, he shoved Scott into a toilet stall and leant back against the door to keep it closed.

'You numb-skull,' he hissed fiercely. 'Haven't you any more sense than to wash your hair – didn't you realise that bloody stuff isn't permanent. Another couple of days and it'll have gone.'

'So I dye my hair. Big deal,' Scott blustered, keeping his voice low.

'Big deal!' Lightning's face lit up in a mocking grin. 'When I happen to know you're not Travers Randal.' Scott blanched and took a step back. 'I know Travers and you don't look anythin' like him. He's twenty pounds heavier for starters.'

Scott felt his mind ticking over and over, searching for a denial that was believable. 'So what were you doing out here for two hours last night?' he said, suddenly remembering the luminous dial on his watch had shifted from 00 to 02, the words flying out of his mouth before he could stop them.

Lightning pinned the younger boy against the wall, his arm pressed tightly across Scott's throat. 'If you intend reachin' Saturday alive, you'll keep quiet, *understand?*' His eyes bored into Scott, his expression ugly; the casual friendship and concern of the past few days wiped out. Scott swallowed painfully and nodded, straining against the arm stopping his breath. '*And quit washin' your hair.*'

Without waiting for a reply, Lightning opened the door and slipped out.

Too shocked and stunned to follow, Scott dropped down onto the toilet seat. His throat felt bruised and he massaged it gently. The guy was a nutcase, his mood swings quicker than lightning. No prizes why the nickname. Nothing to do with being christened Peter Sparks at all. *Of all the rotten luck!* But how would Travers come across someone like that? Falmouth was a huge distance from Exeter. If Travers went anywhere, it would be to play rugby at a school or travel up to London where his parents had a flat. Cautiously Scott pulled open the door and made his way back into the shower room. The hot water had steamed up the only mirror and he rubbed it clear with a corner of his towel, taking a good hard look. He gasped aloud, darting a nervous glance around hoping no one had heard. The face staring back at him was Scott Anderson with brown eyes. How could he have been so stupid? Panicking, he hurried into the dormitory hastily flinging on his track suit, all at once grateful for the rule about not making friends. To their guards he was a prisoner, a number, someone of no importance. Dyeing your hair didn't make you a felon. He bent down to tie his trainers, looping the laces into a double knot that would stay in place, his pulses racing. Should he do something about it? But what? Ruefully, he felt his collar bone, the skin tender. Forget it. Lightning wouldn't dare speak out; he had too much to lose if he really was wandering about in the middle of the night.

Hesitantly, Scott made his way into the corridor automatically glancing into the dormitory on the far side, deserted except for Chris who was scrabbling about on the floor searching for something under his bunk. He was always the last. *Holy crap!* Breaking into a run, Scott tore through the door into the lobby, remembering just in time to collect a bottle of water from the stack near their classroom. Avoiding eye contact he joined the waiting line, their instructor halfway through calling their numbers.

Scott carried his empty tray over to the waiting trolley, stacking his plate and cutlery neatly. Force of habit kept him searching for clues that someone – anyone – existed apart from the guards and their instructor. At the very least there should have been off-stage noises like water running or a distant voice shouting an instruction. Perhaps a cleaning cloth or broom carelessly left behind. Nothing, apart from dishes of hot food and a trolley waiting to be loaded with dirty trays and plates. Obviously the same perverted mind that had created their punishment knew well the effects of isolation and its ability to eat away at healthy minds like a cancerous growth. It had worked brilliantly too. On the coach, guys had clung together taking solace from the company of a stranger. No longer. Over five days, careful schooling had transformed the majority into morose, suspicious individuals who steered clear of their companions, leaving the atmosphere heavy and charged with aggression. Only the friendship of James, Chris, Max and Stephen remained intact. If anything they clung more tightly together. Not talking or using names, overtures of friendship were expressed in a half-smile or raised eyebrow. A few guys responded but not many.

Scott headed for the dormitory still unsure what he was going to do. He wasn't the only one. James and Chris, suffering from blisters, took every opportunity to lie down, and at least half a dozen others – all of them grateful for the extra rest.

Gradually, the sounds of night changed from teeth cleaning and toilets flushing to heavy breathing. Scott fell into a doze, wrapped in a dream of Hilary, her smile like sunshine. He missed her dreadfully. Now he was no longer starving and worn out, he had hours of time in which to fret and her absence was like a constant pain. The thought that she could be asleep on the far side of the wall somehow made it worse. He caught the faint clicking of a latch followed by a scuffling sound like mice and hurriedly slid out of his bunk.

Keeping close to the wall, he peered round the open door to the toilet block. Pinned back at night, the faint red glow from the emergency lighting showed a deserted washroom, a row of shower-heads dangling forlornly like alien bodies on their long, spindly hoses. Taken aback, he tip-toed across the room, ducking down to peer through the gap under the toilet doors. Nothing there but the rounded shape of the metal bowl, its base concreted into the tiled floor. Inching open the first of the half-dozen stalls, he checked for the tell-tale sound of breathing, but heard nothing apart from the dripping of water from a leaky shower head.

Angry at falling asleep, Scott headed back out of the washroom. He stopped dead in the doorway and swung on his heel, staring up at the ceiling, seeing what he'd missed first time round... the ventilation grille above the middle cubicle was no longer flush. It had been moved.

Silent in bare feet, he clambered onto the back of the cistern. Grasping the top of the partition wall, he pulled himself up, aware now that the strange noise had been Lightning's toes scrabbling for a purchase on its plastic surface. Balancing carefully, he reached up and slowly slid the grille to one side, the space beyond it black and uninviting.

Scott flinched, a sudden pain in his throat forcibly reminding him of the folly he was about to commit. Before he could wimp out, he swung his body up nudging the grille slowly back into place. All around, he sensed space and air. Stretching his fingers, he traced the shape of the duct – flat at the bottom where it lay flush with the ceiling, pointed at the top – five-sided. Softly, he rubbed the palm of his hand against its metal surface sensing the miniscule irregularities, which meant iron rather than steel.

He stared round the dark tube unsure what to do next. No point heading towards the yard; there was nothing there.

Forced to wait outside for the tail end of the line to finish their run, he'd have noticed if there had been. Ahead, a series of radiator grilles marked his path lifting the shadow in an otherwise black coffin. A flicker of excitement pulsed through his veins, hastily damped down. Whichever way you looked at it, following someone who had threatened to kill you into a dark tunnel was the height of folly. Scott flashed a grin into the darkness and began to pull himself along on his arms, before he had second thoughts which might quash his resolve. Despite the danger, he had to know. Besides, it just might prove useful to have a fall-back position in case he was recognised.

Ahead, he spotted a glimmer of light. It moved, jerking up and down. How the heck did Lightning manage to get hold of a torch? All their possessions had been confiscated by the police. He'd been lucky to hang on to his drops and his watch, which had been returned when they boarded the coach.

Silently he pursued the flickering light, the woollen fabric of his T-shirt and trousers gliding easily across the metal surface, grateful that he'd left his jacket with its metal zip on the corner of his bunk. Once the initiation was over, their beds had been supplied with sheets and they'd been given a pack with a face flannel, toothbrush and toothpaste but, apart from fresh towels every day, nothing else except for a clean tracksuit and shorts each morning – not even pyjamas. In any case most of his roommates slept fully dressed, they were so tired. And there seemed no shortage of gear. Twice now, they'd got soaked on a run and been sent to change. Scott paused. Somewhere in the building there had to be a laundry. The plastic bins were stacked high each morning with dirty clothes and towels, arriving washed and dried and back on the shelves by evening. Scott had never considered himself squeamish but the idea that a stranger or, even worse, someone he disliked, had been wearing his clothes the previous day left him feeling slightly nauseous. Even knowing they were washed in between made little difference.

Climbing had given him great control over his muscles and he moved quickly, the spark of light intensifying. On either side numerous smaller ducts fed off the main shaft and night noises, an occasional snore and rustle of sheets as someone turned over, drifted up from the dormitory below. Ahead, blue light trickled into the ventilation shaft lifting the solid blackness away. He paused, squinting down through the grille, identifying the bulky shape of a steel workbench, a large microwave standing on it. At last he'd found the kitchen, although it was a pretty peculiar place to put it, tacked onto the back of a building. Perhaps the architect had forgotten that prisoners needed feeding and it had been built as an afterthought.

Edging towards the next shadowy square, he was surprised to find the tunnel continuing, the airflow stronger. Puzzled, he stopped and stared back into the darkness, picturing the building as he'd seen it from the running track. There was no scenery to gaze at and, on the return leg, their path often took them across the bare rock of the hillside, giving him to memorise its stubby shape; the building backed up close to a rocky overhang like a wild boar cornered by the hunt.

Ahead, the darkness had become solid as if a brick wall had been built across it, the flickering light vanished. Excitement and fear in equal measure ripped through him at the thought of discovering a way out. He made to pull himself forward and stopped. Even if it did lead out, what use would it be? They were miles away from civilisation. Besides, they were going back to England in a couple of days.

Scott stared into the empty darkness half-inclined to go back to bed. A trickle of warm air passed across his body reminding him all at once of that day in the spring – the very last day when everything was normal. It was April and the sky had been densely blue. He had freewheeled the slope from the cottage listening to the birdsong, new lambs pushing their noses inquisitively through the bars of the fence watching him cycle past. Nothing would ever be like that again, so what had he got to lose? He listened to the silence, his thoughts confused and bitter, aware that from now on silence would mirror the pattern of his life.

Making up his mind, he inched forward his arms at a stretch. Sensing space all round, he stretched out his fingers to touch the walls. Without warning, a knee struck the middle of his back pinning him down, a hand across his nose and mouth to stop him crying out. A light flashed, instantly extinguished.

TWENTY-THREE

Like a sudden rainstorm lashing down, vivid memories of Sean Terry taking him prisoner swept through Scott's mind, blocking every sensation except the need to keep breathing.

'*Damn young fool*, thought I'd warned you against gettin' yerself killed,' a voice hissed in his ear.

Panicking, Scott got his fingers to his mouth and pulled against the hand. It gripped harder, stopping his breath totally. He choked, the pressure in his lungs like an iron bar.

'I'll let you go – but you promise first to keep quiet. A single sound and it'll be a bullet in the brain.'

Scott dragged his head into a nod of acceptance, desperate for air. This was the second time Lightning had nearly throttled him. He felt the hand pull away, the weight disappearing off his back, and hauled in a vital breath. Painfully he sat up, his head bent forward over his knees, shaking uncontrollably. The light flashed again and he saw they were in a large island of space, pipes criss-crossing left and right like a busy intersection on a motorway.

'Why the hell did you follow me, I warned you?' Lightning whispered into Scott's ear.

Scott rubbed his sore neck, unwilling to confess he didn't have a proper reason, only a gut instinct and an inbuilt hatred of taking orders. He lived the whole of his life taking orders from his dad, never bringing things into the open, and look where it had got him. 'I thought you were a spy,' he croaked. 'I was scared you were going to tell on me… I wanted to stop you… besides, I thought you might know a way out.' He ended the sentence lamely, aware it made no sense.

'You blitherin' nitwit, Scott Anderson. If I had been a spy, I have used a door not crawl through this thing.'

'I was right though, you *do* know who I am.' Scott kept his voice to a murmur. 'So how come you've got a torch if you're not spying on us?' Scott touched the scrap of metal, a small light bulb set into plastic casing, scarcely longer than the top joints of his middle finger. Surprisingly, he no longer felt afraid.

Lightning flashed the light on examining Scott's face intently. 'This old thing?' he said carelessly. 'You have to have friends in high places to get one of these.'

'But they searched us?'

'It fits into the toggles on my jacket.' The lilt in the voice sounded familiar.

'Beau?' Scott gasped in a startled whisper.

'My godfathers! Is my disguise so feeble that a mere babe-in-arms can penetrate it?'

'No! But I…' Scott exclaimed, forgetting to keep his voice low. Instantly, he felt the hand across his mouth, stopping his words.

'If we're trying to keep our visit secret, exclamations of joy are likely to prove detrimental to our cause,' Beau rebuked softly, his voice light and mischievous, all trace of accent gone. 'In this case, silence is definitely golden. No cosy chats – got it?'

Scott nodded his acceptance.

'Okay, I'll tell you what I'm doing here, if you promise to

go back to bed.' Scott felt the warm breath on his neck and shook his head. 'You always were a stubborn cuss…' Beau mumbled. 'Can't you see, I'm trying my best to keep you in the land of the living?'

Scott whispered, 'Thanks, but… '

'No thanks! Okay, I get it. You aren't moving till you know,' Beau sighed dramatically. 'I am trying to discover who's behind the riots and if it's linked to your Mr Smith.' He kept his voice to a whisper. Automatically, Scott leaned forward raising his hand to his ear to catch the words spilling out at speed. 'After Holland, he and his cohorts vanished. Couple months later, the riots started, peaceful rallies turned sour. Then, surprise, surprise, the European parliament brought in a new law to deal with the worst offenders, sending them to these special camps. Every time there's a demonstration, I hang round the edges hoping to get arrested and sent to Europe. So far it's been a dead loss.' He sounded fed up.

'But…'

'But not as Beau Randal.' Scott caught the movement and sensed he was holding up his hands, unable to see them in the dark. 'I have a different identity and fingerprints.'

'How many times have you done this?'

'This is my fourth place in five months.'

Scott stared at the shadowy figure, his mouth dropping open. 'You've gone through this every time?'

'I may be a lot of things but no way am I into self-harming.' Scott caught the teasing note in Beau's voice. 'I promise you, this is by far the worst. The other places were harsh not brutal. *Now* will you go back? If it is the people that kyboshed your dad, they let you escape once before. They'll not make the same mistake twice.'

Scott shuddered then shook his head. 'Hilary's here somewhere.'

Beau pointed back up the slope. 'She's in the unit parallel to ours. I found her last night, and she's fine. But don't even think of trying to rescue her.' He heaved a sigh. 'Come on then, if you're coming, we've only got an hour.' Beau flashed the pinpoint of light into the tunnel ahead.

'But where? ' Scott argued, instantly forgetting the need to be quiet. Beau glared. Scott pointed downwards, saying in a whisper, 'There's nothing behind the building except rock and dirt. If there had been we'd have seen it. This place might be gross but it's too small to hide anything.'

'Yeah, isn't it just.' Scott picked up on the sarcasm. 'Except, doesn't it make you wonder why a small building needs air-conditioning on this scale, unless they're planning a huge extension. Besides, haven't you wondered where the staff live? I can promise you, it's not the local village.' Without waiting for Scott's reply, he slid his long frame noiselessly into the tunnel.

Scott followed, a million unanswered questions zinging round his head like the debris from a meteor shower. Who was Beau working for? Last time Travers had spoken of him he was into athletics. Was it the government? Was somebody, at long last, taking Mr Smith and his ambitions seriously?

The shaft sloped gently downwards, the incline steeply increasing until the air flow formed a tangible barrier, making it difficult to move fast, like swimming against a current. On both sides, tunnels spiralled left and right into the darkness, minute variations in the strengthening stream of air marking each intersection. Scott began to feel rather like a snake lost in the middle of a motorway with roads constantly cutting into it. He tugged the hem of Beau's track suit. 'How do we get back?' he hissed, aware the route back would be tricky without a current of air blowing directly into their faces. 'There's dozens of tunnels down here.'

'No worries,' Beau murmured, not hesitating in his forward movement. 'I've done this before.'

'How many times…'

'Try three. I have a job to do, and it's not finished yet. In case you didn't notice, I left my jacket back there, where I picked you up.' It had been too dark for Scott to notice that Beau like him was only wearing his T-shirt. 'Come on.'

Ahead, the darkness extended as if to infinity. Nervously, Scott flicked a glance behind him. Where on earth were they? 'Beau…'

'*Shush!*' Beau paused. 'Can you hear it?'

Very faintly in the distance Scott caught the sound of music overlaid with voices, like a TV advertisement.

'But… that's impossible.' His tongue fell over the words.

'Not impossible, though I agree it's a puzzle. So why does Agatha Christie spring to mind? Ah, yes, *mirrors.*'

Scott caught the excited tone although he hadn't a clue what was meant by it. Typical Beau – if the tales Travers told about his brother were even halfway true, anything impossible or dangerous he devoured for breakfast. Scott swallowed, his throat aching and sore. If they really were venturing into the lair of Mr Smith, it was beyond scary even for someone like Beau. Thousands of people had died because of this man's ambition to control the world, Tulsa and his dad among them. Scott hovered over the word *dead*. Did Beau already know they'd been killed? Was that why he had urged Scott to go back, because his mother and sister were all that were left? He'd only met with them a few times, before Sean Terry had whisked them away some place no one knew about; still amply long enough to want them as part of the family he and his dad had created.

Beau began moving again, his stocking feet sliding easily across the metal. Scott struggled to keep up, the blurred noise from the television increasing as the ventilation shaft flattened out, its darkness surrendering to shafts of light filtering through mesh screens. Abruptly Beau stopped and curled up into a ball on one side of the grille to let Scott see down.

At first glance they seemed to have blundered into a posh hotel. A vast deserted lobby, its sofas and chairs festooned with scatter-cushions and patterned in muted shades of burgundy and grey; tubs of greenery making an eye-catching splash of colour. Scott counted the squares of light ahead, those in the distance fading into mere pinpricks of brightness. He glanced down at the luminous dial on his watch. It had taken twelve minutes to travel, what… fifty, sixty metres? And they weren't even halfway yet.

Figures drifted into view, a quartet of guys and girls chatting amiably in a foreign language, oblivious to the spectators a mere three metres above their heads.

'What are you looking for?' he whispered as they passed out of sight.

'Know it when I see it.' Beau flipped his finger, pulling forwards to the next grille. He pointed downwards. 'That answers one question, anyway,' he mouthed into Scott's ear.

Scott spotted the flickering screen of a television on the far wall, only its lower half in view. A group of figures were slumped in chairs watching a programme in English. Astonished, he recognised the missing faces from the coach. Catching the sound of a braying laugh, he craned his neck further, identifying the hulking shape of Tyson. Automatically, he flinched back into the shadow, despite knowing he was unseen. And he'd better make sure he stayed that way, for there was something about the guy that set Scott's teeth on edge.

A voice, its accent American, its tones that of someone in authority, broke through the sound track. A pair of elegant footwear, highly polished, came into view, the metal surround of the grille cutting off all but the man's legs from the knees down. The suit was Italian. Scott wasn't particularly into clothes but even he knew the difference between hand-made and shop bought, the material lightweight with a silky sheen, its knife-like creases impeccably cut. 'Listen up! I want to talk to you about Tuesday and you have an early start in the morning.'

The sound from the television dropped to a whisper as the volume was turned down.

'Where to this time, sir?' a voice called.

'How about a nice long weekend in Bilbao, followed by a stop-off in Barcelona for a few hours.'

A muffled cheer sounded.

'So what's in Barcelona?' The guy sitting next to Tyson swivelled round in his seat. Scott found his fists clenching with anger. It was one of the guys that had pulled Hilary off the bike. Unlike Tyson, he'd got away before the police arrived.

'Conference of world ministers starts Tuesday. A couple of demos against global warming have been planned – peaceful ones of course…' Laughter. 'You've done this before; you don't need to know the details.'

'We've not bin to Germany for a bit,' Tyson called out, his voice nasal and quite unmistakable as though anger was never far from the surface. Scott thought of the white powder. He had to be on drugs, nothing else would account for that degree of belligerence. 'I like Germany.'

'You would.'

Scott caught the sneering retort from one of his cronies.

'Don't worry, you go there next week. You can take the new recruits, show them the ropes.'

'Christ, sir,' someone groaned. 'Not another lot. You know 'alf of 'em will get arrested.'

The American's voice cut through the muttering. 'If you

do your job properly, you'll be back here by Sunday and there'll be a nice little bonus waiting.' The words ended on a laugh. The scene reminded Scott of their sixth-form common room and their tutor's friendly little chats. He used the velvet-glove approach too. On the surface it seemed encouraging but in reality brooked no argument – that is if you didn't fancy a visit with the headmaster. Except, these guys were older than sixth formers and definitely not friendly.

There was silence for a moment then the American spoke again, taking off the velvet glove, his tone rasping like sand paper. 'Last week was an intolerable shambles. May I remind you, you're no use to us if you get arrested. There'll be no second chance. I had to call in a whole heap of favours to get you back here. You create mayhem and leave. You get caught – you lose your job and your lavish lifestyle. Understood? No dramatics. I'm talking to you, Tyson! Remember, there's a queue of kids out there anxious to take your place.'

'Yeah, I get it,' was the surly response.

A late-night news bulletin replaced the adverts.

'Turn it up,' the American said taking a step forward. 'I want to listen to this – it's important.'

Scott pressed his nose against the rigid edges of the square-shaped grille anxious to see more. 'Come on, come on,' he murmured to himself. He gave an impatient sigh, seeing the foot move back again.

From the television came the sound of flash bulbs going off and pulses of light poured from the screen. Someone introduced the President of Europe. The man was speaking in English about the forthcoming ministerial conference being held in Barcelona the following week.

'Sir,' a new voice broke in. Scott guessed it to be a reporter. 'Fergus O'Leary, political editor at the BBC. The riots on the streets of Europe… what's the official government position?'

Scott heard the calm voice of the President. 'Naturally, we ignore them. They are insignificant, like fleas on a dog; irritating but that is all.'

A trickle of laughter.

'But, sir, how can you ignore this movement for the restoration of the monarchy? Ten of the twenty-seven countries have openly pledged to destroy the union. I have the list here, sir.'

Scott caught the rustle of paper and guessed the reporter from the BBC was waving it in the air.

'Remember, Mr O'Leary, Europe is not the Middle East; civil unrest does not automatically lead to regime change in a week. We happen to be a democracy with elections taking place in less than a year. The union will stay and I will remain as leader.'

Scott frowned. Okay, so maybe he was tired and exhausted from lack of sleep but he'd heard those words before. Not quite the same perhaps. But where?

He caught a burst of raucous laughter from the guys watching television. 'He's in for a big surprise! How long do you reckon he's got, sir?' someone called out.

'A year, maybe less,' came the response, the man's American accent barely discernible. 'That's the timetable we're working to.'

Scott gasped, the words as clear in his head as if black-out curtains had been cut away letting the sun in. *Remember, Europe is not the Middle East; you cannot expect civil unrest to take place in a day, with regime change following in a week. But it will happen – and within a year – that I promise you.*

How could the President of Europe talk about democracy yet secretly believe something else? It was crazy! Madness! He'd forgotten – that was it. *He'd forgotten.* Scott heard once again the voice that had so disturbed him, the voice accented as if English wasn't his first language, soft… no, not soft… patient, used to being obeyed… *and hellish scary*. No, that was the point. *He hadn't forgotten!*

Beau beckoned. 'What?'

'It's the voice,' Scott gasped, trying to control the hysteria threatening to burst out of him. The words echoed remorselessly, flying through the air like poison darts, and darkness took over. Desperate to be rid of the insidious thoughts, he lashed out with his foot striking the galvanised tube with a dull thunk.

TWENTY-FOUR

Beau's hand clamped hard over Scott's mouth. He caught a sudden pause in the conversation. Terrified, he closed his eyes imagining heads swivelling, pointing at the ceiling… seeing his foot.

He had to move, now, away from the tell-tale square of light, but he was frozen to the spot unable to move a muscle, his head swirling from lack of oxygen. A blur of noise, as someone using the remote flipped through the channels. Scott sensed the arms circling his chest grip more tightly, then he was bodily dragged away and the scene retreated beyond the limits of his vision. He heard movie credits, the voices of the actors in the opening sequence muted.

The space around them widened and Scott felt Beau release him. Still jittery, he took in a breath listening intently for sounds of pursuit. They'd not been heard, his stupid blunder had escaped unnoticed. Gradually, the confusion and terror that had swept over him began to lessen and his racing heart slowed as the weight in his head eased.

'Where are we?' he mouthed.

Beau shrugged. 'Still alive, *no thanks to you.*'

They had left behind the lounge area with its panels of light and were now perched in a central crossing, their heads brushing the metal surface of the roof. Random ducts led off, most too small to crawl through indicating areas of little importance. Straight ahead, the darkness was pierced at intervals by panels of grey, like chalk marks on a pavement.

'What the hell happened?'

'I don't know.' Scott felt his face hot. 'It was the news report....'

'What about it?'

'I heard it before.'

'Where?' Beau's angry whisper scissored through the air.

All of a sudden one of the squares lit up, followed by a second closer this time and a third nearer again. A sense of being tracked from room to room struck Scott and he reared back like a stag at bay. Then the silence was severed by the tap-tap-tap of someone operating a computer keyboard.

Ignoring the impatient tug on his arm, Scott inched forward into the side tunnel, curious to discover who was working in the middle of the night. He stared down into the brilliantly lit room, seeing a work station built across one wall piled high with processors, computer consoles, a scanner and a printer. Just in sight across the room, a coloured quilt draped the end of a bed. As Scott watched a figure passed beneath the square mesh.

'Jameson!' The word was out, winging its way into the room before he could stop it.

The guy paused his wandering, his head cocked listening.

Scott tugged at the grating. Tearing away Beau's warning hand he swung down, his toes gripping the top of the heavy processor. Dropping to a crouch, he jumped to the floor and flung his arms round his friend. Jameson flinched back as if struck, his body rigid with shock.

'What are you doing here?' he said belligerently, the merry ebullience that had been such a charismatic part of his character missing, his eyes exhausted and wary. 'You don't know anything about computers,' he accused. 'They promised…' He stepped back, his glance shifting towards the door. 'I didn't see you come in,' he added in a bewildered tone. He licked his lips, prodding Scott's chest with the tip of his finger, as if testing to see if he was real or a hallucination.

Scott saw they looked painfully dry, crusted flakes of chocolate and something white embedded in the cracks. A surge of anger swept through him recognising that Jameson had been drugged. How could they – Jay had a most brilliant mind, how could they stoop so low?

'Who promised?'

'My friend. His name is Ferdinand. I'm allowed to call him Ferdinand because I'm special staff,' Jameson boasted. 'Everyone else has to call him sir or Mr Aquilla. He gave me this job. Mum and Dad are thrilled.'

'No way. Your mum's worried sick. You've been missing for days. I promise you, she's no idea where you are.'

'That's a lie,' Jameson flashed back. 'They warned me about talking to people like you.' He pulled out his mobile. Scott flinched back 'Bother, I forgot you can't get a signal down here otherwise I'd prove it to you. We can go up to the lobby and phone if you like. It's Frank's birthday in two weeks,' he said, speaking about his younger brother. 'I'm going to send him some money for a new mobile – top of the range it'll be. I can afford it now. He'll like that. And I'll be home soon for a weekend.'

Scott bit his lip, aware arguments were a waste of time. He didn't know how it had been done, probably speech recognition, but somehow Jameson believed he was chatting to his family. Except, that would mean someone had spied on the Brody family even before Jameson had been kidnapped. Scott felt a shiver of disgust rip down his back. Is that what happened to everyone here? Their phones tapped, their minds altered by drugs so they imagined having conversations with their family. His gaze drifted round to the computer, its screen filled with calculations. 'What are you working on?'

'Firewalls. It's a government-backed project. There's loads of us.' Jay waved his arm round the empty room. 'It's an amazing place, exactly like a city with tennis courts and a movie theatre – it's great.' His smile was painful as if the muscles in his cheeks had atrophied. 'There's loads of kids like me. It's government-backed, very hush-hush.' Scott winced sensing the confusion in his friend's head. Jameson put his finger to his lips. 'They say we're not to talk about it because of the spies.' He dropped his head and Scott could almost hear the cogs grinding round and round. He stared at the screen before lifting his head again. 'Why are you here?' he said accusingly. 'You're not a scientist. You know nothing about computers.'

'I'm only visiting.' Scott stared miserably at his friend, wanting to sling him over his shoulder and carry him to safety.

'For pity's sake, get the hell outa there!'

Scott caught the whispered words. He glanced up seeing Beau's furious face glaring down at him.

Jameson's fingers picked nervously at the dry skin on his lips. 'Is there someone with you?'

'No, only me. And I'm going now.'

Scott scrambled onto the desk and swung himself up, Beau reaching down to help him.

Jameson stared up at the retreating figures. Suddenly, as if emerging from a thick fog, his eyes focussed and he gave a painful half-smile. 'I miss my family. Can you tell Jenny to visit – she'd love the sports here.'

'You stupid, *stupid… Words fail me.*' Beau stormed, keeping his voice low. Silently, he slid the grating into place moving swiftly away out of sight of anyone standing below, the overwhelming tension in the silence amply conveying his opinion of the younger boy. Miserably Scott followed, overwhelmed by guilt at his own stupidity. He felt it like a living weight, sucking up the air until he found himself once again short of breath and had to stop. 'He won't tell,' he panted, tears of frustration sweeping across his eyes.

Beau paused to glance over his shoulder, the patch of shadow light enough for Scott to register how angry he was. He swallowed anxiously.

'*Won't tell!* Pull the other one. The guy hasn't a clue what day it is, never mind anything else. I ought to ring your scrawny neck.'

'It's not his fault – they've drugged him,' Scott protested.

'Save your breath for crawling and hope to God that room wasn't wired for sound.'

'*Holy crap! I forgot!*' he gasped the words, mortified by his own stupidity.

'You sure did.' Beau swivelled round, flashing his torch onto Scott's face. 'We'll need a miracle to get you safely out of here now, so start praying for one.'

Beau's long shape vanished into the darkness ahead, a slight slithering sound accompanying his brisk movements forward. Wishing the ground would open and swallow him whole, Scott followed. He knew he deserved everything Beau threw at him. His task was dangerous enough without Scott clod-hopping his way through it. The information Beau gathered must get back to the people who had hired him; that was more important than anything. But at least now he wasn't alone any longer, other people were also aiming to rid the world of Mr Smith – if it was Mr Smith behind this set-up? Although… Scott paused, his arms aching at the pace… everything fitted. The American had spoken about calling in favours to get Tyson back. Was that what happened in the courtroom in Exeter when the magistrate changed their sentence? And

Jameson? What he said about working on firewalls? Could that be Styrus – the virus created by the team his father had been a part of? And the unit? If authorities chose to inspect it – what would they see? A small building in the sticks, coaches ferrying detainees back and forth. Nothing out of the ordinary. Nothing to ring alarm bells or suggest a whole secret world buried beneath it. There couldn't be two sets of people in the world with that sort of power, could there?

Scott shuffled forward, all at once exhausted and in desperate need of sleep. At the intersection he glanced behind him, somehow still expecting to find light and movement. But all was still, silence like a cloak enclosing every centimetre of space. Thank God, they were home free. Abruptly, the murky blackness was dissected by the sound of snoring and, almost before he realised, the open grating leading down into the toilet block was in front of him.

'Get down first.'

Scott nodded, feeling his limbs heavy and dragging. Taking care not to make a sound, he reached down to the top of the cistern, stepping on the floor. He reached up automatically, guiding Beau's feet. 'For what it's worth, I'm sorry.'

'I know. But I wasn't joking when I told you to start praying.'

Scott stumbled wearily into the dormitory, the sounds of heavy breathing reassuring, grateful for one crumb of comfort in an otherwise nightmare scenario. When he got home, he could at least tell Mr and Mrs Brody that he'd found Jameson. He sank onto his bunk, his mind dropping with fatigue. He fought against it, long enough to say that prayer. If only they knew for certain who was behind it!

Abruptly the lights snapped on and a harsh voice hit the air. 'By your bunks. Now!'

Drunk with sleep, Scott staggered to his feet, his vision blurred and misty. He caught sight of several pairs of feet among the familiar knee-length boots of their guards. They were gathered protectively either side of someone in a grey suit – someone with a hugely powerful presence even when you were staring at them half-asleep. Seagar – Wayne Seagar. The name popped uninvited into Scott's head. He'd heard it often enough listening to his father talk about his imprisonment. One-sided conversations, with only a recorder for company, in which his dad had tried to dredge up miniscule snippets of information that just might be valuable to his rescuers. There'd been little enough on the American. He'd been in charge of security, Bill Anderson only meeting up with him the one time. Scott had seen him too, fleetingly, through the thickness of the glass cockpit in a helicopter. Still, the bullet-shaped head covered with a tight crew cut was unmistakable. All this time, he'd been trapped among the very people who had been trying to kill him. The word *kill* felt thick on Scott's tongue and he shied away from it like a startled horse, refusing to dwell on the thousands they had already killed and not lost sleep over. One more would make little difference. And he had blundered into their web like a bewildered fly.

Half-obscured by the guards was a slight figure, his jeans baggy where he'd lost weight. Jameson! Scott rocked-back on his heels as waves of nausea struck him. Why, oh why, oh why, had he been so foolhardy? Why hadn't he stayed put? Sticking his hand into a viper's nest was... *Oh my God! What had he done?* Finding a way out... that wasn't important.

Keeping his eyes on the ground, he watched the progress of feet around the dormitory, aware Jameson had been instructed to identify the intruder in his room. Beau was right. It had been wired for sound. Terrified, Scott raked over the conversation. Had Jameson used his name? If they had CCTV, it didn't much matter anyway.

The figures approached, Scott sensed nervous panic in the guys ranged alongside their bunks. No prizes for guessing what they were seeing… That all-important bus waiting on the tarmac to take them back to England, praying this wasn't a ploy designed to hold on to them for a few extra days. The threat had been present in every conversation involving Mr Reynolds-sir. 'If you infringe our rules, refuse to learn, you will not take the bus on Saturday.' But what had they learned – nothing except violence and terror.

Jameson flanked by two scowling figures stopped opposite Scott. Furious at being woken, the two guards were tapping their batons against the side of their thighs; perhaps hoping someone might step out of line so they could vent their anger. Scott forced his panic down, staring rigidly in front of him. He stretched his fingers to stop his fists clenching, keeping his arms loose and dangling. It was an effort. Dull eyes met his. It was a glance lasting no more than a fraction of a second, long enough to see a spark of recognition struggling to reach the surface like a swimmer caught up in a river choked with weeds. *Don't do it, Jameson. Don't recognise me*, he begged silently, watching the flash of awareness extinguish itself. At last Jameson shuffled on. With relief draining out like water through a sieve, Scott gripped hold of the breath trying to escape his lungs – not daring to move while attention focussed itself on Beau, his face a study of bewilderment, his hand sleepily scratching his head.

Scott caught the words. 'I was definitely talking to my brother. But he isn't into computers so why would he be here?'

The door closed behind the figures, a creaking of bunks the only sound as bodies fell back down, instantly asleep; the inspection one more hideous event in a week overburdened with hideous events.

TWENTY-FIVE

Scott's lids flickered open, the electric light dazzling at 6 a.m. especially after so little sleep. He threw back the covers struggling to climb out of bed, still clutched in the jaws of his nightmare, his head pounding. Air conditioning might be efficient but he'd never get used to it. All his life, he'd slept with his window open a crack even on the coldest of nights. He shied away from the word 'home'. Like the words 'father' and 'friend', the word 'home' no longer existed as part of his vocabulary. That too had gone up in flames.

The top bunk was empty, Beau already up. Scott tore into the washroom and stopped dead, registering a heavy undercurrent of unease permeating through the familiar morning routine. He didn't need to examine the faces of his room-mates; their body-language said it all. Something odd had happened in the night and one of their number was responsible. Doom-laden, harried, heads down pointedly avoiding eye contact, the morning storm of coughs and groans stifled, they moved sluggishly between dormitory and washroom, while dread like a winged bat, silently – ominously – circled the room.

Making sure the cubicle door was firmly bolted, Scott collapsed down onto the toilet seat, reliving his moment of eye contact with Jameson. He'd been let off the hook only because Seagar had stayed by the door. If he had come in… accompanied Jay… Sweat broke out on his brow. Despairing, he buried his head in his hands, his thoughts tumultuous. Like Beau said, he'd never be so lucky a second time. Guys like Seagar didn't get to boss the world about by being sloppy. The man would dig and dig until there was nothing left but bare rock. *And Hilary!* Hilary was in danger too because of him.

His fingers curled into a tight fist and he pounded them hard against his head almost crying at his own stupidity. He had to get to Beau! Warn him! Then get out! He daren't wait to be caught!

Unseeing, he glanced down at his watch. Logic told him he had until nine or shortly after. That's when offices opened their doors and staff logged into computers records, making cross-checking simply a task of pressing a few buttons.

Under cover of the noise from the flushing toilet, he eased open the lock and hurried to the wash basins. He had one shot. Mr Reynolds checked their numbers at the start of the run and again at the end, but no one bothered in between. And they'd seen the helicopter only that one time, that first night. In daylight it wasn't needed; the unit was surrounded by miles of desolate terrain which would deter any but the most foolhardy. When guys fell behind they were left to catch up, forcing the rest of the group to hang about in the yard until everyone was checked in.

With luck, he'd get an hour's start. Head for the hills and hide up until night. There didn't seem to be dogs – at least he hadn't heard any. This way, Hilary might stay safe.

Wishing he had time for a shower, Scott hastily splashed hot water over his face and neck. His hair looked gross, greasy and lifeless… but, thankfully, still hanging onto its colour. He pushed back his shoulders, refusing to dwell on the problems of getting back to England; that could wait until he reached the coast. Grabbing his trainers, he joined the rest of the group in the lobby waiting for their instructor to appear, hoping anyone interested would put his panic down to being late.

Thirty-minutes later they were still waiting. Scott shifted from leg to leg, taking occasional sips of water from the bottle in his hand, hounded by the idea that their unit was being searched for clues as to who had left their bed in the middle of the night.

For the umpteenth time, he glanced down at his watch. It was almost seven. Where was the guy? After the torture of the opening session, their days had followed a rigid pattern, scarcely deviating by more than a few minutes. 6am lights on; 6.30 lined up in the lobby, washed or showered, ready for their early-morning jog. By 8.00 they were back in, allotted sixty minutes to freshen up (shower again if they wanted), change their clothes and, if times had improved, slurp down a hot drink served with bread. In the classroom by 9.00; a second run, longer in the afternoon; then more films, hour upon hour of tortuous images until their nerves jangled and their brains turned to mush. In the nick of time food, as much as they could eat, and then sleep. Scott felt his stomach spasm with nerves. But not today, because he, Scott Anderson, was a damn fool and had set their alarm bells ringing.

As if his thoughts had filtered through the air, the door of the medical unit flew open. As yet, no one had seen inside the little room. On arrival, the guard had pointed to it but cuts and bruises were either ignored or treated in the dormitory. Even that first night, when six of the group had fallen sick from overeating, they weren't rushed off to the sick bay. Instead, guards had appeared in the dormitory. Disinterested and callous, they had checked on the vomiting boys, warning them in execrable English not to do it again because it was *stupide*.

If confirmation had been needed that every word uttered in the unit was recorded, it was that night. No one had called for help and at least half the guys had slept right through, yet guards had still come running.

Without wasting breath on a good morning, Mr Reynolds unbarred the outer door and pushed it open, fresh air flooding in. Scott took a deep breath savouring its clean smell, his headache ebbing slightly.

'Line up outside.'

A guard emerged from the open door of the medical room, his uniform replaced by a tracksuit.

Yet another change!

Timidly, Scott edged his way to the front of the queue to join Lightning. Taking no notice of anyone, he was staring across the yard in a bored fashion, watching the automatic gates slide back open. Now Scott knew who was concealed behind the mask, he realised the guy's boorish behaviour concealed keen eyes, intent on examining every inch of the place.

'Left line… one pace forward. Right line… one pace back.'

For a moment confusion broke out, no one quite sure what they were supposed to do, as if the instructions had been issued in a foreign language. Scott grabbed his chance. 'I have the proof,' he hissed. Beau gave him a startled glance. 'I recognised…'

'Number nine. Get moving. I said one pace forward.'

Scott jumped, the doom-laden words like slabs of granite falling from a great height. Already at the front of the line, he filtered to the back of the milling group, passing Chris on his way up, and taking his place by the side of James at the rear of the column.

With a withering glance, their instructor began checking numbers, the group shifting from foot to foot impatient now to get going; the wind off the hillside blustery.

Restlessly, Scott hacked at a weed growing through the tarmac, unsure what he should do. Now he had the evidence, it was vital he got it to Beau. Dare he wait; try again on their afternoon run? Twelve hours till they were free to go to bed, twelve more till morning. Would he even be alive by then? Raising his head, he peered out along the road the coaches had taken – the road to freedom. Any time now, they'd begin checking prisoners' backgrounds and discover who he really was. His stomach lurched and he dragged in some calming breaths. He had no choice. He had to go. Bending down, he made a show of retying his laces, leaving the double knot loose.

Propping the register against the door to wait their return, their instructor waved the group forward, following the line of runners through the gate, the pace gradually accelerating into a fast walk. A couple of miles to stretch and warm the muscles, followed by a slow jog. Above them the soft navy of early dawn had faded to grey in the east, marking the start of yet another dismal day. Out on the plain the wind died away, the air dank and oppressive. Scott eyed the guard and was relieved to see him speed up, running ahead of the group. He took in a few deep breaths, his muscles sore and bruised from crawling through the air-conditioning ducts and he stepped carefully, angling his left foot firmly down, not enough to rick his ankle but hopefully sufficient to loosen his shoelace further.

At the rear of the line of inmates, their instructor snapped at Scott's heels, striking his cane against his artificial leg, beating out the rhythm of their steps. Scott stared straight ahead, his face expressionless, trying to ignore him. It was one of the tricks Mr Reynolds-sir used to throw them off balance, hitting his cane viciously against a table top or wall during a quiet moment in a film or appearing in the doorway of the dining room, making out he was searching for someone while the food turned to sawdust in your mouth.

By his side, James was also silent. Out of all the guys, he'd lost the most weight and seemed almost proud of his burgeoning fitness, openly boasting that being forced to go cold turkey was the only way to give up smoking – and it was the best thing that had happened in a long time. Although, even after five days, he had little enough breath to spare for talking, puffing and panting his way up rocky slopes. He might be a brilliant companion when you needed time to think, to sort out the panic in your head, but not today when Scott desperately needed the comfort of another human voice. Not the hectoring or bullying tone that Mr Reynolds-sir used – an ordinary voice. It didn't much matter what was said – it was the sound he craved, the silence of the terrain adding to the brooding fear weighing him down.

All at once, he tripped and stumbled forward. Automatically James threw out his arm to stop him falling, his shoelace trailing along the ground. Scott almost laughed at how close he'd come to fouling up again, simply because he'd not been paying attention. He raised his hand. 'Mr Reynolds-sir, my trainer's come undone.'

'Catch up.'

Scott bent down, fumbling clumsily at the dragging lace, trying to decide in which direction he should go. Logically, an escapee should head for the road, keeping it in sight, hoping to reach civilisation before he was missed. He raised his head staring out over the barren landscape, tracking the path the coach had taken, the plain as grey and featureless as the endless cloud base. No! There was too little cover; a running figure would be visible for miles. He must stick to his origin plan. Backtrack round the unit and head for the rocky hillside. He eyed the distant hills, anxiety turning their peaks into menacing blocks of stone and smiled ruefully. One small ray of comfort; at least no one could spot him from a window – there weren't any.

In the distance the strident crackling of an engine dissected the silence. He listened to it coming closer, the half-smile of a second ago wiped away, understanding that escape was never going to happen. With a sense of impending doom, he watched the long-dark shadow of the helicopter approach and felt a rush of air from its rotor blades. Pulling the knot tight on his shoe, he got to his feet, raising his hand to acknowledge the presence of the hovering craft. With his feet heavy against the ground, he sped after the group, the sense of being hunted overwhelming

James nodded as Scott came alongside, but didn't speak his eyes fixed on the horizon, concentrating on keeping up the pace. Gradually the noisy engine faded away, the silence of the air now broken only by heavy breathing and the occasional cough.

Dawn had come and gone leaving heavy clouds already thickening to rain, a layer of moisture trapped by the low cloud base. As they entered the home straight, the unit emerged as a faint blur and an audible sigh of relief swept through the group. It didn't mean anything, the six miles they did in the morning a mere bagatelle compared to the ten or twelve they did in the afternoon. The joint sigh was one of recognition that if it did rain, at least they were heading back in and not out.

Scott couldn't bring himself to join in that communal sigh; that fragile illusion of freedom, made possible by the open air and the empty space, was all he had to sustain him. The moment they set foot inside, he would be doomed.

Gradually, the green-grey outline of the detention facility crept closer, hills draped around it like a shawl of rock and stone. Naturally long-sighted, Scott caught a suggestion of movement, seeing a dark-coloured vehicle heading for the unit. It stopped outside, the angle too acute to follow the action of the gate pulling open. Miniscule figures dropped down from it, hurrying into the building. A moment later others took their place, some pulling a suitcase, others carrying bags. Boarding, Scott watched as the coach backed up, retracing its route across the plain, its dark shape quickly swallowed up by distance.

So that's how they got away with it! The coaches with their windows barred – they were't meant to stop prisoners seeing out but people seeing in. Even the ugly horizontal stripes on the building were there for one thing only – camouflage.

Scott had noticed the solar panels on the roof and hillside, squares of metal and glass, but had not paid them any attention, awarding them only a cursory glance as he ran past, although he had wondered how technology could create heat and light at sub-zero temperatures or on rain-soaked days when the sun became a distant memory. Now, he saw the panels didn't follow the sun, their position was fixed. So that's what Beau had meant by mirrors. Most probably it was reflective glass, angled to transmit images of undergrowth, bushes and shrubs and conceal all evidence of a substantial building. For someone driving past, it would seem insignificant and ugly – scarcely worth a second glance. Only if you really, *really* looked could you unravel the pieces of the puzzle. Even at night, not a single beam of light would escape its windowless walls, the building a dense rectangle of darkness against the night sky. Thermal imaging would show people moving inside, easily explained away by the presence of a detention centre for feral youngsters – those who refused to obey the law. Anyway, who would bother to fly over a desolate area of France and use thermal imagery, unless they were searching for something, or someone?

Scott shivered, the ribbon of sweat down his back icy-cold despite a temperature already in double figures. What sick mind had devised this? And they'd get away with it too, unless he stopped them. 'James?'

His voice must have sounded different because James shot him a startled glance. 'What?'

'Can I trust you?'

'Huh? Trust? Course.' The guy smiled. 'Me and Chris, we're the good guys remember. If I pride myself on anything, it'll be this week...'

'*Holy crap*, James, stop babbling,' Scott hissed. 'This is serious. If I don't get out...'

'Blimey, Scott...'

'If I don't get out,' he repeated, 'can you get a message to my dad...' Scott glanced up, hearing the familiar thwack of the cane. Mr Reynolds-sir paused a long moment, his glance raking. Apparently satisfied, he swung on his heel making his way slowly back up the line, never deviating from the pace he had set.

'Who's your dad?'

'Doug Randall!'

'The sports...' James coughed. 'God, cigarettes have played havoc with my lungs. 'The sports presenter on TV?'

'That's him. I need to tell him...'

'*You horsing around?* With a dad like that, no one will mess with you.'

Scott eyed the squat rectangle of the prison, each thudding heart beat taking him closer. How could he make James understand? How would anyone understand without a day-long explanation? It was all too far-fetched – stories of aliens stood a better chance. But he hadn't got all day. If he was lucky, he had a minute or two. Uneasily, he watched their instructor moving up and down the line. Never long in one spot, he jumped about silently, eavesdropping on anyone brave enough to start up a conversation. Scott felt the tension in the air, the sidelong glances of mistrust.

Suddenly, James threw a life-line. 'Is this to do with last night?' Scott nodded, relieved. 'You knew that guy?'

'Yes!'

'*Jesus!* But how the hell did you get out of the unit?'

Scott opened his mouth.

'No, don't tell me,' James dived in. 'I don't want to know.' He glanced up seeing the figure of their instructor once again heading in their direction. 'So, what's the message?'

'Tell him, *it was the President of Europe who I overheard on the phone.*'

TWENTY-SIX

Scott stared into the gaping mouth of the camera lens, a red light pulsing above it.

'Name?'

'Number Nine – Travers Randal.' The name felt stiff on his tongue, unused for five days.

At the end of their run, they'd been checked off and sent to shower and change. Breakfast of sorts had been waiting. A pitiful fare with coffee from a machine, not fresh like the day before; slices of French bread, cut from a day-old stick and already gone dry, as if it was the cook's day off on a Friday and no was else was bothered. Or perhaps, more likely, a reminder of that first lesson – *one fouls up, you all foul up*.

Told they were to be interviewed, they had waited in the classroom, the screen of unspeakable images no longer playing. Scott stared round the familiar walls, grateful for the rule limiting contact that stopped guys from confiding in one another. Lightning had been called first, Scott last; waiting for what seemed like hours, becoming more and more edgy as their numbers dwindled. A few of the guys had openly boasted that it had to be about jobs, exchanging covetous, greedy looks, the atmosphere once again tentative and uneasy. If jobs were on offer, as had been promised, they were going to have them – no one else.

'And you live where?'

'Falmouth, sir.'

The voice emerging from the rectangular mouth of the speaker belonged to the man he'd overheard addressing Tyson and his mates, rebuking them for being caught; a microphone exaggerating his American accent. No attempt had been made to disguise it – so different from his father's interview with Mr Smith. There, the voice had changed pitch constantly making it impossible to identify. He waited for the next question, a nerve-wracking pause between each one designed to keep the candidate off guard. The absurd idea flashed through Scott's thoughts that the whole mess had involved hidden voices. And only he knew where they all fitted. This voice belonged to Wayne Seagar, its casual vowels and soft consonants perfectly matching the silk suit and expensive shoes of the man standing by the dormitory entrance.

'Family?'

'I have a brother and a sister – Beau and Natasha.'

Beau had passed him a note on his way out of the classroom written on toilet tissue, though where he'd got the pencil... *Keep calm they're guessing. 1-word answers only. GL.*

'My father is Doug Randal. He played rugby for England. He now works in television.'

Scott stared at the camera struggling to keep the muscles of his face relaxed, a sensation of panic flowing through every cell in his body like an angry stream.

'Why are you here?'

'Er... I...'

'*With your background*, why are you here?' The measured tone had hardened.

Scott shook his head. 'I'm not sure what you mean. It was the riot—'

'We have someone with the name Randal in our other unit. Is that your sister?'

Holy crap! Hilary! 'Yes, we were together in Exeter when—'

'Are we to find your brother here, too?'

Scott felt his skin burning. 'No, I... *No!* Tash and I were visiting a friend from uni. We'd stayed the night.' He gabbled the words. 'I was trying for a short-cut when—'

'You know Jameson Brody?'

Scott gasped, taken aback by the sudden change in subject. 'Y-yes,' he stuttered. 'We go to the same school.'

'Falmouth Comprehensive.'

'Y-yes! But we're not exactly friends. I'm into sports. He belongs to the brainy set.'

Stop talking, keep the answers short.

'But you know him?'

'Y-es! But—'

The voice emerging from the speaker cut him off – its tone abrasive, searching. 'How strange you failed to greet him.'

Oh God! 'I didn't recognise him. I was half-asleep. It was the middle of the night and I was exhausted.'

'But you did recognise him. How else would you understand the question?'

'*No!* Not at first! I thought...' Scott stopped, suddenly aware of the huge pit yawning open beneath his feet.

'You may go.'

'*Go?*' he echoed. He swivelled round in his seat and glanced longingly at the door, wondering if it had been a trick question.

'Yes, Number Nine. Leave. The report from your tutor, Mr Reynolds, is excellent. Collect your belongings. A coach is waiting outside to take you back to England. You should be there by Saturday afternoon. Good day.'

Cautiously, Scott stood up. He eyed the speaker but it

stayed silent. It was over. *It was actually over.* Moisture crept into the corners of his eye. 'Thank you,' he said keeping his head averted.

The unit seemed strangely quiet, the classroom deserted; an air of desolation pervaded the corridor, the dormitory walls echoing silently. Feeling a desperate need to hurry, Scott chased into the side-room, a lone polythene bag sitting on the shelves. He was going home. How or why they'd decided to let the detainees out early, he didn't know… and he didn't care.

His clothes felt strangely restrictive, his freshly washed jeans rough against his skin, but so very familiar. Scott stroked the sleeve of his jacket, detecting a faint bloodstain. The tracksuits they'd worn all week were comfortable but symbolised restraint and an absence of free will. Whether he'd be able to wear one ever again, he didn't know.

In the yard, a coach was parked up facing the open gate, its engine switched off. Scott broke into a jog.

Hilary burst from the steps of the coach.

'Tash!'

He grabbed her tightly to him, his head buried in her hair. Never had anything smelled so good.

'Watch it, that's not a very sisterly embrace.' Hilary took a step back, her hand still on his arm.

'I don't feel very brotherly.' Scott smiled, a feeling of total joy springing up, his whole being light as a feather. He stared at the coach, its metal shutters hostile, a grim reminder that he was still on enemy territory. Not for long though. James peered out over the steps and he flashed a smile. He could deliver the message himself now. Impatiently, he glanced down at his watch. In a little over eighteen hours, they'd be back in Exeter. First thing, Hilary must phone the embassy – and track down Sean Terry. Tell him.

'Get a move on, we want to get out of here,' James called.

Scott grinned. So did he.

'*Scott?*'

Scott felt his shoulders move, swinging round before he could stop them, painfully aware of Hilary's nails digging into his arm. He stared into her eyes. Terror swept across them, her skin blanching ash white even as he looked.

'*Scott Anderson.* I thought it was you. Would you believe it? I always thought we'd meet up again. But not here.'

Scott stared down into Hilary's stricken eyes. 'Get on the coach,' he whispered.

'Not without you.' She shook her head, both hands clinging to his.

Slowly, very slowly, he continued the movement of his shoulders. 'Hello, Pete.' He tried to keep his voice casual.

The bony figure of the rogue agent stood alongside the open door to the unit, the corner of a wall a comfortable leaning post. He looked no different from the last time Scott had seen him on the rooftop in Lisse; his sunglasses obscuring a pitiless gaze, firmly in place even in rain, his demeanour relaxed and casual. Even his clothes appeared unchanged.

'So what are you doing here?'

Scott launched his face into a smile. 'I got seven days for affray. I've done my time. Just leaving.'

He pointed to the coach, noticing Beau had joined James on the step, his glance concerned.

'Get a move on, you two – you're holding us up,' he beckoned, his hand urging them to take that step to freedom. Scott caught the note of appeal in his voice.

He took a step backwards, edging Hilary towards the coach. Pete didn't move, his eyes invisible behind their reflective shades, his hands loose in his jacket pockets.

'Sorry, guys. But Scott and I are old friends. When I heard he was here, I didn't believe it.' Scott closed his eyes, rocking back on his heels. How long had they known? He felt Hilary grip his hand tightly. 'I flew straight here. But two old friends? Never expected that. How are you, Hilary?'

'I'm well, Pete. I suppose it's too much to ask, to just let us get on that coach. After all, we've served our time.'

Scott listened to her cool tones with admiration. How did she do it? His own limbs were trembling almost out of control. How amazing she was? He was so lucky to have found her.

'You know, I can't do that, Hilary. At least, not until you've answered a few questions as to why you're here in disguise, impersonating members of the Randal family.'

There wasn't an answer to that. As if replying for him, the coach door slammed shut. Scott jumped. Hearing the engine rumble into life, he watched despairingly as freedom slowly edged towards the gates. Silently, they slid shut behind the moving vehicle sealing them in.

'What are you going to do with us?' Scott managed.

'How about a spot of television while we think about it? In you go.'

Pete still hadn't moved, Scott only too aware there was no need. Resistance was futile. Every atom in Pete's body was on full alert, although you'd never guess it from his casual stance. He reminded Scott of the loose frame of a scarecrow; yet the eyes behind the shades never missed a trick, the hand in his pocket able to move at the speed of a bullet to the holstered gun resting against his shoulder. Scott shrugged his shoulders nonchalantly, faking calm. 'Okay!'

Pete smiled a lazy mocking smile that made the hairs on Scott's arms stand up. Strange, how once upon a time he'd even liked the man, before he knew him to be a ruthless killer capable of murdering a friend in cold blood, without losing a moment's sleep.

'Such a small world. I am constantly amazed at the people you come across.'

With Hilary at his side, Scott walked up the steps and through the open door into the square lobby. What an age it seemed since they first saw it. But if given a choice – face what was ahead or repeat their week from hell – he'd choose the week from hell any time.

Pete pointed to the open doorway of the medical unit, the video camera still glowing red – left on. 'Later on today, perhaps we can have a drink together and chat about old times.' He pulled open the door at the far end, a brightly lit corridor beckoning. 'I suggest you lead the way.'

As if all feeling had driven away with the coach, Scott trailed along the corridor, Hilary matching his steps. He didn't bother to hurry. Whatever was going to happen would happen anyway. He knew where they were heading; he had crawled along this same ventilator the night before. Behind them now were the units that presented a legitimate front to the world; in front of them, a hidden city. What had Jameson said? *With a movie house and tennis courts. Tell Jenny to come and visit, she'd enjoy the sports.*

'What about Jameson?'

'Your pal from school? Nothing! He's a valuable member of our little team. I hear he's clever. Already getting to grips with firewalls. Can't understand them myself. Tragic waste, your dad not wanting to work with us.'

Scott ground his teeth curbing an urge to retort. What was the point, the man's ego was colossal as it was.

The corridor opened up into a wide lobby. Scott recognised it instantly. Built on several levels, it was bigger than he had thought, with his view partially blocked by the framework of the ventilation grille. Shallow half-steps separated areas into private seating, shielded by walls of greenery. Scott touched the leaf of a Japanese maple. Like the rest of the setup it was false, made from some sort of plastic. Something else that gave the impression of being one thing yet, in reality, was something else. On the wall, the vast television screen stayed mute and silent. There was no one about.

Scott pointed. 'You said television.'

'Not here. That's for the use of our work force.' Pete's voice was relaxed, its southern drawl very noticeable. He hadn't bothered to draw his gun, strolling behind them as casually as a tiger with sheathed claws, utterly lethal if provoked. 'Don't bother shouting for help. We don't let things escape our control – not even noise. You'll find every room is sound-proofed.'

At the far end of the lounge area, double doors opened up into a long corridor, doors leading off on both sides like a suite of offices; smart but for middle-management only, not plush enough for the hierarchy, the bosses.

Pete opened a door, casually waving his hand towards a small table ringed by hard-back chairs. In the corner a television was playing, voices speaking in a foreign language.

'Take a seat; someone'll be with you shortly.'

The door closed behind him. Automatically, Scott tried the knob, twisting it round and round. He gave a shrug, grimacing at his own stupidity. 'Haven't a clue why I did that.' Releasing the handle, he hooked his foot round the leg of a chair, crashing down on the seat. 'Hilary…'

Putting her hands on the sides of his head, Hilary twisted Scott round to face her. She stared into his eyes and raised her fingers to her lips.

Scott grimaced painfully. 'Yeah, I know they're listening. I was only going to say sorry. Again.' He dropped his head staring down at the table, his fingers tracing a pattern on its wooden surface. 'Recently, I seem to have spent half my time regretting stuff,' he mumbled, remembering all those times he had behaved like a kid. Getting angry in Switzerland because their holiday had been cut short; furious because his father wanted to do the right thing and help the victims of Mr Smith's ambition, storming out of the house because Sean Terry announced he was moving them to safety, even mad at Tulsa because he'd kept silent out of loyalty to his boss. He raised his head again, dredging up a wry smile. 'Next time, I'll leave you in Falmouth.'

Hilary grabbed his hand, linking her fingers through his. 'You tried, remember. This isn't your fault, Scott. Kids like us; we don't stand a chance against powerhouses of evil.'

The words came out defiantly, wanting listeners to hear. Okay, she might have been taken prisoner but she wasn't beaten. Scott felt a surge of pride. She was so amazing. Even now, totally composed. Most girls would be in hysterics. No wonder he loved her! The thought stopped him dead and a gut-wrenching shaft of pain soared through him. He pictured the Suzuki, a crumpled heap of metal – exactly like his life.

'What?' Hilary's voice was sharp and the pressure on his hand increased.

'I was thinking about the bike.'

Hilary's startled gaze met his, the symbolism not lost. She knew as well as he did that they stood little chance of getting out alive. But there was a chance. Scott eyed the dial on his watch. If Beau or James... He cut the thought not daring even to picture the words in his head for fear of being overheard. He stared round the walls. Somehow he had to buy time – a day, maybe more.

TWENTY-SEVEN

The minutes ticked slowly away. By the time the door opened, Scott felt convinced his watch had stopped and hours and hours had elapsed, not twenty minutes. They'd not spoken much, not from fear of being overheard but because there was nothing to say. No point discussing ways of escape. There weren't any. Even the grilles in the ceiling were too small to climb through. Hilary rested her head against Scott's shoulder, her fingers clasped in his for comfort. It was little enough. The blame was his and his alone. He should have left her with Travers.

They jumped to their feet. He felt Hilary dig her nails in sharply and responded, gripping her hand tightly.

'How charming.'

Scott recognised the stocky figure in the doorway. He may have seen him only fleetingly but it had been long enough to haunt his dreams, a dark menace sweeping to the point of recognition and then retreating again, like the tide on the seashore. When he woke the image was gone, leaving him no nearer putting a name to the face than he had been when he went to bed. Longish dark hair, swept back from the forehead and going grey at the sides; his clean-shaven face was cherubic, with that polished glow that comes from daily grooming, his nails manicured. He wore a diamond encrusted watch on his wrist, and his cuff links sparkled beneath the sleeve of his jacket, his shirt immaculate.

Towering over him, like a gargoyle, was another figure that Scott recognised, the German bodyguard. No silk suit for him. The muscles of his upper arms strained against the coarse material of his jacket, the shoulder on one side distorted by a heavy gun holster. His name… Scott scrabbled through his memory banks. *Arnulf*, his father had called him. He had described him as an ox without brains. He'd been waiting by the helicopter that fateful morning when Pete had taken him prisoner – yet another situation in which there'd been no hope. It was the German's clumsiness that had shifted the balance, awarding him and his dad a precious second in which to run, the shot intended for his dad spinning harmlessly off into space. And they had run. The images flashed past; the chase across the roof tops, the climb down the face of the building – until that fatal gunshot which had so grievously wounded his father.

Pete closed the door and leaned back against it. He grinned at Scott, amused by the expression of hatred on his face. 'I told you once before, Scott. This isn't personal. In any other circumstances you and I could have been great friends. By all accounts, like you were with Tulsa.'

'He was killed saving me.' Scott caught the savage note in his voice.

'I heard. Shame! Good man. Like you, he chose the wrong side, that's all.'

Hilary twisted a lock of hair into place. 'And is it too late to choose the right side?' she said, her voice icily polite.

Scott held his breath, not daring to look at her. She had to be scared like him, but you'd never guess.

Arnulf pulled out a chair and, flipping the seat with his

hand to clean it, offered it to the man Scott had seen across the floor of the United Nations.

'Children! Children! Enough of this squabbling.' Nodding his thanks, the man sat down, resting his hands flat on the table. 'I believe the English are fond of the saying "why stand when you can sit." My dear young people... Scott, I know. And you, my dear...'

'Hilary Stone.'

'American Secret Service,' Pete added from the doorway.

'I resigned,' Hilary spat back. 'Hated what killing did to people like you.'

'I understand. Not a good profession for a delicate young lady.'

A snigger came from the German, hastily wiped off, once again staring stolidly off into the distance.

'I am sure we're all friends here. Please allow me to introduce myself.' The man's English was heavily accented, each syllable slow and marked as if he had learned sentences parrot fashion from a tape. Through the headphones, the man had sounded hectoring and bullying. Now, his voice was as soft as the silk of his suit, the iron fist concealed. 'My name is Vasilov.' He laughed. 'I see that means nothing to you.' He held up a hand offering a blessing like the Pope in St. Mark's Square. 'This is good. Perhaps an amicable solution can be found, after all.'

Scott stayed silent. Was it possible ignorance might save them? He felt a fleeting whisper of hope, instantly dashed.

'My problem with ignorance... so rarely is it ignorance. If you had not turned up here, perhaps I might have been persuaded to believe in it.' Vasilov shook his head. 'A great pity. You so nearly got away with it too.'

'I promise you we didn't plan it. We were arrested – and sent here,' Scott said. 'I can't imagine anyone *choosing* to spend a week here. Please, all we want is to go home. We won't say anything – we don't know anything.'

Vasilov smiled. 'Not true. You know quite enough to upset our plans.'

'So keep us here, till you've done what you want. *Then* let us go,' Hilary suggested.

'Hm! I like your approach, young lady. Pragmatic. Such a pity. A waste, a great waste of obvious talent.'

Scott heard the rigid tone, the man's gaze implacable. This was the man who could drum up killers at a moment's notice. He didn't do caring. 'Are you Mr Smith?'

He was treated to a great burst of laughter. Up until then, the man's gestures and voice had been restrained, held in, like a questing hound on a leash. Scott tried to conceal a shiver. Vasilov had no intention of letting them go, however much they pleaded ignorance. He'd been toying with them all along, like a killer whale playing with its seal prey before snapping its neck in its great jaws.

'I created the identity, yes.'

'So the man at the other end of the phone was Mr Smith,' Scott burst out with the words, unable to stop himself.

A deafening silence fell. Nervously, Scott eyed the two bodyguards, their stance unaltered. The German poker-faced as if incapable of registering thought, Pete propped up against the door, his eyes concealed behind their sunspecs. Scott remembered the piece of wood Pete had picked up from a pile of fragments, after their front door had been blown to smithereens. Casually leaning against the gate, he had whittled it into a shape, not sparing a moment's thought for the man he'd poisoned the night before. Scott bit his lip angrily. Now he'd really gone and done it. Losing his temper like that had scuppered any possible chance of getting out alive. He stuck out his chest defiantly. He didn't care. It had given Vasilov – if that was his real name – something to think about. Besides, right from that moment in the courtyard when Pete called his name, they were doomed.

'Ah! So you did overhear our conversation. I wondered if you had.'

'Then it was me you were trying to kill.'

The man seemed amused. 'Of course! How could I take a chance? You can appreciate, Scott, I would be a fool to let you go, no matter how much you try to convince me otherwise.' Vasilov toyed idly with his cuff link, its diamonds flashing a sparkling rainbow of light onto the walls. 'I flipped a coin, a simple fifty-fifty chance that you had heard. Perhaps… perhaps not. If you had, maybe one day you would recall the voices and be able to put a name to them. And I really wouldn't like that.' Vasilov inclined his head. 'Not good odds. One hundred per cent are the only odds I work with. I have spent twenty years creating Mr Smith. I would not wish to see my work destroyed because I accepted less than an odds-on bet.'

He got to his feet, the German bodyguard at his shoulder, leaving Pete to open the door. 'Kill them.'

'No!' Scott reached forward with his hand as if to pull the man back into the room.

'You won't get away with it,' Hilary shouted. 'Once the authorities find us missing, they'll come searching.'

A bellow of amused laughter echoed off the walls. Vasilov paused, his hand on the knob of the door, a beaming smile on his face. 'My dear young lady; you are so naïve. I told you the odds with which I work. Remember? One hundred per cent – never less. We own the authorities. If I want a file lost – I can assure you it will be lost.' He laughed again, a cruel mocking sound. 'I had intended to let you travel on the coach – to let you enjoy your final hours of freedom.' He shrugged. 'Curiosity got the better of me. I wanted to find out if you had heard our little talk.' He raised a hand, inspecting his nails. 'It makes no difference. The coach will never arrive. Tragically, it will crash into a ravine.' He twirled his fingers nonchalantly. 'Brake failure. Only the driver will survive. Tumbling from the open door of his cab, a tree will stop his fall.'

Beau! James!

'But you can't, there's innocent people,' Hilary shouted the words. 'No one, not even you can be that callous.'

'As I said, a terrible tragedy. The newspapers will love it.'

Too tired even to keep battling, Scott raised his head gazing bleakly at the figure in the doorway, feeling pain in every breath as hope withered. It didn't much matter what he said now; the man was untouchable. But for the sake of Beau and Hilary, he had to try.

His voice cracking with emotion, he spat out, 'The authorities already know you're planning the break-up of Europe. And I'm not talking about the ones you've bribed.' It was a stab in the dark but it found its target. Vasilov hesitated then stepped back into the room.

'Impossible.'

'You said about the odds but you got them wrong too. At best I give you ten to one against.' Scott eyed the three men in the doorway, all three listening intently. All at once, he felt the adrenaline pumping through his veins, banishing his lethargy as if the ligature around the neck of hope had been loosened. 'Tulsa was with me that day. I told him what I'd seen and he passed the message on.' Scott dived into his memory banks, searching frantically for something, anything, to keep their attention. 'Bugging the suite at the UN – that was stupid too. Without that, they might not have believed me. It was a mistake – *your mistake*.' He hurled the words across the room. 'And you were right about the spying. After Mr Smith vanished from Lisse, the Americans were determined to discover where he'd gone. They have spies too, you know. They know about this place.'

Vasilow laughed good-humouredly. 'My dear Scott, a good try; for a moment, I thought you actually knew something.'

A picture of snow swept uninvited through Scott's head and, once again, he watched the little line of cars leaving the UN building. 'They know a Russian is involved. I saw your car through the window.' The figure in the doorway stiffened, the smile replaced by a look of fury. He ploughed on wildly. 'Then I remembered who you were talking to. Except… it didn't make sense at first. Why would this man want to destroy the Union?' He flung the words into the arena. He could be wrong. But he didn't think so. It didn't much matter if he was. Some part of his words were hitting home. Vasilov was definitely shaken, impatient to hear what Scott was going to come out with next. Unconsciously, he crossed the middle fingers of his left hand for luck, his right arm still wrapped around Hilary.

The silence in the room had grown almost painful in its intensity. By his side Hilary hadn't moved, staring up into his face. He forced himself to speak clearly, as if addressing an audience. They weren't to know he was making it up as he went along, some of it true, the rest guesswork and fantasy dressed up to sound like truth. 'Why would the President of Europe… Damn, I never can remember his name.'

'Rabinovitch.' The words hit the air softly.

Scott nodded. 'That's the guy. Igor Rabinovitch. Why would he want to destroy something he was the President of? It's a great achievement that so many countries are working together.' The truth blasted its way to the surface like a rocket. He frowned, pausing while he worked it out. '*Unless…*' He brought his hand out from behind his back and marked the air with his finger. '*He wasn't who he was supposed to be. That's it!* You thought I was the spy. I wasn't… *but he is.*' He caught the look of rage on Vasilov's face and knew he'd guessed right. 'Even the Americans didn't believe that bit at first. But they do now.' Okay, so that bit *was* a lie. But the enemy didn't know and, following a statement of truth, they just might believe it. 'You lied about being Mr Smith… '

'*Shut up!*'

With the speed of a snake paralysing its prey, Vasilov struck out, his fist clenched. Scott felt the blow and reeled back, falling heavily.

'Scott!' Hilary screamed the words. She fell onto her knees helping him up into a sitting position.

'I'm okay.' He fished in his pocket for a tissue, dabbing at his nose. It came away bloody; his jaw and cheek tender and already swelling.

'Killing me won't stop the Americans,' Scott ploughed on thinking of James and Beau. If he remembered right, there were no ravines for miles, the ground flat. Then he recalled the twists and turns of the mountain road they'd met up with half-way into their journey. At least, they'd be safe for a few hours. By that time Beau might have found a way to get a message out. 'They've already worked out that Mr Smith is an organisation, and the President of Europe a mole – a sleeper, you call them.' He watched the fist, clenching and unclenching, and decided to stay where he was on the floor. 'I don't know why the Russians want to destroy the Union, I only know they do.'

'*Get rid of him. Now!* Dispose of the bodies, and get back here. There's work to be done. I'll not let a kid overturn our plans.'

The door slammed, the frame shuddering under the force. A deathly silence fell. Scott stared at the two men, the massive frame of the German, his face as always expressionless, dwarfing Pete by a full head.

Scott got slowly to his feet and pushed Hilary behind him, shielding her body with his own.

Pete slowly drew his weapon, sliding off the safety. Behind him, apparently uninterested, Arnulf was bent down, casually tying his shoelace.

'Good performance,' Pete drawled. 'But then you always were a gutsy kid. I'm almost reluctant to kill you.'

'Then don't.'

'Sorry, kid.' He aimed the barrel at Scott's chest. Still using his old gun, Scott thought idly, recognising the dark shape of the Colt pistol. 'As I told you before – this isn't personal, it's business.'

'Is that how you square your conscience, Pete?' he shouted wildly, stepping sideways to avoid the black muzzle. 'Pretending it's someone else's fault – nothing to do with you – that it's not you pulling the trigger. My God, I hated Terry but he's worth a million of you even on bad days.'

Pete's face darkened. Scott watched the finger on the trigger tighten and shut his eyes.

TWENTY-EIGHT

Blasts of noise reverberated round the room, then a further sound of a chair hitting the ground.

Scott didn't move, waiting for the fatal blow. Then, feeling Hilary's breath still warm on his neck, he slowly opened his eyes to see Arnulf bent over Pete's body spread-eagled on the ground.

He sank down onto a chair, his legs like jelly, and grabbed at his head, the noise of the gun-shots still echoing against the bones of his skull. Behind him, Hilary stared in speechless bewilderment. Scott pointed. 'Wh… who…'

The stolid lines of the bodyguard's face erupted into an impish smile, all at once transforming him into an ordinary big guy. 'Name's Haupt. American Secret Service – ASS for short. Appropriate, don't you agree?'

'Th-th-then…'

'*I was the guy that saved your ass on that roof?*' He chuckled. 'Yeah! It was all I could dredge up at the time. Thank God, we got lucky today. Vasilov hates blood – turns his stomach. Come on. We need to get you out'a here.'

Hilary stepped up. 'What do you want me to do?'

The agent removed his jacket, the butt of a gun protruding from a brown leather holster strapped to his rib cage. 'See if you can find something to tie this guy up with.'

Scott stared at the sprawled figure on the floor. 'But he's dead.' He heard the words but they didn't make much sense. This was all wrong. Pete couldn't be dead. It was him. He should be the one lying there. He felt dead, all sensation gone, neither his sight nor hearing processing information. Even his tongue felt heavy in his mouth. In the distance, he caught the sound of voices and wondered who they belonged to.

Righting the chair that had fallen across the body, Arnulf stepped onto it, easily tall enough to reach the ceiling. He lifted a panel to one side, exposing a shallow false ceiling.

Hilary scrabbled behind the television set. 'This do?' She held up a thick black wire, the plug and connection still attached at either end.

Arnulf nodded. 'We've got to hide the body in the roof space. We'll use the wire to lash it to one of the beams. Stop it falling. You first, Hilary.'

'What about the noise?'

'No worries – it's only the hired help carrying out their orders. Besides, silent as the proverbial grave this place. Apologies – bad joke.'

Scott gazed blankly at the hole in the ceiling, finding it difficult to focus. As if in a trance, he watched Hilary climb up onto the table. Arnulf picked her up, shooting her upwards like an express elevator.

She disappeared and he caught a faint scuffling noise. She reappeared, leaning back down. 'There's a narrow ledge by the wall. If we can drag him that far, we can lash his legs to the beam.'

'Go for it! Twenty yards that way,' Arnulf pointed down the corridor away from the main lounge, 'is the laundry room. You'll need to take care crossing it. It may be staffed but you should be okay. You can't hear yourself think with those machines.'

'Okay and…'

'Far side is a staff cloakroom. Drop down into there and straight into the engine room across the corridor.'

'We need to break cover? Can't we get to it from the roof space?'

'Not unless you've got a chisel handy to break down the wall.'

Hilary stared at him, her eyes big.

'It'll be okay.' Arnulf patted the small hand, which was tightly gripping the edge of the metal framework.

Hilary eyes filled with tears, her smile watery. She wiped them away with the back of her hand. 'Don't worry about me. I'm saving up my nervous breakdown till we get out of here.'

'We've not come this far to fail now.' The big man grinned up at her. 'Besides, Sean Terry hates losing agents and I'll never hear the end of it, if I manage to lose you two. You'll be fine. Even if you are seen, no one knows who you are. There's dozens of kids around here, you could easily be one of them. And the engine room won't be manned,' he added quickly. 'On the far wall is a turbine. That's your way out. It's caged for safety but it comes off. I tried it one time, when I was searching for a fire exit, in case I ever had to get out quick.

'Don't forget to wedge the blades; you'll be cut to ribbons else.' He twisted round, pointing down at the floor. 'Scott, pass me Pete's gun, you can use that. *And get a grip;* I need your help to lift the body into the roof space. They may find it in a couple of hours but, hopefully, by then you'll be long gone.'

Scott stared down at the body on the floor, a bright stain on the back of the jacket where the bullet had penetrated the man's heart. Vaguely, he recalled the ripped jacket worn by Tulsa soaked with blood. Confused, he stared up at the figure on the chair.

Arnulf followed the direction of his gaze. 'I carry a spare, small calibre.' He pointed to his ankle. 'Does the job and doesn't make a mess like the Colt Pete carried. Came in useful today. Can you use a gun?'

'I can. Scott? For pity's sake…' Hilary's voice quivered.

Scott stared at the tear on her cheek. Like a bolt of lightning, his senses hurtled back, reality hitting home. *They were alive. They were actually alive! They'd been given a second chance.* Bending down, he dragged the gun clear of Pete's body trying to avoid looking at the dead face, its sunspecs knocked aslant when the body hit the floor. The weapon was surprisingly heavy, heavier than the one Tulsa had carried. He stepped up onto the table and passed it up.

'I'm…'

'No sorries, Scott. We're alive that's all that matters.'

Scott nodded, his smile hesitant. Catching hold of the metal framework, he swung himself up into the ceiling space.

Unlike the dark cavern of the air-conditioning unit, light from below filtered through the panels, leaving a sombre dusk quite different from the hostile darkness of the metal tube. Above him, no more than shoulder height, was a flat roof supported by a double row of stout wooden uprights. Scott stared at them uneasily, wondering how far underground they were and how much weight they were carrying. Recalling the gradual slope of the air duct, he reckoned the roof to be just under the surface. Most likely, loose rock and earth had been scattered on top for camouflage.

It was a long narrow space, cluttered with the usual builders' paraphernalia, lengths of cable running from one end to the other. Down the middle ran a galvanised air duct which rested in a cradle on short metal stirrups. Spaced evenly, these were bolted onto transverse beams, the light framework of the false ceiling pinned to the underside. On either side, partition walls of double block work poked up into the space, reflecting the run of the corridor below with its office-like rooms, the space between the blocks filled with polystyrene foam for insulation. At the far end was a solid brick wall. If Arnulf was right, the cloakroom lay just beyond.

He leant down putting his weight on the metal strips used to keep the panels in place.

'These'll never hold us.'

'Use the beams. You'll be okay – you can't weigh more than a hundred and forty pounds.'

'A hundred and forty-five,' Scott managed to keep his tone light.

Arnulf gave a brief nod and, lifting the slumped torso high into the air, held it steady. Scott grabbed at the arms and pulled. The head flopped backwards, the dead eyes staring up at him. Scott felt his stomach lurch, wanting to throw up. Keeping his face averted, he edged back along the beam, slowly dragging the body after him, its jacket snagging on the rough metal. One of its arms flopped down, jerking erratically across the ceiling panels, the ring on its left hand rapping noisily.

Hilary shot him an anxious look and passed across the long piece of wire. Feeling sick as a dog, Scott worked it under the knees and, looping it round the beam, used the end with the plug to tie a knot.

'That's good enough.' Arnulf popped his head through the hole in the ceiling.

Scott wiped his hands down his jeans. He crawled to the opening, ignoring Hilary's sympathetic gaze. 'What now?'

'When you get out, someone should be waiting.'

'Who?'

'No idea.' Arnulf stepped back down onto the floor and shrugged on his jacket, the button straining to fasten across his chest. It was weird, as if the fabric contained magical properties that changed the wearer into a wax work, his stance instantly becoming rigid and wooden again. 'Got a message a while back that Terry wanted me out. Took no notice, then a couple of nights ago someone contacted me.'

'Who?' Hilary repeated.

'No idea. Never did see the guy's face. Told him about my fire exit and he checked it out. Said he'd be back but never showed.' Scott grimaced, guiltily aware he was responsible for Beau not keeping his promise.

'If no one is waiting, head straight for the hills. There's a good path, six or seven miles will take you to a village. Tourists occasionally use it in winter for skiing. Go to the hotel, ask for Elsa. She's a friend. Incidentally, she was the one Terry contacted first. Tell her.'

'Aren't you coming?' Hilary said, a pleading note in her voice.

A flicker of amusement broke into the stolid face. 'Impossible! I'm too big to go crawling around up there. One false move and I'd bring the whole lot down. Besides, if I don't return...' He left the words unsaid. 'When you catch up with Terry, warn him not to storm this place. It's rigged to flood the air-conditioning with carbon monoxide. And there's a load of innocent kids still here; at least half your group besides regular staff.'

'I thought they'd already left,' Hilary said.

'Not this lot. These are the kids they offer jobs; the ones without families, with no one to ask why they didn't return, and always the most easily led by that communist claptrap. Hurry now, before they come looking.'

'Won't Pete be missed?'

'I'll tell them he volunteered to burn the bodies in the furnace.'

A shiver of outrage and disgust swept through Scott, all of a sudden glad Pete was dead.

'See you back in the States.' Arnulf made to fit the panel back into place.

'Wait.' Hilary put out a hand. 'Promise you'll get out. We owe you our lives.'

'I'll do my damnedest,' he said and closed up the ceiling before she could say anything further.

'Do you think we'll ever see him again?' Scott whispered, following Hilary's jeans-clad legs along the beam, the sole of her trainers flashing like the scut of a rabbit. He moved slowly, uncertain how much weight the narrow beams could take, although neither of them was exactly large.

Hilary called over her shoulder, her reply lost in a whirring of machinery coming from up ahead. He didn't bother asking her to repeat it. It didn't matter anyway. It was unlikely Arnulf would get out whatever the man said about Sean Terry hating to lose his agents. No way could he just walk out. His only chance was if a rescue party was already waiting, like he said.

Shinning over the partitions proved easy, and within moments they were facing the brick wall. Below them, the noise of the machines in the laundry room sounded like a symphony orchestra at full gallop, the drum in the washing machines thudding heavily as it spun round, with metal fastenings on clothes slapping noisily against the metal frame of the driers. Scott sat back on his knees examining the wall for gaps. Nothing obvious apart from a neat hole incised through the brickwork where the heating duct passed through. He tugged at Hilary's sleeve. 'It's a dead end. We have to go back.'

Shrugging off his hand, Hilary got gingerly to her feet, keeping her head bent to avoid hitting it on the roof. Holding onto one of the uprights, she edged slowly along the wall, testing every brick with her fingers. She pointed triumphantly. In the darkest corner of the apex where the roof met the outer wall, successive layers of brick were missing, leaving a gap large enough to crawl through. 'Whoever sussed this out was a genius.'

'It was Beau.'

Astonished, she swung round, her mouth half open ready to ask a question. Losing her balance, her arms whirled frantically teetering on the edge of the light-weight panels. Scott grabbed her, pulling her upright.

'Don't do that,' she said crossly, brushing away his hand.

Scott grinned with relief. 'Which, save your life or scare you?'

'Both! You did say Beau, didn't you?'

'I did, but it's a long story. I'll tell you later.'

'I'll keep you to that if there is a later. I'll go first, I'm thinner than you. Here,' she slipped out of her jacket. 'Hold this.'

Clasping the low wall with both hands, she positioned her head, torso and one leg along the narrow ledge, keeping her weight on her second leg. Balancing carefully, her face turned sideways, she began to slide up her other leg. Scott could see the effort it was taking to keep her balance on the narrow brick shelf, the hand on the nearside of the wall white with strain. She rested a moment then, carefully repeating the manoeuvre, inched her foot down the far side, tumbling down off the wall and out of sight. Scott caught the sound of her feet crunching against some loose mortar and heard a whispered, 'Give me your jacket and be careful – the ledge this side is pretty dicey.'

Mimicking Hilary's action, Scott lay prone on the wall. It was a close fit, his back scraping the low roof. Unable to see anything, he scrabbled for a foothold on the rough ledge and felt Hilary grab his foot guiding it down onto a solid piece of brick.

Below them, the washroom seemed bathed in silence. Scott hoped that meant the place was deserted, rather than someone reading a newspaper while sitting on the toilet. Keeping one hand firmly on the wall, he knelt down and carefully prised up the panel nearest them.

'It's safe,' he called over his shoulder and lifted the panel away.

The washroom was quite small, with just enough room for a toilet and wash basin. Showing Hilary how to clamber down, using the top of the cistern as a foot rest, he ran over to the door and eased it open. The corridor was silent.

'What about...?' She pointed to the hole in the ceiling.

'Oh heck, I forgot about that. We daren't leave it.'

Leaping back up onto the cistern, he tried to fix the panel across the hole. The flimsy material snagged on the edge, leaving a gap.

'It's not straight.'

He shrugged. 'It'll have to do.'

Tentatively, he eased open the door to the engine room to be greeted by the hum of well-oiled machinery. Facing them was a vast control panel covered in dials, its flashing knobs proof that it was working hard. Above it, heavy iron brackets set at intervals pinned a nest of piping to the ceiling, the far wall covered with yet more levers and dials. Scott recognised a gadget similar to the one that had stood in the garage at the cottage, but on a much larger scale, which controlled the output of electricity from the small wind turbine on the hill.

On the far wall, iron steps led up to a platform. At waist level, a vast cylindrical drum connected a giant fan, quietly revolving within its rigid polymer casement, to the main air-conditioning unit. Its sides were of fine steel mesh and through them daylight was trickling. Scott flew up the steps and tugged at the metal cage, ducking under the pipework to attack the far side. 'Arnulf was right. It's only held by screws, and it's hinged at the bottom.' He pointed to a curved metal flange lying flush against the brickwork of the wall. 'If I can loosen this side and lift it clear, we'll be able to climb through, no problem.' Leaning out over the steps, he stared round. 'There has to be tools somewhere.'

Hilary nodded and, heedless of the noise, began ferreting about in the drawers in the base of the console. 'This any good?' She waved an electric screwdriver in the air and, pulling out a wrench, held it up. 'Or this? There's all sorts in here.'

'I'll take the screwdriver. Thanks.' Scott pounded down the steps, leaping back up two at a time. 'Watch the door, will you.'

Within seconds, the first of the screws had dropped with a sharp click onto the metal platform, six more rapidly following. Scott tugged at the side of the cylinder and it broke loose. He pulled the half-piece away and it fell back resting against its hinges, and leaving a large gap.

Scott leaned back down over the railings, smiling triumphantly. 'Come on, Hilary, let's get out of here.' Then he froze, his victorious smile wiped off. Tucked under the platform, almost lost in darkness of the corner, were a row of long, black cylinders, the letters CO – carbon monoxide – stamped in black, a faded yellow triangle cut through by an exclamation mark visible only on the top layer.

Scott sank down on the edge of the platform and buried his head in his arms, his feet resting on the top step. 'I have to go back,' he muttered.

'*What!*' Hilary screamed. She tore up the steps and peered out through the slowly revolving blades. 'You crazy or something. We're out of here, home free. An hour ago, I wouldn't have given us one chance in a million of making it out alive.' She dragged on his arm, trying to force him to his feet. 'It's still daylight, Scott. Come on, please, I'm begging you. Whatever it is, leave it.'

'I can't, it's Jameson.'

'*Jay!* You said Beau.' She sat down beside him, clutching Pete's gun to her lap. 'Jay's in London… isn't he?' she finished uncertainly.

'That's just the point,' Scott said, his voice rising close to tears. 'He's here. Didn't you get woken up in the night?'

'No! One of the girls said there was a ruckus in the boys' dorm but I took no notice.' Hilary screwed up her face. 'I was asleep. Why…'

'Jay took that job, the one we were so worried about. It landed him here. I mean, what are the chances?' Hilary stared. 'It's crazy, I know,' Scott agreed. 'I keep thinking I'm going mad.' He pointed to the blades of the turbine, its thick sheath of curved metal splattered with the desiccated remains of squashed insects. 'I feel like one of them. One moment carefree, flying around outside sipping nectar; the next, dragged inside and squashed. There's nothing those insects can do. And there's nothing I can do either. I have to go get him,' he said miserably, his hands trembling. Holding them against his chest, he added in a sombre tone, 'They've been using drugs on him.'

'In that case, I'm coming with you.' Hilary leaned her head against Scott's shoulder. 'We started this together. We'll finish it together.'

'Not this time.' Scott's smile was painful, mirroring his eyes. 'I've done you enough harm. Besides, you have a family.'

'So do you,' Hilary retorted. 'What about your mother and sister?'

'It's not the same without Dad,' Scott replied simply. 'Anyway, I need you to go for help. Arnulf said someone would be waiting. Tell them about the gas.' He pointed to the cylinders, a dark forbidding mass of huddled metal.

Hilary twisted sideways, poking the barrel of the gun hard into his chest. He flinched back. 'You suffering from a death wish, Scott Anderson? What the hell are you trying to prove? You're a stupid, *stupid… fool!* I could kill you for being so stupid. You can't possibly go back on your own. What happens if they've already found Pete? I'm the only one that knows how to use a gun, remember.' She waved it belligerently through the air.

'It'll be all right, I promise,' Scott shook his head, nervously eyeing the barrel of the pistol once again aimed at his heart, hoping Hilary wasn't crazy enough to have released the safety. He pointed with his finger to the pipes carving through the air. 'I'll use the air conditioning pipes. I've done it before.'

'*You've done it before?* When?'

'Last night. I told you, I found Jay.'

Hilary sighed heavily. She leaned in, the barrel of the Colt pressing heavily against Scott's ribs, kissing him fiercely on the lips. 'Okay! This time I'll stay but don't you dare get killed – you hear?'

TWENTY-NINE

Scott stared down into a laboratory, brightly coloured graphics spilling out from computer screens. Just visible at the far end of the room, a white-coated figure was writing on a clipboard. Back turned, he moved steadily from screen to screen copying information. Scott caught the sound of laughter and noticed two guys huddled round a monitor, a third rushing over from the far side of the lab anxious to join in the merriment. How could they be so cheerful? Weren't they aware that an execution had been ordered not an hour since. Scott stared angrily at the figures. Of course they weren't – only Vasilov knew that. These people were part of the hidden city, either because they believed or because of the money they were earning. What had Seagar said… something about a bonus and a luxury weekend away? Even among sixth-formers, most openly admitted that money was their goal when choosing a career. But money before principles was something else again. And what about guys like Jameson who needed drugs before they could be persuaded to join the movement. If they didn't eventually accept the regime, were they also disposed of? Scott shuddered, suddenly icy cold. *He had to find Jameson and fast.*

He had eventually found his way into the air-conditioning unit through a plate fixed to the underside of the large galvanised duct. Used for maintenance and cleaning, a series of screens in ascending order of density, designed to rid the incoming air of particles of debris, had been welded across the pipe-work close to the turbine and had blocked any entry at that point.

At first Scott moved quickly, blessing the building's need for lights even in the daytime, the illuminated rectangles easy to follow. He soon found that light also meant people, and dropped to a slow crawl, holding his breath every time a door opened or shut. Despite this precaution, he'd nearly been caught crossing the lounge area and the incident had left him shaking with fear. Two girls in jeans and T-shirts were collecting up rubbish from the night before, putting it into black bin bags, casually plumping cushions on the sofas. He stopped, hoping they wouldn't be long, but when he went to move again the metal button on his fly caught in the grille. Stupidly, he'd tugged at it. It flew out and he overbalanced, banging his elbow on the metal wall, the sound reverberating along the duct. One of the girls had glanced up curiously calling out to her friend. At that moment the girl had switched on the vacuum cleaner, her friend's warning lost in a roar of sound. With a shrug and a final glance upwards, the girl had continued her work, picking up an empty crisp packet off the floor. It had left Scott really rattled and, under cover of the noise, he had scuttled along the pipe-work desperate to put distance between him and the cleaning staff, uncaring of the direction. He felt like the bird that, last spring, had built its nest in the roof space above his window. Every night, until its young were fully fledged and flown away, he'd gone to sleep to the sound of rustling and the patter of tiny claws as the birds settled down for the night.

Retracing his steps to the main duct, he crawled to the next turning, listening intently for the identifying click of a computer mouse. He peered down, seeing the monitor dark, the bank of computers turned off. For a moment he was scared, and then he saw feet protruding from the bottom of the quilt.

Trying to make as little noise as possible, he hopped down to the ground seeing his friend fast asleep. Flicking on the computer, he tiptoed to the door and tried the handle, relieved to find it locked. Returning to the desk, he waited impatiently for the machine to boot up. Quickly connecting to the music centre, he searched for Jameson's favourite piece – Vivaldi's *Four Seasons*. Turning the volume high, he shook his friend awake. He looked ghastly, his skin blotchy and feverish.

'Is it tea-time? I must have fallen asleep.' Jameson sat up. He stared vacantly. His eyes focussed. 'Sc…'

Scott put his finger to his lips, mouthing the word – quiet.

'I didn't tell them,' Jameson whispered. 'They wanted me to, but I didn't. I said it was my brother.' He leaned back closing his eyes. 'I'm so thirsty,' he moaned.' He pointed to the glass of water on the bedside cabinet. 'Can you pass it for me?'

Scott carefully held the glass to his lips, Jameson's hands shaking too badly to hold the glass steady. He drank eagerly like a man that hadn't seen water for the longest while, gulping it down.

In the background, the solo violin flew through a series of loud cadenzas. Scott got to his feet. 'Jay, I'm taking you to hospital. Okay?'

The boy in the bed nodded tiredly. 'Okay, but can you help me dress? I really don't feel too good.' He closed his eyes, then started awake shivering violently. 'What am I doing here? Why aren't I at home?'

Holy crap! Scott got him to his feet and fumbled his arms into his jacket, not bothering with shoes, aware of the enormity of the task ahead. Hilary was right. He did need her, he'd never manage alone. 'I've phoned for an ambulance. It's waiting for us outside. But, first, we have to get you out of here.' He pointed to the door, Jay's eyes following dully. 'That door's locked so we're going through a tunnel.' He kept his tone patient, articulating each word slowly like speaking to a child. He pointed to the ceiling. Obediently, Jay stared up into the gaping hole. 'It's not far but you have to keep quiet – no one must hear you. Promise?' He climbed onto the desk, pulling Jameson up with him.

Jameson stared round the room, his eyes slowly zigzagging towards the door, stopping to examine every item of furniture as if he had never seen it before.

Scott waited, forcing himself to stay calm, every nerve in his body jangling and on edge, hoping that Hilary had escaped and was among friends. It was all taking far too long. At any moment someone could come in, but he daren't hurry his friend.

Jameson turned back, a puzzled frown on his face as if he was trying to work out why they were heading up into the roof, when there was a door. Raising his hand, he pointed upwards. 'Home is that way?'

Scott hauled in a breath. 'Yes,' he said firmly, '*home is that way*. But you have to be quiet. One sound and we won't make it.' Scott gazed at his friend, noticing the whites of his eyes were deep yellow. He really was ill. Even stepping onto the desk had seemed to exhaust him.

'I can do this, Scott.' Jameson lifted his foot into the air. Realising what he wanted, Scott bent down making a step with his hands. 'But I hurt, really, really bad. It's like every bone in my body is on fire. But I'll hold it together, I promise. Just get me home.'

By the time they reached the main lounge area, Scott's nerves were shredded, flinching at every sound, and he felt shattered as if he had traversed the entire globe several times over. But apart from his slow and obviously painful progress, Jameson had kept his promise and hadn't uttered a sound. Even so, they'd been forced to stop every few metres either because there was someone about or to allow Jameson to rest, his breathing becoming more and more ragged.

For the umpteenth time he urged his friend on, promising they were almost there, the glow from the lights below emphasising the suffering on Jay's face. Before Hilary had removed the gun from his ribs, she had made him promise that if rescuing Jameson was impossible, he would let it go and get out. Adding, 'I thought the kiss might make you see reason.' He'd been glad to give that promise. The idea of meeting up with Vasilov or Seagar again was something he daren't give thought to. Now, after seeing how ill Jay was, it was a promise he was willing to break aware, that if positions were reversed, Jay would never think twice about giving his life for a best mate.

All at once, the light changed and Scott spotted the open grille. They'd made it. Triumphantly, he half-turned seeing Jameson collapsed in a heap behind him.

'Scott?' Hilary's head ducked up in front of him. 'Thank God.'

'What the hell are you still doing here? I told you to go – get away.'

Hilary grinned. 'You know me – hate taking orders. Besides, I thought you might need some help. *Oh my God*, I was right.' She pointed with trembling fingers at the body slumped on the metal floor. 'Is that Jay?'

'I think he's dead.'

'Budge up. Let me see.'

Scott swung down onto the ground allowing Hilary to take his place.

'He's not dead, he's just fainted,' she called, bending over

Jameson's inert form. 'When you need water, why, oh why, isn't there ever any around? Scott, you'll have to pull him out by his arms.'

Distraught, Scott shook his head.

'Oh, for goodness sake!' she snapped. 'He's unconscious, he won't feel a thing. And hurry. We've just about used up our ration of luck for the next fifty years.'

Pulling at the slumped figure, Scott dragged him down onto the floor, wincing sympathetically as Jay's legs crashed to the ground. If he wasn't dead before, he soon would be. With Hilary helping, he hoisted Jay over his shoulder, staggering across to the steps, pausing on each one to take a breath, the weight of the unconscious body pressing against his shoulder making it harder to draw in air.

Footsteps sounded in the corridor and he froze. If someone came in now, they were helpless.

'Go on, Scott, four more to go. We can make it.' Scott felt the sharp edge of the gun barrel.

'You can't,' he protested, his breath coming in fits and starts.

'Yes, I can. It's my job remember. Three to go.'

Still no one had come in; the footsteps silenced. Hitching Jay into an easier position, he pulled up another step. In the background came the sound of running water from the toilet and his breath eased.

'Two steps, Scott.'

He pulled up again, his arm on the metal banister keeping him upright. Even play fighting, Jay had never been easy to carry, both taller and heavier than Scott. But now, it was as if an iron weight had been attached to his feet.

Hilary darted past. 'Too bad if they come in now,' she called and jammed the butt of her pistol into the narrow space between the shaft and rotor blades. They swayed, gradually falling still.

Laboriously, Scott manhandled the inert body down onto the platform, viewing the turbine with dismay. Easy enough for a small person to scramble through but Jay...

'Jay, *Jay*, can you hear me?' He patted his friend's face.

Jay stirred and sat up, holding his head. 'Are we home yet, Scott?'

'Almost. Hilary's here.'

'Hilary? What's she doing here? That's right, she's your girlfriend. About time, too.'

Hilary patted his arm affectionately. 'Jay. I need you to crawl.'

'Okay, if you say so. Where to?' He stared vaguely, his gaze wandering, without focus.

'You go, Hilary,' Scott hissed. Then, in a louder voice: 'Hilary will show you the way.'

The sultry heaviness of the morning had cleared away, but the day had kept its promise of rain and a fine drizzle filled the air already darkening towards night, although it wasn't cold – at least not yet.

The fresh air seemed to revive Jameson. He sat up looking about him in a dazed fashion. At least he was conscious, for which Scott was grateful but it was still a huge mountain they had to climb. The only sensible way was for Hilary to go and get help – but he doubted she would see it like that.

'Take his other arm, Hilary. Let's see if we can find some shelter.'

He got Jameson slowly to his feet. They faced out across a platform of rock overlooking a long narrow gorge, as if someone had taken an axe to the mountain and split it apart; its slopes strewn with loose boulders and a brisk wind funnelling along the gap. The turbine had been built into the rock face about halfway up, the slope below them strew with loose boulders. On either side of the long winding chasm, mountains continued their steady climb towards the summit, their shadows daunting against a sultry sky. A sudden gust of wind caught Scott unawares and he heeled back, stumbling over a rock, which rattled noisily to the bottom of the gorge. What an astonishing place? A death trap for the unwary.

Slowly, with Hilary taking Jameson's weight on the other side, they staggered a few steps, anxiously looking for a pathway. Without warning, the sound of applause broke the silence. Vasilov emerged from behind a shoulder of rock, a mocking smile on his face. He clapped the palms of his hands slowly together, the sound hollow in the pure air.

'Oh no,' Hilary gasped.

'My dear young people. Did you really imagine that Seagar would fail to install CCTV in that young man's room... ' He pointed to the silent form leaning against Scott. 'With a rat somewhere in our organisation that we needed to flush out. So kind of you, Scott, to demonstrate how it got into a locked room without using a key. Actually...' He raised his fingers, his smile fixed and never flickering. 'We had two rats. Once we found the body of our man, it was but a simple matter to unearth the traitor. And while Seagar dealt with the security issue, some friends and I thought to take a short walk. Very pleasant at this time of the afternoon. You never know what you will find... as I have proved.

'Please don't make a fuss. I never carry a gun...' He undid the button on his jacket and held it wide open. Scott spotted the neat pistol tucked in the waistband. 'But for you, I make an exception.'

Scott stared at the man's right hand, noticing his knuckles grazed and swollen. 'You beat Arnulf.'

'Oh! Was that his name? I never bother to enquire about the hired help. In any case, in my book traitors deserve to die. I simply made sure it would happen. I dislike blood, but like this weapon, on occasions I make an exception. Now, are you coming with me quietly? I can't wait all night; you've caused me enough trouble.' The tone of voice changed. 'I'm happy to shoot you here if you prefer.'

Hilary had not said a word, standing motionless by Scott's side. Suddenly she screamed, the shrill sound echoing on and on through the silence of the mountain range.

As if she had gone berserk, she cannoned into Scott, aiming punches at his chest, screaming wildly all the while. '*I hate you, Scott Anderson*. This is all your fault. You wouldn't let it alone. You just had to play the big shot and go back for your friend. We'd have been free. Don't you realise – free!'

Alarmed and scared, Scott took a hurried step backwards, trying to keep out of range of the flailing arms. Vanished was the calm figure, the person forcing him back and back a shrieking virago.

Vasilov laughed. 'What a delightful end to a great friendship.'

'*Friendship!*' Hilary hurled over her shoulder, poking Scott hard in the chest. He hurriedly backed away, determined not to hit back. Hilary surged forward again, almost spitting into his face. 'I'm sixteen, Scott. I don't want to die because of you and your stupid ideas. *I want to live.* Get it? I want to live. I'll change sides – do anything, crawl, beg – if it helps me to live.'

'My dear young lady. Why didn't you say so before? Do step aside while I remove this pest. Then we will have a talk. I can always use a loyal servant, especially one that wants to live as badly as you.'

Hilary cannoned into Scott, knocking him to the ground and topping down on top of him.

Winded, and as much use as a beached whale, Scott caught the scrape of metal against plastic, a rush of wind, and then a sound he knew well… the crack of gunfire – two shots.

Gun in hand, the stocky figure of Vasilov stared at Hilary, his mouth open with astonishment. Half-upright, both arms at a stretch, a smoking gun clasped in her fingers, Hilary stared back; her finger poised to fire again, her gaze steady and her expression calm as if the fracas of a moment before had never happened. Slowly, his amused expression vanished, wiped away. Scott watched him crumple to his knees then tumble in a heap on the ground.

Silently, Hilary got to her feet. She walked across and stared down at the body. 'He deserved to die, Scott. Don't ask me to be sorry 'cause I'm not. Not one bit.'

'B-b-but,' he stuttered.

Hilary shrugged. 'I couldn't think of any other way of reaching the gun. You didn't think it was for real, did you?'

Scott slowly sat up, his breathing still painful from the pummelling. 'I – I – *Holy crap*. Okay, I admit it. I did,' he said shamefaced.

Hilary laughed. 'After all this time, Scott Anderson, you thought I'd turn you in for a rat like Vasilov. I must be a better actress than I thought. Give me a hand. We need to hide Vasilov's body before any of the guards come looking.'

'Push it over the edge. With luck, they'll think he tripped.'

The Russian's body was heavy, the fabric of his jacket constantly catching on the rough ground. Scott watched it slowly tumble out of sight. Strange, like Hilary he found himself quite devoid of pity.

He straightened up, surreptitiously rubbed at his chest bone. Acting or no acting, he'd have a massive bruise tomorrow. But who cared? At least they'd have *a tomorrow*. He swung round in panic, hearing the familiar click as the bolt on an automatic was drawn back. Then a voice cut through the twilight.

'*Vos mains en l'air.*'

THIRTY

Scott leaned against the canvas side-panel of a truck, no energy and no hope left. Once the guy with the automatic had realised they didn't know French, he had switched to English, calling for back-up on his radio. None of the men guarding them had asked questions but Scott had the distinct impression that they were waiting for something or someone.

He scrolled back over the events of the day. An endless day. Even now it wasn't late – a little after five. It was the onset of darkness that made it seem later, the sky swathed in rain-clouds behind which the moon would hide. He recalled the words of the Russian dismissing any chance of escape. He should have guessed they would have outside patrols. Hilary's head rested tiredly against his shoulder. If they were asked he would admit to shooting Vasilov. Her pistol was gone but, so far, no one had been harmed. Quite the reverse, the soldiers lifting Jay into the truck. Now, he lay on a makeshift bed covered with a blanket. But, at least, so far they'd not been dispatched back to the detention centre. It didn't matter anyway; he had no fight left. They had won.

In the distance, he caught the sound of an engine. Someone was on the way to get them. Abruptly, it cut out. A door slammed. The noise too rough for a car more like a jeep.

Someone shouted. Unbelieving, Scott leapt to his feet staring in bewilderment at the two figures coming into sight. Even hating the man, there was no one on earth he'd rather see this minute, other than his dad and Tulsa, alive and well. But Sean Terry, his jacket flapping loosely round his bony frame, meant everything was all right.

'Scott! Is that really you? Hilary, too! If I was a believing man, I'd say it was a miracle.' The Irish tones swept through the burgeoning darkness as the agent shinned over the tailboard.

'This chap's come to look at your friend. I hear he's in a bad way.' He pointed with his thumb over his shoulder indicating his companion waiting to follow him into the truck, a small red cross clearly visible on the lapel of his uniform jacket. '*Hell!* By rights, you should be dead. I might have guessed you'd find some way to stay alive.' The maverick agent stared grimly into their faces. 'When my man reported Pete had got you, I feared the worst. He doesn't let people slip through his fingers…'

Scott grabbed at the word. 'Your man? *You mean Beau?*'
Sean Terry nodded. 'Then he's in terrible danger – you have to get him…'

'*Easy! Easy!* It's okay.' Sean Terry patted him on the shoulder. 'We got the coach safe already. So, Doc, what's the verdict?'

Scott slumped back down onto the bench, his legs no longer able to support him. He watched the medic insert a drip into the back of Jameson's hand. 'Is he going to be okay?'

'The drip should help. But his pulse is all over the place. Drugs?'

Scott nodded, hoping he wouldn't be responsible for yet another death. There were so many, he'd almost lost count. 'He said he was thirsty and his eyes have gone yellow.'

'Liver, I expect. Some sort of allergic reaction to whatever they pumped into him. But at this stage I'm only guessing. The drip will help steady his blood pressure but there's nothing more I can do till we get him to hospital and run some tests.' The medic stood up staring keenly at Scott and Hilary. 'You two look in bad shape, too. Can I help?'

'Tired but okay,' Scott answered for them both.

'If you're sure?' He broke into a different language which Scott didn't recognise. The guidebook, he'd skimmed through on the plane, said that Switzerland was home to numerous languages, including French, German, Italian and something called Romansch, the sounds much crisper and harder than the French language spoken among the soldiers. One of the soldiers got to his feet saluting and replying in the same tongue. The medic switched back to English. 'This chap says they've got a couple of guys back there with bullet wounds in them. Know anything about it?' He grinned at the expressions of alarm confronting him across the truck. 'I don't mean the bullet wounds. Our lads said one of their patrols bumped into them shortly after picking you up and they opened fire.'

'I expect they were looking for us,' Hilary cautiously volunteered.

'Aah, right.'

'Obliged,' Sean Terry called after the disappearing figure.

'Who are they?' Hilary broke in.

'Swiss army on manoeuvres,' Sean Terry said casually. 'Happens every year with permission from the French. There's not much flat ground in Switzerland. This time, though, the US of A asked to borrow them for twenty-four hours.' The agent grinned suddenly, his blue eyes losing their bleak look, as if laughing at some inner joke. 'I guess you could say these lads are the Swiss branch of the American services. And, thank God for it. If those guys had found you first, we'd have had two more corpses on our hands and been in a right mess. Who's your friend?' His keen glance raked the makeshift bed.

'It's Jay, I mean Jameson, from school. He was kidnapped and brought here. I had to get him out. The carbon monoxide. *Holy crap!* I forgot the carbon monoxide.' Scott made to leapt off the back of the lorry and found a rifle pointing at his chest.

'Are we prisoners?' he gasped, sitting down again.

Sean Terry laughed. 'Not exactly. They're under instructions to keep you safe at any cost. Which means you ain't going nowhere without them.'

Scott produced a weak grin. 'Reminds me of that Dutch policeman. He followed me everywhere too.'

'Do I hear my name taken in vain?'

'Beau!'

Before the soldiers could react, Scott had leapt off the back of the truck and ran across to Beau, hugging him tightly. 'It's amazing! I'm so sorry,' he yelled.

Beau pushed him away, regarding him intently. 'What on earth for, kiddo?'

'For putting you in danger.'

'Me! In your dreams. Safe as houses, I was.' Beau wrapped a friendly arm round Scott's shoulder and steered him back to the truck, calmly pushing aside the barrel of the gun aimed at his chest. The soldiers regarded him warily, not quite sure what to make of this badly dressed apparition who exuded confidence, even when ringed by soldiers with automatic weapons.

Beau called out in French. The soldier nearest to him nodded and, parking his automatic against the side of the truck, disappeared into the dusk.

Sean Terry raised an eyebrow.

'I asked if there was anything to eat or drink. I'm sure these two kids are starving, I know I am.'

The gadget attached to Sean Terry's chest squawked loudly.

'Hang on, I need to get this,' he muttered. 'Yes, sir,' he said more loudly, speaking directly into the receiver. 'Quite safe. One minute…' He swivelled round, his expression once again businesslike, as if his lapse into jollity was a once in a lifetime occurrence, his tone of voice terse. 'What's this about carbon monoxide?'

'Arnulf, your agent. He said to tell you they would flood the place with gas if it was ever stormed,' Hilary reported. 'It's true, we saw the cylinders. It's haunted me ever since. Dozens of innocent kids will be killed. He saved us and they killed him… '

'Whoa! One thing at a time.' Sean Terry held up his hand, speaking rapidly into the radio-mike. 'I suggest using the backdoor and get the place secured.'

'The army are invading? Because of us?' Scott burst out.

'Sorry to disappoint,' Beau grinned. 'It's actually because of me. Tracing the headquarters of the bad guys.'

Scott pulled a face. After all they'd gone through, it would have been nice to hear that the President of the United States had given orders personally for them to be rescued.

He looked up to see two soldiers appear round the side of the truck, their hands clutching mugs of coffee and packets of biscuits wrapped in cellophane. Beau got to his feet and, nodding his thanks, handed them round. 'First thing I do when I get back, after taking a long shower and changing my clothes, is visit the finest restaurant in Oxford for a rare steak.'

The whirring sound of helicopter engines broke into the silence of the twilight. 'That's the signal to begin.' Still munching, Sean Terry got to his feet, peering round the flaps at the back of the truck. 'This time we're making damn sure they can't escape by air.' He sat down again. 'So, Stone, it's nice to know for once that you're actually glad to see me. While we wait for news, how about you fill me in?'

She shook her head. 'No, this is Scott's story. I only know bits – and I'm in a hurry to forget, not remember.' She shuddered. 'But how come you're here, Beau? Wait a moment, you're not that guy at the rally in Exeter, are you?'

'So much for not being recognised. That's twice now,' he complained.

'But the mark on your face?'

'Vegetable dye, it'll wear off.' Beau grinned. Leaning back against the canvas sides of the truck, he stretched out his long legs. 'Without it, I'm far too good-looking, never would have got away with it in a million years.'

'And the scar on your neck?' Scott gazed at the twisted mass of broken flesh. He'd be glad to get shot of this place too. He picked up his mug of coffee, wishing it was tea. Coffee might be okay in a crisis but tea was still better. 'It's pretty realistic.'

Beau's eyes sparkled. 'Pretty realistic! That's an understatement. It's totally brilliant.'

'You mean it's a transmitter?' Hilary leaned forward to touch the scar, running her fingers across it. 'It's lumpy.'

'And waterproof. Knew every step I took. Clever blighters, these Americans. Good job too. Without it, we'd have been scuppered.' He sat up abruptly. 'University's going to be deadly dull after crawling around the insides of a pipe for a week.' He paused. 'Apropos of nothing at all, your mate, James, was drivelling on and on about a message he had to give to Doug Randal – *your dad*! Can't wait to hear that story. He said, "Tell Dad to phone the President of Europe".'

All of a sudden, Scott collapsed into helpless giggles. He wasn't sure why but it was so funny.

Hilary grabbed his hand, peering at him closely. 'You okay?'

Scott gave a loud hiccup and hastily covered his mouth. 'I guess so,' he gasped, as a second spasm of laughter wracked his body. 'It's…'

'Reaction,' Beau chimed in. 'Gets you like that sometimes.'

Scott shook his head, swallowing down the bubbling gales of mirth. He wiped his eyes on his sleeve. 'I suppose that might have something to do with it,' he agreed. 'I was desperate to get a message to you. If you remember, I tried before that last run.' Beau nodded. 'All I could do was tell James. *And he got it wrong.* Like a Chinese whisper.' Suddenly serious, he aimed his words at the American listening intently.

'That phone call I overheard at the UN…'

'You mean… *that was the President of Europe.* What the devil is the man's name?'

'Igor Rabinovitch,' Beau's lazy tones broke in. 'Born in East Germany in the nineteen-seventies.'

'Hmm! Go on.'

'The man on the other end was called Vasilov. I noticed his car leaving the UN, and recognised the Russian flag.'

'Naval attaché, Russian embassy.'

Sean Terry rounded on Beau. '*Do you know everything?*'

Beau grinned, lightening the tension in the air. 'What about him, Scott?'

'We met him today,' Scott said soberly. 'He gave the order for us to be killed.' He paused to exchange glances with Hilary. She shook her head warningly and he hurriedly lurched into a brief account of what had taken place that morning, the horror of being recognised moments from freedom.

Without replying, Terry switched his attention back to Scott. 'So, which one is Mr Smith?'

Scott shrugged. 'Neither. He just laughed when I accused the President of Europe.'

'So who the hell is it? This man – Vasi…'

'Vasilov,' Beau corrected.

'Yeah! Him too. Is he Smith?'

'No. I only figured it out a minute ago, when you said the US of A had borrowed the Swiss army.'

'Don't follow.' Sean Terry glowered.

'How could one person ever possess the sort of power needed to create a nuclear explosion? Look at Geneva – they were after us in minutes. And that Norwegian woman whose car was blown up? When Hilary said he wouldn't get away with it, Vasilov just laughed. Told us the coach would fall into a ravine and everyone would be killed bar the driver, and reports of the incident would get lost.'

'You saying the Russians are behind it?'

'I think so.'

'Makes sense,' Beau said. 'When the wall came down, the Russians lost out big time. Managed to get rid of the US for a few years, only to find Europe breathing down their necks. You think Smith is a sort of code-word?'

'For the break-up of Europe, yes,' Scott agreed. 'If they manage that, the Russians...'

'Become top dog again,' Sean Terry added thoughtfully.

'Bravo, youngster!' Beau applauded, clapping his hands loudly together to the astonishment of the watching soldiers.

'What's going to happen now, Mr Terry?'

'Why the hell can't you call me Sean?' Scott shrugged. 'If you're right...'

'He is,' Hilary said fiercely.

Scott blushed and Beau grinned. 'Love's young dream.'

'If you're right,' the American repeated his words, 'the Russian representative to the UN will be called in to explain himself and, with luck, asked to leave. And if things go real well, Ambassadors in other European countries will get their knuckles rapped too.'

'Is that all?' Scott said, disappointment marking his voice.

'You can't touch people like Vasilov; accuse him of jaywalking and he'll claim diplomatic immunity all the way to the Pole. Forget it.'

'Not this time,' Scott said, his face creasing up into a grin.

'Scott?' Hilary stared beseechingly, her face starkly white.

'You know something I don't,' Sean Terry snapped.

'He's dead.' Scott said. 'We shot him.'

Beau gave a long whistle of surprise.

'Was it you, Stone, or Scott?'

'It was me.' They spoke together. 'Does it matter?' Scott added. Sean Terry's blistering glance reminding Scott of a laser, able to cut through metal and see through lies.

Beau sat up, his gaze flipping from one to the other. 'It probably matters to the Russians. They won't be very pleased.'

'It was self-defence. He'd already tried once to kill us. And he admitted killing your man – Arnulf. And Scott would have been dead now if I hadn't,' Hilary begged. 'Will I have to stand trial?'

'Not a chance. US agent acting in the line of duty.'

'Ex-US agent. I retired, remember.'

'Did you? I guess I forgot to put the papers in.' Sean Terry's bleak eyes looked across at the young American girl, a hint of affection in their gaze. 'And once the story's been leaked to the press, that'll be that. Newspapers love a good spy mystery. Tell them, he's a spy working for the Russians; they'll be in seventh heaven for months. You'll probably get a medal.'

'But what about Rabinovitch? He's got to be punished.' Scott said.

Terry rolled his head as if the muscles in his neck were stiff. 'What you've just said, no way is it enough to put him on trial. You overheard a conversation – period. But I can promise you, the fall-out from the rumours will lose him the election and, in the next couple of years, a load of important people will lose their jobs.'

'But, that's so wrong.' Scott thumped his fists on his knees in frustration. 'He's a murderer!'

Sean Terry dumped the dregs of his coffee onto the ground and stood up, his expression bleak. 'Yeah, *ain't life a bitch!*' In the air, the muttering of the distant helicopters was joined by a new noise. It came close, the staccato rattling of its engine filling the air. 'Come on, helicopter's landing to get your friend to hospital.'

He nodded at the unconscious figure; drops of liquid from the saline drip sliding steadily down a plastic tube into the cannula in Jameson's hand.

After a moment or two, white-coated medics came into view carrying a stretcher and an oxygen cylinder. Manhandling the stretcher into the truck, they carefully transferred Jameson onto it. He stirred and moaned. 'Scott.'

Scott bent down and took his hand. 'It's okay, Jay. These guys are going to get you well again.'

'Then, can we go home?'

'Yeah, you can go home.' He bit his lip to stop himself adding: *But I can't. They blew my home up.*

'They'll be taking him to the hospital in Clermont Ferrand. Why don't you two go with him?' Terry broke in. 'Beau too. You'll find the other members of the coach there. We put them in a hotel for the night ringed by soldiers, so you'll be quite safe.'

Scott scrambled down onto the ground, turning to help Hilary. The soldiers ringing the truck stayed still. Their job was done. The kid and his friends were someone else's problem now.

'Get a good night's sleep and tomorrow you can get your lives back on track. We'll finish up here and join you later, once this little lot's wrapped up.'

'I haven't got a life to get back on track, Mr Terry.' The words spilled forcefully out of Scott's chest. 'Men like Vasilov and Rabinovitch have destroyed it, remember?' he said, his tone bitter.

'Scott?' Beau put his arm round Scott's shoulders. He shrugged it off.

'What the hell are you ranting on about now?' The agent gazed at Scott bemused.

'That guy, Arnulf. He put his life on the line for us – just like Tulsa did. Except you don't care about any of that, as long as your precious America is safe. Now he's dead and whose fault is it? It's mine!' He turned away, shielding his face. 'I seem to make a habit of killing the people who care for me,' he spat the words out bitterly, 'like Tulsa and my dad.'

Sean Terry started. 'But Bill's not dead,' he called sharply. 'We got him out. Didn't you know?'

'*Not dead!*' Scott echoed stupidly. 'But they found his body. We saw the flames.' He swayed and grabbed Hilary's hand.

'Hell! Someone give this lad a seat before he collapses.'

Beau leapt off the back of the truck, calling out in French. One of the soldiers sprang to his feet, pushing Scott down onto an empty fuel drum.

'Beau, tell those medics to hang on a minute. This is important.'

Beau nodded and disappeared at a run.

'Dad's alive?' Scott quavered.

'Hell, yes! Last time I heard, he was busily sorting out a computer somewhere in the North Sea.'

'But how did he get there?' Scott echoed stupidly, his head full of cotton wool.

'Doug and me, we took him.'

'I don't understand.'

'I thought we'd have a day or so. Tulsa had already left to get you when that old guy, the farmer, he phoned. He'd been tending to one of his sheep which was about to lamb. Said there was, "*one of them bloody foreigners,*" Sean Terry quoted, his Irish orgins once again overriding his Washington accent, 'hanging around the lane and he wondered if they had anything to do with that business last Easter. Your dad rang me. I told him to get out straight away and contacted Doug.'

'But the body?'

'Bill got off a lucky shot. Stopped the guy in his tracks. Doug had his quad bike and they headed for the river, where I met them. I guess that's why they torched the place. Revenge! I tried to phone Tulsa, to warn him not to let you go home, but I was too late. After that, I was playing catch up for a while.'

Beau came into view. He nodded. 'Waiting.'

Hilary shook her head tiredly. 'But the men at headquarters? Someone was killed there too.'

'Not our guys. It was our booby trap, though. After Pete, we moved around. If you'd rung in, you'd have got directions.'

Hilary flushed guiltily. 'My mobile was shot to pieces and I'd never bothered to memorise the number. Didn't think I'd ever need it again.'

Scott sat silently. He listened to the explanation but none of it made any sense except the one bit... his dad was alive. How or why, he didn't care. He was alive. Now, he really could get his life back on track. Tears swept across his eyes and he brushed them away, thinking of his mother and sister. At last, he'd know what it was like to be part of a family. And he didn't care where – not now. He got to his feet, no longer tired, eager to take up his life again, and smiled at Hilary, his eyes sparkling with confidence.

She stared at him astonished. 'Feeling better?'

'I'm fine. Couldn't be finer. Sean?'

'Finally,' the agent exclaimed. 'Why the sudden change of heart?'

'I couldn't call you that before, because I never trusted you.' He held out his hand.

Sean Terry walked over to where Scott was standing and they shook hands. 'I know you didn't, kid, and I respected you for it. But why do I get the feeling you're about to ask a favour?'

'Because I am.' Scott's expression changed, becoming serious again. 'The danger, it's not gone, is it – not all of it, anyway?'

'Nope. But I gave you a promise back in Geneva, that we'd sort it; that still stands. Tonight brought us a heck of a lot closer to the finishing line. But, until that time comes, you'll have to remain hidden. That Rabinovitch guy, he won't lose power or influence overnight and the Russian can't have been working alone. It was all too big.'

'I guessed all that,' Scott said, 'because you said that the guys from the coach were being guarded by soldiers.'

'Yeah! Sadly, from that point of view, nothing's changed. Except, this time, Hilary, and I'm damn sorry to do it to you, you'll need a new identity too.'

'But, why?' Hilary gasped out, her manner uncertain.

'When it comes to the trial, you'll both have to give evidence; your dad too, Scott.'

'But I don't want to leave Falmouth,' Hilary protested. 'I like it there. I've just made friends. Scott?'

'That what's I said.' Scott wrapped his arm around Hilary's shoulders. 'Except this time, it will be different. We'll be together, won't we?'

Beau chuckled.

Terry glowered. 'So that's the favour.' He turned staring out into the dark sky, then swung back. 'Okay, I promise, but I don't like it. To keep you safe, it's going to have to be way out of reach.'

Scott grabbed Hilary's hand. 'I don't think either of us care where, do we, Hilary?'

Hilary laughed, 'You might not, but I do. What about my "A" levels". I was thinking of becoming an actress. I've had plenty of practice in the last week.'

'Not happening,' Scott grinned back. 'Come on, let's get Jay sorted. We can quarrel about where we're going afterwards.'

A buzzing came from the radio-mike. 'Terry here. Casualties?' He directed his piercing gaze at Scott, and his bleak blue eyes brightened. 'That was quick. Go on.' He listened intently making brief comments now and again. 'How bad? Right!' He swung round to his eavesdropping audience and nodded triumphantly. 'We got them. That guy Aquilla is already singing like a bird. Claims he's a scientist – that's it. And the American Seagar swears he wasn't in on the killings, although I doubt a jury will believe him.'

He spoke into the mouthpiece. 'By the way, you'll need to send a recovery team into the gorge behind the unit. You'll find the body of the head man there. My agent took him out. Great gal she is too. One of the best. She'll be a big loss to the service.'

Hilary blushed and laughed. 'I'm still leaving.'

Sean Terry nodded. 'Pity, if you'd stayed I could have partnered you up with that German guy – Haupt.'

'Arnulf? You mean he's alive?' Hilary's voice rose into a squeak.

'Pretty badly beaten but he's tough, he'll make it.'

He spoke into the microphone. 'When Haupt recovers consciousness, tell him I owe him nine years' back salary.' He grinned and switched the receiver off.

'I'm still leaving.' Hilary repeated. She held out her hand.

Her boss nodded briefly and shook it. 'Yeah, I guess. Now, get out of here Scott Anderson and take Hilary with you, before I have a change of heart and send her to the North Pole and you to the South.'

EPILOGUE

The sub-marine nosed its way to the surface, a light covering of ice swirling across the stretch of inland water. A stiff breeze straight from the Artic kept the dark grey waves of the strait snapping at the sides of the cigar-shaped hull like an angry, snarling dog. Waiting patiently, close to shore, was a power launch, courtesy of the Canadian Coast Guard.

Further out to the east, sunrise had already taken place, the early-morning sun busily throwing out tendrils of warm air, softening the snow and ice that had fallen onto the northern land mass.

The hatch to the conning tower opened and a handful of men descended the deck, sufficient to hold the launch steady as it came alongside. To the east, an anonymous shoreline with a ribbon of hills had become plainly visible. Running into the shoreline was a deep valley whose waters bottomed out at hundreds of feet, permitting safe passage for coastal vessels and even tankers ploughing a course through to Alaska and New Brunswick. To the west, sea and sky marked the horizon; but only the captain, the navigation officer, and one seaman knew exactly where they were. Orders had arrived for the navigation officer on screen and in code the moment they left US waters. The captain already knew, advised by top brass, and he had been on hand to welcome their guests aboard. But only the one seaman, the oldest of the group, had visited the spot before. As a youngster in 1989, and still green about the gills, orders had taken them north where the oil tanker, the Exxon Valdes had gone aground in Prince William Sound. They had stayed for six long weeks, while the clean-up operation began, checking that the Ruskies weren't about to poke their noses in, and he'd visited the island. Roberts lifted binoculars to his eyes. For years he'd been one of the lads descending the deck; not these days, seniority kept him up top. Casually he scanned 360 degrees, not expecting to see anything except perhaps for a whale or two. Last trip had taken them off to Alaska and he'd spotted the rare beluga – a large white mass driving its body through the water in search of food. He stared at the rolling landscape of Prince Edward Island. Good place. He might go back one day when he retired.

The captain appeared with the two passengers, all eyes trained on them. Both wore greatcoats provided by the American Navy against the bitter Arctic wind. And both were young, little more than kids. Even bundled up, you could tell by their easy stance.

Silently wishing them luck, Roberts idly followed the path of the launch as it bounced across the waves, squinting slightly to keep it in sight as it headed for a jetty on the southern tip of the island. Okay, so he needed specs to read but he was still fit and healthy – even at forty-eight. His thirtieth year in the service and his final one. By now, he knew it all by heart; all the drills off pat. Anything they threw at him, he had done a dozen times before. But no regrets. It had been a good life, even though curiosity had to be put to bed before you signed on the dotted line. Uncle Sam expected total allegiance and he'd been happy to give it. Still, it would have been nice to know their story. It had to be a good one, if the captain came up onto the bridge at the crack of dawn especially to shake their hands.

The working party headed back up, a warning klaxon sounding impatiently. Impulsively, he hung back for another look. Okay, it was none of his business, still–

Waving from the end of the jetty were three figures – a man, a woman, and a young girl. The launch pulled alongside.

'Roberts?'

He called automatically, 'Yes, sir. Sorry, sir.'

'Roberts. *At the double.*'

The boy in the launch leapt onto the wooden jetty, hurling himself into the man's arms.

Roberts smiled and stowed the binoculars. He ducked under the metal cover of the conning tower, grinning at the irate faces of his mates waiting impatiently to close it. It was a good day after all.

The End